SWEETER THAN DREAMS

SWEETER THAN DREAMS

OLGA BICOS

KENSINGTON BOOKS

KENSINGTON BOOKS are published by

Kensington Publishing Corp.
850 Third Avenue
New York, NY 10022

ISBN 1-57566-070-9

First Pinnacle Paperback Printing: June, 1995
First Kensington Hardcover Printing: January, 1996

Printed in the United States of America

For my sister, Leila, because I love her.
And for my knight in shining armor, Andrew.

Part One
No Prey, No Pay

When the Trouble All Began . . .

Chapter One

April 1728, St. Kitts Island, British Antilles

Love never entered into Quentin's plans.

Quite the contrary. A man of business, Quentin Alexander Rutherford, Viscount Belfour, heir to the Earl of Carrick and all his lands, had long ago outgrown such romantic notions. Lust, he could credit. He'd experienced that fine sentiment for a good portion of his thirty-odd years rakehelling his youth with the London blades he'd once called friends. But love? That tender emotion bloomed only in the hearts of poets, those who needed life wrapped up in dreams rather than the harsh realities it had dished up for Quentin. The weak, the young, the fanciful . . . Viscount Belfour was none of these.

Yet, staring down at the gold-edged invitation in his hand, Quentin could only imagine that someone in his household still held hopes for bringing love into his life.

"Stevenson," he murmured, tapping the vellum against his bare chest. It appeared his steward had stooped to matchmaking.

Naked on his tester bed, Quentin lay sprawled atop the counterpane, his only companions the stacks of unanswered correspondence sparking white in the flame of the silver torchère at his bedside. He dragged his hand through hair as dark as shadows as he read what were most certainly Stevenson's broad strokes, assuring the Lady Godrich that Viscount Belfour would attend her soiree—an evening that would no doubt feature the lady's most eligible daughter torturing the keys of the pianoforte.

Quentin tossed the card and threw his arm over his eyes. "The sentimental old fool."

He peered toward the mullion window, where light from a few stars glimmered on the horizon. A hopeless insomniac, he slept little—but this night his dreams had robbed him of even those few precious hours.

"And not even a whiff of dawn," he murmured.

There was no hope for it. He wouldn't find sleep this night. The monotony of correspondence had not lulled him as he'd hoped. Perhaps it was for the best. Too many nightmares lurked in the corners of his mind, ready to pounce at the first wink of sleep.

He pushed back the yards of mosquito netting that curtained the bed. The testered monstrosity was a forest of dark walnut. Undulating bands of leaves, berries, and flowers sprouted from the posts and trailed across the canopy, giving Quentin the sense that he should hack a path out of the bed each morning with a machete. But the grandiose bed had suited his mood when he'd bought it and the matching pieces. He'd thought to lose himself in the jungle of it.

Toasty warm fur brushed across his ankle as he stood. A ginger tail flicked past his bare calf. Quentin picked up Aloysius in the palm of one hand as nearly two stone of animal sunk the tom's belly into his fingers. The meow that followed was a mere squeak, the effort of a proper greeting too much for the overweight beast.

"You must learn to earn your keep, Aloysius," he whispered against the orange coat. "The mice feast and dance in my halls while you stay snug in my bed."

The cat purred, happy for the attention.

Tucking Aloysius under his arm, he walked to the floor-to-ceiling window framed in a waterfall of crewel-work chintz drapes. He shivered against the predawn breath of the trade winds and thought of dressing. He could go downstairs and read the contracts Arnold's messenger had delivered the previous afternoon, perhaps push off the visions of his nightmare by focusing on the maze of numbers. But instead, he touched his fingers to the cold pane of Bristol glass, not quite able to wipe away the cobwebs of his dream.

Of course, he knew what had triggered the nightmare of Clarice and the baby. The earl's unexpected arrival.

His father had come to St. Kitts.

"Bugger him," Quentin whispered into the cat's pricked ears.

He could still hear that familiar voice. *Dammit, Quentin, I demand the courtesy of an audience at the very least!* It echoed from his memories, leaching into the bedchamber with the potency of a malignant air.

Seven years. Seven long years.

Just when he'd convinced himself his father wouldn't come . . .

Quentin closed his eyes. The memories of the day's disastrous afternoon twisted and turned inside his head, making it pound. He could picture his father as he'd appeared poised at the gilded entrance to the receiving chamber that afternoon. The earl had been a mere shadow in that cavernous doorway, until he'd swept into the room in a flurry of rich velvet and lawn lace, demanding the attention of each and every soul in the chamber.

It surprised Quentin that the memory could still bring him pain. He'd thought himself beyond foolish notions of family.

With a sigh, he propped his shoulder against the window and gave up his fight, allowing the past to wash over him. It was no longer the walnut darkness of his bedchamber that surrounded him, but the gilded splendor of the room that had become a confusion of contracts and files over the past months. He could see himself clearly beside Stevenson, hovering over the ledgers, hearing his father's voice. . . .

"For the love of God, man, I'll not be left at the doorstoop like some leper!"

The Earl of Carrick, confidant of kings and lord of God-knows-how-many estates, strolled into the chamber, the model of pomposity and artifice. As usual, he was dressed in the latest fashion, down to the gold-tipped amber cane and maroon tricorn in his hands. The rich brocade waistcoat of robin's-egg blue and the skillfully tailored jacket showed off a figure still lean despite the passage of time. His father, of course, had always been the epitome of style. Apparently, the stifling tropics hadn't curbed his appetite for fashion, even as the moist heat threatened to stew the earl in his own juices like a pot of boiled clams.

Seated behind the desk, Quentin folded his arms across his chest and leaned back into his Turk chair. "Well, look what the tide dragged in," he drawled to Stevenson beside him.

The Earl of Carrick crossed to the center of the room, his red-heeled shoes falling soundlessly on the French wool carpet. His gaze scanned the chamber overflowing with papers and gilded with riches, finding fault or favor, it was difficult to know which. "It was a hell of a crossing from England on that merchantman, Quentin. I presume you'll at least allow me the courtesy of speaking to me. Or do you plan to throw me out bodily? That's what it will take to be rid of me."

Quentin propped his quill on the foolscap before him. "It's quite tempting, I assure you."

The earl's chest puffed out, a gesture Quentin recognized as a precursor to anger. Even that small memory wounded, mocking him with its unmistakable message: *You know me. You can't shed your past so easily, lad.*

Quentin sat very still for a moment. "Get the hell out of my home," he whispered, giving up his pretense of indifference.

"That's certainly an odd greeting after seven years!"

"It's no greeting at all, my lord. Goodbye and Godspeed."

"Dammit, Quentin!" His father's fingers fisted around the swan grip of his cane. He glanced at the waiting Stevenson, seeming to struggle for composure before the servant. Finding it, the earl hissed in a more controlled voice, "You won't answer my letters. I had no other recourse but to seek you out."

"A mere seven years after my parting."

"I've come a long way to speak with you!"

Seeing his father lodged like a barnacle, Quentin stood to make his own exit.

"For the love of God, man! Will you never forget the past?"

Quentin managed a smile, knowing at least this lie would come easily. He'd rehearsed it often enough these past years. "But that is precisely what I have done, my lord. Forgotten."

"I'm your father, dammit. You can't change that, no matter how much you wish to ignore the fact!"

"On the contrary, I'm rather good at ignoring." He crossed his arms and leaned against the walnut shelves. "I learned from the best."

A pained look crossed the earl's face. "Don't, Quentin. I'm here to make amends, not fight. You've changed, made a success of yourself." He glanced about the room, taking in the gold leaf of the painted ceiling, the imposing marble fireplace and delicate French furnishings—excesses that made an odd contrast to his son's simple waistcoat and shirtsleeves. "Why, by all accounts, you've made quite a fortune for yourself here. After all those years of watching you waste your life . . . you're a son to be proud of now. I'm sorry about our differences in the past—"

"Differences?" Quentin asked mildly. "Is that what you call Clarice's murder?"

The earl blanched, his face turning almost the color of his powdered wig. "That was a long time ago, Quentin. Haven't I been punished enough? My sole heir has abandoned me, threatened never to marry and sire a child. Everything I have ever worked for stands to escheat to the Crown—" As if sensing its inadequacy, the earl cut short his tirade. He lowered his eyes, then looked up to meet Quentin's gaze with a surprising expression of remorse. "You're my son, Quentin. My only child. You'll never know how it pains me not to be a part of your life."

The muscles across Quentin's chest tightened. God, that his father could dare. That he could even for an instant speak of a reconciliation.

"My life has nothing to do with you—or your wishes, my lord," he said stiffly. "Not anymore."

"Oh, so you'll turn your back on it all!" the earl shouted,

losing his pretense of control. "Your family? Your good name? The title?"

"I haven't turned my back on anything." Quentin gave his father a cold stare. "I just choose to wait until you are six feet under to enjoy it."

The salvo scored. The earl's mouth dropped open, then seemingly hung lax for the span of two breaths. Soon enough his lips snapped shut and a fire kindled in his blue eyes. "I won't give up, Quentin. Not this time. I'm staying in Basse Terre until you come to your senses. You may choose to turn your back on your family, but you're my sole heir, dammit, and like it or not, you will do your duty!"

Quentin dug his fingers into Aloysius's fur as his memories receded. He could feel the perspiration inch down his forehead as he let out a long, slow breath. His eyes scanned the jungle of walnut furniture in his bedchamber, his heart winding down from its brush with his vision. *His duty.* Quentin had the sudden image of his father leading one of his prized stallions to the stud pen, and laughed.

"Not this time, old boy."

But soon enough, his laughter died. The only sound in the room became the steady clicking of the basket clock and Aloysius purring in his arms.

"Damn him." Quentin stroked back the cat's ears, suddenly sick to his soul. "Damn me."

Revenge was supposed to be sweet, certainly better than this melancholy lodged in his heart. Seven years he'd toiled to become the grand lord his father would respect, making his fortune in trade, filling his plantation home with riches the earl himself would covet. Seven years he'd garnered powerful government connections both on St. Kitts and in England, scheming for the day he would dangle his successes like a carrot, waiting for the satisfaction of seeing his father's face when he realized he could touch none of it. Not the fine Palladian palazzo Quentin had built, not the acres of cane, not the shipping business—not his coveted heir.

He thought he'd finally feel something. . . .

"Perhaps revenge was too long in coming," he told Aloysius.

He stared out beyond the waving pane of glass, thinking of Clarice. "God. No wonder she haunts me. There's no pleasing the dead now, is there?" he asked the cat.

With a muffled squeak, Aloysius jumped from his arms to the Turk carpet. Quentin raked a hand through his hair, then strode with purpose to the clothespress. He dressed quickly, suddenly wanting to leave the forest of walnut vines and flowers, needing to snuff out the shadows of his dream. Stevenson, with his own curious sources, had informed Quentin the earl was staying at the Cockerel at Basse Terre. Quentin hadn't responded, knowing from experience that soon enough he wouldn't give a damn.

In the meantime, he couldn't sleep and there was work to be done. Taking a brace of candles and his correspondence in hand, he made his way to the contracts stowed away in his receiving chamber.

It wasn't until the wax pooled in a thick ring at the base of the taper stick that his eyes wavered from the parchment. By dawn, he'd reasoned out how to add to his already bursting coffers. He glanced at the angels painted on the cove ceiling—guardians that out of whimsy he'd commissioned some brilliant Italian to paint for him. His angels were his companions there at Rutherford Hall. He liked to think that in their own silent manner they guided him.

The ominous bang of the door slamming shut snatched Quentin's attention. A sliver of dawn streaked across the blue and gold of the carpet as his steward rushed into the chamber, rounding the settee to reach the desk.

"The *Falcon* was boarded," the harried man shouted as his powered wig slipped askew. Unearthing a handkerchief from deep within his sleeve, Stevenson wiped his brow in anxious pats. "Stripped of its cargo. Half the crew deserted. They just barely made port."

Quentin pushed back his chair, slowly standing. "Kincaid?"

"I'm afraid so. Sneaked clean past the patrols. That pirate has raided us again!"

Quentin stared at the contracts, shaking his head. "I'm actually impressed. That's the third time this season."

Stevenson adjusted the pigeon curls of the wig to hover directly before his ears. "I'll send another note to the Council. Of course they say Heartless Kincaid has enough government men in his pocket to assure no one gives a damn who he raids. But perhaps if we petition to increase the ships patrolling—"

"I think not." Quentin twirled the goose quill between his fingers, staring at the dancing flame of a candle. "I think it's time we take matters into our own hands."

"Other than hiring a small armada to protect each ship that sails . . ."

"Take a look at this." Quentin shoved the contracts to his steward across the rosewood desk. "I assume that with the money Arnold has offered, I can afford my own flotilla."

"Yes, yes . . ." Stevenson's keen eyes scanned the figures as he dabbed at his forehead. "But if I may say so, sir, money isn't quite the point. This pirate, Kincaid, is fiendishly clever—"

"And so must we be, then." Quentin tapped the pen against his chin, his plan taking shape. "Kincaid needs more of a challenge. We've made matters entirely too easy for him and his Brethren."

"But, sir, you can't seriously suggest—"

"I can," Quentin said with a purpose few ignored. "Indeed I can," he whispered, thinking to give himself some other focus than his soured revenge. He glanced up at the painted angels on the ceiling glittering with candlelight and dawn. There came a slow, steady smile. "I'd be delighted to give Mr. Heartless Kincaid a run for his money, despite whatever protection he's managed to buy in the Council."

Stevenson flung up his hands in surrender. "All right, all right. But if you choose to add capturing a pirate to the endless list of my duties," he said, pointing a gnarled finger to one of the many stacks threatening to suffocate every inch of space in the chamber, "I shall need an assistant."

Quentin steepled his fingers and peered at Stevenson, finding the request odd. Stevenson had served as Quentin's steward for seven years and had managed the plantation for Quentin's grandfather ten years before that—without help or complaint. Still, glancing over the Moroccan-leather-bound ledgers jamming the mantel, crowding even the plum-blossom splendor of the St. Cloud wall sconces, Quentin thought perhaps help wouldn't go amiss.

"Are there any servants on the plantation who can read?"

Stevenson shook his head, frowning. "Not a one . . . except. It's near June, is it?" His face lit up like a taper. "I've just had a most remarkable thought, sir. Miss Leydianna Carstair should be coming to spend the month with her mother and father. She's very good with her letters. And can cipher, too."

Quentin glanced up. "A woman?"

"But not just any woman," Stevenson said, enthusiasm budding in his voice. "A brilliant young scholar she is. Fiendishly sharp with the books. Oh, yes, remarkably clever. I trained her myself."

"Did you?" Quentin asked lightly. He was always a bit wary when his steward waxed eloquently about a woman. He shifted through the papers on his desk until he came across the familiar cream vellum. He flipped the Lady Godrich's invitation over, staring down at Stevenson's distinctive script. *With great pleasure and equal enthusiasm I look forward to attending your charming soiree* . . . "And why, pray tell, would you train a woman to cipher?"

"I've known the young miss since she was a child," Stevenson began, taking no notice of the card Quentin fanned before his face. "She spent a fair bit of time in the manor doing odd jobs. I caught her one day in the library with one of your grandfather's prized books on her grimy lap, back when I ran the estate for his lordship, God rest his soul." Stevenson's eyes misted over with sentiment. "Trying to teach herself to read, she was." He smiled wide enough to show a missing first molar. "And well, with me and Mary not having any children of our own, you might say I took her under my wing. She has a brilliant mind for numbers. A ingenious talent, really."

Quentin continued to wag the gold-edged card back and forth. Something more than memories accounted for the gleam in Stevenson's rheumy blue eyes. Oh, yes.

Quentin glanced back at the Lady Godrich's invitation. Stevenson's efforts the last weeks to press the young lady of prime breeding on him actually surprised Quentin. His steward was well aware of Quentin's resolve: There would be no marriage, no heir to inherit his father's name and riches.

But this Miss Carstair—the daughter of one of his servants, a woman of possibly limited means— that could be another tactic altogether. It had been quite some time since Quentin had taken a mistress.

A fleeting image danced before him. Arresting gray eyes that sparked intelligence—then nothing.

Curious, that I should remember her eyes . . .

"I know the chit," he said to Stevenson, finding a fading memory of a chestnut-haired girl sitting on a hillside near his sugar mill. "A little mouse of a thing, isn't she?"

"A mouse?" Stevenson echoed. "Why no, sir. I would hardly describe Miss Carstair as a mouse. Intelligent, lion-hearted, yes— but not a mouse. Why, she's saving to buy some acreage for herself and her parents. To start her own plantation. Now, would a mouse do such a thing?"

Still unable to recall a clear image of this monument of industry, Quentin examined his overly enthusiastic steward with a touch of misgiving. He was, of course, very familiar with her parents: a sugar maker apt to cause trouble on the rare occasions when he'd too much rum in him, and a sour-faced matron who worked in the kitchen with Mrs. Bailey, the housekeeper.

"No, no, no," Stevenson continued, his voice most emphatic. "A mouse is entirely inappropriate. Why, Leydi—" Stevenson paused to rattle out a chuckle. "That's what me and the mistress always call her. It suits the girl, for someday she'll be a great lady indeed."

Quentin frowned. He hadn't seen this much life in his steward in a good pass of the moon.

"Never did care much for her parents. You'll know Carstair." A sharp look came to Stevenson's watery blue eyes before he gave a superior sniff. "A very dull fellow, if you want my opinion. And entirely too fond of that Cape Horn rainwater they sell in town. But Leydi is nothing like him. . . . Why, the girl has half again more brains than God allows most men. Miss Carstair would get through this work in a month's time, no trouble."

Quentin allowed his secretary to mutter on, only half listening, until he recalled Stevenson's first words. "You say she's here for only a month?"

"Yes, sir. When she visits her parents. She's off the island the rest of the year."

"And she spends the other eleven months . . . ?" The chit he remembered could hardly be of an age to go off flitting about the islands.

Stevenson gave his forehead another thoughtful swipe, then tucked the handkerchief back in his sleeve. "She's always a bit . . . vague on that very point. The location seems to change—quite often in fact. I believe last year she mentioned Montserrat. Yes, the last she spoke, she was working on Montserrat. As a book-keeper on a plantation there. But that mustn't dissuade you, sir. Knowing my Leydi, I'm sure she'll have fine references."

Quentin stood to pace to the window, tapping the invitation against his hand. He pulled back the velvet drapes and peered beyond the rippling glass to the fields of gold swaying with the morning breeze. He tried to imagine this mysterious mouse of a girl running loose about the Caribbean. A bookkeeper no less—a woman who seemed to completely disregard the rules that applied to her sex.

He glanced back at his steward's overly innocent features. He smiled. Oh, yes, Stevenson had intrigued Quentin with his little mouse.

He crushed the invitation in his hand, knowing he didn't want Stevenson's Miss Carstair, no matter how tempting. It had been a long time since he'd allowed himself happiness of that sort. In the shadow of his father's arrival, a mistress was the last thing he wanted.

"Miss Carstair sounds very enterprising," Quentin said, strid-ing around Stevenson to his desk, "but I think it would be best for all if we allow her some peace during her short stay on Rutherford Estate. She's here to visit her parents, after all." And Quentin would stay well away from her and any other prizes his steward might dangle before him.

"But, sir—"

"Make inquiries in town for someone else."

"I really think—"

Quentin tossed the crumpled invitation to his steward. Stevenson caught the balled paper in one hand. It took only a moment for him to realize what he held—evidence of his matchmaking.

"Someone else, Stevenson." Quentin said. "A man, if you will."

Stevenson flushed the color of his red velveteen jacket. Instantly, the older gentleman's shoulders stiffened. He sniffed dramatically. "As you wish, your lordship."

Quentin bit back a smile. Stevenson used titles only when his steward wanted to distance himself from some objectionable course on Quentin's part.

"Why don't you go to the kitchen and ask Mrs. Bailey for some of those fine scones," Quentin said, flipping through the pages of a ledger. "And a pot of coffee. We'll begin discussing our plans for Kincaid when you return. Perhaps we should send for a representative from His Majesty's Navy; we need not work on his capture alone."

"As you say, your lordship."

Quentin listened to the door click shut behind Stevenson. He shook his head and glanced up at the angels above him, seeking an answer to his steward's odd machinations. But, as always, the painted faces remained silent. He heard a low squeak and peered down. Aloysius circled his boot.

"A lady bookkeeper?" he told the cat, crouching down to give the animal's ginger head a pet. "Next he'll be smuggling women to me in the guise of the bootman."

But catching sight of the honeyed fields of cane beyond the window, the room mellowing with the touch of morning sun, his thoughts became less than merry. The momentary amusement of the contracts, Kincaid, and Miss Carstair faded as he again thought of the questions that had plagued him through the night.

No marriage, no children—that much he had promised Clarice's memory. It left little else.

He smoothed back Aloysius's ears, feeling beneath his fingers the rumbling purr. He expected the earl to make another attempt to persuade him to return to the flock, perhaps even a third foray after that. But soon enough the earl would return to

England and the pleasure of bedeviling his father would vanish. He would remain, as always, alone with his memories of Clarice.

Quentin told himself he didn't feel lonely.

He told himself he didn't feel anything.

He thought that, given enough time, he might even believe it was true.

Chapter Two

Devil's Gate, Island Hideout of Daniel Kincaid

Leydianna Carstair loved to daydream.

Oh, she did her best to dress the part of a sensible bookkeeper. She tortured her chestnut curls into a tight braid that roped down her stick-straight spine to her hips; she armored herself in practical cotton gowns, tidy aprons, and buckled shoes, all very appropriate attire for her position. She adopted an air that said she suffered no nonsense.

But the fact was, Leydianna—or Leydi, as most called her—was a consummate daydreamer.

She could without a moment's notice lapse into fantasy, envisioning herself part of any of the daring schemes the buccaneers of Devil's Gate recounted over tallow candles and strong rum. At the drop of her simple lace cap she would relive adventure after riveting adventure from one of many books she devoured under the shade of a banyan in the compound's courtyard.

At that very moment she was engrossed in a particularly grand daydream. She saw herself parry the sword thrust of her masked opponent, driving the rascal back across the quarter deck. Her knee boots thundered on the wood as she countered a riposte of the fiend's saber, lunging to the side as he missed his mark. *Take that!* she responded mentally. With a twist of her wrist she engaged the fellow's sword, flicking it into the air—

There came a hard jab to her rib and Leydi snapped alert. No longer did she see her masked enemy bearing down on her from across a ship's deck. It was quite a different fellow pounding the floorboards of the antechamber where she stood. Her employer, Daniel "Heartless" Kincaid, stomped across the satinwood, his great black boots striking in a cadence crafted to intimidate. Leydi sighed deeply. More's the pity. Kincaid looked to any not familiar with his gentler side as if he had every intention of string-ing her up.

Biting her lip, Leydi watched the full skirt of his knee-length coat furl behind Kincaid like the Black Flag itself, skull and bones hitched on a breeze. Though she liked her pirate employer quite a bit, had worked as his bookkeeper these past eight years, this show of temper was all too typical. More than once she had lapsed into daydreaming in the middle of just such a tirade. But she was sorry she'd been so deep in her musings that she'd missed half his bellows. In the three decades Daniel Kincaid had commanded the quarter deck of the most feared pirate sloop on the high seas, the *Plague,* he'd perfected three expressions of command: menacing, murderous, and a death-dealing stare that could twist the bowels of the hardiest swabbie. It was the latter expression he fixed on Leydi now.

She glanced up at her best friend standing beside her, thankful Gabriela had had the presence of mind to nudge Leydi from her fantasies with a dig of her elbow. Taller than Leydi and wear-ing a gown as flamboyant as Leydi's was plain, Gabriela de Sousa looked just a touch bored.

As usual, Kincaid's anger was wasted on Gabby, the quadroon who kept Kincaid's house as diligently as Leydi toiled over his books. Gabriela was used to the pirate's censure and took a per-verse pleasure in ignoring him. Leydi frowned, sensing troubled seas ahead.

"Yer not a pair of pirates, fer the love of God, to be swilling rum and swearing blue fire like the best of the Brethren!" The morning light streamed through the louvered windows of the cottage, shining against the graying temples of Kincaid's queued hair—the only blemish to attest his near-fifty years. "You're me housekeeper." He scowled at Gabriela. "And me bookkeeper." He glowered at Leydi, then stabbed the air before him as if his finger were a sword. *"Not* a pair of luckless cutthroats. Pay me heed, gels. There'll be no more sharing a wee gram of rum with the men. No more playing games of blind and straddle until the cock crows—"

"Has Cy been complaining again?" Gabriela asked, a lilting accent from the Brazils teasing the edges of her voice. She pressed a hand to the hip of her gown. The scarlet brocade draped over a lace corseted bodice and underskirt, accenting her lovely figure. Her exotic green eyes tilted catlike, the color shining in stunning contrast to her café-au-lait complexion and shoulder-length brown curls. "Bah." She shook her head at Leydi. "I told you to let Cy win, *caro.*"

"Do hush up, Gabby," Leydi whispered, stepping on the toe of Gabriela's pretty gold-buckled slipper while keeping her smile fixed on Kincaid.

"Ladies practice tatting and needlepoint," Kincaid sputtered, ignoring Gabby's sarcasm as he gathered steam for his familiar harangue. "They learn the latest dances . . . these are the things that should occupy ye gels. Now, for the next month," he said, referring to the time Leydi and Gabby would venture away from the pirate's hideout to visit their mothers on St. Kitts, "I care not what ye do. But when ye return here to me and Devil's Gate, I've made a list of suitable activities—"

"He's going to teach us tricks, *caro,*" Gabby said, clapping her hands before her, "so we can entertain him like a pair of dancing bears."

Kincaid's lips curled into a snarl. "Marooning ye might be my first trick," he bellowed, "so don't ye tempt me, gel!"

"So we had a little fun." Gabby swaggered forward. Her accent from the Brazils was always more pronounced when she goaded Kincaid, and it was thick as cane syrup now. "But it is nothing to do with you, Kincaid." She waved one hand aside in a dismissing gesture. "But all I hear is this trouble we cause—"

"Last night I found ye with yer skirts hitched to yer waist and that devil, Murdock's, hands around yer breasts! Don't ye tell me that weren't true fear in yer eyes when I found ye fighting him off. Damn me, I had to maroon the sorry dog. I'm short one man now, thanks to your tempting—"

"Tempting!" Gabby blushed in her fury. She planted both fists on her hips. "Murdock is an animal. He thinks the sheep flirt with him when they bleat."

Leydi wriggled between the two, pushing a palm to Kincaid's chest and wedging a shoulder against Gabriela as she eased them apart. "In just a few hours we'll be on our way to St. Kitts—"

"And when ye return, they'll be no more acting like yer a wee Mary Reed and Anne Bonny! I did not bring ye here to turn ye both into a pair of female pirates, damn yer eyes."

"Then why *did* you bring us here?" Gabriela asked.

Gabriela's question stole the wind from Kincaid's sails. He stood, openmouthed; the room grew deadly quiet. Outside, the shouts of Kincaid's men preparing to sail filtered through the cottage's louvered windows, the only sound in the room.

Leydi didn't understand the sudden tension. The position Kincaid had offered her eight years earlier had been a godsend. It had meant honest coin—well, honest enough—with which to make her dreams come true, and she'd never thought to question his offer. She'd merely believed he'd been guided by whim that day he'd offered her a position in Basse Terre, that she'd impressed him by skillfully haggling with Bertie, Gabriela's mother, for a set of buttons she'd bought in Bertie's shop while Kincaid watched.

But Gabby's question and Kincaid's silence implied something more. Something perhaps not so innocent . . .

"The wages I pay purchase yer fine clothes and jewels," Kincaid stammered into the silence, then turned away. He shook his head, seeming to battle with himself until he murmured, "I needed the help. There's no better reason than that, wench."

Gabby's steady gaze could have bored a hole into the back of Kincaid's fine velvet coat. "Sometimes I truly hate you, Kincaid."

The pirate turned on his heel, his expression a warship prepared to ram. "Listen to me, ye snippet of Eve's flesh. I should let ye rot in the brig for the manner ye speak to me. Let yer arse—"

"Kincaid!" Leydi stepped in, dispelling her own unease to keep her two friends from each other's throats. "There's better to do here than argue with Gabriela. For heaven's sake, did you assign a man to tend my fields while I'm gone?" she demanded, knowing only too well how to distract Kincaid from Gabby.

"Rot that damned tobacco of yers!" he shouted, only too happy to switch his attack to Leydi.

"Now, Kincaid, you were only too willing to risk such a wager on the turn of a card. I won that concession fair and square."

"Fer the love of all that's holy, I had three queens! What were the chances of losing, I ask?"

Leydi smiled, only too happy to provide the information. "According to Mr. Malcomer's book, *Winning at Brag,* the odds are precisely—"

"Rot Mr. Malcomer! And rot yer damned tobacco! Ye'll not rest until ye turn every last bloodthirsty pirate on this island into a blasted farmer, damn ye!"

"There are many here with families who seek a more honest way to make a living than pirating, Kincaid. If I'm right, no one on Devil's Gate need go 'on the account' seeking Spanish treasure again. The buccaneer life has taken its toll on too many as it is." She gave him a measuring look and lifted her brows. "Though it pains me to say it, a man your age might consider retirement—"

"My age! Why, ye blasted woman, there's room in the brig fer ye as well. 'Tis a fit place for both," he said, swiveling between Gabby and Leydi. "That's what's needed here! A bit of discipline—"

"Daniel," came the lilting voice with its Spanish accent.

In unison, all three turned to the arched entryway leading to the hall. Her genteel figure swathed in a severe black gown thickly encrusted in gold metallic threads, Kincaid's lady love, the Lady Consuelo, waited at the threshold. She wore a mantilla of Belgian lace draped over ebony hair now graced with strands of silver. From her ears dangled diamonds the size of Kincaid's thumbnail. But the right ear flashed gold where a second hole, directly above the diamond, had been pierced by the mate of the pirate's hoop.

Leydi stifled a sigh of relief. Even when Leydi's best wasn't enough, Consuelo always managed to protect Gabriela from Kincaid's temper.

Kincaid stepped to Consuelo's side, taking her hand as he drew her into the room. "What I'm suggestin', my dearest heart, is that a spell in the brig might not go amiss." As Consuelo seated herself in an oak elbow chair, Kincaid slid a glance toward the two younger women. "A rat bite or two would give these two a noggin of sense."

"Leave the girls be, Daniel." Consuelo's near-black eyes tilted seductively as she touched her fingertips to the cleft in Kincaid's chin. "Their ship leaves within the hour. For once, won't a kiss and a wave do for a farewell?"

"Aye, 'tis like yer sex to stick together," he grumbled, but Leydi could see by the way his gaze feasted on Consuelo that the storm had passed.

"I'll not say a word more." The gold flecks in his near-emerald gaze sparked with the beginnings of forgiveness. " 'Tis my bane in life that I've a soft spot for green eyes," he said, giving his familiar farewell. Leydi returned his grin, knowing the parting words fit only Gabriela. Leydi's eyes were nothing better than a cloudy gray.

"Off with ye," he said, giving a rare smile to both women. "And Godspeed. Cy lad," he shouted back toward the hall. "Come get the hoydens."

Without waiting for further comment, the two women picked up their bags and made their way outside the cottage-style house with a final wave to Kincaid and the Lady Consuelo. Once the louvered door closed behind them, Gabriela leaned against the rail leading down to the center courtyard, where a contingent of sheep kept trim the grass of the surrounding compound. She hugged her sides, laughing.

"I could barely control myself, *caro,*" she said, catching her breath long enough to speak. *"Dio mio,* it's a sight to behold when you start bullying that pirate."

Leydi frowned, not liking ill feelings between two people she

cared for so much. "I was just trying to make a point—I won my
tobacco fields fair and square." She slid a disapproving glare to
her companion. "Unlike you, Gabby, I pick my battles," she
added, referring to Gabriela's penchant for goading their pirate
employer.

The door slammed open behind them. Both women turned
to see Cy Cuthbert, Kincaid's second-in-command, step out of
the cottage, a small trunk balanced on his broad shoulder and
a large leather bag in his hand. Neither burden seemed particularly taxing to his hulking figure. His blue eyes shifted from one
woman to the other, and though it was difficult to make out his
expression beyond the barrier of his full red beard shot with
gray, Leydi had little doubt it was filled with disapproval.

"What are ye ruddy imps up to now?" he asked, dropping the
trunk and leather bag to each side. He was dressed in a jerkin,
cotton waistcoat, and canvas breeches—clothes befitting a pirate's man but for the fact that the garb was immaculately clean.

Gabriela waltzed forward, a wicked smile on her full mouth.
"Leydi was just telling me how she cheated Kincaid out of his
fields playing brag."

"I most certainly did not cheat," Leydi said stiffly. She
smoothed the apron over her brown dress with a sharp tug and
slipped her long braid over her shoulder with a prim sniff.

Gabriela's teeth shone white against lips just a shade darker
than her skin. "I wonder. Perhaps given something you *really*
wanted, if even you, my little Puritan, might be tempted to guide
fate." Gabriela tilted her face to one side, measuring Leydi with
a look. "Or perhaps, *caro,* you don't know how?"

"The lass knows how to cheat," Cy said with a wink to Leydi.

"Every good card player knows how," Leydi answered, repeating Cy's very words when he'd taught her that particular art.
"That way, you know when you yourself are being made the
dupe. But no matter, winning is a simple question of calculating
the odds."

"But sometimes, *caro mio,* we must make our own odds, no?"
Gabriela wiggled her fingers, as if slipping a high card into the
cleavage of her gown. "Tamper a bit with what life gives us."

Cy glared down at Gabriela, his expression that of a father

tending to an errant child—a role he often served with Gabby. "And why are ye so bent on causing trouble on such a fine day, lass? I've a mind to take you over my knee and teach ye the lessons yer mother's neglected."

Gabriela's green eyes narrowed, wiping away her playful look. Picking up her bag, she scooted around Cy and skipped down the stairs. "I think it will be Kincaid who gets his lesson," she threatened.

The sailor shook his head, watching Gabriela slip away. "She'll come to a bad end someday with that temper of hers."

"Leave it be, Cy," Leydi whispered. "Kincaid will be long gone when we return in a month's time. They'll not see each other for the summer. Perhaps their feuding will come to an end after such a long parting." But before Cy could add a good dose of skepticism to the neat scenario she'd painted, Leydi added, "Now, you won't forget to feed Nigel?"

"Nay, lass. If I can keep the lads from skewering the monster on a spit and eating him for supper, he'll be whole and hearty by the time you return."

"And you'll do a proper dunging of the fields I've set out—"

From inside his vest pocket he slipped out a familiar piece of foolscap, the instructions she'd left with Kincaid. "And water yer tobacco patch. Look over the plans for the sugar plantation yer drafting. Find the new plant for the dye ye've been promising the Lady Connie"—he thumped the list with the back of his hand as he read off each duty—"I'll do the lot, rest assured. Have I ever come short of what ye bid of me, lass?"

She patted his shoulder and gave him a smile. "You're a good man, Cy. Kincaid's lucky to have such a fine second-in-command."

Cy picked up the small traveling chest and shifted it back onto his shoulder. "Aye, so I let him know meself on occasion."

Feeling a bit more light of heart, Leydi fell into step behind Gabriela on their march to the lagoon. A hymn of birds sounded from the woods covering the cone-shaped peak behind Kincaid's pirate hideout. The perpetual clouds that floated over the dripping forests kissed the tips of the trees in the distance like a mystical shroud. On the island floor, brilliant gold and violet from wood anemone, hibiscus, and flowering ginger spotted the carpet of vines and grass. But when she heard the raucous cries of the giant parrots that made Devil's Gate their home, Leydi experienced her first wrenching pain of regret at parting.

Have patience, she told herself. Soon—within a few short years—she would never have to leave again.

"The devil take Kincaid," Gabriela said, hiking the trail beside Leydi. "Be *ladies,* says he. Well, what are we now? A pair of hens? Of course we play cards and drink sometimes with the men. What else is there to do on this godforsaken island? *Dio!*"

Leydi said nothing, knowing she too enjoyed the freedoms allowed on this island far from her mother's critical eye. Perhaps the drinking contest with Theo *had* been unwise, but over the past years she'd discovered she had a fair stomach for rum.

"Kincaid would have us both hobbled in his house slaving for him if he had his way, *caro.* Sometimes I think that man will drive me to murder. Truly, I'm sick and tired of listening to his complaints, doing his bidding. Someday he'll show me the respect I deserve."

Leydi frowned, hearing the old bitterness in her friend's voice. She remembered Gabby's strange challenge to Kincaid earlier. *Why did you bring us here?*

"We don't have to work for a pirate, Gabby," she said gently.

"Don't we?" Gabriela answered with a sudden sharpness. "Tell me you would ever leave Consuelo? Or Cy and the others?"

Leydi placed her hand on Gabriela's shoulder. "I wouldn't leave a one, as well you know. But most of all," she added with heartfelt emotion, "I wouldn't leave you, my friend."

For a moment the fire in Gabriela's eyes banked. The taller woman looked down on Leydi with an expression that bordered on regret. "You've a gentle soul inside you, Leydi. What a pity there's those who would take advantage of it."

"I take as good as I get," Leydi assured her.

An answering grin curled Gabriela's mouth. "Perhaps you are right." She pinched Leydi's cheek affectionately. "And you have me to keep Kincaid from leg-shackling you to his ledgers. Or your mama from bleeding you dry of all your spirit. Ye need someone to make you see there's more beyond those columns of numbers you cipher and the pages of your books. What's your newest treasure, eh?" she said, reaching into Leydi's satchel. She tried to snatch out the book. "Another of Defoe's adventures, I'll wager."

"Oh, something like that," Leydi chimed, swiveling away with a delighted smile before Gabby could grab the book.

A silent communication pulsed between the women. Over the eight years they'd shared a single-room cottage on Devil's Gate, a bond had developed between them—a link as strong as any between blood kin, or perhaps stronger, because it was a relationship created out of choice. Almost three years set them apart, Gabriela being near five and twenty. Cy called them a strange pair: a tall quadroon with a nose for trouble, and a petite bookkeeper whose every move was governed by Kincaid's fortunes.

And yet, Leydi saw clearly why they had come together, like two pieces of a puzzle box searching to fill the lack in the other. Gabby would venture anything quite fearlessly, and yearn for moderation in her life— while ever-practical Leydi would smooth over her friend's misdeeds and dream of the day she would find Gabriela's flamboyance to experience her own true-life adventure.

"Still, he cannot tell us how to live our lives forever," Gabby whispered almost to herself. Then, glancing at Leydi, she added, "I may not come back from St. Kitts this year. I've often thought of staying on at Basse Terre with my mother. Helping her with the shop."

"Oh, Gabby, no!" But thinking of her friend's happiness, she put aside her own selfish need for companionship. She squeezed Gabby's hand. "You do whatever will make you happiest. But I'll miss you, Gabby."

The two friends stared out over the freshwater harbor, nearly invisible from treacherous shores that kept Devil's Gate a haven from other ships. The twisting path that would lead them down to the lagoon and its sandy beach wound back and forth like a whip cracking its tip. The sloop, whose shallow draught permitted her to glide into inlets where no English frigate could follow, waited—the chariot that would take them to their next port of call, Dominica. From there, they would part company, Leydi taking a lugger to Montserrat and Gabriela transferring to a skip heading for Guadeloupe. They would meet again on St. Kitts, with no one the wiser about Kincaid's hideout.

"Let's go." Gabby started down the path. "As Kincaid says: No prey, no pay."

Leydi hesitated for a moment, watching Gabriela skip down the curve of the hill toward the lagoon. One last time, her eyes sought the mountainside, where clouds lined a lone peak, hiding its beauty from view. The forests tipped with jewel-colored flowers appeared as precious as the treasure Kincaid hoarded.

Gabriela thought not to come back to Kincaid's island—while Leydi never wanted to leave.

The wind kicked up, tickling her ears until a low buzzing began. Slowly, the sound took shape, mimicking the harping and carping that she knew awaited her at her parents' bungalow at Rutherford Estate. *Your hair looks abominable, Leydianna. You should cut it. Fix your braid, for goodness' sake.* Almost without thinking, she grabbed her cherished braid protectively, hair that brushed past her hips despite her mother's pleas that she cut it to be fashionable. She wanted to slap her hands over her ears, to snuff out her parents' voices. *Leydi girl, can you spare a few coins for a man with a thirst—you know your mam. . . .*

The voices started to roar in her head as she clutched her tapestry bag. *I'll need much more money than that if you expect me to get anything other than the scratchiest wool for my new gown. . . . Have you gained weight . . . Leydi! Your bosom looks to burst in that dress. Tighten your corset.*

"Daydreaming again, *caro?*"

Leydi looked up at Gabriela, once again standing beside her. She shook her head and reached into her bag for a handkerchief. "It's just hot, that's all." Quickly, she wiped her brow with a shaking hand. But inside her head, a voice warned: *Don't go back. They'll take everything—even your dreams if you let them.*

Quickly, she silenced her unkind thoughts, reminding herself that her parents had led difficult lives. It was only natural that their labors had left a mark. *Labor we were obligated to do for your welfare, daughter.* Her parents had chosen to pay for her lessons with dear Mr. Stevenson those years she'd lived with them at

Rutherford Estate. They hadn't used the meager coin they'd managed to save to buy back their papers of indenture or make their own lives easier. But for those lessons, Leydi would never have made her way off St. Kitts.

"Caro?"

She smiled, licking her lips and throwing her braid over her shoulder as she shoved the kerchief back into her bag. "I'm fine. Come on. Cy's waiting."

Slowly, she made her way down the path to the lagoon. Turquoise waters shimmered around the hull of Kincaid's ship, reflecting the color of the sky. Leydi bit her lip.

The island was called Devil's Gate. Her fortunes turned on the whims of a man called Heartless. Still, as she followed Gabriela down the path to the lagoon, she was overwhelmed by a sense that she was leaving paradise for a month's stay in her own kind of purgatory.

Chapter Three

St. Kitts. Rutherford Estate, June 3, 1728

Quentin watched Argus Carstair skip out the door of the daub and wattle bungalow. The sun dappled past the palm-frond thatching of the bungalow's roof, flitting over Argus's plain-as-pudding face. The man's mouth broke into a smile as big as morning. In his hand, Argus cradled what looked like a fistful of coins. He weighed the silver in his palm, laughing as he pocketed the lot in his woolen breeches.

"He'll be off to town now," Stevenson said, stepping up behind Quentin. Both men had been out to the boiling house, checking on the new pans Quentin had ordered. The sight of his sugar maker looking fit to dance a jig on his doorstep had caught their attention.

"No doubt, he'll be leaving by way of my stables." Quentin's gaze followed the hulking figure swiveling past banana fronds and palmettos. "Did you know he keeps a horse there now?"

His steward's only response was a prunish expression of disapproval.

As Quentin gazed on, Argus plucked up a gardenia to wave

under his red-veined nose. He ducked his tricorn-capped head beneath a blossoming crepe myrtle and disappeared down the garden path to the stables.

"My good sugar maker asked me just yesterday if he might use the stables for his mount," Quentin said. "Until he can make permanent arrangements for the animal's upkeep elsewhere. A rather fine bay gelding, I must say." He glanced down at Stevenson. "I wasn't aware I paid so well."

"You don't," Stevenson snapped. "It's Miss Leydi's money that's paid." He shook his head, making the pigeon curls of his wig dance across his ears. "The lass returned just three days ago and already it's started. If they could cut her up into little pieces and sell her for a profit, she'd be baled and stacked for sale already. But even Carstair knows better than to kill the goose that lays the golden eggs."

Quentin could think of very few occupations that would give Carstair's daughter the blunt to purchase a blooded horse. The one that came most glaringly to mind had nothing to do with bookkeeping. He frowned. Frankly, he couldn't imagine the little mouse he remembered—despite a very fine pair of gray eyes—garnering such a wealthy protector. He tried to recall when he'd seen her last. Could it have been as long as three years? *Certainly enough time for some blooming . . .*

"If you're interested, the story lies beyond that door," Stevenson said, nodding his head toward the Carstairs' bungalow.

Perhaps it was his steward's tone—anger, with just a hint of something more punishing, a pity that reached beyond even Quentin's stalwart guard against the weakness of sympathy. Perhaps it was merely the long, sour day of endless moist heat and the boredom of one too many worthless contracts crossing his desk. Whatever the reason, Quentin followed Stevenson's unwavering stare to the bungalow door.

Details that would never have caught his attention before etched into focus. A painted ceramic door handle replaced the bungalow's practical iron latch; just beyond the window, a lovely shawl tipped in Belgian lace lay draped over a bent-cane rocker. The costly garment was tossed over the slats as if it were of little worth to its owner. Chintz curtains draped the window. A wool runner brightened the doorstep.

The crushed shells of the path crunched beneath his boot heels as Quentin walked toward the bungalow, drawn to the mystery of those luxuries. Despite a day of grueling business commitments, two images clashed to lure him irresistibly forward: a mouse of a girl sitting on a hillside, watching his mill as if it were a gold mine—a temptress dispensing money with an ease that promised a foolhardy belief in her charms.

When he and Stevenson climbed up the porch, the door stood ajar, Carstair in his jubilance for his coin having failed to latch it. Angry voices drifted from inside.

"—A waste of money! Lord in heaven, Leydianna, have you learned nothing these years? He'll just go into town and drink himself into a grave."

"He bought the horse just as he said he would. He doesn't always drink."

"And a fine plow horse it will make for your grand dream of a plantation! What need have we for such an animal? Look at this house! The carpet is threadbare, the dishware is cracked—"

"The carpet is new and of a fine thick wool—"

"My house is filled with old and ugly things! And yet you give five quid to your father . . ."

The angry tirade continued, stealing inside Quentin, stroking memories he'd hoped long since buried beyond reach. The words coiled around his heart, shifting into the familiar patterns of his past. *I'm tired of paying for your markers and fancy women! You're nothing to me but a preening peacock—a wastrel. Good God, have you no pride, boy? No sense?*

Regrets he'd managed to corner into his dreams these past seven years plundered past their carefully constructed restraints. He thought of his father's arrival last month—the man's stubborn refusal to leave Quentin alone.

Quentin pushed the door with his fingertips and watched it ease open with not so much as a creak. As Stevenson promised, the tale lay inside—but not the story Quentin had imagined.

The mouse had not blossomed into a temptress. The mouse had changed very little, if at all.

She was dressed in uncomplimentary brown, a shade that her square-shouldered stance carried with infinite familiarity. She was so small, only the full shape of her breasts saved her from being waifish. The spray of freckles across her nose and the pixy tilt of her silver eyes made him think of an elf. A thick rope of sable hair swept down her back. Its tip brushed temptingly against a delightful backside unhampered by hooped petticoats. The hair was the most extraordinary thing about her. That and her hands fisted with white-knuckled tension at her sides.

By contrast, her mother wore a splendid skirt of the softest light blue wool, propped by a surplus of packaging. An impressive length of lace adorned the cuffs of the fitted bodice. A fichu at the bosom and a band around her throat showed an elegance not customary for a woman of her station. Quentin had never taken notice of the clothes worn by servants, but the disparity between the mother's extravagance and the paucity of the daughter's dress showed too glaringly to be ignored.

Three years before, when he'd seen Lcydi on that hillside, he'd thought of a mouse. Studying her now, he didn't so much see a plain girl as a pretty girl wrapped in plainness.

His gaze flicked over the tableau of mother and daughter. Tight lines marred Mistress Carstair's aging face. The daughter's countenance held only the color and expression of sudden shame. The moment nudged at the haunts of his past, prickling his conscience, making him want to do something to alter the scene.

"Your Lordship." The mother bowed her head in the merest brush with respect. Her daughter did nothing, just blinked owlishly at Quentin with those wonderful gray eyes. The shame was gone, replaced by a fleeting wonder and then a braced-back resolve. He watched as she rested the fingers of one hand on the scrolled walnut tea caddy beside her, looking suddenly as if not even a hurricane would dislodge her.

Here, then, was Stevenson's tale. The dutiful child buying the love of her parents. From experience, Quentin knew the ending only too well. Money could purchase oh so many things. Love, however, was not one of them.

"Miss Carstair, my steward informs me you have a talent for

bookkeeping," he said to the daughter, surprising himself with the words—with his need to interfere.

"An extraordinary talent!" Stevenson sputtered into the shocked silence.

"Stevenson needs assistance for a few weeks. Nothing too taxing, just a bit of ciphering, a little organizing. Perhaps you're interested?"

Leydianna Carstair looked nowhere but at him. She had the ability to make a person feel as if they had her complete and utter attention. It was a talent that made a man take a second look. Quentin narrowed his gaze on Miss Carstair, seeing something more than wonder in her silver eyes. Perhaps relief.

"Your lordship, my daughter is here for but a month. Surely a mother can expect a brief time with her own child—"

"Her wages will take into consideration any inconvenience to you, good mistress," Quentin said, sure that money would sway the mother. "I'm sorry to indispose you, but Stevenson considers my situation quite dire. I will speak to Argus on the matter. I'm sure we can come to some agreement beneficial to all."

"Perhaps it is I who should speak for Leydianna," the mother continued, her lips primped into a forced smile. "She is my only daughter . . . you understand, my lord?"

Quentin knew that gleam of avarice. Mistress Carstair wouldn't trust the girl's father to bargain the best price.

"I understand only too well, madam. You must value your time with your daughter a great deal."

"Most certainly, my lord."

"Then I think we'll let Miss Carstair negotiate her own wages. If she has half the head for business Stevenson leads me to believe, she'll no doubt do herself justice." Before the mother could argue further, Quentin turned for the door. "Come speak to Stevenson at the manor," he told Leydianna, his hand already extended for the knob.

"But, your lordship—"

He turned, his eyes on the mother. His expression was that of a man who knew her livelihood depended on his good graces. The greedy old eyes turned away, whatever protest she'd devised dying on her lips.

"Good day, ladies," he said with a smile he used on business acquaintances and fools.

Outside, Quentin walked briskly toward Rutherford Hall, knowing he'd just made a terrific blunder of the next month. Good Lord, now he'd have the chit constantly underfoot. He'd have to hunt up odd jobs and such for her—worthless projects he wouldn't fear she'd bungle. He should have left the mother to her bullying. He shouldn't have given in to that infernal tug at his heart that made him want to give the little mouse more worth than the upbraiding he'd interrupted.

He grimaced at Stevenson stepping lively alongside him, an unusual spry bounce to his step. The old codger had gotten his way and he was too sure of Quentin's regard to hide his satisfaction.

"You never hired anyone to help you with the ledgers, did you?" he accused Stevenson.

"No, sir." His servant caught up to Quentin's wider stride with an awkward hop, nearly losing his powdered wig. "I thought perhaps I might manage alone. But offer me assistance of the caliber of Miss Leydi, and I cannot refuse."

"Indeed," Quentin said.

Surprisingly, he wasn't angry at Stevenson's manipulation. What he felt was a strange combination of curiosity, anticipation, and annoyance. Damn the little mouse for letting herself be bullied. And then he smiled. *Damn me for being foolish enough to intercede.* Just because for a moment he'd been recalling his own aching past with his father.

Well, it was only for a month, he told himself. And perhaps his little charity work would ease some of the boredom that lately held sway over his days.

He thought of the accounts waiting for him, his meeting the next day with the Council representative, a military man he hoped could further his plans to capture that pirate, Daniel Kincaid. But soon haunting gray eyes clouded his vision.

Though he allowed his expression to show nothing, a definite pique was beginning to brew inside him. *That silly brown dress,* he thought. That awkward mobcap shadowing her pretty face. And her ridiculous show of relief when he'd offered her work.

He'd wager that unlike her mother, she hadn't a clue what a man like himself could buy from a woman.

"A strange bird, that Mistress Carstair," Stevenson said, shaking his bewigged head. "When I first asked if I might tutor Miss Leydi, the mother haggled with me, making it clear she begrudged every penny and hoped dearly I'd refuse to teach the girl. I never took a farthing from her, of course—a circumstance that suited us both. I always had a suspicion Mistress Carstair begrudged Leydi those lessons—begrudges her everything. Such an unnatural mother."

"Really?" Quentin picked up his pace, already picturing the pile of correspondence waiting in his study. "Frankly, I see nothing the least bit unnatural about her."

Leydi uncoiled her mother's fingers from her arm. She scarcely noticed the red half-moon marks left behind on the delicate skin as she stared at the door, too happy to care. *Happy and puzzled and intrigued.* So many emotions riddled through her mind, it was difficult to snatch the words out of her head to describe them.

She had seen the elusive Rutherford heir face-to-face but once—on the hill outside the sugar mill, where she'd been making notes for her own enterprise. But dear Mr. Stevenson had spoken of his patron often. The steward's accolades and Quentin's own dark heroic looks certainly made him prime material for the knight-in-shining-armor rescue he'd just laid at her feet.

A smile tugged at her lips. For an instant, while he'd stood before her in his woolen coat and leather breeches, she *had* allowed her eyes to blur a bit, imagining him with a plumed visor and lance under arm coming to slay her dragon. But soon enough she'd vanished the fantasy, happy for the strange reality of his coming to her parents' bungalow.

She still couldn't quite believe Lord Rutherford, famed entrepreneur, master of this plantation, had actually stood before her mother and complimented Leydi on her expertise for book work. She would have gambled a month's wages that the man didn't even know of her existence, much less her talents as a bookkeeper.

"Oh, aye. You've caught his eye," her mother said, pinching Leydi's chin between her thumb and forefinger. She tugged her daughter's face up to hers. Calculation molded Elaine Carstair's face, making her features appear unusually harsh. It was a look that Leydi hated, an expression that made her wonder if it was possible that a mother might not love her own child.

"Come, daughter," Leydi's mother said, plucking at the lace scarf, watching the plank-board door thoughtfully. "We've a bit to discuss before I send you to that dragon's lair."

Under her mother's firm lead, Leydi sat down. The slats of the chair bit against her shoulder blades as she waited, her small pleasure at Rutherford's vote of confidence slowly ebbing from her. There were few matters on which her mother held no opinion. Money was not one of them.

"Now then," Elaine began crisply, pacing before Leydi, her high-heeled slippers tapping against the floorboards when she stepped off the wool rug. "I know you'll not take my counsel and refuse his offer, so I'll save my breath with the asking. But you're not to accept his lordship's employment for a quid less than I say." She yanked back the few curls that escaped Leydi's braid, tucking them behind her daughter's ear. Her mouth curled in definite distaste.

Leydi grabbed up the long rope of braid protectively, not wanting another lecture on the "unfashionable length" of her hair. "I'm sure his lordship will be more than fair about my wages."

Her mother sniffed disdainfully. "We'll just see about that. Now, you will, of course, dress properly for the big house," her mother continued, examining Leydi from the tip of her mobcap to the toes of her buckled shoes. "His lordship isn't the rabble you're used to, and I want you to take the extra effort to make your father and me proud. For the hundredth time, you must tighten your corset." Her eyes narrowed on the braid again. "And do something about that dreadful hair."

"I'll wrap it around my head in a crown," Leydi said to forestall her mother's suggestion that curls three-fingers long and tucked up in her cap were more appropriate to her station and age.

"It's so much more practical," she added in an even voice, hoping her vanity didn't show too glaringly.

"Have it your way, then, but keep it neat. You'll not want to draw attention to yourself any more than you have already."

Her mother stared down at Leydi's bosom. A flush crept with unerring heat up Leydi's neck to her cheeks. Her mother's mouth pinched at the corners.

"You're such an innocent, Leydianna." She shook her head, the sausage curls beneath her pinnet rolling with the motion across her ears. "Don't you know what that man's offering you?"

"He wants help with his ledgers. I'm to work with Mr. Stevenson . . ." she finished lamely, wishing with all her heart that what her mother implied wasn't true. The knowing look her mother gave her struck up images of Murdock's brutal attack on Gabriela. Leydi peered down at the tips of her shoes.

A deep suffering sigh sounded just above her head. The *tap-tap* of her mother's heels against the floorboards struck up their rhythm. "If I'd had my way, you would be married by now and out of harm's way. I told that idiot no good would come of his grand plans for you."

"I wish you wouldn't call Kincaid that. He's helped so much—"

"Oh, yes, encouraging your silly notion of owning your own plantation."

"Have patience, Mother. It shouldn't be much longer now. I've already put in my bid at the government office. They say they're encouraging the smaller plots with the change in government, trying to stop the absentee ownership of the larger plantations—"

"Dreams, like everything else you talk about. Your father will ruin us quickly enough if left to his own devices. Good Lord, you sent him to buy two plow horses and he comes back with a gentleman's mount, as happy as you please. You're such a fool, Leydianna. You take after Kincaid in that at least."

Leydi held her counsel, knowing from past experience that when her mother began her tirades about Kincaid, it was best to stay silent. Eight years before, in one short meeting, Kincaid had persuaded Elaine Carstair to allow her fourteen-year-old daughter to work for a pirate—though in all fairness, Leydi wasn't sure her mother knew Kincaid *was* a pirate at the time. That agreement had been their last. And her mother was just as sore a subject with Kincaid.

"That idiot might tolerate your daydreaming, but I'll have none of it now," Elaine continued, nervously plucking at the lace of her sleeves. " 'Tis clear to me his lordship will pay what price is needed, and I'll not have any of your antics of giving money to your father for a horse or a plow, or anything else for that matter. I expect to see the entire amount in my palm to make sure Rutherford's not taking advantage of your soft nature." She stabbed Leydi with a sharp look, waiting to see if her daughter understood her dictates. "Still, I am your mother, and I would do less than my duty if I didn't warn you before sending you off to the big house."

In a rare display of warmth, her mother sat down in a chair opposite hers and took up Leydi's hands between her own. Despite the heat inside the baked walls of the bungalow, her mother's skin felt cool and dry.

"I know we've had our differences, child. 'Tis clear to me you don't think me much of a mother, though your father and I have broken our backs and sacrificed our youth to provide our best for you," she said bitterly, igniting Leydi's keen sense of guilt. "It's not many a girl that's educated, Leydianna. Of your station, none. It was my money that paid for Mr. Stevenson's lessons, don't you forget. So I've at least bought your respect, if not earned it."

Her mother leaned forward in her chair. Her hazel eyes gleamed gold with the morning light streaming through the window behind Leydi. "I advise you to listen carefully to what I've to say now, for your own good. You'll have noticed the master is a handsome man. I can assure you that he can be charming as the devil himself. Any man can be if he wants something from you. You watch yourself. Though I've always tossed it up to no more than kitchen gossip, I can't in good conscience let you go to the big house without a warning."

Her mother licked her lips as if unsure of her words, piquing Leydi's curiosity. "What is it, Mother?"

Elaine's fingers squeezed around Leydi's two hands. Some

strong emotion flickered in her eyes. "Seven years ago, before his lordship came to St. Kitts, they say he had a mistress. A beautiful woman, the story goes, but not one so honorable—a woman of experience with men and their ways." Her gaze flitted over Leydi's head. She sighed, then met her daughter's curious stare once more. "Some say she tried to blackmail him, and she got only what she deserved. I'm not sure I can be a judge of that. Nevertheless, gossip has it she crossed his lordship." Her mouth pressed into an uncompromising line. "You take care of yourself in the big house, Leydi. Though I've never known his lordship to consort with the help, you're innocent, and sometimes that's enough to tempt them."

Elaine's nails pinched into Leydi's fingers painfully. Leydi stared down at her hands, watching them leach of color. "Mother? What happened?" she asked, too curious not to urge her on with her story.

"They say he killed his mistress." Her mother's voice attained a haunting edge as she added, "When he found she carried his babe. Have a care, Leydianna. For once, listen to your mum, and have a care in that great house."

Chapter Four

They say he killed his mistress when he found she carried his babe.

Her mother's warning pounded with the beat of Leydi's heart as she followed Mr. Stevenson down the corridor of Rutherford Hall. The tale was right out of one of her books, as eerie and dramatic as a Greek tragedy. *And certainly as fictitious,* she assured herself, her eyes shifting from a tapestry featuring a boar hunt to a coved niche harboring three white marble muses. Though handsome beyond good sense and reeking of wealth and breeding, the man Stevenson held in such high regard was no lecher capable of murder. Abandonment, perhaps—no one expected the aristocracy to accept the consequences of their actions.

Nor did she believe for one instant that she might "tempt" his lordship as her mother had suggested. Only in her imagination would a man like Quentin Rutherford pay her the least attention. In real life she could conceive of Rutherford cavorting only with pampered young ladies, the kind that wore French silk and ate sweetmeats with darling little pouts on their lips as they chewed. The only thing Leydi had a habit of chewing was her nails.

Leydi trained her eyes on Mr. Stevenson's bewigged figure

bobbing ahead. Goodness, she'd lived on an island brimming to the gills with pirates and not so much as a single attempt had been made on her person. She wouldn't fear one titled gentleman.

There was a slight thickening to the air around her, reminding Leydi of age and preservation. She suspected the tapestries lining the seemingly endless corridor were originals, perhaps even centuries old. Many retained their vibrant earth tones despite their obvious age. The woven cloths gave the long hallway a medieval feel, contributing to the castlelike atmosphere of Rutherford Hall.

Leydi's eyes scanned the dentil work of the ceiling, then perused down the polished oak floorboards covered with costly wool runners. She raised her eyebrows when she realized the sconces were Chinese porcelain, each worth a field laborer's wage for a year. Apparently, like many wealthy young men during their Grand Tour, Rutherford had garnered a taste for the finer things. Though it had been almost a decade since she had walked these corridors as a servant, she certainly didn't remember such opulence when his grandfather had owned the plantation. Rutherford must have spent a fortune renovating the house.

Reaching the end of the corridor, Leydi wiped her moist hands on her apron. Mr. Stevenson stopped before enormous carved oak doors whose elaborate scrollwork could have done a cathedral proud. A queasy flip squeezed her stomach as she wondered what kind of man needed the exorbitant luxuries she'd seen. And would her meager talents as a bookkeeper be sufficient to please?

"Miss Leydi?"

Smiling encouragingly, Mr. Stevenson signaled her to precede him into the room. Giving herself a mental pinch, Leydi straightened her shoulders. She'd never doubted her abilities in finances before, and she wouldn't start now. There was no more demanding a patron than Daniel "Heartless" Kincaid, for goodness' sake. It was her mother's fear that had kindled her doubts, not her own.

Marching ahead, she pictured the small tract of land she'd been saving to purchase for her parents' plantation. With the coin she earned here, she might very well buy the plot within a year's time. And once she had them established on their own plantation on St. Kitts, Leydi would never need to leave Devil's Gate again. Taking a deep breath, she brushed past dear Mr. Stevenson and stepped inside Rutherford's stronghold.

Within two paces Leydi stopped. She blinked, almost rubbing her eyes to clear her vision. Everywhere she looked were piled papers, ledgers, estate books stacked drunkenly to either side . . . there seemed no end to the clutter. And dark. The chamber was as dark as a lair.

It was such a stark contrast to the perfectly manicured rooms she had passed that it took a moment to realize she was still in Rutherford Hall. Yet, beneath the disorder, she could indeed see the frivolous French furnishings of equal quality to those in adjacent chambers. Her gaze skipped from one toppled stack to the next. A comforting warmth seeped into her heart as she realized just how much Rutherford needed her services.

From the receiving chamber's corner, Quentin watched Stevenson hover over his prize pupil with an enthusiasm that bordered on irritating. Stevenson ushered the girl into the room, guiding her to the plushest chair and presenting it for her ease as if he were seating the queen mother. She thanked the old codger with her young-girl smile. Stevenson flushed, beaming his own grin.

Quentin leaned a shoulder against the walnut paneling, not bothering to make his presence known. In the dim light of the room, the girl appeared a study in brown. Brown hair, brown clothes, brown buckled shoes crossed demurely at her ankles. Only her dimpled chin—angled at a slant one might term provocative—and the long braid worn in a tight crown around her head prevented a completely generic appearance. But despite these notable traits, the overall effect had been achieved nicely. She was a little brown creature, a mouse, no doubt molded that way by a less-than-stunning parent fearing they might be outshined.

Quentin realized then why he'd accepted Stevenson's little game, allowing his steward to shelter the girl from her mother. Leydianna Carstair challenged Quentin, a man who had made the bulk of his fortune taking something another had spoiled and turning it into treasure.

Stevenson glanced up from his pupil, seeming to notice Quentin for the first time. He adjusted the wig threatening to slip over his ear. "With Miss Carstair's help, things should be tiptop in no time," he answered shamelessly.

"Do you think so?" Quentin drawled. "Shall we ask the opinion of your protégé? See if she shares your faith? What say you, Miss Carstair?" He glanced around the room, noticing that indeed he'd allowed matters to pile up. "How long will it take to make this disarray . . . tiptop?"

Seated in the chair, Leydi felt her smile freeze on her lips. She could barely make out Rutherford's features in his darkened corner and had a near-irresistible urge to fling open the drawn curtains. Inspired by the shadows, she thought he made a rather admirable dragon: eyes glittering, nose flared as if ready to attack any who would disturb his hoard. But it was the edge to his voice that startled her. Kincaid sounded just the same right before he pounced.

"Well, my lord," she began, licking her lips and reaching for her braid before she remembered she'd moored it around her head in a crown. "It appears that you contacted me just in time. Otherwise, you might find yourself entombed in your own paperwork."

The dark brows flared. He appeared not the least amused by her attempt at humor. She nibbled on the tip of her finger. Humor at least had always worked on Kincaid.

With a deliberateness that could be called only natural grace, Rutherford pushed off the shelves and stalked toward her. "Ah, then you agree with my good steward's assessment that I am in desperate need of your services?" As he drew closer, his dark eyes shone midnight blue in the meager light. "Well, perhaps you're both right."

Rutherford circled Leydi, disappearing behind her chair. She swallowed the lump in her throat and wondered if the rich and pampered lord had ever been "desperate" for anything.

"I presume I can get started today?" she asked, satisfied that her voice did not shake. Again her eyes surveyed the crammed chamber. "If I'm going to be of any help, I will most certainly have to begin soon."

"The room is at your disposal, Miss Carstair," Rutherford said from somewhere behind the armchair. "Stevenson will be working in another office in the wing opposite. You may remove yourself now, Stevenson. Miss Carstair seems eager to begin, and I do so hate to keep a lady waiting."

"But, sir—" Stevenson sputtered.

Making sure the little mouse remained huddled in the berth of the chair, Quentin grabbed Stevenson's sleeve and pulled him out of earshot. "You practically presented the girl as a gift. All that was missing was a pretty ribbon tied in a bow. You're not having second thoughts, are you, old man?"

"No, of course not, sir. Leydi will do a fine job of this mess." Stevenson cleared his throat, looking distinctly uncomfortable. "It's just that—" He glanced at the back of the armchair, where Leydianna's petite height was completely concealed. He stepped closer to his employer, lowering his head to whisper, "It doesn't seem quite proper, sir. The young lady. Here." He wagged his eyebrows up and down. "Alone."

Quentin smiled. Hooking an arm around Stevenson's elbow, he guided his steward toward the door. "Ah, but she won't be alone. I'll be right here beside her, I assure you."

"Yes, well. That's my very point. You see, sir." Again Stevenson lowered his voice, attempting to keep his treasured protégé innocent of this rescue. "I'm not sure that would be quite the thing."

Quentin suspected he wouldn't be able to keep his laughter in check much longer. "If I understood you correctly, the lady spends the year touring the Caribbean without chaperone or husband. I suggest her reputation, what's left of it, needs little or no protection. Now, I have spirited her away from the 'unnatural mother' you so feared, which I assumed was precisely your intent from the first. Don't worry, Stevenson. I plan to make very good use of our little mouse."

"Sir, if I might just add one observation," Stevenson said, looking decidedly uncomfortable, not quite struggling but not quite keeping pace with Quentin as the door loomed closer. "She is such a *young* lady."

"The younger the better, I always say," Quentin added, nodding to Miss Carstair, whose winsome face was now peeking around the cushioned back of the armchair. "I do love youthful enthusiasm. I thought that's why you picked her out for me."

"I didn't exactly 'pick her out' for you, sir," Stevenson said, now starting to bristle. "If you recall, I distinctly said it was *I* who needed Miss Carstair's expertise with the ledgers—"

The door slammed before his steward's face, guided shut by the heel of Quentin's boot. He turned back to Miss Carstair, who kept her eyes trained on the exit as if it were the doors of Bridewell Prison closing before her. For just a moment she actually resembled a mouse. A frightened, cornered mouse. But just as quickly she rose from the chair and faced Quentin, giving her apron a smart tug. The gesture made Quentin smile. It reminded him of a knight lowering his visor for the charge.

Crossing his arms, he leaned back against the doors. For the first time in too many years he realized he might actually be enjoying himself. "My, my. So eager to get started, Miss Carstair?"

"I've quite a lot of experience with matters of *finance,*" the lady said pointedly, seeming to have gotten the gist of his conversation with Stevenson. "If you tell me what's needed, you can be on your way. I require no supervision. . . ."

"But I intend on a great deal of supervision," Quentin said, strolling forward. "In fact, I plan to make quite a nuisance of myself. I so do like the personal touch. Let's get started, shall we? Your gown." He stopped before her, his eyes fixed on the plain cotton dress. "I don't care for the color."

She stared at him as if he'd just spoken in a foreign tongue. "You don't like the color of my dress?"

"It's not very flattering. A shade somewhere in the vicinity of dung-brown, is it? I've seen you before. You were wearing brown then as well. Brown shoes, brown skirt, brown cap. I'm sorry, but it just won't do." And then, with deadly earnest, "Don't wear it again."

Leydi felt the heat scorch her cheeks as she snapped her hanging mouth shut with a click of her teeth. Not only was the question entirely too personal, it rang disturbingly familiar, edging on one of Gabriela's diatribes about her lack of fashion. "It's practical," she answered tartly. "And I assure you, the color of my clothes won't impede my ability to organize your papers."

"Practical?" he repeated with a smile. "For a practical book-keeper?" he said, inching closer. "And I presume this is practical as well?" he asked, reaching behind her.

It wasn't until the braid fell down her back that Leydi realized he'd slipped the pins from her hair. She twirled away, stumbling into a small tripod table behind her. She had the satisfaction of seeing the fragile piece of furniture crash against Rutherford's shins. She thought he bit back a wince.

He looked amused as he straightened the mahogany tea table, but then his eyes shifted to the tip of her braid, where it drifted near the back of her skirt. All signs of humor vanished.

"I imagine it's quite beautiful." The way he spoke, it was as if he could see her hair unbound, curling and twisting around her seductively. She'd never had a man look at her in such a manner, as if she were some delicious confection and he couldn't wait to take a bite. His dark blue eyes drifted to hers. "I'm surprised your mother hasn't convinced you to cut it."

Leydi caught her breath, shocked that he could come so close to the truth. But then she told herself she shouldn't be surprised by his insight. Rutherford was a man who'd made a fortune through speculation.

"Do you always counsel your servants on their sense of fash-ion?" she asked with a sharp look.

"Only when what they wear offends me," he answered, reach-ing up to brush a curl from her face, his fingers lingering there.

That touch seemed to paralyze Leydi, making her feel hot and cold at the same time. All manner of things swept through her mind, daydreams about knights and kisses—her mother's warn-ing against Quentin. She picked up the tip of her braid, worrying the hair between her fingers, wondering if perhaps her mother had been right after all. Perhaps Rutherford was a dangerous man, and she, a simple bookkeeper, was quite out of her element.

Suddenly Rutherford's offer of employment seemed more like a trap than an opportunity. Yes, indeed, Leydi determined, almost losing herself in those dark blue eyes. Perhaps it was time to make a prudent retreat.

She turned for the door. "If you care so much about fashion, you might mention to Mr. Stevenson that his wig needs refitting," she informed Rutherford over her shoulder. "The thing tends to list a bit starboard."

Just as she reached the doorknob, his hand covered hers. "Poor man. He's completely bald, you know." With a feather-light tap of his finger, he tipped her face up to his. "But I still have great hopes for you, Miss Carstair."

He was smiling like a boy. It wasn't an expression that fit his sophisticated good looks. The grin appeared awkward on the aristocratic planes of his face. And perhaps it was that awkwardness she responded to. Truly, he was being outrageous. And though a wiser tongue counseled retreat, a stronger voice inside her wanted to keep that smile on his face.

Leydi crossed her arms before her. "What exactly have I been hired to do here, Rutherford?"

His smile broadened. "Rutherford, is it? Why, Miss Carstair, I do believe that's the first time anyone seeking employment has ever referred to me as such. Mind you, I'm not overly fastidious. But I'm afraid I require a bit more respect from those I hire. Your lordship, sire . . . prince of my heart . . . will do nicely." He rested a hand on the door behind her and leaned over her. "But I'll settle for Quentin from you, little mouse."

Quentin watched Miss Carstair slip under his arm, not so easily cornered. But at least now she was smiling at his teasing. He found he liked that smile. It made him want to keep grinning down at her—until her simple gesture grew, changing her expression into something infinitely delightful. Supremely sweet.

His eyes centered on that inspiring mouth the same coral pink as the roses that grew in the gardens out back. Dear Lord, that expression of unselfish innocence was enough to steal a rational man's breath away if he weren't on his guard against it.

And then he heard her whisper up to him coyly, "Prince of my heart? Well then, I suppose it's a fine thing I haven't been hired yet."

She nudged him aside and yanked open the door. Catching

him unawares, she almost managed to slide past before he pulled her back inside and placed his full weight against the oak. The door clicked shut.

"Book work, my dear brown mouse. I need you only to keep my ledgers." He lowered his face to whisper in her ear, "But I grant you an open invitation for anything else, if you are so inspired." When she pulled on the knob again, he added quickly, "At thirty pounds a month."

Immediately her tugs at the doorknob ceased.

"Oh-ho, I see I have your attention now. Make it thirty-five." He held one hand over his heart, bowing his head graciously. "To compensate for my ill sense of humor."

She looked him straight in the eye. "You're offering me thirty-five pounds a month?"

"Forty, if it tempts you."

It more than tempted; it seduced. "But that's outrageous," she sputtered. It was much more than Kincaid paid, and she thought *him* overly generous. "For book work?"

"I'm quite at your mercy, Miss Carstair." He gestured to the paper-festooned room. "As you can well see."

She gave him a lingering glance. Her sweet gray eyes narrowed as if searching deep into his character. He tried for a moment to look utterly benign, a harmless gentleman of finance.

Apparently coming to a decision in his favor, she stepped back from the door. Miss Carstair marched to the drapes. In one powerful stroke he'd thought beyond her tiny size, she thrust the curtains open, flooding the room with light. Without missing a step she reached the nearest pile and picked up a letter. "April twelfth," she said, raising her eyebrows as she read the date. "Near two months. I presume this correspondence has gone unanswered?"

"It was my birthday," he improvised. "I wasn't up to doing business that day."

She pinned Rutherford with a no-nonsense glare as she read the date on the next letter. "May third?" And the next. "April twenty-third?"

Quentin leaned on the table he used as his desk, crossing his arms over his waistcoat. He hadn't realized how much his father's unexpected appearance had affected his business dealings. Other than a few pet projects, he *had* let a few things go to seed.

The light streaming through the mullion windows shone directly on Miss Carstair as she leaned over the desk. Perched there, she reminded Quentin of a little brown hen as she examined the piles of papers. Indeed, she looked as if she were ready to pounce on each and swallow it whole. Watching her, he had the curious notion that despite her little show of bravado, before him was innocence—stripped bare, and with little armor to protect her.

The very notion disturbed him, extinguishing the joviality of just minutes before. He thought of her vulnerable expression when he'd walked in on her mother's rantings. Thoughts of his own past swelled over him. A host of memories pressed forth, memories of a self-absorbed aristocracy in the king's court, of an uninvolved mother and manipulative father. With the deluge came the one memory he found most unbearable, a phantom that in past years he'd managed to keep to his drunken binges and nightmares.

Clarice.

He frowned. Perhaps it was a mistake to invite innocence into his life.

Quentin turned from the sight of Miss Carstair and examined the herringbone edging of the rosewood desk. *What foolish nonsense,* he told himself, dismissing his qualms. Why should he deprive himself of any gift, especially Stevenson's little mouse? In the meantime, he might teach Miss Carstair a valuable lesson or two. He'd made enough mistakes to counsel a dozen men, certainly he could add to the education of one ill-used daughter.

Leydi shifted through sheet after sheet, shaking her head. She turned to meet Quentin's gaze with a stern expression. "This is all quite untenable, my lord."

"Each day I live with the shame of it, Miss Carstair."

Choosing to ignore his sarcasm, Leydi took her evidence in hand and advanced on the viscount. "I'm sorry to say, my lord"—she waved the sheets below his nose—"but the situation is more dire than I thought."

"Dire?"

"Indeed. I will require at least the afternoon to acquaint my-self with these papers, organize an efficient filing system, priori-tize what needs immediate attention and what might wait." She gave the room another assessment. To Quentin she looked like a general planning an assault. "Why, you might as well have a tray sent around with supper. I shall not resurface until well past that time."

"And you won't need my presence until then?"

"Correct, my lord."

Her confidence amazed him; it was a striking change from the girl he'd seen in her mother's bungalow. He smiled, just a bit. Why not let her have a go at it? To be honest, he didn't much care if the room filled with papers burned to the ground. "The tray won't be necessary, Miss Carstair. You will be dining with me. Dinner is served at eight."

"I don't think I will be ready—"

"I insist, Miss Carstair. Consider it a business meeting. With the good Mr. Stevenson in attendance."

Leydi pressed that lovely mouth closed. "As you wish, my lord."

"It is my deepest desire, Miss Carstair," he answered with equal formality. "Until eight o'clock, then. I'm sure you know your way around. A tug on the bell pull will bring George to attend you. Oh, and Miss Carstair," he said, almost in afterthought, not able to leave without this parting remark, "wear green. That would suit your eyes nicely."

As the door shut behind him, Leydi pursed her lips, seeing her coins would be hard earned indeed. Again her mother's words reared up in her mind. She frowned.

There was a great deal attractive about her dragon, certainly enough to be wary. She straightened the apron over her skirt. With a lift of her chin she marched up to the door to make certain it was properly shut, and she would not be disturbed again.

"And good riddance," she said, speaking out loud. "Wear green, indeed. The beast."

On the other side of the door, Quentin leaned against the carved wood, listening to her softly spoken epithet.

"A mouse?" he whispered to himself, pushing off the door and continuing down the hall, for the first time not giving a damn about his father's presence on St. Kitts.

Chapter Five

Leydi sat back on the heels of her shoes as she knelt before the piles of papers she'd stacked in a semicircle around her. Thus far, she'd managed to organize all but these remaining odds and ends. Now she set them on the floral carpet like pieces of a puzzle—which they were. All related to one event. Something mysterious and disturbing.

She worried the end of her braid between her fingers, biting her bottom lip. In her two and twenty years, Leydi had never turned her back on a mystery. She wasn't about to do so now.

She knew her way around ledgers and contracts, and she could learn a lot about a person reading their papers. Whether he knew it or not, Rutherford's story had been set out before her in these unanswered bits of correspondence, haphazard filings, and unsigned contracts now set out on the carpet's formal design. All dated back to the beginning of spring.

Something had happened to Quentin Alexander Rutherford in early April. Something disturbing enough to make a man who kept impeccable records become suddenly careless.

Something that intrigued Leydi more than it ought.

A small squeak from behind her startled Leydi. She glanced

around to discover an immense ginger cat padding the blue and gold of the thick wool, wending a path toward her.

"Hello," she said, giving the animal a friendly stroke. "Not shy, are you?" she asked as the cat immediately curled up next to her leg and began purring.

She lay down alongside the tom on the carpet, smiling. "You are enormous, you beast," she said, scratching under his chin. She missed Nigel, her own pet. Even though Nigel wasn't warm and cuddly, ever since she'd saved him from the stew pot, he'd tended to stick by her side, making her feel wanted. "I do hope Cy treats Nigel half as nice as you're treated here, you big spoiled thing," she told the cat.

Impervious to her teasing, the cat had an expression of pure feline ecstasy as she scratched behind his ears. With a laugh, Leydi tumbled onto her back and patted the carpet beside her. The audacious fellow climbed onto her stomach, making himself comfortable on her apron. Stroking the cat, she sighed, then stared up.

For the first time, she noticed the most beautiful mural of angels painted on the cove ceiling. Fluffy clouds emerged from the gilded molding surrounded by cerulean blue sky. The light from the candelabrum played across the painted heavens, giving the work an almost Titian quality. The mural seemed to reach down, transporting Leydi to where angels smiled with lifelike cherub faces.

Reaching beside her, she grabbed one of the pages of correspondence she'd found as she petted the ginger beast perched on her stomach. This letter was of particular interest—an offer to sell six male slaves to Rutherford Estate. Its bold strokes assured Quentin he could never make a go of his plantation if he didn't buy more slaves before harvest time.

"And I must agree," she told the angels above her. Going over the estate books, she'd noticed that Quentin had few enough slaves, their purchase dating back to the years the plantation was owned by his grandfather. "The place barely pays for itself. Not that he isn't rich as Croesus already, but if he increased the acreage and doubled his workforce, he could make a tidy sum in sugar."

Staring at the angels, her mind began wandering, floating through the whimsy of clouds as she searched for an answer to this new mystery. His books suggested most of Quentin's money came from speculation. He'd invested in enterprises as small as rudimentary manufacturing works and as grand as coal mines in Wales. There had even been a business with the China trade and some commerce in Russian iron bars and rods. Lately, his own shipping company had suffered some losses. "Losses he could more than make up if he should choose to run Rutherford Estate in a serious manner," she told the angels.

Still, she couldn't fault his decision not to buy slaves, though she didn't know if his reasons were entirely altruistic. On Devil's Gate, many of the men who lived under Kincaid's democratic rule as buccaneers were runaways. She'd heard horrid tales of their treatment and thought their stories would move even the hardest heart.

No, Leydi didn't agree with the purchasing of humans—whether they be indentured, like her parents, or black slaves. Her love for Gabby and her mother, Bertie, both free women of color, made her particularly sensitive to the misery of the slaves who started new lives on Devil's Gate. Though he didn't speak of his past often, Kincaid had recounted enough stories of the cruelty he'd suffered during his own years as an indentured servant that it was no wonder he'd accepted these runaways with open arms.

"I think the dragon must abhor the injustice of slavery," she said to the ceiling, her imagination giving answers where there were none. "That's why he hasn't bought a man since he became master here." She picked up her braid, brushing the tuft of hair at the tip across her chin as she drifted off into her imaginings. "He thinks, as I do, that soon there will be grand machines to do all this miserable work."

She thought of the experimental equipment she'd read about in his Moroccan-leather-bound books—the plans she'd found for the water-powered mill. On several pages she'd even seen ingenious sketches for machines that could aid in the harvesting of cane. She herself had advised on similar equipment when she'd drawn up her plans for a plantation on Devil's Gate—plans that to date Kincaid had allowed to gather dust. As her eyes drifted closed, she smiled up to the angels and buried her fingers into the cat's warm fur. "I wonder. I truly wonder . . ."

Outside the receiving chamber, Quentin prowled down the corridor, coming to retrieve his latest acquisition—one Leydianna Carstair. He was in a thunderous mood; in his hand he held his father's latest missive. Like all the others, he didn't bother to open it. He'd stopped opening these pleas for reconciliation ever since he'd discovered the first letter was not, as he'd hoped, a note informing him of the earl's forthcoming departure.

Damn the man to hell. Did he really think Quentin could be so forgiving? Good Lord, he couldn't abide these appeals for sympathy from a man who in his lifetime had spared his own son none.

But as he entered the room, Quentin reined in his anger. He wouldn't take out his foul mood on the Mouse and risk frightening her off. When he saw Miss Carstair lying on the floor surrounded by piled papers, the lappets of her mobcap trailing behind her head like ribbons, he eased the door shut quietly behind him and stepped soundlessly inside. She seemed so intent, he didn't wish to disturb her.

"You know, dear angels, I'm sure he's really quite nice," he heard her murmur. "Painting you there—that's obviously the act of a sensitive man. That and the fact he refuses to purchase human beings as slaves."

Quentin leaned back against the doors, biting back a smile as he crossed his arms before him and listened. So the Mouse tended to daydream. And she was quite loud about it, too.

"Why, he has few enough servants, and every one of them is paid only too handsomely. And they all respect him so. He's probably just a darling old dear," she said, still completely unaware that the "darling old dear" was listening. "Not a dragon at all. Mother can be so mean at times, telling me that vicious story."

It didn't take much imagination for Quentin to realize what

vicious story the Mouse had heard. But before he could add that burr to his already bursting temper, the room itself captured his attention. In the dimming light of dusk and tallow candles, he hadn't noticed the chamber's startling transformation.

In just a few short hours, the Mouse had managed to change chaos into order.

He stepped over to the nearest table, a sofa table where ledgers had been organized. He glanced over to the long mahogany cabinet whose Chinese fretwork was now hidden by lined-up contracts. Small scraps of paper flashed from the top of each pile. He picked up one, careful not to make a sound, and read the scrolling spidery script: *Is the offer for the tobacco or the sheep? Or both? Unclear.* He picked up another such piece, then another, reading them both. Good Lord, had she read all the correspondence? Every contract? And given her opinion on each?

"And not even married," he heard the Mouse continue, her eyes still closed as she petted Aloysius purring loudly on her stomach. "Were I a fine lady, I would set my cap on the dragon. Or maybe it's his past that's problematic? Maybe they're foolish enough to fear him?"

Quentin smiled as in one breath she called him a dragon, then blithely pronounced any who would fear him fools. Quietly, he returned her scraps of paper to their proper places. Perhaps he'd been too harsh on the Mouse. He paced back to the door, determining then to send George to find her. He'd not embarrass her by waking her from her musings now.

"I could be the Lady Anne," he heard her say as he started to close the door behind him. He stopped, shamelessly listening for just a moment more.

"Lady Anne, yes, yes. A very important person who dresses in elegant gowns and satin slippers. Someone he wouldn't be able to ignore, I would be so beautiful and important. . . ."

With those final musings ringing in his ears, Quentin shut the door. He stepped down the hall, his father's missive crumbled and forgotten in his hand. Poor Mouse. She hadn't a clue the dragon had no plans to ignore her.

* * *

The supper table extending down the length of the yawning candlelit room could have seated a small army. As it was, only three souls graced its marquetry. Quentin Rutherford and his steward exchanged pleasantries across the sea of Flanders linen as Leydi's fingers played absently with the tip of her braid and her gentle gray eyes stared at nothing but empty space. . . .

"Lady Anne, your hair—forgive me, but I can't keep from touching it. It's like spun gold in the light."

"Oh, Viscount." Leydianna laughed, slapping Quentin's hands away playfully from the thick tresses flowing over her shoulder. She spread the loose curls to their best advantage so they draped over the emerald satin of her gown. "Nonsense, it's an ordinary brown, and we both know it." She sighed, taking a sip of claret. "But that does sound terribly romantic. How you do say the most lovely things."

"Only for you, dearest heart," he whispered, his dark blue eyes cherishing her from the jeweled combs in her hair to the silk slippers.

"My mother told me to be wary of you," she confessed from behind the wineglass. "She was quite displeased that I agreed to have supper with you tonight."

"Your mother be damned—and anyone else who should keep you from me. Until we met, my days were filled with darkness. I toiled over accounts, making my fortune only to keep sheer boredom at bay." Quentin leaned closer, his eyes filled with love and longing. "Lady Anne, you have brought sunshine into my life. Allow me to bathe in its warmth. Marry me, sweet love. This very night. This very minute—"

Her fingers tightened around the crystal goblet; her breath caught. "I wouldn't dare. We've only just met. I couldn't be so bold. . . ."

"But it's only soup, Miss Carstair."

Leydi looked up from her glass, dazed from her daydream by the odd mention of soup. She blinked. Directly to her left, Quentin Rutherford watched her from the head of the supper table, a puzzled expression on his handsome face. Standing beside him, a tall black man in a servant's uniform waited patiently as he held out a silver tureen of soup.

With growing horror she realized she'd done it again, lost herself in fantasy. The only similarity between the present scene and her imagined vision of seconds before was the crystal wine goblet in her hand and Quentin's dark blue eyes fixed on her.

"It's turtle soup," he added helpfully. "It's quite good, actually."

With complete and utter mortification, Leydianna wondered how long she'd been staring at nothing, daydreaming as Quentin watched on. Had she spoken out loud? She glanced across the table at Mr. Stevenson, tendrils of panic sprouting from her heart as she tried to discover how big a fool she had made of herself. The older gentleman was busy spooning up his soup, his wig veering slightly over his left ear.

Taking his lack of interest as a good sign, Leydi gulped a healthy swallow of the claret. When she dared a glimpse back at Quentin, he was patiently waiting for her decision on the soup.

"Please," she said, nodding her head toward the delftware plate with its charming view of Venice painted at the bottom. In a swallow, she emptied the wineglass and held it out for more.

"As I was saying, Stevenson," Quentin stated, his voice mellow as the servant topped off Leydi's soup and turned to Quentin's bowl, "I agree that the salt ponds on Nevis show promise, but the price Simmons asks is a prayer." Taking up the wine decanter, he refilled Leydi's glass.

Everything in his quiet manner put her at ease that she'd not made an incredible ass of herself. Goodness. It wasn't like her to go dodding off in the middle of supper, she thought, taking another drink.

"Wait a month, when Douglas's tobacco crop is ready to harvest, you'll see Simmons will drop his price. He'll be needing . . ."

Leydi gave thanks to every saint whose name she could remember that all seemed on proper course now. She peered over at Quentin and frowned. He certainly fit the part of the chivalrous suitor in her daydreams, looking quite handsome with his dark hair queued and unpowdered. He wore a simple black coat, breeches, and a matching moiré waistcoat. She fiddled with her glass sullenly. She could just imagine what Rutherford would do with the knowledge that he was the object of her fantasy. Particularly after his horrid teasing that afternoon.

"And tell Terence again I've no need for those slaves he's so intent on selling to me."

"And why is that?" Leydi asked. It was the very question she'd asked herself earlier. "I mean, I read the letter when I was organizing your papers and I must agree that you could use more slaves. At harvesttime, certainly."

"Because it's barbaric," he said simply. Returning to the soup, he added, "Visit the slave mart at Basse Terre and you'll see. It took me only one trip to decide against it."

His response was so much in line with her own beliefs that Leydi set down her spoon and took a moment to study the man seated beside her. As he continued his discourse on the salt ponds with Stevenson, she searched his face for more answers to the mysteries she'd unearthed in the receiving chamber.

She'd found so many riddles in those papers she'd read, enough apparently to fuel her romantic daydreaming clear through to dinner. She studied Rutherford's profile in the light glittering from the branched candlesticks in the silver rococo centerpiece. She tried to find anything that might explain or corroborate her theory that some startling event in the spring had wounded Quentin. She peered closer, hunting for any signs of moodiness or evidence of recent catastrophe in his life.

"How is the soup?" he asked, catching her staring.

Her gaze fell back to the delftware bowl. "It's grand," she murmured, disappointed. Other than slightly red-rimmed eyes, his handsome face revealed nothing more expressive than the austere lord of the manor.

"I'm so pleased," he said with a smile.

Leydi sighed. She hated mysteries. Basically because she couldn't resist trying to unravel them.

Finding the soup indeed tasty, Leydi dug in with a bit more spirit. He hadn't even commented on her plain brown dress— her thrown gauntlet. Despite the admirable pay he'd offered, she'd wanted to make it understood she would not scurry back to her parents' bungalow and change her gown just to curry his favor. He'd purchased only her expertise in book work and nothing more.

Not that she owned anything other than plain brown dresses, she reminded herself, stirring the soup listlessly. She couldn't really say when it had happened, but over the years she'd actually begun liking the clothes her mother had insisted she wear, finding the circumspect gowns with their simple white aprons, the plain kerchiefs and mobcaps, indeed very practical. She remembered Rutherford's disturbing reference to her mother's influence that afternoon. He had certainly put a different light on that motherly advice. She picked up her braid, twining the end through her fingers. Perhaps Gabby was right; perhaps Leydi had allowed her mother to bully her of late—

"I say we ask Miss Carstair her opinion," Quentin said, interrupting her thoughts. "Something tells me she can be quite inventive if the need arises. What think you?" he continued, turning to Leydi as she filled her mouth with soup. "How would you go about hunting a pirate like Kincaid?"

Leydi choked. Her spoon clattered to the bowl, splashing soup in every direction. Horrified and gasping for breath, she grabbed for the wineglass while Rutherford pounded on her back. When she managed to catch her breath, she swabbed at the fine Flanders linen now ruined with large green blotches.

"You were speaking of p-pirates?" she sputtered. "Oh, I would definitely stay clear of the Brethren of the Coast, my lord. Truly. A dangerous lot."

"Exactly what I advised," Mr. Stevenson said with a decided nod that sent his wig dangerously steering off his head in the direction of his soup. "Likely to target more of your ships if you get on the wrong side of Heartless Kincaid."

"I've already been targeted," Quentin said, waiting for the room's single servant to clear the soup bowls and set the next course. "Or what do you call three boardings in two months?"

Three! Leydi silently cursed Kincaid as she scrubbed the soup stains with her mangled napkin. He'd sworn to stay clear of the Caribbean after Jack Randall's hanging in Jamaica. He said he was hunting in the Pacific!

"You're sure it was Heartless? I mean," she added when

Quentin stilled her hand from its useless attempt to clean the linen, "you wouldn't want to go after the wrong man. I understand Heartless Kincaid preys only on ships in the Pacific these past years—since the Royal Navy has started rounding up pirates in the Caribbean. And no one has seen Heartless himself in near a decade. It could be someone else altogether."

"His ship, the *Plague,* is quite distinctive, Miss Carstair. And though no one caught sight of the pirate himself, his men made no attempt to hide the identity of their leader. They touted it proudly, I understand."

Leydi frowned. Drat that man! Next time they met, she would call Kincaid Mindless instead of Heartless.

"Three boardings in such a short time?" she said, hoping she sounded casual in her interest, reaching for her braid and torturing it through her fingers anxiously. "How truly unlucky for you, sir. But I'd wager to say he's had his fill of you." She cleared her voice when it squeaked. "Odds are, you'll never see that pirate again."

"I disagree." Quentin took a sip of wine. "I intend to bring the man down, and I've the promise of the government's help to do it."

Fear clawed at Leydi's throat. Rutherford looked like a man with a mission. A dangerous man.

"Well, since you asked my opinion, I would say only a dunderheaded fool would go after Heartless Kincaid," she snapped, failing miserably in her attempt to keep calm. She threw her braid over her shoulder and struggled with some excuse to get Rutherford off Kincaid's scent. "And with your own situation being what it is . . . well, are you a man of business or a mercenary? You have an entire room filled with . . . with . . . unanswered obligations." She waved her hands for effect, true fear brimming from her voice. "You've had to hire me to relieve poor Mr. Stevenson of a colossal burden. And you want to launch into this escapade of . . . of . . . pirate chasing? Well, let me tell you, sir, pirates are dangerous people," she said, gathering steam. "Blackbeard was known to chop off a finger rather than show the patience to wait for his victim to hand over a ring. And Rock Brasiliano roasted Spaniards alive," Leydi continued, unaware she had the men's complete and rapt attention, "simply because they wouldn't tell him where they kept their pigs!"

"Rock Brasiliano?" Quentin steepled his fingers. "I'm not familiar with the name."

"And the Barbarossa brothers, Captain Devil," Leydi counted off on her fingers, "Koxinga and Edward Low—why, they're vicious, vicious men. And believe you me, a man like Heartless is worth two or three Captain Devils."

"You seem rather knowledgeable about pirates."

But Leydi wasn't listening to Quentin. She was too embroiled in her own fears and worries. "And they died so horribly. They say it took two dozen thrusts of the sword and half as many bullets to stop Blackbeard. They hung his head from the bowsprit of a ship while sailing up and down the James River. They put Captain Kidd in an iron cage, and tarred his body to preserve it as a warning to others."

Her eyes glazed over with the horrible images. Her hand crept to her own neck, where the kerchief she wore tucked into the laces of her bodice had grown uncomfortably tight. "Just a few years ago, forty-one *good* men were hung from Gallows Point for acts of piracy."

The room became incredibly quiet. Stevenson had stopped eating; Rutherford was staring at her. Even the servant who'd removed the dishes stood transfixed beside the cupboard, where a spirit lamp kept the side dishes hot.

"It was horrible," she said weakly, taking her hand from her neck. "We all cried buckets that day when we heard the news."

Quentin played with his fork, mystified by Miss Carstair's performance. In almost a single breath the Mouse had gone from spouting about the bloodthirsty Brethren of the Coast to showing quiet sympathy for the very men she'd just warned him against. Along the way she mentioned obscure names with the finesse of a pirate aficionado who made it her business to know such rabble and their reputation.

"I agree with Miss Leydi," Stevenson said from across the table. "Your efforts are best suited to business, not capturing a pirate."

"Do eat your fish, Stevenson," Quentin said in the same mild tone he'd used the entire evening. "It's quite ghastly when it's cold."

Quentin ate his own meal thoughtfully, going over the Mouse's strange behavior now that she was quiet. He'd thought her odd enough when he'd caught her daydreaming in the receiving chamber, something she seemed to indulge in with disturbing frequency if he'd read that glazed look in her eye correctly at supper. Now, this curious discourse on pirates. He was beginning to think the poor Mouse was more than just browbeaten by a miserable parent. He was beginning to wonder if she wasn't just . . . well . . . a bit tetched.

Watching her now, he could see she hadn't touched her food. He guessed she was furiously thinking about something. Soon enough he expected to see that lovely coral-pink mouth begin to move, another silent discourse to which only the Mouse would be privy. He returned to his own meal, disbelieving that he might actually find "tetched" intriguing in a woman.

As the dishes were removed and fruit and dessert served, Leydi wished desperately she could leave. Providence had given her the opportunity to discover Rutherford's plans before it was too late, but she didn't know how much longer she could just sit there as the man planned the demise of the only person who'd shown her an ounce of kindness. Tomorrow she would go see Gabriela and Bertie at the shop—tell them the horrible news. Yes, that was a good plan. Bertie was sensible. She would know what to do.

"Well, I'd best be going," Leydi said, waving away the syllabub, ready to make good her escape. She dipped her fingers into the finger bowl, then yawned for effect before wiping her hands.

Quentin stood beside her. "Of course. You must be tired from your work." He took her hand and led her to the door, watching her braid swing provocatively across a backside not obscured by the hooped petticoats that were all the fashion. "And tomorrow will be another full day."

Leydi froze mid-yawn. "Oh, no. I can't tomorrow. I . . . I have a prior commitment. In town." *With Gabriela and Bertie!* "It's really vital . . ."

Quentin nodded. But to Leydi he appeared less than understanding. "I thought my considerable wages enough to buy your time, Miss Carstair."

"Yes. Of course. It's just that . . . ." She struggled for an excuse. It was imperative that she do nothing to jeopardize her position with Rutherford. Not if she was to keep track of his plans for Kincaid. "It's the dress," she said, grabbing for inspiration. She tried to look embarrassed. "I . . . I wanted to surprise you and buy a new gown." Good heavens, she prayed Bertie had something suitable. "Something . . . green."

"I'm flattered." Quentin watched her closely. Nothing changed in his expression, but somehow Leydi thought he hadn't believed a word she'd said.

He reached for the door behind her. "An emerald green," he said, nodding as she slipped past him into the hall. "Yes. That color will look lovely with your eyes."

Before she could escape down the corridor, he tilted her head up to his. His eyes seemed to stare into her own, arresting in their intensity. His gaze dropped to her mouth. Leydi felt her stomach take a flip. Suddenly, she wished she hadn't touched that soup.

"Yes," he whispered almost to himself. "Quite lovely."

"I'll pick something spectacular," she said, backing away. She tried to tell herself now was not the time to fall for one of Rutherford's spells. She had her duty to think about. She turned, planning to hurry off, doing her best to shake off the compelling magic of those dark blue eyes. "Truly, I will," she called back over her shoulder.

"And Lady Anne."

Halfway down the hall, Leydi stopped. She recognized that peculiar cadence in her name—not Leydianna, but *Lady Anne,* two distinct words. The name she'd called herself in her daydream.

Leydi went cold as she heard the sounds of Quentin walking up behind her. She refused to turn around to look at his face, to see the satisfaction that would surely be there. She stared at the trio of muses in the alcove to her left, as if Calliope or Erato in all their marble splendor might somehow grant rescue. She told herself she couldn't possibly have spoken out loud, that she wasn't that much of a dunderhead.

But there seemed no other explanation for his use of the name Lady Anne. And she wanted to die, to perish right then and there.

She could sense he'd stopped directly behind her, could feel his breath on the back of her neck as he whispered, "You're proving to be a very difficult lady to ignore, Mouse."

She heard Rutherford turn, then chuckle as he stepped down the hall, returning to the supper hall—while Leydi died a million deaths of complete and utter humiliation.

"He's watching us." Gabriela nodded her head toward the man waiting across the street. She and Leydi stood outside her mother's shop on Palace Street, where a frantic Leydi had practically pulled Gabby's arm from its socket in her haste to tell her friend the tale about Kincaid.

"Don't be ridiculous," Leydi said, looking over Gabby's shoulder. A wagon pulled by oxen obscured her view, followed by a woman balancing a sizable basket on her head, calling out in accented English, "Mangoes! Fresh mangoes!" But when Leydi did catch a glimpse of the man almost hidden in the shadow of the colonnade and a tinker's stand, she thought for a moment that he might indeed be watching them.

He wasn't particularly ominous, just tall and slim, his shoulders not quite fitting the open jacket he wore, as if it were borrowed. His hair looked a dark russet, though it was difficult to tell from where Leydi stood. For a moment, their eyes met, until he turned his back to them, seeming to examine the wares in the lacemaker's shopwindow.

"Look, Gabby. We have bigger problems to solve than some swain trying to catch your attention. Have you heard a single word I've said?" She tried to keep her voice steady while conveying to Gabby the danger they faced. "Rutherford is after Kincaid! He's working on a plan to capture him this very minute! He's managed some official aid in the matter, despite all those bribes Bertie dishes out." She stepped closer, whispering, "He even asked my opinion on how to do the deed!"

"He was there yesterday, as well," Gabby said, her green eyes peering back across the street. "And the day before that. Always waiting under the colonnade across from Mama's. Perhaps he's taken a fancy to me."

"Gabriela! They are going to hang Kincaid on Gallows Point if we don't do something!"

"Don't be overdramatic, *caro.*" Gabriela fingered the lace fichu tucked into the neckline of her hooped gown. "I think he's quite attractive—in a young sort of way."

Before Leydi could stop her, Gabriela wiggled her fingers in the man's direction, granting him the full force of her smile. The man, now leaning against the wall of the shop, didn't seem to notice.

Leydi grabbed Gabby's arm and yanked her around. "Lord in heaven, Gabby, I know you and Kincaid have had your differences, but I never thought you wished him ill. Don't you care what happens to him?"

Gabriela's eyes grew brittle bright. "Kincaid can take care of himself. He doesn't need our interference."

"How can you not wish to help? Aren't you the least bit concerned? We owe him so much—"

"Yes," Gabby said sharply, "I know exactly how much my mother and I owe Kincaid—for the shop, for bringing Mama here to St. Kitts. For my useless job as his housekeeper. Well, he owes us as well."

"I don't understand," Leydi said, confused by Gabby's mulish expression.

"Kincaid has no need of my help, *caro.* He never has and never will. Now leave me be. I've business to attend to."

Gabriela danced around Leydi's reach and hurried into the dirt street before her friend could stop her. She wouldn't let Leydi ruin the day with her talk of Kincaid. Skirting around a slow-moving carriage, waiting for a troupe of hogs to pass, she searched for the gentleman. She'd spotted the fellow across the street yesterday, dressed in a jacket and slops, the loose breeches favored by naval men. When she'd seen him standing under the golden eagle emblem of the lacemaker's shop, she'd realized she'd seen him before, standing in that very place. Was it the day she'd returned from Devil's Gate? She couldn't recall exactly.

At first she'd been wary. Her dark, exotic looks had a habit of attracting the wrong sort—men like Murdock, who thought that because she was beautiful and a quadroon, she was at their disposal. Damn Murdock, and all others like him.

As the wagon passed, she spotted the redheaded fellow again and smiled. The past days, he hadn't approached Gabriela or her mother, just watched silently from his post. She'd come to think him more a nuisance than a danger. At the moment he was making a valiant effort to look anywhere but at Gabriela.

He was indeed good-looking in a rangy sort of way, with red hair that curled at his temples and dark, brooding eyes. Though it wasn't her intention to encourage him, it wasn't in her nature to hide, either. She wanted to know what he was about.

Ignoring Leydi's cries to stop wasting time, Gabriela ventured toward the flower vendor's stall on the street just past where the man was waiting. A friend of her mother's, the vendor smiled as Gabriela plucked up a bright red rose and mouthed her thanks. Holding the long-stemmed flower under her nose, she walked down the raised path, making her way slowly toward the gentleman in the shadows.

As she approached, she saw him stand taller, stepping away from the support of the wall. He took his hands from his pockets, watching her with wary eyes. His gaze was so intense that for a moment Gabriela's step faltered and she wondered if she hadn't made a mistake—until she saw the flicker of desire.

She slowed her approach, holding the rose below her chin as she plucked off its thorns. Desire Gabriela could well understand. Too many men had proclaimed that emotion to her. "I need you, Gabriela." "I want you, Gabriela." "You're so beautiful, Gabriela." Oh, yes. She knew all about that lovely passion.

Her mother always said Gabriela had been blessed in her mixed ancestry—in her had flowered the best the two races had to offer. She was tall, with full lips and long limbs, like her grandfather. Her brown hair fell in tight ringlets just past her ears. Her skin was a dusky tan, several shades lighter than that of her mulatress mother. Her eyes were green and slanted over high cheekbones, part of her grandmother's Portuguese blood. But despite all the attention her figure and face had garnered, Gabriela had yet to find what she wanted most from life. True love.

Gabriela tossed the thorns to the ground, holding the sailor's eyes with a smile. Ever since she'd been old enough to understand the romantic story of her grandparents, Gabriela had prayed for such a love in her life. Bertie always told the tale with great emotion, and over the years that image of true love had seduced Gabriela until nothing else would do.

It was a wonderful story—her grandmama had been near death in the Brazils when her uncle, the owner of a rubber plantation, had sought the help of one of his slaves, a man known for his talents at healing. Soltan had saved Maria's life, and had been granted his freedom for his success—but he had sought a greater prize. Maria herself. The two had run off together, carving a life for themselves in the jungle, living with the local Indians. Her mother, the daughter of that union, had married a trader, a man half Indian himself.

But unfortunately, Bertie did not have Maria's luck with love. Her husband had left her destitute. It was Kincaid who had saved her from the fate that awaited abandoned women on the streets of São Paulo. Since then, her mother's soft heart and eternal youth had taken Bertie from one heartbreak to another—her biggest being Kincaid.

But Gabriela was nothing like her mother. She wouldn't settle for the drippings that pirate had given Bertie by setting her up in her own shop. Gabriela wanted true love, like Maria's and Soltan's. She would settle for nothing less.

Twirling the rose in her hand, she stopped before the redheaded sailor. There were many military men in Basse Terre, the conflict with the French being so recently settled. And from his manner and the expense of his clothes, she judged he was an officer, possibly even part of the royal patrol that hunted pirates like Kincaid. She deepened her smile, refusing to be intimidated by any man, military or not.

She held out her rose. "Here. For your vigilance. Now be a good boy and leave me alone. There's nothing for you here."

He took the rose, his eyes never leaving hers. They were brown, and looked nice with his dark auburn curls tied back in a queue. Closer up, she saw that he had freckles and lines that said he was older than she'd first thought.

"Am I so obvious, then?"

Gabriela laughed, less intimidated now that she had him smiling. "Yes. I'm afraid so."

"You're her daughter?" he asked, nodding his head toward the louvered windows of Bertie's shop.

The question puzzled Gabriela, making her wonder if it was her mother he'd come to romance. Not that it mattered. He'd get nowhere with Bertie, who was totally enthralled by that lothario Hugh Piton—a man half her mother's age. Gabriela didn't much care for Hugh, sensing the relationship meant only more heartbreak for her mother.

"May I ask your name?" The man gave her a lopsided grin, not waiting for her answer. "I mean, if I'm to be totally dismissed, I'd like to know your name, at least."

"Gabriela," she said, a bit more at ease. "Gabriela de Sousa."

"Then you are her daughter."

The smile faltered on Gabriela's face. She'd just been manipulated into answering his first question.

"Clever man," she told him, her smile not so nice this time. Behind her, a hand tugged at her elbow, pulling on the lace trim of her sleeve.

"Let's go, Gabby," Leydi said through gritted teeth. She looked anxiously at the naval officer. "We don't have time for this, for goodness' sake."

"All right, *caro,*" Gabriela said, turning away from the man to speak with her friend. "Just let me tell this fellow, he can't . . ." But when she turned back to give her parting remarks, the man was gone.

Gabriela looked up and down the colonnade. There was no sign of him. He'd vanished.

"Come on, Gabby!"

"Did you see where he went?"

"We've more important things to discuss!"

As Leydi pulled her away, Gabriela glanced down and frowned. The rose lay on the plank boards of the raised walkway, the crushed petals staining the wood where the man had been standing.

Chapter Six

Even the weather conspired against her fears, Leydi thought, watching the sunshine flood the cheery shop, making it nearly impossible to worry on such a day. Unlike most concerns on Palace Street, Bertie had forsaken the shelving space provided by a narrow door and small-paned windows. Instead, two enormous louvered openings flanked each side of the entrance. Light shone on nearly every barrel of Holland gin and French cognac, flashing across shelved boxes of Netherlands lace and stacked chinaware, inviting the buyer to conduct a close scrutiny of European and West India goods alike.

In the center of the shop Leydi balanced atop a cane stool as Bertie finished hemming the satin gown she'd unearthed from her back room. Afternoon shadows danced across the plank floor and shifted over the floral print of Bertie's gown. The room smelled of dried herbs and strong tobacco.

Leydi fidgeted from one foot to the other. "Ouch!"

"Don't move an inch, or I'll prick you," Bertie warned, speaking around a mouthful of pins. She wore her dark, curly hair turbaned in a colorful scarf patterned in red and yellow. Large gold hoops swung from her ears, brushing across her neck. She knelt down beside the stool, getting a closer fix on the hem.

Leydi stood with her arms stuck straight out, looking much like a scarecrow, she thought. But the gown was almost worth the trouble of the fitting. Unlike anything Leydi had ever worn, it was an elegant dress, with clean lines consisting of a bodice open in the front to show an embroidered stomacher. Though a bit impractical, the wide hooped skirt made Leydi think of grand ladies and moonlit soirees. The material was perfect, an exquisite emerald satin with a hint of cream lace and a row of pink baby roses decorating the three-quarter-length sleeves and square neckline.

"This gown should lull any of Rutherford's suspicions," Leydi said, wishing she could put her arms down but knowing there were enough pins in the dress to stab her into an early grave.

"Pirate treasure!" Bertie said, her dark eyes shining with her smile. "Part of a trousseau shipped on a Spanish galleon. I pity the bride-to-be—the clothes were *muito belo,* very beautiful," Bertie translated. "I sold all but this one. I was saving it for a special occasion. Hold still, *menina!* You thank Daniel next time you see him, eh?"

"Oh, *sim,*" Gabriela said, popping a bit of candied fruit into her mouth. "Let us all bow and give thanks to the great Daniel Kincaid." She turned to look out the window.

"Gabriela!" Bertie's singsong intonation as she said her daughter's name always made Leydi smile. Unlike her daughter, Bertie had a heavy accent. "It gives a woman wrinkles to be so sour all the time." She shook her head and pinned up another inch of hem. *"Menina,"* Bertie said, calling Leydi "little girl" in Portuguese, her special name for her, "you think this man you work for is dangerous? He will hunt Daniel down?"

"Rutherford's trouble, all right," Leydi said, picturing in her mind Quentin's determined expression when he'd discussed his plans to capture Kincaid. "Do you have any idea how we can stop him?"

Bertie shook her head. Taking the pins from her mouth, she shut the sewing basket and gestured for Leydi to hop down from the stool, having finished the hem. "But we will think of something, eh? To save our dear Kincaid." She jogged her head to her daughter brooding near the window and winked at Leydi. "And sourpuss there *will* help us."

Behind a japanned screen decorated with two willowy cranes standing among tall reeds, Leydi paused as Bertie went about the business of helping change her gown. She held up her braid, waiting for Bertie to lace up her dress, when she felt a distinct loosening of her stays.

"What are you doing?" Leydi said, twisting to peer over her shoulder.

"Loosening this thing before it stops the breath in your lungs!"

"Stop," Leydi said, trying to dance out of Bertie's reach.

"Yes, *Mãe,*" Gabriela said, peering over the screen. "You'll spoil Leydi's plans to hide her breasts. You know how it pleases her mother to make her daughter most unattractive."

"Do hush, Gabby," Leydi said, pushing Bertie's hands away to lace up her own gown. "That's simply not true."

Gabriela pulled on Leydi's long braid of hair. "Elaine ties up everything of beauty Leydi has, lest she appear an old toad next to her daughter."

Leydi said nothing to Gabby's baiting, examining the dark patterns on the floorboards made by constant douses of rainwater and scrubbing. It was only too true that her mother seemed to try her best to make Leydi less attractive. But Leydi guessed Elaine's motives were much more complicated than simple jealousy.

"What are we going to do about Rutherford?" she asked, coming around the japanned screen, veering the conversation to more important matters.

"Not *we,*" Gabby said, both fists resting on the padded hips of her smart muslin striped gown. "You, *caro.* You will be our spy."

"Spy?" Leydi said, tucking her braid up inside her mobcap. "Don't be ridiculous. I can't spy."

"Who else," Bertie seconded from behind the counter, where she put away her sewing box. "You work for him, don't you? You can encourage him to take you into his confidences."

"Yes, *caro!*" Gabriela said enthusiastically. "Why, he's even asked for your considered opinion. You could influence him. If you take the right tack." She gave her a sly glance. "The dress is a good start."

Leydi scowled. "You want me to charm him with my womanly wiles? Odds are very poor of my succeeding there." Leydi pushed through the many pots and pans hanging by iron hooks from the exposed rafters and followed Gabriela to the counter. "Rutherford would eat me up in one bite if I tried to fool him that way," she said, remembering her embarrassment when he'd overheard her daydream. "No, I know a better way."

Setting aside a lacquered box filled with goose quills, she motioned both women to lean closer. "Quentin Rutherford is a man of finance. He prides himself on his reputation for speculative ventures." She beamed a pleased smile, thinking her strategy quite sound. "I've read over his books and I've an idea or two on how to help his finances. I'll make sure to advise him on a few good bargains, enough to catch his interest, then I'll lull him into further confiding in me with a venture I've been looking into for Kincaid. If I succeed and fatten his purse, he'll certainly trust me."

"She might be right," Bertie said, thinking.

"Yes," Gabby said. She gave a dramatic sigh. "Though boring in the extreme, I suppose that will work just as well as my plan."

"Trust me, Gabby. I wouldn't be a very good temptress, even wearing that beautiful gown. But a business wizard." She nodded with assurance. "Now, *there* I quite excel."

Gabby leaned her elbows back on the pine counter, staring out the window. "Still, you would think that with all those books you read, *caro,* you could come up with something more exciting."

Leydi picked out a candied lemon peel from a canister on the counter. Certainly she yearned to compose some enticing adventure where she could heroically save the day. She smiled, for an instant allowing herself to weave an image of her yielding a cutlass, taking the dragon to task.

She took a bite of the candied fruit, thinking out loud dreamily. "If I were to take inspiration from my books, I'd have us dress up like pirates and play Anne Bonny and Mary Reed. Now, there's two who knew how to get what they needed from men." She laughed. "We could kidnap Rutherford and threaten him with cutlass and pistol until he swore to forgo his revenge against Kincaid." She sighed, knowing this was no time for daydreams. Her first plan was by far the wiser course.

"Well," Gabby said languidly. "At least it's not boring." Peering more intently out the window, Gabby stood up from the counter. "Speaking of boring. Look, *Mãe.*" She nodded her head toward the window. "Isn't that Hugh?"

Bertie turned with a smile, almost shining with the name of her beloved—until her gaze focused beyond the window.

"And who is that woman he's with, I wonder?" Gabby asked too innocently.

Bertie's ebony eyes narrowed like daggers. Grabbing up the cumbersome hooped petticoat, she marched to the door, her heeled mules gliding in a ground-eating pace. With a questioning glance to Gabby, Leydi followed, just missing the door as Bertie slammed it open.

She peered around Bertie's shoulder, wondering what all the fuss was about. And then she saw him—absolutely the most beautiful man it had ever been her pleasure to lay eyes on.

He stood on the raised walkway just outside the shop, oblivious of the chickens pecking the boards for food. He wore a felt tricorn, a waistcoat of calamanco over a linen shirt and woolen breeches, the simple clothes of a laborer. His stockings were threadbare and his buckled shoes old. But the disreputable clothing took nothing from his beauty.

His hair was the color of mink, a beautiful rich brown, tied in a ribbon at his neck. Eyes a startling pale blue were rimmed with thick, sooty lashes. His proportions were perfect, broad shoulders and slim waist, as if God had decided to make a model of what man should look like. Right now he leaned over a young woman with burnished curls beneath a straw milkmaid's hat tied with ribbons behind her head. She flushed daintily at something he said.

"Hugh?" Bertie called out. When he didn't seem to hear her, she stamped her foot and yelled, "Hugh!"

The man turned, his movements languid, his expression tame, as if he'd not a worry in the world. When he saw Bertie's fulminating expression, he merely smiled warmly. Seeing Bertie, the woman who'd been preening under his regard turned tail and ran briskly toward the colonnade on the street opposite the shop.

"À Dieu, Monique!" Hugh called to the woman, shaking his head in appreciation for her swing-hipped walk. Leydi had the impression that any minute he might kiss his fingers to his lips. Instead, he turned with a sigh toward Bertie. As soon as he saw her, he held out his hands. All his considerable attention and appreciation turned on Bertie—as if the woman minutes ago never existed.

Leydi looked up at Gabby standing beside her. Gabby crossed her arms before her lace stomacher and nodded her head toward the approaching man, the lappets from the pinnet cap she wore swaying with the movement. "Mother's latest," she said as they both turned to watch Bertie stride out to meet Hugh on the walkway outside the shop.

Gabby leaned out the door for a better look, making room for the more petite Leydi beside her. "And Mother looks none too pleased."

As both women watched, Hugh engulfed Bertie in a tremendous bear hug. He swung her around until her feet left the ground. Before Bertie could utter a word of protest, Hugh kissed her right then and there, for all to see, in a most disconcerting manner—intimate enough to make Leydi blush.

"The best is yet to come, caro," Gabby said, her expression filled with distrust.

While Bertie teasingly tried to swat his hands away, Hugh scooped her up in his arms and carted her back inside the shop like a groom carrying his intended. Gabby and Leydi stepped aside as Hugh glided past, dipping Bertie down to the floorboards in another heartfelt kiss.

"Hugh!" This time Bertie managed to struggle out of his embrace. "Who is that woman?"

Hugh kept staring into Bertie's eyes, his own pale blue gaze shining with an intensity that made the airy shop seem suddenly hot and stuffy to Leydi. There was no other way to put it—he caressed Bertie with his eyes, watching her as if he hadn't any idea what Bertie was talking about.

"Bertie, *mon coeur,* even a few hours without you breaks my heart."

Gabby rolled her eyes heavenward.

Just as it appeared that Bertie might give in to his charms, she ducked as Hugh reached to embrace her, keeping clear of him.

"The woman, Hugh! Who was she?"

"Woman?" He actually looked confused.

"That . . . that . . . Monique!"

The look of confusion vanished as his eyes glazed over in a look of dreamy contemplation. "Ah, Monique . . ." He seemed to shake off his stupor. "Monique, *chère,* she is my cousin. A dear, dear woman."

"Cousin?" Bertie echoed, looking unsure.

"Yes, *mon petit chou.*" He folded Bertie into his arms, whispering in her ear, "Ah, Bertie, how I have missed you." He lowered his mouth to hers.

Bertie melted, simply melted, right there before Gabriela and Leydi, like sugar on a boiling plate. "Cousin?" she said, returning Hugh's kiss with equal ardor. She began motioning with her hand behind her back for Leydi and Gabby to leave.

Gabby shook her head in disgust, but stepped outside the shop just the same. Leydi followed close behind her, holding her heated cheeks up to the breeze. The two friends kept walking down the street silently. Gabby shook her head.

"She's really lost all her senses this time."

"Oh, I don't know," Leydi added with a note of optimism. "He didn't seem a bad fellow." She frowned. "Though he was rather young."

"Younger than her own daughter. A *bebê!*" Gabriela shook her head again.

"Don't be so hard on Bertie. She has a good heart." Leydi sighed, thinking of her own travails and what lay ahead. "Do you really think I can persuade Rutherford to leave Kincaid alone?"

Gabriela glanced down at her. "Why not?" She stopped on the walkway and took Leydi's chin in her hands. "With your genius for bookkeeping and such, you'll have him eating out of your hand in no time with the promise of more gold. Now, I'll bring the dress by as soon as *Mãe* is finished with the alterations." She winked at Leydi. "You never know. You may find you have hidden talents that will aid our cause."

Felix Bishop walked his horse up the considerable drive of Rutherford Estate, wondering what he would do about the daughter. A pity she had seen him. He might have to do something about that.

He'd spent the last month and a half scouting De Sousa's shop without notice. Perhaps that's why he'd grown careless. The mother seemed too preoccupied with that young swain of hers to notice his presence. The daughter, apparently, had no such distractions.

He handed his horse to the stable hand, his mind still fixed on the daughter's connection to Kincaid. What role did Gabriela de Sousa play in this drama? She was a beautiful woman, with the exotic looks of an Egyptian princess. The entire ride out of Basse Terre, his thoughts had wandered to those haunting green eyes and full mouth. It truly would be a shame if she were involved with the Brethren, and with Kincaid in particular.

Felix stepped up the stairs of the Palladian mansion of red-brick and cut stone. From the central structure sprouted two impressive wings. The opened colonnades supported by Ionic pillars connected the stables and kitchen to the main house. A bit overwrought was his first impression, reminding him of that Frenchman's castle, De Poincey, a monstrosity now in ruins that included a grotto and a secret underground passage to the church in Basse Terre a mile away. But even in its grandeur, Rutherford Hall looked desolate, isolated in the lonely countryside at the base of the old volcano, Mount Misery.

He raised the knocker and gave the door a good thump. He hoped Rutherford was home, impatient to get on with his business. He wanted Daniel Kincaid to hang. He wouldn't rest a day until the man paid for his crimes.

Felix had been four years old when Kincaid and his men had

landed on the Bishop plantation and massacred Felix's family. His mother had hidden Felix, the youngest, in an empty water barrel. He'd been so scared, he stayed in that musty barrel for more than a day. By the time he'd crept out, they were all dead. His father, his mother, two beloved brothers, and his sister.

All Kincaid's doing.

It had taken him twenty-five years, but Felix was patient. He knew God would make sure Kincaid paid for his murderous ways. And Felix intended to be his tool.

The door opened. Felix stated his business to the waiting servant and was shown inside. He'd passed through the reception hall, where paintings from some Italian master crowded the walls, and stepped into a parlor.

Everything in the room was grand—the vaulted ceilings, the walls paneled in rich wood. Apses finished with half-domed ceilings housed marble statuary worthy of the finest collection. Felix sat in one of two leather-backed Portuguese chairs and thought of the simple ways he'd been raised to cherish by the man and woman who'd adopted him on Monserrat. He smiled, still having fond memories of his youth in that plantation house despite the tragedy that had brought him there. This room, with its overabundance of riches, left him cold.

"Lieutenant," Rutherford said, stepping into the room. "I just came in from a long ride. I wasn't expecting you today. Did we have a meeting I forgot?"

Felix shook his head. For a moment, Rutherford's appearance took him by surprise. Unlike his polished surroundings, Rutherford looked disheveled, wearing only his waistcoat over his shirt, breeches, and riding boots—no jacket or neck cloth. And though his hair was tied back in a neat queue, Rutherford was unshaven, his eyes bloodshot.

"We had no appointment, my lord," Felix said, standing. "I came across a new development—one I thought might interest you."

Quentin picked up Aloysius, asleep in the chair opposite Bishop. Too tired to be polite, he sat down and dropped the cat on his lap, stretching his legs out before him. He'd had a ghastly day, beginning with another sleepless night. Neither work, nor rum, nor the long ride to the heated sands of Mount Misery had chased away the darkness lodged inside him.

Good Lord, Clarice haunted his dreams and his father bedeviled his days. He felt like a prisoner in his own home, unable to travel to Basse Terre for fear that his father would accost him on the street and make a scene. Now he was beginning to fear sleep. The past month, Clarice had gained a hold on his dreams that she'd not had since her death seven years before. When he woke from his short fits of slumber, it seemed the very shadows seethed with visions of her. Clarice calling to him; Clarice dancing with him. Laughing with him. Dying in his arms.

Perhaps it was a good thing Bishop had come then, he thought, despite a pounding head and his lack of concentration. Quentin ran his fingers over the cat's rumbling fur. The lieutenant's feverish resolve to trap Kincaid always provided distraction.

"I'm interested in any new developments that will aid in Kincaid's capture," Quentin said, gesturing for Bishop to be seated. "You have my complete attention."

"I asked a few questions in town, and I have reason to believe one of your servants is connected with Kincaid. It might explain why you have so recently been targeted by the pirate. It wouldn't be the first time a servant has sought revenge against his employer for some imagined wrong."

Quentin stopped stroking Aloysius. There were few enough souls living in the bungalows on the grounds. He kept a small staff at Rutherford Hall, and only the field hands the law required for his acreage. The idea that someone would betray him was not at all to his liking. "Now you do have my attention. The name?"

"Leydianna Carstair. From the intelligence I gathered, her mother and father both work for you."

Quentin stared nonplussed—then burst into loud guffaws, sending Aloysius running from the room. "The Mouse? Sir, you couldn't be more wrong than to suspect Miss Carstair . . . why . . ."

And then he stopped laughing.

For a fleeting instant, he remembered Miss Carstair at dinner. Her strange speech about pirates. Her anxious gray eyes.

"What is it?" Bishop asked.

Quentin's tired mind attempted to put together the bits and pieces scrambling through his head. It didn't seem possible. He told himself he was just catching a bout of Miss Carstair's overactive imagination. Not the Mouse. She was too sweet—too young. A woman.

And she traveled about the Caribbean unfettered. No one seemed to know her whereabouts for eleven months out of the year. In one sitting she'd recounted more information about the Brethren than Quentin had heard in a lifetime of running his own shipping company in the pirate-infested waters of the Caribbean . . . and she'd begged him to leave off his attempts to stop Kincaid with an urgency that almost suggested her own neck might be feeling the noose.

Quentin smiled as a curious anger rushed through him. *The Mouse, a pirate's woman.*

There was, of course, little or no reason for him to feel betrayed. She owed Quentin no allegiance. And yet, that was the exact emotion that boiled inside him. Betrayal. It had been a long time since he'd shown anyone the kindness he'd bestowed upon the Mouse by hiring her. How interesting that it should be repaid in such a manner.

He glanced up at Bishop. It would be an easy thing to tell the lieutenant of his suspicions. But he knew with a certainty he didn't want anyone else involved in this skirmish. He intended to seek his own retribution.

"Your investigation has gone seriously astray," Quentin heard himself tell Bishop. "Leydianna Carstair has nothing to do with Heartless Kincaid." Quentin stood, wanting to get rid of Bishop as quickly as possible. He needed time to think. To try to decide what he should do. "But since you've come all this way, may I offer you some refreshments?"

Standing, Felix shook his head, more than a little confused. In the past, any effort to hunt Kincaid down had been obstructed by those in the government he suspected were in the pirate's pay. But this time Felix had held the hope that Kincaid wouldn't get away. At last the pirate had run afoul of the wrong sort, a titled gentleman with his own fleet.

Now Rutherford was hiding something, though he'd been careful not to give too much away. That surprised Felix, mostly because it was Rutherford who had come to him in the first place, seeking to rid himself of Kincaid. Felix put on his hat, watching Rutherford carefully.

Everything had been fine until he'd mentioned Miss Carstair. The woman, then, he thought, nodding his head to the viscount. Apparently, she deserved a closer look.

"This Miss Carstair does work for you, does she not?" he asked Rutherford.

"As a matter of fact, I have recently hired Miss Carstair to do some book work for me. She grew up on Rutherford Estate, and my steward was wise enough to see her talent and teach her well. Despite her gender, she promises to be quite indispensable. Have you met the lady? Mild as milk toast. I sincerely doubt she could have any involvement with pirates."

"The fact remains, she is friends with the owner of a shop in town, Bertland de Sousa, and her daughter. That shop has been selling goods very similar to those you reported stolen from your ships."

"That means little enough. As I recall from the bill of lading, there was nothing unique. This De Sousa woman could easily have bought the goods from someone else, not necessarily Kincaid himself."

"I have other reasons to believe Mistress de Sousa is connected with Kincaid," Felix said, pressing Rutherford. "Both she and the daughter."

Both men's eyes met, a silent challenge. "But nothing concrete against Miss Carstair," Rutherford said softly.

Felix shook his head. "Not at the moment."

Rutherford smiled, an even turn of his lips that did little to suggest amusement. "Then let me say in her defense that my steward has known Miss Carstair since she was a child. He'll stand witness to her fine character. And she came highly recommended by a friend on Monserrat. He wrote her a splendid letter of introduction. She works for him year-round, so you see, she's quite busy. She has hardly the time or the interest to commune with pirates. I'm hoping to steal her away, myself; she's proven to be quite talented in organizing several projects."

"I see," Felix said, wondering why Rutherford was trying to protect the woman, which he most certainly was. "And your friend's name?" he asked casually.

"Averns. Matthew Averns. Been a friend of the family for years."

Felix nodded. "Well then, perhaps I am mistaken after all."

"Yes, Lieutenant. I believe your time is better spent searching out Kincaid and not investigating a gaggle of women."

"Of course. Good day, your lordship. Next time I hope to bring you more promising news."

Felix turned on his heel and left, knowing full well that it would be useless to contact Matthew Averns. By now Rutherford would be plotting to send the man word to cover for Leydianna Carstair. His protection made it more probable that Miss Carstair was involved. Rutherford knew something, something that made him think the lady needed protecting.

In the end, he could do nothing to help her. Not if she was cohort to that murderer Kincaid.

As the door shut behind Felix, Quentin stared at its elaborate scrollwork. The ghastly sleepless night and his haunting dreams receded into the machinations of the present.

Yes, indeed, the Mouse's odd behavior was beginning to show something other than bizarre as a motive. He tugged on the bellpull, summoning George. For a moment he questioned this ardent refusal to hand her up to Bishop, despite his suspicions.

Perhaps it was the lack of sleep. Perhaps his father and memories of the past had pushed him beyond reason. Whatever the cause, Quentin's gaze misted over, bringing a clear picture of the Mouse when he'd seen her in her mother's bungalow. He didn't consider himself a sensitive man—it wasn't like him to be nostalgic—but he admitted her beaten expression had touched a memory of his own miserable childhood.

Perhaps he could even understand her seeking the power and protection of a pirate like Kincaid. He thought of how helpless she'd looked in his reception chamber, daydreaming. It made him smile to think of her lying on the carpet with Aloysius, speaking to the very angels he'd painted to keep him company in his self-enforced exile.

Yes, there was something about the Mouse that made a man want to take her under his wing.

The door opened and George stepped inside, bringing him out of his reverie. He wished suddenly his reasons for protecting the Mouse could be as laudable as faith in her innocence. But the truth was, he wasn't that noble. He'd buried his innocence years before with Clarice. He never looked for goodness in anyone. Not anymore. Most certainly, not in himself.

He knew he had only one reason for keeping Bishop off the Mouse's scent. He didn't want the overeager lieutenant guiding his game of cat and mouse. If she was behind the attacks on his ships, Quentin would make it his business to find out—and deal with her appropriately. He would set his own trap.

"Sir?" George prompted.

"Call Stevenson in here immediately. I have an urgent message I need delivered to the Averns plantation on Monserrat."

Chapter Seven

Leydi stood on the stone floor in her stocking feet. She'd discarded her brown dress for the emerald satin Gabriela had brought just that morning. The brocade heeled slippers and a matching lace cap waited on the counterpane of the tent bed behind her. Bertie had done the alterations overnight and Gabby had hurried to bring the gown to the bungalow, wanting Leydi to wear it that day.

The woman in the gilt gesso mirror looked nothing like a sensible bookkeeper. Nor was she the elegant Lady Anne. But she would do, Leydi thought with a smile. Oh, yes. She would do nicely.

Before she could change her mind, she uncoiled her braid from around her head and fingered out the waves until her hair was loose and reached past her hips. The late morning sun from the window reflected off the Spanish-walled room where she slept in her parents' bungalow, turning her hair a burnished gold. The far-off cries of green monkeys and bananaquits blended with the rustle of palm trees as the breeze whispered past.

She turned to see herself in the mirror propped on the commode. She had to admit, the combination of the dress and her loosened hair made her feel transformed. "I think I'll surprise him," she whispered. And then she frowned. When had she started wanting Rutherford to admire her?

She thought of him too often of late—and it had nothing to do with her worries for Kincaid. Too many times she reflected on Quentin Alexander Rutherford without the least fear for her pirate employer. She envisioned herself flirting and smiling and dancing. She daydreamed. And Quentin, with his dark good looks and admirable figure, was always the man in those dreams.

Pressing her lips together in a flat line, Leydi shook out the folds of the dress. She knew what fueled her overactive imagination—Rutherford had done her a kindness by hiring her to work for Mr. Stevenson. In her mind she'd turned the dragon into a knight atop a noble steed. And she'd met his angels and his fat old cat.

Like a reader poring over the worst to be had in the coffee shops for a penny, she'd combed through the pyramids of books and contracts, making herself believe there was nothing but these papers in his life. No wife, no children—just a lot of money and a big, empty mansion. She glanced over to the pile of travel and adventure books peeking out of her satchel in the room's corner, her only companions. A copy of *Gulliver's Travels*, Dampier's *A New Voyage Round the World*, and *Robinson Crusoe* stuck out at odd angles from the tapestry bag. She sighed. She could well understand the kind of loneliness she'd imagined for Rutherford.

She stuck out her tongue at her reflection. "You silly thing. Dreaming up romantic fantasies about a man who's out to see Kincaid hang. And just because Rutherford made you see yourself as a woman."

That was, in fact, the problem. When Quentin looked at her, he didn't look dreamy like that Frenchman, Hugh, when he'd held Bertie. But there was just as much heat in Quentin's blue eyes. Enough to make Leydi want to be desirable.

She supposed that's precisely why he did it. Like the bored, titled gentleman he was, he had nothing to lose by flirting with the help. He wouldn't know how much it meant to Leydi—that at last a man had noticed her.

She sat down and picked up her brush. She began brushing her hair with great care— the only vanity she allowed herself. With her hair flowing over her shoulder, she could shut her eyes and believe she was just as alluring as Lady Constance in *Constant Constance,* one of her favorite books because of its intrepid heroine. She'd worn her hair down a time or two on Devil's Gate—but no one seemed to notice. The men just smiled and treated her like one of them. Which was probably for the best.

She pushed back the strand she'd been brushing and picked up another. Still, she had hopes that someday one of those men would look at her differently—would ask her to marry and have a family on Devil's Gate, as many had done with other women. She would love to have children of her own, little ones to cherish and teach about all the marvelous things there were to learn in the world. At twenty-two, she felt too often that she was running out of time.

"But it won't be Rutherford," she told her reflection. "So you can just stop dreaming. Keep your mind on the matters at hand and be sensible."

She stood and picked up two strands of hair at her temples, holding them back off her face. Still, there was no reason she couldn't look nice. And the dress had given her the excuse she'd needed to ride into Basse Terre yesterday. It was best to wear it today and smooth over any suspicions he might have about her errand.

She turned, trying to think how her hair would look best. She didn't want to be late for her meeting with Rutherford, so she'd best hurry. Leydi gritted her teeth, trying to hold back a visible cringe when she thought of him calling her "the Mouse" again.

"Well, perhaps today he'll think differently," she told her elegant image with a wink.

Behind her she heard the door swing open. In the mirror she saw her mother's reflection as she stepped into her room. Leydi turned around.

"Take it off," her mother commanded, her lips barely moving.

"Mother, I . . . it's a gift from Gabby and her mother."

"It's a whore's dress. Take it off."

Leydi flushed and looked down at the simple gown with its beautiful lace trim and embroidered stomacher. "It may be a bit grand, I'll admit, but it's not—"

"It's for him, isn't it?" her mother said, taking two quick steps into the room. "To make him see you like a woman. To make him want you."

Leydi shook her head, confused and upset because her mother had come so close to the truth. But Elaine made Leydi's innocent musings sound ugly and horrid. "No. No, I wouldn't do that, Mother. I'm just his bookkeeper. I don't—"

"Take it off!"

The expression in her mother's eyes burned right through Leydi's chest to her heart. It was as if she weren't seeing her daughter at all, but someone else—someone who frightened and angered her.

Her mother reached out and twisted a handful of Leydi's hair in her fingers. She let the tendrils slip through her palm and stared down at the curled ends dipping down to Leydi's hips. "You don't even know what you're doing, Leydianna. I won't let you make yourself a fool for that man."

Her mother grabbed the front of the gown and pulled. The sound of the beautiful satin tearing echoed through the small room. Leydi closed her eyes. She didn't want to see the hate in her mother's eyes—the crazy, crazy hate Leydi feared was not for the dress, but for her own self.

For the longest time, nothing happened. The only sound in the room was the cry of laborers in the fields, the calls of monkeys and birds. And then she heard her mother weeping.

Leydi opened her eyes. Elaine held the back of her hand to her mouth, as if trying to stop her sobs. She was staring at the front of Leydi's gown. Leydi glanced down. The delicate satin had been torn to her waist, ruined beyond repair.

"What have I done?" her mother whispered through the fingers covering her mouth, still trying to catch the cries. "Oh, Leydianna, forgive me."

Her mother grabbed her, hugging her, crying even harder. Leydi closed her eyes. It was a familiar scene. Only when she was her most cruel did Elaine Carstair show her daughter any kind-ness.

Leydi reached up and cradled her mother as Elaine continued to pour out her tears. It was an odd ritual, one Leydi had never understood. As if Elaine couldn't abide the evidence of her own ugliness. The sight of it seemed to unlock whatever morsel of love she held in her heart.

"Leydianna, you don't know. The dress, your hair . . . Leydi-anna, you're my only child. I have to save you. I must *save* you."

She wanted to ask: Save me from what? Rutherford? *When you're the only person who has ever hurt me in my life?* But there had been too few moments of tenderness between her mother and herself. And so she grasped what little Elaine offered.

"Hush, Mother. I'm fine. You're right. The dress isn't appro-priate. I'm making a fool of myself wearing it to do book work."

"Yes, dear. Completely inappropriate." Elaine gulped back her sobs, still holding Leydi with the genuine affection Leydi so craved. She pulled back and stared at the ripped cloth, touching it lightly. "I shouldn't have done that. I don't know what came over me. Forgive me, darling." She pulled the lace and torn fabric back in place, futilely holding it there. "Here. Let me try . . ."

Leydi guided her mother's hands away. She held the dress against the embroidered stomacher, keeping it in place. "It's all right. That won't be necessary."

"Or possible. It's ruined," Elaine said in a reedy voice that showed what had to be true regret. "I'm sorry. So sorry."

"I said it was all right," Leydi assured her. Giving her a quick hug, she whispered, "I have plenty of other dresses. Take your mirror back to the front room for me and I'll change."

"Yes, darling," Elaine returned the embrace, then brushed the curls from Leydi's face. "Do you forgive me? About the dress, I mean? I was trying to protect you, stop you from making a terrible mistake. I told you to be careful with his lordship. But I shouldn't have torn the gown."

"Don't give the dress another thought." Leydi smiled, feeling strangely close to her mother. She almost wondered if it wasn't worth the loss of the beautiful gown to see her smile like that. "Now, I won't be but a moment."

On her way to the door, the cherished mirror cradled under her arm, Elaine called back, "And, Leydianna?"

Leydi turned, still smiling. "Yes, Mother?"

"Your hair, dear. Do something about your hair. I do wish you'd let me cut it. It's so untidy that way."

The fleeting happiness vanished from Leydi's heart. Her smile felt brittle on her mouth. "I'll braid it, Mother. Nice and tight. There won't be a hair out of place."

Quentin stared at the back of Miss Carstair's head. She was studying some figures Stevenson had put together. Despite two hours of pointed remarks on his part, the mysterious emerald gown she was to purchase in Basse Terre yesterday had yet to be mentioned. She was, as usual, entombed in brown, and making no excuses for it.

He suspected there would be no new colorful dress. Bishop's suggestion that the gown had been a ruse loomed more likely. She'd grabbed for the first excuse so she might scurry off and report to Kincaid's people about his plans for the pirate. Strolling around the desk, Quentin smiled, his fingers trailing absently over papers and notes Miss Carstair had carefully organized on the rosewood. A shame really. He thought he'd at least have the pleasure of seeing her better dressed.

Yes, indeed, the lieutenant appeared correct about the real purpose behind Miss Carstair's trip to Basse Terre yesterday morn. The Mouse could very well be in cahoots with pirates.

Silently, he stepped behind Miss Carstair. As she studied his contracts, he in turn examined the few tender curls that had escaped the braid she'd tucked up in her mobcap, the tidy white scarf tied over her shoulders, and her busy fingers wrapped around the quill. He watched her poke the tip of her quill in and out of the inkwell, gaining a rhythm of sorts. *Dip, dip, scribble, scribble. Dip, dip.* A machine of industry. Jotting her notes on a scrap of paper, she wrote faster than most people could form a thought.

He folded his arms across his waistcoat and tried to decide if the Mouse's falling in with pirates was the act of a supremely naive woman—or someone with dastardly guile. Either way, it was his goods the pirate was stealing. That made Miss Carstair his for the catching.

He picked up one of the contracts, staring unseeing at the sheet as he plotted his strategy for the day. His bookkeeper was becoming a happy distraction. *Better to tease and bait the Mouse than face the fact he'd not slept in two days, thanks to the earl's bothersome bleatings.*

He sighed. His father's pursuit had become tiresome in the extreme. And Clarice . . . he'd come to St. Kitts to forget those dark days in London. He couldn't abide the sense that even here he'd become a prisoner—particularly of his own regrets.

Dear Lord, he needed to sleep. He leaned back against the walnut shelves, thinking of the trouble it had taken him to muster the energy to shave and dress that morning. As it was, he'd not bothered with a coat, despite George's urgings, determined to stay cool in only breeches and a waistcoat. He almost laughed at the ironic interest he'd taken in the Mouse's lack of fashion.

He peered at her bent head. Her shoulders were huddled over the contracts, those pieces of paper holding a world of interest for her. This afternoon Miss Carstair looked particularly brown. Even her expression was pinched around her mouth, as if the clothes had begun to transform her. She was entirely too serious, focusing all her energy on clearing the months of correspondence he'd ignored, when he didn't give a damn about the papers. He stared out the window at the cerulean blue sky punched with drifting cotton clouds, wondering what he might do to liven up the next hours.

"Here now," she said, pointing a slim finger to a set of numbers drafted on the vellum. "Only six hundred barrels." She shook her head. "As you can see, that reduces your profit considerably." She began scratching out the numbers.

Quentin snatched the quill from her hands. "I'll be in ruins in a sennight. Can nothing save me, Mouse?"

Her response was a pinched-mouth silence. He knew the name

annoyed her—as did his sarcasm. He wondered how long she would allow it.

Quentin pretended to examine the numbers over her shoulder, something of no interest to him at the moment. But the gesture gave him an excuse to get close enough to smell her scent. Lavender? "Seven hundred and three seems more the right of it," he said absently, not paying the least attention to the sum.

"Look again," she said, tapping the figure. "It's six hundred and not a farthing more."

He smiled, hearing the anger in her voice. Apparently the Mouse took insults to her ciphering skills with less humor than those to her dress. He handed her back the quill, though he stayed close to her shoulder, whispering in her ear, "Yes, I see you're right." *Lavender. Definitely lavender.* "Six hundred it is. Quite a disaster for a profitable enterprise." He leaned still closer, his cheek almost brushing her hair, wondering at her use of scented soap when she tried so hard to hide her beauty. "Shall we look at another, then, Mouse?"

She didn't bother to inch away from him, as if the gesture might somehow give him a modicum of satisfaction she couldn't afford. But that prunish expression stayed. She looked as if she'd just tasted something foul. *Mouse, Mouse, Mouse,* he said to himself with a smile.

"Here," he said, reaching for another letter, recognizing Gellman's seal. "I've high hopes for this coffee crop."

"But look at this price," she said, setting the quill's feathery tip to the number. "That's quite too high."

"Do you think so?" Quentin shuffled through the papers until he unearthed four other letters. "If we act quickly, the price is quite reasonable. Look here." Despite himself, he found his mind searching out, fitting the pieces of a puzzle as he arranged the letters across the desk. He pointed to the first letter. "Derrick asks if I've extra seed cane. He makes a decent offer, but suggests he has a fine crop of tobacco and would I accept a portion as payment instead?" He pointed to the next letter. "Williams seeks tobacco, but can pay only in sheep, something Derrick has no interest in—and Billings," he said, pointing to the next letter, "wants sheep, but has only these salt ponds on Bonaire." He stared at the pages, the complicated negotiations already setting to work in his head. "And Gellman. What do you think he wants for his coffee?"

Leydi shook her head, caught up as he was in the drama of finances played out on the desk. "I've no idea."

"He's trying to buy Billings's salt ponds, of course. We start here," Quentin said, the same odd excitement washing over him that came when numbers fell together. He pointed to the first letter. His grandfather had always told him he had a merchant's heart. "And end up here," he added, shifting his fingers across the papers.

"And double your profit when you sell the coffee."

"Triple, actually, when I sell to Struthers on Jamaica, who has overextended his commitments and hasn't enough bean to fulfill his own contracts."

"But that's amazing," she said, shaking her head, staring at the papers. She glanced up at Quentin. "That's really astonishing."

He leaned back against the shelves, smiling at her awed expression. He hadn't seen this much interest come his way from Miss Carstair since he'd suggested her extravagant month's pay. "Have I impressed you, Mouse?"

Immediately, her enthusiasm dimmed. Her lips pruned once more into tight-lipped disapproval. "I really detest that name. It's demeaning and unnecessary. Must you use it?"

"But I thought that was the point, Miss Carstair." He gestured to her clothes. "All this brown. Why, I assumed it was for my benefit . . . so I might see you as truly nondescript. A mouse."

"If this is about the emerald gown, I bought the dress, as I told you—"

"Good. I'm quite eager to see it, actually. I'm glad you settled on green. I believe I said it would go quite nicely with your eyes."

"Well, you won't. See it, that is," she continued, staring down at her hands. "Because . . . well, because I've decided it was entirely inappropriate. I'm a bookkeeper, not some strumpet to parade her wares before you."

The slight tremble to her voice caught him off guard, as did her vehement tone. To Quentin, the Mouse was a diversion, a game—he wasn't prepared for so strong a show of emotion at his teasing. Taking her by her shoulders, he pulled her out of the chair and turned her to face him, wondering about that quiver in her voice.

She stared at the tip of her shoes, not looking up at him. "I thought it was fine in the store. But the light must have been off. When I tried it on this morning, I saw it was garish." Her lips were pressed in a bloodless line. "An ugly color. It did nothing for my eyes, I assure you. My mother hated it, in fact."

"Your mother," he said, unable to hide his distaste.

"She was wise enough to see it wouldn't do at all." She looked up, meeting his gaze with an unblinking challenge. "But the color of my gown won't make the least difference in my skills at bookkeeping. It's really no concern of yours what I wear."

He looked into her brittle-bright eyes, the green more prevalent with the emotion she tried to hide. *My mother hated it.* Oh, yes, the mother. The woman who dressed in grand silks while she clothed her daughter in simple brown muslin.

A tidy scenario appeared in his mind, coming together with the same intuition that guided his business dealings. The Mouse, splendidly gowned in her new clothes. Her envious mother seeing her daughter blooming in her beauty.

It was the mother, of course. The Mouse probably looked splendid in her dress. That's why she wasn't wearing it.

An anger like none he allowed for himself steamed inside Quentin, threatening to release with the grandeur of Mount Misery's past eruptions. He took Miss Carstair's arm and pulled her none too gently to the window. He yanked off her mobcap and threw it to the floor. He proceeded to take out the pins from her hair, throwing them to the carpet as well.

Leydi tried to pull away, but he wouldn't let her. He kept tossing the pins, amazed at how many she'd stabbed into her head, until the long rope of braid fell down her back. She slapped his hands away, ducked under his arm. He grabbed her by both shoulders, giving her a smoldering look that told her to stay put.

"You pay me to do your books, not to wear green dresses," she told him stiffly. "You can call me Mouse all you want. I don't give a damn." She lifted up her chin and crossed her arms, daring him with her eyes. "Perhaps I should come up with something equally charming to address you?"

But no matter how hard she tried to hide behind her anger, he could still see the hurt.

Immune to her baiting, he unraveled the braid. Her hair was astonishingly long, falling past her hips to brush the back of her softly curved behind. It felt like silk. In the light of the window it was the color of shadowed gold. And it transformed his little Mouse into a beauty.

"There, Mouse. Does your mother think your hair is garish and ugly as well? Does she wrap it up in this braid, telling you it won't do, like the gown?"

"Leave me be," she whispered.

Again that slight tremble, as if this unveiling had hurt her somehow. At the same time, she spoke with an odd show of strength. He thought she was doing her damnedest not to cry.

He let the tendrils slide from his fingers almost with reverence, then slowly arranged for a few strands to fall over her shoulder and down past the curve of her breast. He stroked the hair once more, surprised at how much he wanted to touch it—it wasn't the reason he'd given himself for loosening it. He brushed a few last curls from her face and tipped up her chin.

She stared straight at him, her eyes filled with tears and thunder.

"If you act like a mouse, that's what I shall call you, Miss Carstair." He held her chin, then wrapped a lock of hair around his finger. "Is that what you want? To hide all this for your dear mother's sake?" He gestured to her hair, meaning so much more.

"You don't understand," she said under her breath.

He smiled. "Then why don't you explain? I'm all ears, I assure you."

She shook her head, frowning, watching him now with a touch of wonder. "How do you do that? Smile when you're the most angry?"

Her remark caught him off guard, her words too perceptive by half. Her comment and her probing expression created an odd connection between them. It seemed they shared enough in common that with astonishing ease they might slip past the façade each had erected to keep others from seeing too close.

Quentin frowned. He didn't want anyone peeking at those painful truths. He planned to teach his little Mouse her lessons, but he wanted no schooling in return.

Before he could deliver a suitable retort, there came a loud pounding at the door. A resounding *thud* followed, as if someone had just thrown their body against the carved wood. The knob rattled. Garbled shouting echoed in the hall. Both Leydi and Quentin turned just as one fierce voice rang out true and clear.

"Damn you, Quentin! I know you're in there. Stop hiding and meet me like a man! Let me in, I say. Out of my way, you bastard!"

More shouts followed, then another assault of pounding against the door. Leydi turned to Quentin, looking for some clue, some notion of what was going on. But she discovered only an expression of intense concentration. As she watched, he took two steps toward the door, then halted. There was a loud crack, like pistol firing, and then all was quiet.

Leydi grabbed her loosened hair and began braiding it quickly. She flung the finished braid over her shoulder and followed behind Quentin as he took one careful step after another toward the door. He no longer seemed to know she was in the room, his full attention on what was happening in the hall.

"Aren't you going to open it?" she asked as he stared at the door, not moving. Too curious to wait, Leydi stepped around him and grabbed the handle, opening the door a careful crack.

Only George stood in the hall in his blue Yorkshire cloth suit. The tall black servant seemed to weave a bit, the cellar keys clanging at his side. She gasped when she saw there was a trickle of blood at his left temple. In his hand he held a white slip of paper.

"Are you all right?" Leydi asked as she ushered in the dazed servant. George's thin but stately figure stumbled forward. With one hand he cradled his dark, curly-haired head.

"Yes, ma'am. I'm feeling fine."

"He didn't leave without a struggle, I see?" Quentin helped guide George into the armchair. He took out his handkerchief and pressed it to the wound, stanching the flow of blood. He spoke in an amazingly placid voice.

"No struggle, sir," the congenial George said, wincing as Leydi took the handkerchief and added more pressure. "It took Mr. Stevenson firing his wheel lock. But his lordship conked me upside my head real fine with that cane of his, yes he did." He glanced up at Quentin. "But I'm thinkin' he meant me no harm. Most likely, his lordship be wishin' it be your head, sir."

"That is certainly true, George. Any other casualties?"

The black man shook his head, then sucked in a breath with the move. "He left this note, sir."

"You'd best have Mrs. Bailey take a look at your head, George," he said, taking the missive. Without even sparing the paper a glance, he threw it into the cold hearth. "Hurry on, now. She'll know the trick to keeping the swelling down."

"Yes, sir," George said, standing now with a bit more starch to his back. Then with a gleaming white smile to Leydi, "Thank you, miss."

"If you need something for the pain," Leydi said, watching him go out into the corridor in a steady step, "I've an infusion that will help."

With a salute and a smile, George strode down the hall. Leydi turned to Quentin and nodded her head toward the hearth. "Why did you do that? You didn't even open it."

He stared at the white slip of paper. Taking the flint and steel from the tinderbox on the hearth, he lit some kindling and tossed it at the coals. "I think you said it best, Miss Carstair. It's really no concern of yours what I do."

His words hurt. Just minutes ago he'd held her in his arms, arguing that she should allow herself a touch of beauty. Now his midnight eyes seemed to look right past her. But it was the suddenness of his violence that confused her most. She shook her head. "I don't understand you."

"That's good, Mouse," he said, his voice devoid of any emotion. "I'd hate to lose my mystery so early in our acquaintance."

Leydi took a careful step toward him, bewildered by the meanness of his smile, the fierceness of his expression. For a moment he seemed lost in thought. He had the astonishing capacity to make a person feel as if they were no longer important—no longer even in the room. She watched as he glanced up at the ceiling with an intensity of purpose that made her look up as well.

"I keep thinking they want to say something," he surprised her by saying. "That if I would only listen well enough, they would talk to me and impart their wisdom." He gave her a bemused smile. "I'm sure you understand, Mouse," he said, turning for the door. "I'm certain all manner of objects speak to you."

Dismissing her and the angels, he turned and walked into the hall. He shut the door with a resounding *click* behind him.

He was cruel, she told herself. Cruel and horrible and so many other things there weren't enough words to describe his meanness. But at the same moment he'd been incredibly vulnerable in his show of temper. It made her want to know what lay beneath the fierce emotion.

Without wasting even a breath, Leydi dove for the hearth. She'd always been too curious for her own good, she scolded herself. But she grabbed the burning slip of paper just the same. She dropped it to the brick hearth, slapping out the flames with her hands. She stared back at the doors. She bit her lip. Quickly, she opened the missive.

The seal had melted off; half the message had been burned away. There remained only a few words legible.

Come . . . forgive . . . the Cockerel.

There was a signature at the bottom. It read:

Your loving father.

Chapter Eight

Leydi peered at the knave of diamonds, wondering what her chances were of piling yet another card on the tower she'd built on Bertie's counter. She glanced out the window, flicking the card, with its charming woodcut design of a foot soldier, back and forth with her thumb. Down the street was the Cockerel—a popular boardinghouse in Basse Terre. She'd walked past the native stone structure three times on her way to Bertie's, almost circling the boardinghouse before continuing on to the shop.

Gabriela had just finished dousing the floorboards with water from the rain barrel out back. It was Saturday, and Leydi had managed to coax a ride from George, who'd driven the Rutherford gig into Basse Terre early that morning. Though the sun was just peeking over the thatch and tiled roofs crowding the streets to the water, Bertie had yet to make an appearance from her night out with Hugh. Giving up on her mother, Gabriela had thrust ajar the door and louvered windows, determined to open the shop herself.

Leydi dropped the French deck to the counter and walked out toward the door. Watching Gabby start to sweep the doused floor, she grabbed for the broom herself. "Here. Let me help."

Gabriela snatched back the broom and gestured to the cane stool beside the counter. "You sit, *caro*, and talk to me. *Mãe* will be hours yet with Hugh, and I'm too curious to wait that long. What have you to report about Kincaid?"

Leydi glanced out the door and down the street already lined with vendors. She could just make out the carved-wood façade of the Cockerel's upper story. With a sigh she returned to the counter and plopped down on the stool. Picking up the deck, she thumbed through the cards. "Since that one night at dinner, Lord Ruthless hasn't spoken nary a word about pirates, much less Kincaid. I suppose my wizardry with his books hasn't bought me his confidence yet."

Gabby stopped sweeping. She raised her brows. "Lord Ruthless?"

Leydi studied the cards as she shuffled and shrugged. "Well, I don't call him that to his face—though I'm tempted to," she said, thinking of the incident with her braid.

She'd spent most of the night trying to unravel the significance of his odd goading. A part of her argued that he'd wanted her to fight her mother—that by unraveling her braid, forcing her to show the beauty Elaine urged her to hide, he was acting as an advocate of sorts. That he'd wanted to prove she was safe being a woman around him.

And yet, the arrival of his father had changed him. Changed them both. Suddenly, it had been Leydi taking the lead, wondering at the bizarre motives behind Quentin's estrangement from the earl.

She could still see that odd expression of intense concentration on Quentin's face. His blue eyes had turned cold and darkened to a near black as he'd stared at the door. Last night she'd thought of little else, wondering if the father was behind Quentin's sudden lack of interest in his business concerns, the correspondence he'd allowed to languish—the contracts he'd ignored since spring.

She sighed, watching Gabby sweep. "No, I don't call him Ruthless to his face. I've the good sense not to goad him into dismissing me, not if I'm to help Kincaid. *He* calls me Mouse. Quite often, in fact. Whenever the mood suits him."

Gabby started to laugh, then shut her mouth with a snap when she saw Leydi's sharp expression. "Well, you must have something to report. Haven't you nudged the conversation a bit? Did you bring up Kincaid at all?"

Leydi shuffled the cards more quickly, then fanned them out in her hand. "The timing didn't seem right." Catching Gabby rolling her eyes, she added, "It's a delicate matter. I don't want to press things and make him suspicious."

Gabby continued sweeping, obviously not convinced. "Did he at least like you in the dress?"

Leydi tried to look busy. Flipping out the knave again, she gingerly lined up the card over the two steepled gables of the house she'd built. "I haven't worn it." She dropped the card into place. It stayed . . . for a second . . . before the entire structure tumbled down, the cards flying from the counter to the floor. "Damn and blast," she said under her breath.

"No dress, no news. *Caro,*" Gabby said, coming to stand beside her. "Something tells me you're not much of a spy."

"Well, I'm no Lady Constance. One of the heroines in my books," she explained, picking the cards off the floor. *"She's* quite a wonderful spy. Saved the Crown plenty during the battle of Blenheim." She stacked the cards back into a nice even deck. "Rutherford caught me off guard, is all. I'll do better next time. You'll see."

Gabriela pursed her lips and gave Leydi one of her cryptic glances. Putting the broom away, she wiped her hands on her apron and adjusted the lace pinnet she wore over her ringlet curls. "Well, maybe he's forgotten all about Kincaid and there's no danger?"

Leydi shook her head. "He doesn't strike me as the kind of man that would forget a slight done him. By the bye, that suspicious gentleman you saw across the street a few days back? He came to the house yesterday. To speak with Rutherford."

"You're sure it was the same man?" Gabriela asked, instantly alert.

Leydi nodded. "Red hair. Very serious eyes. I saw him just as I was leaving."

"Merda," Gabriela cursed under her breath. She began pacing

before Leydi, her hooped skirts swaying, her buckled shoes tapping against the floorboards. "My mother told me she's seen the same fellow outside for weeks now. Most probably spying on the shop owned and run by Kincaid—selling goods he's stolen. Now this character visits your Lord Ruthless, a man you say has sworn to stop Kincaid at any cost." Gabriela looked up at Leydi, her green eyes bright with sudden concern. "Perhaps you were right to worry for Kincaid."

Leydi rose slowly. "He was dressed like a sailor, Gabby. Do you think he could be part of the patrol? Good heavens, he could be a government agent. Mr. Stevenson told me Rutherford has asked the Council's help in hunting down Kincaid."

"That's what you must find out, *caro*," Gabby said, stabbing a finger to Leydi's collar.

The door to the shop swung open and Bertie waltzed inside, belled skirts almost catching in the door as she slammed it behind her. There was fire in her black eyes.

"*Animal, bastardo, ingrato . . .*" Bertie seemed to struggle for yet one more expletive. "*Imbecil!*"

"*Mãe!*" Gabby gave a wink to Leydi. "You can't be speaking of your beloved Hugh?"

Bertie's gold hoops swung to brush her shoulders. "He has been unfaithful to me."

"*Ave, Mãe.* This surprises you? It was only a matter of time before that womanizer showed his true colors."

Bertie stayed by the counter, but her dark eyes seemed to fill with tears. Again she cursed, then shook her head. "I loved him!"

Leydi gave Gabby a questioning glance. She'd never seen Bertie like this.

"He was too young for you to love," Gabby said gently, stepping over to her mother and putting her arms around her.

Bertie sniffed, the anger in her eyes saying eloquently she refused to shed tears for Hugh. "Yes, I knew this. But I fell under his spell just the same. The French can be so wonderfully . . . intense. I lost my heart, *Gabriela*. Your foolish old mother lost her heart."

"*Mãe*, please. He's not worth your tears—"

"How right you are!" Bertie said, squaring back her shoulders and brushing away the moisture from her cheeks. "This supposed cousin, this Monique. I caught him kissing her right outside his bedchamber—while I slept inside, still warm from his lovemaking. He has no conscience. He has no heart."

"He has no shame," Leydi added.

"Criminoso! Animal!"

Gabriela patted her mother's shoulder soothingly, seeing the storm was over with her mother's healing anger. Leydi certainly thought she had good reason to be upset.

"He tries to tell me, this is only a friendly kiss—from one cousin to another," Bertie sputtered. "But I see passion in that kiss, *menina*. Oh, that man has ruined me forever."

Gabriela gestured with her head toward the door. Understanding, Leydi made to leave mother and daughter alone. Giving Bertie a quick kiss on the cheek, she hugged the woman who'd treated her as kindly as her own daughter over the past years.

"Oh, Leydianna, I hate for you to see me like this. Men, they are not all so untrustworthy. You should fall in love, *menina*, marry a good man," Bertie said, starting her familiar litany about hearth and home.

"You take care, Bertie," Leydi said, pulling away with a sad smile. She could commiserate with Bertie and her unrequited love more than she cared to admit. Of late, Leydi had wondered if perhaps her future would never be more than the emptiness of balancing Kincaid's books.

Outside, Leydi strolled down a walkway whose uneven planks made it hazardous to traverse from one storefront to the next. In the street, the strident voices of vendors hawking their wares blended with the chatter of fishermen coming home. She told herself she was looking for George, or the Rutherford gig, but somehow she ended up in front of the Cockerel.

She stared up at the whitewashed building with its distinctive square-cut stone quoins and window borders. Perhaps it was seeing Bertie's tears, or her own melancholy, but suddenly she wanted to go inside. She wanted to hunt out the man who had signed that note "Father."

Before she lost her courage, Leydi swept across the narrow threshold. Through the paneled hall and out past the back door, she traipsed round the courtyard jungled with decorative palms and crepe myrtle. She found Leon McClellen, the proprietor, sweating in the kitchen as he piled up wood for the stove.

As soon as he saw her, Leon wiped his hands on his apron covering his breeches and waistcoat and doffed his tricorn hat. His sunburnt face cracked into a smile and his blue eyes danced with welcome. Leydi knew most of the tradespeople in town through Bertie and Gabriela.

Leon walked toward her in the rolling gait of an old tar. "What can I do for you, Miss Leydi?" he asked, clasping her hand between his two in a hearty shake. "What brings ye to the Cockerel. Shall I get Martha fer ye?" He turned to call for his wife over his shoulder.

"No, don't bother Miss Martha. Please. I do have a favor, but perhaps you might help me just as well." She held fast to her courage and said in one breath, "I understand the viscount's father is here. Well, I'm just a bit curious about the man—my family working for Rutherford so many years and all." She felt so awkward, stammering to Leon like this. She thought it best to say straight out what she was about. "There's rumors at the house. Strange rumors."

Leon nodded, a keen light coming to his pale blue eyes. He looked left, then right, as if checking to see if anyone watched, then looped his arm around her elbow. He pulled her toward a private corner of the courtyard. "Strange goings-on, isn't it, lass? The earl turning up like that. What do ye make of it, eh?"

"I really don't know." Leydi's heart pelted so hard in her chest it actually pained her.

Leon shook his head. He peeked over his shoulder once again, then leaned closer, whispering, "Martha and I asks ourselves, why's the earl staying here at the Cockerel and not at Rutherford Hall? I hires a chaise for him now and so often, and he always comes back with murder in his eyes. And every day—he's not missed a one, mind me—he sends a missive to Rutherford Estate with one of me two boys, but he's not received a reply." He raised a gnarled finger dramatically. "Imagine, lass, not a one. From his own son—his heir. No, there's bad blood there. I'm certain of that."

Leydi licked her lips, thinking of the horrible shouting outside the door and the note Quentin had tossed into the fire without reading. "You're sure he's the earl? Perhaps he's an impostor of some sort?"

"Nay. Not with them same blazing blue eyes. He's the look of the son, all right." Leon shook his head again. "Sad to see such a quarrel among kin. Poor gentleman's in the supper room right now," Leon said, nodding his back toward the house. "Drowning his sorrows in a flagon of ale." He patted Leydi's hand. "Yer sure ye won't stay and speak to Martha a bit. She'll be right mad at me if I let ye leave without even a hello."

Leydi shook her head. "I'll miss my ride if I stay too long. Please, don't let me keep you from your work. I'll just show myself out."

Leon wiped his brow with the back of his arm. "There's work a-plenty, and that's a fact. 'Tis a full house tonight. Well, good day to ye, then, Miss Leydi."

Leydi waited until Mr. McClellen stepped back into the kitchen. Not wanting to be caught nosing around where she had no business, she strolled slowly through the courtyard garden, then quickened her step once she was out of McClellen's sight. Her breath coming in uneven pants, she steered through the narrow back door into the hall. Biting her lip, she stopped before the supper room and inched the door open—just wide enough so she could peer inside.

A lone figure sat in the far corner, wreathed in shadows. He was a gentleman, by his attire. A very rich gentleman. The velvet coat was of the finest material, boned to flare extravagantly from his waist. The amber cane leaning next to the table shone gold at the tip. She wondered if it wasn't the same cane that had conked poor George on the head.

She leaned her cheek against the doorjamb, watching the man silently. There was something infinitely sad about the way he held his shoulders. Despite the richness of his attire, he was bent over his flagon of ale like a tired old soul. She wondered what could be so terrible to weigh down those shoulders. What had built this wedge between father and son?

Suddenly, the man pushed the ale aside, the gesture quick and violent. The flagon teetered, just finding its balance on the edge of the pine table. Quentin's father dropped his head into his hands. His shoulders began to shake.

He was crying.

Leydi stepped back from the door, staring at the dark timbers in the hall. She thought of the words she'd seen on the charred paper. *Come. Forgive. Your loving father.*

Her throat grew tight. She closed her eyes, again seeing the earl crying alone in the shadows of that empty supper room. Whatever had happened to make Quentin turn his back on his father, the earl felt the loss greatly.

Come. Forgive.

Her fingers curled around her drawstring purse. She bit her lip almost painfully. Why couldn't Quentin forgive? Her whole life, she'd wanted her parents to say those words to her, to welcome her, to ask her forgiveness for past misdeeds. Quentin's father had done just that.

Come. Forgive.

Leydi knuckled away her tears and silently made her way to the street. Outside, she blinked at the sudden brightness and searched the street for George.

She told herself she had no business being angry at Quentin. She didn't know the reasons behind the estrangement. It was none of her business, really. Her only interest was Kincaid and thwarting Rutherford's plans. Still, she couldn't understand not finding the heart to forgive a parent. And she wondered as she walked down the crowded street, dodging a curricle that thundered past in a cloud of dust, what it would take to make Quentin see the same.

Gabriela sashayed past the groping hands of one of the tavern's customers, her backside just missing the outstretched fingers. She gripped the shawl that she'd looped over her head, scanning the room that smelled of rum punch and stale straw for her quarry. She just managed to creep forward through the crowd of bodies. This was the third tavern she'd visited. And though she thought herself relatively safe in these establishments run by the very families she'd grown up with on St. Kitts, she knew trouble would find her if she wasn't quick enough to get out of its path.

Most every proprietorship did trade with Kincaid. Here at the Stone Elephant, he provided a fine French brandy. Their regard for the pirate had given Gabriela, the fatherless child of a free woman of color, the respect she would never have otherwise. Many knew her mother worked closely with him.

But rather than endearing Kincaid to her, Gabriela resented his protection. He had refused to give her the one thing she wanted from him—she had too many memories of the pain he'd caused her mother. Bertie's small heartbreak over Hugh was nothing compared to the months of tears she'd shed for Kincaid. Even when they'd been most happy, Kincaid hadn't been faithful to Bertie. Only Consuelo held his fidelity.

Putting aside her sour thoughts, Gabriela searched the darkest corners. The tallow candles on the tables barely gave off enough light to see where she was walking. She could swear the rushes hadn't been changed since Whitsunday; the room smelled dank and sour. And then she saw him, sitting back against the timbered wall, listening to a musician play the treble lute. Tonight he wore trousers, a shirt, and short coat. His burnished red curls were tied back in a pigtail, and his brow was furrowed.

Her heart in her throat, Gabriela strolled toward him. The room was crowded with sour-smelling bodies. Most gave way, and she swatted aside the few who didn't. A fixed smile on her face, she wondered over the wisdom of her plan as she caught the redhead's eye. But she had little faith in sweet Leydi's ability to spy. And though Kincaid had hurt her and Bertie irreparably, it was his money and protection that had given her an easy life and an education. She must check her bitterness long enough to stop what harm might befall him.

The gentleman didn't return her smile, but slid across the bench seat to make room for her just the same. Gabriela lowered her lace shawl to her shoulders and took the bench across the table, a safe distance away.

"You left in a hurry the other day," she said, speaking just loud enough to be heard over the lute's mellow strumming. She gave her most seductive pout. "That wasn't very friendly."

He picked up his rum and took a slow drink. His dark eyes looked black in the candlelight. "I believe I was dismissed right and proper. If I remember your exact words, 'Now, be a good boy, and leave me alone. There's nothing for you here.' "

"A girl needs to be wary these days." Taking his glass, she drank a sip of the rum, her eyes on his over the rim.

"You don't strike me as the careful sort."

She laughed, her voice seductively low. "Let's just say I'm discerning."

He took his glass back and set it aside. He leaned forward on the table. She could just make out the boyish freckles. They made an odd contrast to the deep lines around his mouth that spoke of age. "Why exactly are you here, Mistress de Sousa?"

Gabby held her lace shawl closed at her bosom, holding back a shiver, feeling suddenly very unsure of her plan. "I happened to be out and I saw you sitting here. You looked lonely. I thought you might wish my company, that's all. And you're right; I was rude the other day." She reached out and placed her fingers gently on his hand. "Let me apologize for that now."

"Come to grog shops often, do you?" he asked with a twist of his mouth.

Gabriela tried to sound sweet as she answered, "The proprietor is a friend."

He nodded, and then stood. He threw a few coins on the table. Their patter on the table echoed in a hollow ping in Gabriela's heart as she realized he was going to leave.

"A moment, *senhor*," she said, her voice losing some of its smoothness. "I don't even know your name."

"It's Felix, Gabriela," he said, holding out his hand. The palm was callused. His fingers were long and tapered. "Felix Bishop. And I plan for you to know much more than that."

Gabriela stared at his outstretched hand. This sudden offer took her by surprise. He'd been so distant, sitting across that table. So cold. Even now his dark eyes showed none of the desire a woman would expect with his proposition. But she knew she'd hesitated longer than was proper for her plans. He didn't seem the least put off as he grabbed her hand and pulled her to her feet.

Felix guided the daughter toward the door, silently fuming. He'd had a ghastly day. Kincaid had managed to grease enough palms in the government that everywhere he turned, Felix came up against a wall of incompetence or outright protection of the fiend. It seemed no one wanted the scoundrel caught. The few he'd not bribed outright owed their loyalties to the pirate through their livelihoods: Kincaid's pirating kept half of Basse Terre equipped with goods.

But the last stroke had been Rutherford's defection. It had been a mistake to mention the woman; Felix realized that now. Once again his meeting at Rutherford Hall had turned into a useless chat over coffee.

And now one of Kincaid's own had sought him out. He wasn't quite sure why. The way his investigation was going, he was no threat to the pirate. But the woman was beautiful, with dark, creamy skin and an exotic beauty he found he couldn't resist. He was lonely and frustrated enough to take what she offered and damn her and Kincaid both.

Outside, he turned for the nearest alley. He rented a room from a very proper woman who'd made it clear she expected no female visitors. He wasn't about to be led to the mother's shop, Kincaid's den, for slaughter. In the alley he'd have the privacy he needed.

Finding the narrow street abandoned, he pulled Gabriela into his arms. There was just enough light from a window above them to make out her features. He hesitated for a moment, surprised to see fear in those lovely green eyes.

"Not so fast, love," she whispered, her breath coming sharp and warm as if she'd just run the block. "A lady likes at least the illusion of romance."

He ran his fingers through her hair, taking the two combs that held back the curls and dropping them into his pocket. The tight ringlets just touched her shoulders and were surprisingly soft through his fingers. He brushed his thumbs across her high cheekbones. She was tall for a woman, almost of a height with him. He looked deeper into those exotic green eyes, trying to understand the hesitation he saw there. She'd seemed confident enough in the Stone Elephant.

He tentatively brushed his mouth against hers, once, twice. He could hear her breath catch at even that slight touch. He frowned, not sure he was up for her games.

"Have I made a mistake? Isn't this what you want?" he asked, reaching up and cupping her breast over the striped muslin. He leaned forward to kiss her again. He was hard and hot and not in the mood to show patience.

She stumbled back against the alley wall. This time there was true fear in her face, enough that he stayed his hand and stood watching her.

She licked her lips and gave a good attempt at a smile. She fumbled with the folds of her skirt. "I find you very unromantic, Felix Bishop. But then, I shouldn't be surprised. The way you crushed my rose."

He didn't say anything at first, just studied her in the dim light as he crossed his arms. "What's this about?" he asked, giving her a graceful way out, something she looked right ready to do.

She gave a shallow laugh. "It seems it is I who made the mistake." *A big one,* Gabriela thought to herself, clutching the bone handle of the knife she'd hidden in the pocket inside her skirt.

"I've plenty of money, if that's what you're after."

Gabriela shook her head, feeling quite sick. For an instant, when his hand had squeezed over her breast, she could think only of Murdock's brutal attack. But it wasn't time to turn fainthearted.

"Please, I . . . I'm a bit new at this," she said by way of explanation. "But I would like to see you again. Perhaps you could come by the shop—"

He barked a laugh. "Is this a joke?" He took a step forward, his hands outstretched. "Do you think—"

"Don't come any closer," Gabriela warned, holding the knife before her with both hands. She tried to remember everything.

Cy had taught her about using a blade. But despite his loyal tutoring, she was afraid she wouldn't be able to strike this man.

Felix took one look at the pig sticker in her trembling hands and shook his head. He turned as if to walk away. At the last minute he lunged for Gabriela. He grabbed the knife from her hand and threw it down the alley. He pushed her up against the stucco-and-timber wall and pinned both her hands there.

"You tell Kincaid that he'll have to do a lot better than to send his strumpet if he wants to get rid of me." He stared at her, those intense eyes seeming to look straight into her soul. And then he kissed her, bruising her mouth with a passion that stole her breath.

He pushed off the wall and walked away. At the entrance to the alley he turned and said, "I'll see him hang yet."

Gabriela watched him disappear. When he was gone, she let her head fall back against the wall and tried to still her galloping heart. Slowly, she walked to where he'd thrown the knife and picked it up. She touched her lips with her fingers and remembered the fire in his eyes when he'd spoken his threats.

"Dear God," she whispered. He wanted Kincaid dead.

Chapter Nine

He could never forget the smell of roses. Sweet. Cloying. Clarice's scent.

As he watched the rain dash against the mullion window, Quentin thought he could almost smell the memory of it. Roses.

It was the dead of night. He sat in the window seat in the hall. He wore only his breeches. No shoes. The water pooled and streamed down the glass, making Quentin think of weeping. Clarice had always found tears easy. She'd cried for a pendant of table-cut diamonds. She'd wept for seed pearls and a pink topaz suite of a necklace, bracelets, and earrings. Much of anything could bring on a torrent. He lifted the dram glass to his mouth and sipped the rum.

Yet another night he wouldn't sleep.

"Go away, Clarice," he whispered to the shadows.

He'd had the dream. Again he'd held Clarice in his arms and watched her die. And heard her confession about his father's role. Those visions brought back a suffocating anger, making even the mattress of superfine swan's feathers torture.

"God. How long can a man go without a decent night's rest?" he wondered out loud.

Aloysius peeked around the door to his bedchamber, then padded down the hall to wrap his plump body around Quentin's ankle. With a smile, he bent down and picked up the tom. "So. You have a heart after all, leaving that warm bed to find me."

The half-empty dram glass rested abandoned on the window seat as Quentin cradled Aloysius in his arms and listened to the cat's rumbling purrs. "What do you think, Aloysius? Shall I go mad from lack of sleep?" He pressed his chin to the cat's warm fur. "I'm sure I've heard somewhere that's possible."

Aloysius responded with a raspy lick of his tongue across Quentin's cheek.

"As sweet a kiss as any I've had of late," he told the cat.

That much was true. There'd been nothing but a few fevered gropings for release in Quentin's life since Clariċe, all very forgettable, almost perfunctory. His refusal to take a bride had become legend on the island; his lack of interest for the local crop of eligibles incited whispers of a dark past. But Quentin didn't mind. He had no time for women. And little inclination since Clarice.

The Mouse, of course, had changed all that.

Tucking Aloysius under his arm, Quentin stepped barefoot down the corridor and stairs. He knew his way around the manse well enough to require no light, but once inside the receiving chamber, he lit a taper. He carried a brace of candles to the center of the room and set it down on the rosewood table he used as a desk. Seeing the tidy piles of missives, he smiled. In three days the Mouse had brought them all to heel. He'd even watched her bully Stevenson into adopting her method for organizing the considerable correspondence that arrived each day. He had to admit, she'd surprised him a time or two with her abilities.

Sitting in the Turk-worked chair, he looped one leg around the arm and dropped Aloysius to his lap. He stared up at the ceiling. The flickering flames of the candelabrum provided just enough light to see his angels' faces.

"Well, what do you think? Shall I seduce her?"

He waited, but there came no response.

"Unfortunately, it wouldn't be difficult," he told the angels, scratching behind Aloysius's ear. "That's what makes it so tempting. She looks at me with those gray eyes full of need. Oh, yes, she's quite mine for the taking, whatever her relationship to this pirate might be. And yet . . ." He laughed. "Dear God, what a surprise—" He ruffled the cat's fur and whispered in his ear, "I still seem to have a conscience."

He sighed, too tired from lack of sleep. Taking a deep breath, he leaned his head against the pillowed headrest of the chair. "And my conscience advises against using the Mouse for a mistress."

He made himself think of Clarice. He closed his eyes and pictured her, the dramatic red curls, the guile shining in her amethyst eyes. Clarice had been tall, with a slimness that was almost unfashionable, but quickly forgotten with the provocative attire she favored. She made an art of tempting men, of making them fantasize about what it would take to fulfill the appetites she displayed when she met your eyes. It was a challenge few could resist. Quentin certainly had not.

He told himself he preferred women like Clarice in his bed— women who knew what they were about, who could give as good as they got.

He didn't want innocence. He didn't need devotion. He'd never involve himself with a woman who held her heart in her eyes for all to see the tenderness offered there. A woman who seemed to blossom when a man showed the slightest hunger for her.

These were the attributes the Mouse offered—a sweet sense of purity, a desire to give all. He remembered her charming little fantasy about Lady Anne, and he wondered if he was the first man to show interest in her, she seemed so susceptible.

"No, I won't take her to my bed," he told the angels. "But I want to . . . oh, yes. I want to."

A part of him wanted to strip those little brown dresses from her and bury his fingers in that seductive fall of curls. He wanted to see her naked before him, to feel her hips beneath his as he tangled them together in artless passion. He wanted that naiveté she exuded with the ease of the lavender scent she wore. He wanted that incredible sense of purpose she'd given his books focused on him, on his mouth, on every heated part of him. And he'd a notion she could do that—give over everything to pleasing one man.

"I shall have to settle for knowing what she's about with her pirate," he told himself. "But I've a thing or two left to teach the Mouse." That life was cruel—that you shouldn't give so much. "She needs a harder heart," he thought out loud. The Mouse shouldn't try to please so well, whether it be him or her pirate or her mother.

"That much I can teach her," he thought with sudden bitterness.

In *Constant Constance,* the heroine, Lady Constance, seemed quite capable of these feats of espionage. But waiting with her shoulder blades pressed against the Chinese wallpaper in the Empire Room, Leydi wondered if perhaps spying weren't a bit beyond her.

She held her breath, then peeked around the doorjamb. The hall was empty. Not a shadow. Not a sign.

Dear Lord, what could possibly be taking so long? She clutched the tablet she held in her arms and released her breath. She'd spent the entire morning waiting for Lieutenant Felix Bishop to make his appearance.

After she'd returned from Basse Terre the previous day, pleasant chitchat over tea with Mr. Stevenson and a bit of tactful probing had revealed Bishop was due at Rutherford Hall the next day. At a quarter past ten Sunday morn, Bishop had indeed walked into the Grand Hall. For the past hour Leydi had been waiting, hoping to time her exit just right. Her heart thundered so loudly in her ears, she'd been fooled once or twice into peering past the doorjamb to find the hall empty.

The distinctive *click* of the receiving door sent Leydi ducking back into the Empire Room. She listened as Rutherford bid the lieutenant good day—a gentility that was answered only by the muffled steps of Bishop's boots on the carpeted runner.

Counting silently, Leydi held her place, then plunged into the corridor, her gaze fixed at the toes of her buckled shoes beneath the hem over her gown. When she collided into the wall of male chest, she almost sighed with relief. *Success!*

"Oh, excuse me, sir. I didn't . . . see . . ."

The words died in her throat, as did the rest of the speech she'd rehearsed the past hour. The lieutenant's tall figure elbowed around her as if she were no more bother than a gnat. But she'd gotten a good look at his face before he'd stepped past. Whatever Bishop had discussed with Lord Ruthless, the man was not pleased.

Well, at least she'd managed the collision if not the introduction she'd needed. Squaring her shoulders, she marched down the corridor to the receiving chamber, ready to put the second half of her plan into action.

She knocked loudly, but rather than waiting for Rutherford to answer, she stepped inside, the tablet outstretched before her like a shield.

"I've those figures you asked for on the salt ponds, and you're right, the yield should be more than ample for our needs. Now, I've taken the time to make a few suggestions on equipment, new processing techniques, effects of weather, and other such variables. If you'd care to take a look."

She held the tablet out to him, bold as brass, as if she had every right in the world to be there. Which she did not. She'd snatched this duty from Mr. Stevenson—and spent half the night going over her calculations. At this very moment she was to be working on another matter entirely.

Rutherford said nothing, just assessed her with those azure eyes as if she were some enterprise that hadn't quite produced its promised yield. His silence got the best of her. "Mr. Stevenson and I finished early with the day's correspondence," she said by way of explanation for her presence there. "And I thought you'd want these figures you asked for as soon as possible."

Quentin took the tablet from the Mouse and stared down at the sums, not really seeing the figures. There was a strength of purpose to her that made him wary. He'd just spent the last hour hearing Bishop spout about the danger Quentin allowed by keeping her near. And he was inclined to agree that the Mouse could be trouble. But not the kind Bishop had suggested.

He sighed, taking a look at the tidy figures she'd penned. She must have worked all night; he'd spoken of the salt ponds to Stevenson only yesterday. Of course, she had some nefarious reason for taking over a job he'd requested from his steward. He thought if he gave her enough time, she'd get to the point.

"I ran into a gentleman in the hall," she said, answering his silent suspicions. "Actually, he practically bowled me over." This, followed by a dubious-sounding laugh. "He seemed quite official—I've seen him here a time or two before. Is he here about Gellman's coffee?"

Quentin looked up, catching myriad furtive emotions in those pewter-gray eyes. She was talking about Lieutenant Bishop, but he judged by the way she mangled the end of her braid in her hands and her tight smile that she knew Bishop had nothing to do with the coffee venture. He put down the tablet, wondering just how much the Mouse had guessed about Bishop's purpose there.

"Lieutenant Bishop has been quite helpful on an entirely different matter."

"Not the coffee?" she fished innocently.

"The pirate," he answered with a smile.

He watched her throw her braid over her shoulder and adjust the mobcap. She shuffled through the papers on the desk as if she might find something of use there. "So you won't heed my advice and leave off your pirate hunting?"

He held out his hands in mock apology. "You've done such an admirable job of clearing my obligations, Mouse, I find myself quite free to aid the lieutenant's search for the culprit."

Her eyes widened, then turned the gray of storm clouds. He thought she looked just a touch pale. "Perhaps I've done my work too well, then."

The irritation in her voice really made it difficult not to smile. "Sit down, Miss Carstair. I have a few additions I'd like to put to these figures."

Quentin listened as the Mouse debated her findings on the salt ponds, infinitely distracted by the lavender scent spiraling up from her neck. As she leaned over the desk, her fingers tap-

ping on the figures to make her point, he found himself forgetting Bishop's dire warnings and just enjoying the sight of her.

The past week he'd seen all too quickly beyond the mobcap
and brown clothes. His gaze drifted to the curve of her full
breasts outlined by muslin, the sweet shape of her arms and
fine-boned hands. He thought of those delicate hands clutching
at his shoulders, her talented fingers lacing through his hair as
he kissed her. He had to forcibly remind himself of his decision
of the night before. The Mouse was not the woman for his bed.
He wanted to know only about her involvement with Kincaid.

But she seemed to ignite desire in him simply with her presence as she laid out calculations on yield per square foot. His
hunger was obvious enough that she stopped mid-sentence, just
to stare at him questioningly. For an instant her silver eyes peered
up at him, promising only eagerness to please, without price.
Tell me how to help, they seemed to say. *I want to please you.*

Quentin shuddered, feeling that look too deep inside himself.
It seemed to catch a spark, drawing him to the point where he
actually leaned closer to her. The Mouse startled from her pleasant pose and moved quickly to continue her calculations, her
voice sounding reedy and just a bit out of breath.

He told himself it was the lack of sleep. He usually had more
discipline than this. He reminded himself he had a mission to
fulfill with Miss Carstair—and it had nothing to do with the seduction she unwittingly invited.

He forced himself to listen to her analyzing weather patterns
and averaging rainfall. She was utterly thorough, surprising him
again with her expertise. He glanced up from the figures, about
to say as much, when he discovered her staring up at him and
not at the numbers.

"Was it Lieutenant Bishop who hit George the other day? The
man who was screaming to see you outside the door?"

His father. She was speaking about the earl.

That surprised him.

"It was no one of importance," he said carefully.

The Mouse frowned. "But now that I think about it, it didn't
sound like the lieutenant. Somehow I imagined . . . oh, I don't
know. Someone older?"

He wasn't prepared for her interest in his father; she'd caught him off guard. Of course she would have heard the servants gossip. He knew her mother had been telling tales about his past. The Mouse seemed a curious woman—curious enough to make this mistake.

"It's this number that has me most concerned," he said, steering her back to the figures on the ponds. He wouldn't speak about the past—not to the Mouse. Not to anyone. "That's quite inventive, but is it accurate? If we're going to make a success of the enterprise, we'll need to make sure we have a plan if these figures don't work out."

She didn't answer him at first, just stared at the sums. And then she whispered, "It's strange that a son should refuse to see his own father."

Quentin put down his quill. "We can debate the salt ponds tomorrow, if you prefer," he said, making it clear he would not discuss the earl. "I've plenty of other matters I need to attend to today."

Her soft gray eyes met his. There was a depth of sadness there for him to see, and no attempt to hide it.

Quentin cursed softly. He stood, pushing back his chair on the carpet as he turned away. For a moment he felt the same violence surge through him that had kept him awake most the night. Imagine, his father begging forgiveness when he knew— he knew!—there could be none. Not for the past. Not after seven years. It was a burden they would all have to live with.

And now the Mouse had brought it all back.

Damn all—this night he needed to sleep, even if he had to drink himself into oblivion to accomplish it. The lack of sleep was the only reason he could give himself for the effect she had on him.

"It's just that he seemed so angry," she prompted when he didn't speak, heedless of the danger. "And poor George . . . I was just curious if—"

"Don't," he said, turning to face her. "Don't be curious. Don't wonder. Don't interfere."

It almost hurt to see her eagerness checked. He knew from experience the Mouse could be tenacious. She was staring at him now as if he were a puzzle and she'd just solved one sad part.

He wouldn't have it. He couldn't abide this little show of insight on her part, as if she had just read his soul. It was he who was investigating her, not the other way around, damn her.

"You've heard that old saw—curiosity killed the cat?" he asked, pacing toward her. "And with all the work you've done, Mouse, I would hate for a small misunderstanding to put an end to such productivity." He watched her take a step back, like an innocent lamb stalked by the wolf. He found he liked the illusion—found he wanted to play that part.

He took up her hand. With his fingertip he lightly caressed each knuckle, continuing up to stroke the soft skin of her wrist. "You know, you quite dazzle me with your talents. . . ." The practiced speech came to him without thinking. It had been a long time since he'd played the rogue, but it was a role with which he was infinitely familiar. When she would step away, he held tight to her hand, not allowing the distance. "I must confess, it's a struggle to concentrate on pirates, ponds, or pounds when you're about." He lifted her hand to his mouth and placed a kiss on her exposed wrist.

She snatched back her hand. He could see she was breathing hard. Her lips were pressed together, so tight they'd lost their color. "I only wondered who he was," she said, her voice full of hurt. "You don't have to . . . do this."

He smiled but continued forward. He cupped her cheek in his palm, looking for the green in those lovely gray eyes. "What exactly am I trying to do, Mouse?"

She met his gaze straight on, this time keeping her ground. "You think I'm a fool—but I'm not. If you don't want to answer my question about the earl, you need only to say as much. You don't need this . . . charade . . . to scare me off."

He almost corrected her, tempted to tell her just how little acting he was doing and how much he desired her. But she was right. If he'd wanted to seduce her, he wouldn't go about it in such a fashion. Mindless flatteries were not the path to the Mouse's heart. But he was tired now of their play, and so he said simply, "I won't speak to anyone about my father."

She shook her head, watching him now as if she pitied him. "I hope you know what you're giving up, turning your back on him."

He raised his brow. He hadn't expected this noble insistence. He felt outflanked, the way she'd challenged him. Enough that he attacked, knowing most definitely how to change her tune. "Let's discuss a topic that seems just as dear to your heart. Felix Bishop has put forth an ambitious plan to capture Daniel Kincaid," he improvised, thinking to steer her from her talk of the earl. "Would you care to hear it??" He looped a curl that had escaped her braid around her ear, then brushed his thumb across her cheek. "Would that interest you, Mouse? Hmm?"

Leydi swallowed hard. But her heart still jammed in her throat, making it difficult to speak or breathe. His words came from nowhere and hit with the force of cannon fire. For a moment her silly imagination had allowed her to think she might help Quentin meet with the man she'd seen crying in the shadows of that supper room. Half the night, as she'd put together these calculations on the salt ponds, she'd wondered about the rift between father and son—imagined herself bridging that gap. And now, unthinkingly, she'd allowed her daydreams to goad her into speaking out of turn. In defense, Rutherford had hit with a keenness that was frightening, striking where she was most vulnerable.

"Lieutenant Bishop in particular seems determined to rid the seas of that scourge," he said, continuing his assault with a smile. "With the Royal Navy's patrol at his disposal and my own fleet of ships, he's come up with something quite brilliant. You see, Miss Carstair, he's discovered a favored route of Kincaid's. Bishop has gathered some intelligence that the pirate will be there by month's end."

Leydi shook her head, as if she could deny the disaster she saw unfolding. Everything she feared was coming true—her ineptness at spying, Bishop and Quentin's plans against Kincaid. "It's a fool's errand to try to capture such a notorious pirate," she whispered, her throat gone dry.

"Perhaps," Rutherford said, leaning closer so that she could feel his breath against her neck. "But I think we'll succeed. What say you, Mouse? Not a bad plan?" he said almost gently. "Do you think Kincaid will hang?"

Leydi scrambled back, holding her hand to her own neck. "I shall think on it, my lord—since you asked my opinion. Your plan may have a flaw or two you may not see in your enthusiasm to capture Kincaid. I understand the pirate can be very resourceful."

He crossed his arms and leaned against the desk. "Indeed. But perhaps you underestimate my resourcefulness."

Leydi glanced down at the desk. At that moment her eyes found something to fight with—to show Rutherford he should beware. It was the kind of weapon that came most naturally to her. She picked up the sheet of paper with the figures she'd quickly tallied, a talent she'd had since an early age.

"Don't take my sense of caution too lightly. Anyone can make a mistake, no matter how splendid his resources." Her finger landed on the vellum sheet like the point of a sword. "For example, that figure. The number is wrong. It should be 53,452, not 53,756."

Quentin stared for a moment, wondering what she was up to. That was a rather important contract she'd picked out. Having just done those sums himself, he didn't even bother to look over the figures. She couldn't honestly expect him to believe that she was capable of summing ten rows of numbers, each in the thousands, in the blink of an eye—an equation he'd done himself on an abacus.

"You're wrong, Mouse," he said, quite sure of himself. "I seldom make mistakes. Certainly not when it counts. The number is 53,756."

She picked up the abacus from the table, holding it out to him. "My point exactly. In business, as in life, a certain amount of self-possession can be helpful. But take it too far, and the same characteristic can be foolhardy, leading to very bad results."

"Why, Mouse, is this a warning?"

Her answer was to hold the abacus once more.

Humoring her, he did the sums, clicking the numbers rapidly on the beads . . . and discovered she was right. *She was right!*

That quickly, in a mere glance really, she'd seen the error and calculated the correct sum.

He was still staring at the beads when he heard her say, "I just wanted to make a point."

He glanced up, watching her gather her papers. She didn't even bother with a smile of triumph, she just made for the door. At the threshold she looked back and said, "Don't make the mistake of going after Kincaid."

He watched the door close behind her. He put down the abacus and stared at the numbers. He was tempted to do the sum again—but then 'he smiled.

"*Touché*, little Mouse. *Touché.*"

He'd lied about Bishop's plans for Kincaid, of course. The poor lieutenant had no notion of the pirate's route. But his fabrication had gotten the response Quentin had wanted. Oh, yes. The Mouse was in deep with pirates.

"Pour me another dram, Bertie."

Bertie shook her head. "You'll get wool headed." But she poured the drink just the same into the pale green glass.

"Not Leydi, *Mãe,*" Gabriela said, joining her friend in a drink at the counter of the shop. "Cy says her stomach's lined with lead."

"I wish I could get wool headed," Leydi said almost to herself. "Lord in heaven, Bertie. What can we do? The patrol will be out looking for Kincaid—they'll trap him for certain."

Bertie shook her head. "I've seen Kincaid in worse fixes, *menina.* I'd not worry overmuch about him. If Rutherford thinks he has special intelligence about Kincaid, you can be certain Daniel knows about it. He has *muito* friends." She leaned over to give Leydi's hand a comforting pat. "Why, if *we* know about Rutherford's plans, it is no secret at all."

"Do you mean to do nothing, then, *Mãe?* Just sit here like hens and let the rotter hang?"

At that surprising defense from Gabriela, Leydi choked on the rum. She put down the dram glass, seeing Bertie, too, was amazed by her daughter's concern for Kincaid.

"And what do you suggest, daughter?"

Gabriela frowned, staring at the golden rum in her glass. "Well, we should do something, at least. You can't just rely on Kincaid's spies. That pirate and I might have our differences, but even I couldn't forgive myself if he hangs and I could have done something to stop it. He'd probably haunt me." She shook her head and took another sip.

Bertie seemed to think a moment, looking at her daughter with a touch of speculation.

"She's right," Leydi said, hoping to sway Bertie. Like Gabby, she couldn't just wait around and hope everything turned out well. "You wanted me to play spy, and I have. Shouldn't we put the information to some use?"

"All right," Bertie said, corking the bottle and putting the rum behind the counter. "We'll send Cy a message. If anyone knows how to get a warning to Kincaid while he's at sea, it's Cy. Hand me my writing desk, *Gabriela*. I'll pen the note now."

As Leydi and Gabby watched, Bertie opened the lap desk and retrieved her vellum. Putting pen to ink, she quickly wrote her message. Using the pounce pot, she sanded the same and sealed it. She placed the folded paper into the embroidered linen pocket she wore under her apron. She gave the message a pat. With a smile to both women, she said, "Now rest assured Kincaid will be fine."

Not the least bit at ease, Leydi kept silent just the same. She helped Gabriela put the glasses away as Bertie went about the business of closing the shop. Soon Leydi would meet George to return to Rutherford Hall. All day her argument with Rutherford had haunted her. When she'd come across George taking the gig into town to run errands, she begged a ride, hoping to discuss this new development with Bertie and Gabriela.

"Do you really think it's enough to send Cy a warning?" she asked Gabriela. Outside the shop, Bertie was gathering up the frying pans and sadirons she'd arranged in an open-air display with cedarwood pails and yellow queen's ware. "It seems so useless, waiting like this."

Seeing her mother was busy outside, Gabriela leaned closer. "*Mãe* relies too much on Cy and Kincaid. She thinks those two can never make a mistake." She seemed to think a moment, then whispered urgently, "I, too, had a run-in—with Bishop. He's determined to capture Kincaid." She squeezed Leydi's hand. "He says he won't rest until he sees Kincaid dead."

"Dead!"

Gabriela motioned for her to keep her voice down. "Yes. And it seems he's guessed our connection to the pirate, mine and Mother's. Enough in this town deal with Kincaid through *Mãe's* shop to give us away, though it surprises me any would be disloyal enough to speak to a naval officer. Kincaid pays well for silence."

"Then we must do something!"

Bertie walked inside, dragging in the trestles and boards she'd used in her display. Both Leydi and Gabby fell silent. Gabby checked the cash box, rifling through English and French guineas and Spanish pistoles and doubloons, looking closely for French sous disguised through clever alchemy to look like the more valuable Spanish moidores. Leydi helped pack woolens and linens on the shelves. Just as Bertie locked the front door, there came a terrific pounding.

"Mon petit chou, please, I beg you . . . torture me no longer," wailed Hugh's distinctive voice. "I must see you."

"Go away, Hugh," Bertie said. "Better yet, go find Monique. Your cousin!" she added with a bit more bite.

"She means nothing to me, Bertie. You are my love, my heart! Each day without you, my soul dies a little more."

Bertie leaned against the door, folding her arms over the lacings of her bodice. She played with the gold hoop in one ear. "If I open this door, your soul will reach heaven sooner than pleases you."

"Do with me what you will, Bertie . . . I deserve your scorn. But don't ignore me, my love. Give me a chance to explain."

"That around a willing woman you can't keep your breeches laced? That needs no explanation for me."

"Why won't you listen to reason . . . Bertie?" More pounding. "Bertie! Open this door! *Merde!*"

Bertie ignored the pounding, picking up a crate of oranges, but Leydi thought she saw a bit of a smile on her full lips. She clapped her hands free of dust from the crates and pushed back a curl that peeked out from the colorful scarf she'd tied around her head. To Leydi, the black woman looked just a touch younger and even more beautiful in the dimming light. She could understand why Hugh bewailed his loss.

"You go out the back, *menina,*"Bertie said to Leydi. "I cannot bother with this nuisance," she said breezily. As Hugh continued to pound on the front door, Bertie walked out the back. Leydi could hear her taking the stairs to the second floor.

"How long has this been going on?" Leydi asked, nodding toward the door.

Gabriela shrugged. "He hopes to win her back with his persistence. But I know my mother. Forgiving she may be, but she's not so gullible to lose her heart twice to someone who's betrayed her."

"What about Kincaid?" Leydi whispered, leaning close so Gabriela could hear over the pounding.

Gabby smiled, taking Leydi's hands in her own. *"Caro,* what would you say to a little adventure?"

"You know I'll do anything to help Kincaid."

"What I plan will take only money—I'll do the rest."

"You'll do nothing without me," Leydi said, already reaching for her drawstring purse and the coins she kept there.

"Actually, *caro,*" Gabby said, counting the money Leydi handed to her, "the idea is yours."

"Mine?"

Gabby nodded. *"Mãe,* she will send Cy his note—only it will not be the message she thinks." Gabby walked behind the counter and picked up the lap desk. Snatching a sheet from inside, she said, "I will ask Cy to send the *Fortune,* the ship Kincaid keeps at port at Devil's Gate, and sign my mother's name. The *Fortune* isn't known as a pirate ship and should be fairly safe coming to St. Kitts. I'll let him know that it is of the utmost importance that Cy have the ship off shore, near Old Town Road, the night the moon is a quarter full. That will give him just enough time to get here, but not enough time to challenge my plan."

"And the plan?"

"You yourself said it would serve these men right if we should abduct them, hold them at sword point and threaten them to leave off Kincaid—"

"I was speaking of Anne Bonny and Mary Reed, two of the most notorious women pirates ever to sail these waters."

Gabriela shook her head. "Not us, *caro*. But I know where to find men who will kidnap those two for a price." When Leydi looked hesitant, Gabby added, "It's the best we can do on such short notice. Listen, *caro*, no one will get hurt. I'll write to Cy to keep clear until he reaches the inlet there. We'll have the men we hire bring Rutherford and Bishop bound and gagged to the shore. With the ship on the horizon, the men will need only to warn the lieutenant and your Lord Ruthless that Kincaid got wind of their plans and then they'll let them go. Those two will see it is useless to pursue any other intelligence against Kincaid. The threat alone will do. No one will get hurt."

"Then we meet with Cy at Old Town Road and explain what's happened," Leydi finished for Gabby.

"Exactly. All will go well. With this and what I have," Gabriela said, holding up the coins she'd counted, "we can at least tempt a few men to agree to our plan. But we'll need the promise of more when the job's done."

"Money won't be the problem," Leydi said, her heart racing as she thought of the danger they courted. She couldn't let anyone harm Kincaid, a man she loved like a father—but she didn't want to see Quentin hurt.

"*Caro*, if you can think of anything else . . ."

Leydi shook her head. "No. No, I can't. Still." She turned and grabbed up Gabby's two hands. "You promise those men double if no harm comes to Rutherford."

Gabby nodded. "Don't worry. I know just who to ask. You'll see, *caro*. It will all turn out for the best."

Part Two

Walking the Plank

Chapter Ten

Gabriela waited patiently for Bertie to fall asleep. The house was full dark; both mother and daughter had been in bed nearly an hour. Thus far, Gabriela's nightly excursions had gone without notice by virtue of the fact that her mother trusted her implicitly. Tonight's tiny betrayal smarted a bit, but creeping inside her mother's room with the stealth of a thief, Gabriela reasoned she acted in Kincaid's best interest. Certainly the result, if not the method, would be to her mother's liking.

Quietly, she hunted among the garments hanging from wooden hooks on the wall for the gown Bertie had worn earlier that day. Discovering the fine feel of chintz, Gabby searched for the linen pocket beneath. She found it soon enough and the treasure inside: her mother's letter to Cy. Gabriela switched the missive for the one she'd written in a fine attempt at her mother's bold script, then slipped back into the hall.

Tomorrow Bertie would send the note off to Cy, Kincaid's second-in-command, and Gabriela's plan would be set into action. With her mother's name penned at the bottom, Cy would follow the letter's instructions without question.

Gabriela crept back into her room. She pocketed the coins

Leydi had given to her and added her own savings. Listening once more for her mother's gentle snores, she skipped down the steps and out the back door, slipping into the darkened street behind the shop.

Half running, half walking, she navigated the road still muddy from the previous night's sudden downpour. She bemoaned the absence of her pattens, but the wooden overshoes would have prevented the stealth and speed she needed to find the men who could kidnap Rutherford and Bishop. Holding tight to her hooped skirt with one hand and clutching her shoulder cape with the other, she hurried past two sailors staggering down the street, well in their cups. When she reached the colonnade, she stepped up on the raised walkway and grabbed her drawstring purse, darting a look behind her to see if the sailors continued their course down the street or had doubled back to cause trouble.

A hand reached out from a shadowed doorway. Fingers like grappling hooks latched on to her elbow. In one fluid motion she was pulled into the darkness.

She fought, trying to free her wrists. She kicked her captor in the shins. The man pushed her up against the wall, knocking the breath from her. She thought of the purse tied at her waist, scheming on how best to hide it—to get away. She grasped for her knife, when a man's face, his breath smelling of mint and rum, lowered to hers.

"We meet again, fair Gabriela."

Bishop. She stopped struggling. Letting her eyes adjust to the dark, she could indeed make out his features. "What do you want? Are you following me?"

She saw his eyes glittering with the moonlight. She could hear his breathing, harsh and shallow. He pressed against her, his thighs brushing her skirts.

"Following you? No. I've been waiting here, anticipating this little midnight excursion of yours. I didn't want you to catch me by surprise this time," he said.

Against the wall, Gabriela knew she should be afraid. She was on her way to hire someone to kidnap this very man precisely because she thought he was dangerous. And yet it wasn't fear that made her breath catch in her throat.

As she watched, Bishop reached up with one hand and stroked her cheek with the backs of his knuckles. It was an oddly gentle caress, nothing like Murdock's attack. No one had ever touched her like that, as if she were made of glass and might break.

"Did you give Kincaid my message?" he whispered, his mouth very close to hers.

"You've made a mistake," she said, putting as much conviction in her voice as she could. "I don't know this Kincaid. The other night I wanted only to talk." She licked her lips. "You looked lonely, sitting there at that table by yourself."

"You're such a poor liar. You should have left me there, Gabriela. At that table, alone. Lonely," he said, now stroking the bottom of her lip with the pad of his thumb. His eyes focused on her mouth. "It would have been better for you if you had. Better for both of us."

"What do you want?" she asked, her heart pounding from fear—and something else. Something she didn't want to acknowledge.

"That's the puzzle. I shouldn't want anything from you, one of Kincaid's minions. But since I kissed you, I can't seem to forget," he whispered. "I keep wondering what it would be like if you didn't fight me. If you kissed me, just once, with that lovely mouth. It's dangerous thinking, Gabriela."

"Because of Kincaid?" she asked. He'd put into words the same odd feelings she'd battled since that night in the alley when she'd threatened him with her knife. She could feel the heat of his body. She realized she wanted that heat to surround her, to swallow her up. He had the most intense eyes, so brown, they were almost black. In the dim light of the moon they looked bottomless.

He inched up her chin so their mouths were close enough to kiss. "Yes. Kincaid, for the most part. But there's other reasons," he whispered as he brushed his mouth across hers.

Gabriela closed her eyes as his lips pressed against hers. Her mother had spoken often about love. She described it as an irresistible force that drew a woman to a man. It was a force Bertie could never seem to turn from, a force Gabriela had never experienced in her near twenty-five years. Until now.

She found herself kissing Bishop even as her mind warned her to retreat. She reached up with her hand and brushed his cheek once, twice, then cupped his face in both hands as she kissed him again and again. She was holding in her purse money she must use to trap him—to threaten him to abandon his pursuit of Kincaid. But instead of trying to escape, she stopped thinking altogether as he moaned softly, opening his mouth over hers.

His body stayed close. She could feel the muscles of his chest beneath his waistcoat, his thighs touching hers through her skirts. The wall behind her prevented retreat. But she didn't want to escape.

It was Bishop who finally pulled away slowly, as if it cost him to do so. He stared at her, those dark brown eyes taking in every detail of her in the moonlight, then shook his head. He looked like a man waking from a dream.

"Dear God, I'm a fool," he whispered under his breath. "Here," he said, slipping something into her hand.

He gave her one more haunted look, his dark eyes almost beseeching her. Quickly, he turned and left.

Gabriela watched him hurry down the street. She knelt down to pick up the lace pinnet that had fallen from her hair when he'd kissed her. She heard the raucous laughter of the drunken sailors, the grunts of a nearby pig wallowing in the mud, the music from a tavern. She could just make out the shadow of Felix as he crossed the street and turned around the bend, falling out of sight.

This time he'd given no message to pass on to Kincaid. His mission, it appeared, was for her alone.

She looked down at her hand. She held the combs he'd taken from her hair the other night in the alley.

An irresistible force.

She took a deep breath, waiting for calm. For courage. She was a fool to allow what had just happened.

Stabbing the combs into her head, she headed for the harbor, more determined than ever that her mission succeed. She was careful this time to make certain she wasn't followed. Whatever had just happened between her and Felix Bishop, she still had her duty to Kincaid. Damn him.

"Here ye are, mate," the barkeep said, serving Felix his second glass of rum. The grog shop was dark and smoky, reeking of day-old fish and ripe bodies. But Felix was in no mood to be choosy. He stared at the cup, as if he might find answers to his moodiness there—which he knew he would not.

Was it her beauty? Certainly her exotic allure would be difficult for a man to forget. Her gold skin and green eyes. The silky ringlets of hair. That full mouth. Or was it merely something so simple as the fact that she was the forbidden fruit?

Or did he just hate Kincaid enough to want to hurt her?

Felix didn't consider himself a cruel man. He believed in justice. In right and wrong. Kincaid had destroyed his family, taking no more mind to the carnage he'd left at the Bishop plantation than he had for any other of his assaults at sea. Years earlier Felix had made himself the instrument of his family's revenge. But that revenge would be paid by Kincaid, and Kincaid alone.

A pair of tars elbowed up to the counter beside him, laughing and thumping their empty glasses on the counter. Felix moved aside, his thoughts only for Gabriela de Sousa. A part of him said she was false. She was the daughter of a free woman of color, a shopkeeper—and yet she spoke and dressed like a lady. No doubt, those jeweled combs he'd returned to her were part of some pirate booty. He told himself her association with Kincaid was enough to taint her.

But what he'd seen under the colonnade hadn't been tainted. She was just as lovely and sweet as he remembered. Just as irresistible.

Felix took up his drink, letting the gut-rot rum burn down his throat. He cursed himself for the idiocy of what he'd allowed this night. He had to concentrate on Rutherford. Rutherford was the key to his vengeance. If he could get the man to back him in his plan to take Kincaid down, then maybe Felix could finally get some rest.

After Kincaid hung for his many crimes, only then could Felix think of loving a woman, marriage, and a family. Of finding someone who made his blood burn as hot and ready as the lovely Gabriela de Sousa.

Rutherford. He was the key.

This time her daydream was about her parents.

Not her real parents. Leydi never daydreamed about Elaine or Argus. She dreamed only about happy times and good things.

In her fantasies her mythical parents held her in their arms as if she were someone to cherish. They brushed away her tears instead of causing them. They gave her presents; they advised with concerned patience. They asked for nothing, giving only love.

And they looked surprisingly like the Lady Consuelo and Daniel "Heartless" Kincaid.

"I suppose that makes an odd sort of sense," she told Aloysius, purring on her chest. She lay stretched out on the carpet in Rutherford's receiving chamber, her favorite spot of late. "A man of daring like Kincaid is just like the heroes in my books. In fact, he reminds me a great deal of that intrepid spirit Dampier—he, too, was a pirate, you know. And the Lady Consuelo, well, imagine having the fortitude to leave a prominent family, a husband, and a fortune, just to follow your heart? She lives beyond the conventions of society to make her own rules."

She looped Aloysius's whiskers through her fingers. Her childhood with Elaine and Argus hadn't been a bad thing. She had, after all, spent her time working to become a better person. But sometimes it hurt to think she was trying to earn their love rather than finding it free for the taking.

"If God allowed a person to pick their parents, it would be Consuelo and Kincaid I'd choose," she admitted with more firmness than she ought. "And I'm sorry if that sounds disloyal. I admire them so."

She smiled, realizing she was speaking about a pirate and a fallen woman. But both had offered their friendship these past eight years without exacting a price.

Reaching up, she mussed Aloysius's fur with her fingers, making it stand on end until he looked twice as fat. "I wish you could meet Nigel." She missed everyone on Devil's Gate, Nigel in particular. "Though, come to think of it, you might not take to him overmuch. He's a silly beast. Steals Gabby's ribbons when we give him the chance. I've even had to lock them in a drawer, he's such a thief."

She sighed, then looked back to the desk where Rutherford's books waited. She gave Aloysius a quick kiss between the ears. "It's back to the salt mines for me."

Standing, she flicked her apron smartly over her skirts, then picked up her braid and brushed the tip across her chin. She bent over the rosewood table and studied the numbers Rutherford had left her.

But her mind seemed not the least bit fit for work this morning. She kept hearing her mother's hateful words of the night before. *How could you give Argus money? You've no notion of what's proper, Leydianna.*

Last night Elaine had stormed into her room, waking Leydi from a delicious dream about a darkly handsome suitor—who looked enough like Lord Ruthless to make her blush. When she'd wrung the sleep from her eyes, she and her mother had gone another round about Argus. Her father had taken to drinking last night. He'd been singing at the top of his lungs in the front room, sounding like a cow in need of milking. No amount of arguing would convince her mother Leydi had not given him the coin for the rum.

Leydi stroked her cheek with the tuft of hair at the end of her braid, brushing it back and forth where Elaine had slapped her. Despite her ready temper, her mother never really hurt her. But more and more Leydi was finding it difficult to bite her tongue and not fight back.

She looked up at the ceiling. The morning light through the Bristol glass made the angels painted there appear singularly inspiring. "Why not wish for better parents when the ones you're given can be so unfair?" she asked them.

But soon her anger ebbed and Leydi smiled, thinking that Lord Ruthless had been correct when he'd mentioned her predilection for talking to objects. The angels in particular seemed rather sympathetic. Their painted expressions of concern gazed down from the cove ceiling lined with fluffy white clouds. Leydi sat down in the armchair, her petticoats whooshing up with her unladylike drop into the seat. She folded her arms behind her head and stared up at the ceiling.

"Perhaps I shouldn't be so quick to judge Elaine," she told the angels. "After all, I wouldn't be sitting here doing sums and analyzing yields but for her urging Mr. Stevenson to tutor me."

She peered at the angel on the right, thinking he looked skeptical. "Well," she said, "I do ask myself how long a person must pay because their mother and father did their duty as parents? If I had children, it would be my greatest wish to give them a better life than mine."

She twisted for a superior angle in the chair. Leaning back, she arched over the arm, letting her braid trail across the carpet as she addressed the small angel in the corner. He looked about to roll his eyes, as if her reasoning were hopeless.

"Of course, I won't be spending the rest of my days trying to please them . . . I've petitioned the Council for that plot of land just outside Old Town Road. Once Elaine and Argus are established on their own plantation—"

And what if it's not enough? the angel asked with a full-blown frown.

Leydi pursed her lips and let out a long stream of air. It was, of course, her greatest fear. That nothing she could give her parents would buy her freedom.

You can't buy their love, a different angel ventured with an almost wistful expression.

"Perhaps not," Leydi answered. "But I can try."

Bang. Leydi flailed upright, just saving herself from falling over the arm of the chair to the floor. On the rosewood table a pile of books had just been dropped into a stack reaching her nose.

She turned in the chair. Quentin stood at her side, his arms folded over his waistcoat, a bemused smile on his arrogant face.

"Daydreaming, Mouse?" He glanced up at the ceiling, giving

the angels painted there a thoughtful stare. "I'm not sure I like sharing my angels with you."

"Lord Ruth-Ruth-Ruth-Rutherford," she sputtered out at last, almost voicing her mean-spirited name for him.

He watched her for a full minute. She noticed he looked very tired. And he'd not shaved. It wasn't the first time she'd suspected he didn't sleep well. What surprised her was that he could still look so handsome despite those bloodshot eyes.

"Belfour, dear Mouse," he said, taking a step closer to her chair. "It's Lord Belfour—my title. Not Rutherford. That's just my surname, you see. You may call me Lord Belfour if you like." He set both hands on either side of the chair, leaning forward, making her press back into the seat to keep a civil distance. "But I so long to hear the sound of 'Sweet Prince' if you would but give it a try."

She pressed her lips together. "I don't know how the ladies resist you," she said with an edge to her voice, precisely because she did have trouble resisting the rogue. "You can be so utterly charming when you choose."

"Oh, ho! Sarcasm from the Mouse?" He took her by her hands and pulled her up to her feet, bringing her flush against him in a mock embrace. "Don't resist," he whispered. "It's so much more fun if you give as good as you get."

She slipped free and graced him with a look that said she was not the least bit intimidated by these false romantic gestures. She paid him no mind at all—even if her heart thundered like gunfire in her chest. With what she considered great aplomb, she sat back in her seat at the desk. She pushed aside the pile of books he'd dropped there and, taking the first tome, she opened the book before her. "Let's have a look, shall we?"

"All work and no play, Mouse? How very dull."

"Efficient, Lord Belfour," she said with a smile. "That's why you hired me. I am very efficient."

Quentin scanned the cleared room. "Yes, the place does seem a bit more spacious of late." Almost playfully, he picked up her braid and began stroking it against his hand. "It makes a man wonder what other talents you might possess," he said, raising his brow, his eyes centered on her mouth. "You can be so very thorough."

There came a soft knock of warning. The door opened and Leydi released the breath she'd been holding, saved from having to respond to the provocative statement. George strolled toward them, his back straight, his blue suit almost regal in its neat state despite the heat. He carried a folded piece of paper on a salver. Leydi thought she recognized the seal.

Almost apologetically, George held the paper out to Quentin. The writing on the outside was identical to the script on the missive Leydi had saved from the fire—the very slip of paper she now carried in the pocket of her apron.

"This just came, sir," George said, waiting for Quentin to take the note. "The boy insisted you'd want to read this one."

Leydi's hand wandered to the pocket of her apron. She pressed her fingertips against the linen, feeling the charred remains of the message crinkling inside.

"You've too soft a heart, George," Quentin said, his face suddenly as cold as stone. His hand closed around the paper and he crumpled the note into a ball. He dropped it back onto the salver. Both George and Leydi stared at the crushed paper. With an audible sigh, George turned on his heel and quit the room.

Leydi peeked up at Quentin. She had never seen a man look so tired, as if he hadn't slept in years. She knew it was dangerous thinking to imagine what brought about those sleepless nights. But it seemed so likely that this rift between father and son had caused his anguish—just as it had made the earl shed those tears in an abandoned supper room.

She bit her lip, studying Quentin. Today he wore only a waistcoat, no jacket. When she looked closer, she saw he'd mismatched a few buttons at the bottom, making the cloth pucker just a bit. His hair was tied at his neck, the black curls sleek and shining in the morning light. But if his unshaven face and rumpled clothes hadn't given him away, his eyes surely would have. They were narrowed on the door, and definitely red-rimmed from lack of sleep.

Leydi stepped closer, reaching up with her hand to touch his shirtsleeve. At the last possible instant she thought better of the

gesture and shrank back. She told herself she shouldn't interfere—it was none of her concern. She shouldn't always try to
make things right between people. For Quentin and his father;
for Gabriela and Kincaid. She remembered only too well
Quentin's warning yesterday. *Don't be curious. Don't wonder. Don't
interfere!*

And yet. *And yet . . .*

She couldn't help but remember that poor soul at the Cockerel. Couldn't help hearing his tears over and over inside her
head.

"Can't you even read it?" she asked softly.

At the sound of her voice Quentin turned those blazing eyes
from the door to her. Before she lost her nerve, she reached
into her pocket and retrieved the slip of paper, knowing then
why she'd brought the missive. She'd meant to share it with him
all along, despite her better judgment.

"I read it." She held the note out for him to see. "I can tell
you what it says if you've not the courage to read them yourself—"

He grabbed her hand, stopping her from unfolding the paper.
"I know what it says."

"No. I don't think you do," she said, truly believing her words.
"If you knew—if you only knew—I'm sure you—"

"You're wrong." His voice was like a gust of wind from Mount
Misery. "You are very wrong."

"There are only three simple words left," she argued for that
lonely man crying in that supper room. "Come. Forgive. Your
loving father . . ."

Quentin turned away, as if he could no longer bear to listen.
"Get out, Miss Carstair."

But Leydi couldn't seem to stop herself. She reasoned it was
Kincaid she should worry about, that she should leave now, before she said something she'd regret. But she couldn't keep from
speaking. Through some flaw in her character, she thought of
her own situation—of her parents and her hollow life with them.
And she had to fight for a father begging for a second chance.

"You don't know what you're turning your back on," she whis-

pered. "I saw him," she confessed. "I went to the Cockerel and
I saw him. He's miserable. He was crying—"

"Yes, he's rather good at that," he said harshly. "Crying when
it suits him."

"I know about self-serving tears. He was alone in a dark room.
That was no act. Whatever happened between you and your father, he wants to make things right—"

Quentin grabbed her hands and pulled her toward him.
There was no softness to him. He was all hard bone and muscle
and solid resolve. And there was violence in his gaze. "Is that all
it takes to buy your forgiveness, Mouse? A few heartfelt tears.
What would you do for me if I shed some for you?"

"He's your father . . ." she said, unable to understand the
stark hatred she heard in his voice.

"And that forgives all, that he's my father? Hmm? My flesh
and blood?"

"Yes," she whispered.

"You foolish little thing," he said under his breath. He tipped
up her chin to look at him. "And you would forgive anything?
Any wrong a parent might do you?"

Thinking of all the things she had forgiven over the years, she
answered with quiet certainty, "Yes."

"So sure, Mouse?" He traced the curve of her face with his
finger. "So absolutely sure?"

It was possibly the only thing she could be sure of—all those
years of neglect and hardship she had forgiven. She raised her
head and said with conviction, "I'm very certain."

He sighed, his fingers combing back the fine curls around her
face that had escaped her braid. With his red-rimmed eyes he
stared at her hair, then grabbed up a length of her braid, brushing it across his cheek. There seemed an odd significance to the
gesture—a meaning that puzzled her as well as left her chilled.

"Go home, Miss Carstair," he said. "And take your undying
forgiveness with you. You may have need of it."

Leydi stepped away. Something in his tone frightened her.
She looked up at the angels, telling herself the mural proved he
had a heart—that he was, for all his accumulated wealth and
mean-spirited words, a sensitive man.

"They'll not help you," he said, watching her with hooded eyes. "I had them painted there years ago. And they haven't helped me a goddamned bit."

Leydi stumbled back toward the door, fearful of this sudden violence and what it meant. How it could hurt her. When he'd spoken his threats against Kincaid, his tone had been almost playful compared to his words now.

She wished she'd stayed silent and kept that silly note in her pocket. She hadn't salved any wounds with her prompting—hadn't brought father and son any closer. And now Lord Ruthless looked more dangerous than ever. She turned back to the door, glancing over her shoulder. In the morning shadows she recalled she'd once likened him to a dragon brooding over his hoard. For the first time since she'd met Quentin, he'd made her truly afraid of him.

The door closed behind the Mouse. Quentin stared at it, overwhelmed by the sense that he'd been shut in. That's what he'd done for the past seven years. Bottled himself up on this little island. Away from his memories of Clarice and his father. Only they'd not left him alone. After seven years those haunts had followed him to his island hideout.

He stared at the crumpled paper, the half-burnt missive he'd taken from the Mouse. With an oath he smoothed the paper out on the table. The words she'd spoken lay smudged on the vellum, clear for him to read.

Come. Forgive. Your loving father.

The rage that filled Quentin almost frightened him. He thought back to the years he'd begged like a puppy for his father's approval. He'd been like the Mouse then, believing that anything his parent did was right. That the flaw lay in him, in Quentin. And when he realized no amount of effort on his part would gain him the love and acceptance he craved, he'd sought the opposite. He'd become a useless wastrel, gaming and whoring with the money his father gave him, then using notes when that source dried up.

Until Clarice had told him about the baby.

When she'd come to Quentin, explaining she carried a child—his child—he'd been able to find the goodness inside himself again. That's what Clarice had given him. That hope. He'd been able to see through all the ugly rebellion. In that baby he'd imagined—*At last. Someone to love!* Not like Clarice, whose violet eyes could never quite hide her avarice even as she moaned her release beneath him. But a child. Someone who could accept him and everything he had to give.

That's what the earl had denied him.

In a sweep of his arm, Quentin cleared the ledgers and papers from the desk, watching them tumble to the floor. He stared at the clutter, breathing hard.

Now the Mouse asked him to forgive? She didn't understand that some hurts reached so deep, they touched your soul, twisting it—making it dark and ugly. It was an important lesson. One he planned to teach the Mouse.

He drew on the bellpull, calling for George. Perhaps it was even a kindness he did her now. She shouldn't trust everyone. Good Lord, she'd involved herself in the life of a man she knew nothing about. She must learn not to look for the goodness in every man—even a pirate.

Not to look for the goodness in him.

But as he told George his plans, pretending it was the kindness it appeared and not a dastardly plan to dish up pain and teach lessons, he carefully avoided looking at the angels on the ceiling.

Chapter Eleven

Leydi stared down at the small but not insignificant stack of coins. The pieces of eight glittered gold against the flowers embroidered along the edge of her mother's tablecloth. The tiny hoard represented every last coin of her wages she'd been able to wrestle from Elaine's greedy grasp.

"Is it enough?" she asked Gabriela.

"More than enough, *caro.*" Gabriela slid the money across the linen into her purse. Ringlets of black hair tipped across her cheek as she glanced over her shoulder, as if expecting Leydi's mother to burst in on their secret conference. Both women were ensconced in the corner of the bungalow's front room, obscured by afternoon shadows and a creamware set. Any who bothered to look would see only two young ladies enjoying a cup of tea and gossip.

Leydi stirred the tea indolently. She'd had a miserable night mulling over her confrontation with Lord Ruthless, hearing over and over his ominous threat: *Go home, Miss Carstair—and take your undying forgiveness with you. You may have need of it.*

She glanced up at Gabby and nibbled her bottom lip. Today her friend looked resplendent in a satin gown with loose turned cuffs, all a charming shade of peach. Leydi peeked down at her own brown muslin, thinking the color suited her mood. She hadn't even mentioned yesterday's debacle to Gabby, too guilt-ridden that she might have hurt her chances to help Kincaid.

"Hiring three seamen to kidnap Rutherford—one of the most well-respected, not to mention wealthiest, men in the district—and a naval officer . . ." Leydi shook her head with a touch of disbelief.

"But it will work. You yourself said there's few enough servants here on the plantation; taking Rutherford should be simple. And I've found Bishop has a habit of wandering about Basse Terre late at night. The men we hired will nab them, tie them up, take them to that inlet just outside Old Town Road. Kincaid's sloop will be waiting menacingly, spars and rigging alight with the quarter moon."

"Later, we meet up with Cy onshore," Leydi finished, repeating by rote the plan they'd devised. "The men wave a few scabbards and pistols, give a harsh warning or two, and Rutherford and Bishop are set free on the beach to find their way home."

"Trust me, *caro*. It will happen just like in one of your books. Now, enough doomsaying. In a few short days Rutherford and Bishop will know who they're dealing with. And if anything goes wrong, Cy will be there to bail us out—though I hope it won't come to that." Gabby's mouth curled in a secretive smile as she tied the drawstring purse to her waist. "This time, Kincaid will owe us."

Leydi glanced up, catching that glint in Gabby's eyes. "Is that what this is all about? Kincaid owing us?"

Gabriela shrugged. "It's a good plan just the same, *caro*, whatever my reasons—so why does it matter?"

The front door opened. Elaine Carstair stepped inside wearing a loose wrapping gown whose peacock blue did nothing for her sallow complexion. She was holding a package tied up with an enormous red ribbon. The bow flopped charmingly over the sides of the box.

Elaine glanced at Gabby, barely hiding her disapproval in the crimp of her mouth. Her mother had never countenanced Leydi's friendship with Gabby, a quadroon. But she accepted the

De Sousa women with the same testiness she tolerated Kincaid—a necessary evil.

Her wide hooped petticoats swaying, she skirted the table. Elaine held the package out to Leydi. "Mr. Stevenson brought this." She set the wrapped box on the linen between the teacups. "It's for you, Leydianna. From the master of the house."

Leydi stared at the package, blinking hard as if it might vanish in a puff of smoke. A present was the last thing she expected after Quentin's violent dismissal. And yet the box was indeed tied up with a red ribbon, branding it a gift.

"From Rutherford?" she asked. "Are you certain?" It didn't seem possible after yesterday's battle between them. Quentin didn't strike her as a man who forgave a perceived wrong lightly.

"Mr. Stevenson was quite clear," Elaine said crisply.

Leydi eased forward in her chair, drawn to the gay wrapping and festive bow. The fog from her sleepless night began to lift and an unwilling smile touched her lips. She stroked the silky ribbon with her fingertips. An apology of sorts? From Lord Ruthless? At the very least, the package seemed to suggest he understood why she'd pressed him about his father.

Her heart swelled with unexpected emotion as she thought of Quentin swallowing that tremendous pride of his. He'd looked fit for murder when he'd dismissed her. This truce showed great heart on his part.

The silk purse of coins tied neatly to Gabby's waist flashed like a beacon. A pinprick of conscience jabbed Leydi's heart. She bit her lip, torn between her loyalties to Kincaid and the emotions engendered by this small token on Quentin's part.

"Open it," her mother commanded, the edge to her voice showing she was losing her patience.

With trembling fingers Leydi pulled the ribbon loose, then folded back the paper. It was an enamel box painted with a beautiful pastoral scene, set in richly gilded scrolling. A thing of beauty.

"Go ahead, *caro,*" Gabby said behind her, excitement threading her voice. "See what's inside."

Taking a deep breath, Leydi opened the lid, then peeled back the tissue paper. Nestled inside was a set of combs more lovely than any piece of jewelry Leydi had seen worn by Gabriela or even the Lady Consuelo. Each comb was in the shape of an eagle, the body a baroque pearl, the spread wings, gold set with table-cut rubies.

Leydi was actually frightened to pick them up, afraid that this moment of happiness would vanish with the swiftness of all her daydreams. She couldn't imagine Quentin giving her such a gift.

"There's a note, *caro*," Gabriela said behind her. "Read the note!"

Caught up in Gabriela's and her own excitement, Leydi opened the folded sheet of vellum.

"For those beautiful tresses of spun gold," Gabriela said, reading the note out loud.

Leydi stared at the words. The lovely note could have been concocted by her own overactive imagination, it seemed so sweet. She tried valiantly not to give romantic fancy to the bold script—tried not to imagine that, just as in her dreams, Quentin admired her for more than how well she did her sums. She picked up the tip of her braid, worrying it between her fingers, embarrassed and delighted he'd guessed her hair was her one conceit.

"You'll have to send it back, of course," her mother said in a flat voice. "It's an entirely inappropriate gift."

Leydi turned to her mother, blinking back the stars from her eyes. "W-what?"

Elaine grabbed the box from the table. She stuffed the tissue and card over the beautiful combs and slammed the lid shut. Her gestures were quick, furtive. "Take this back to the house on your way home, Gabriela," she said, pushing the box into Gabriela's hands. "Ask for Mr. Stevenson at the servant's door," she whispered, her voice catching as if she were fighting back tears. "Make certain you give it to him—no one else. It will be a godsend if the staff doesn't get wind of this," she said, wringing her hands, "though it's probably too late for that."

"But it's so lovely . . ." Gabby met Leydi's eyes. *"Caro?* Are you sure?"

A dark sense of foreboding crept over Leydi. There was panic in her mother's voice. Leydi had heard the same fear the day Elaine had torn the beautiful emerald gown.

She clutched her hands into white-knuckled fists, her fingernails biting into her palms. *Not the combs,* a voice inside her shouted. *Fight for the combs!*

"Yes. Of course," she heard herself answer, unable after all to go against her mother's wishes. "My mother's right. It's entirely inappropriate."

The words came unthinkingly—she always obeyed her mother—but even as she spoke, she realized the gift *was* too grand. She looked back at her mother's face, the sense that something was not right gaining a foothold in her heart. She remembered her terrible fight with Quentin, recalled her impression that he wasn't a forgiving man. And yet, he'd written: *For those beautiful tresses of spun gold.*

Leydi studied the enamel box. The box alone was worth a small fortune—the combs inside, a fantastic treasure. Used to seeing such at Devil's Gate, she hadn't realized the enormity of the gift. She frowned, tilting her head as she examined the painted surface of the enamel.

For the first time, she saw the present as her mother would see it—a treasure too grand for a bookkeeper. A lover's gift.

Leydi blinked, confused. She watched Gabby take the box from Elaine, her friend's sharp eyes full of questions. Leydi had the sense that she was in the middle of one of Quentin's complicated negotiations. The moment reminded her of Gellman's coffee—when she'd watched Quentin take disparate elements to achieve a result Leydi never would have suspected from analyzing those components alone.

Slowly, methodically, like sums coming together, something not so nice forged in her head as she stared at the torn wrapping paper and red ribbon. She was surprised by the villainy of her thoughts. And then she recalled his warning against her meddling in his life. *Go home—you may have need of your undying forgiveness.*

"What a shame," Gabby said with a sigh. She reached out and stroked back the curls that inevitably escaped Leydi's braid near her face. "They would have looked lovely—"

Gabby's voice faltered. Leydi glanced up. Gabby was staring at Leydi's mother. Elaine seemed transfixed by her daughter's hair. In her eyes there was a clarity of purpose.

"Take the box back," Leydi said in a hoarse voice. "Take it back for me, Gabriela."

Gabby nodded. With the intuition of a sister, she leaned down and gave Leydi a quick hug, an excuse to whisper in her ear, "I'll take the box, but don't you do anything foolish, *caro.*"

Gabby kissed her on the cheek, then peered up at Leydi's mother. Elaine's face looked pinched, the lines of age more obvious with her sober expression. Her tired gray eyes remained fixed on Leydi's braid.

The door shut behind Gabriela. There was an unsettling quiet in the room as mother and daughter stared at each other. Her mother was first to break the tableau, taking two clipped steps toward Leydi. Elaine bit her lip, as if trying to stop her tears even as they welled in her eyes.

"I told you to be careful with Rutherford."

Leydi shut her eyes, knowing from years of these scenes what had brought on her mother's misery. The combs. Those beautiful combs. So inappropriate for a bookkeeper. But little enough for a lover.

"Mother." Leydi stood. "It's not what you think."

"How can it not be?" her mother wailed. "Such an intimate gift for a servant? For the love of God, Leydianna, I'm not stupid. Do you think I've never been young and foolish? Susceptible to men like Rutherford? I suspected the truth when I saw you in that dress. Dear God! What are we to do?"

"Mother, please! You're wrong. I don't know why he sent the combs."

But she did. At that moment, seeing the tears streaming down her mother's cheeks as Elaine collapsed into a chair, Leydi knew exactly why Quentin had sent the gift.

The box had been delivered to her mother, not Leydi. He'd made certain Elaine would know who'd given the present, making dear Mr. Stevenson an unwitting tool for his plans. It was only to be expected that her mother would wait around for the unveiling, curious as to what the lord of the manor would give her daughter. The combs were, as her mother suggested, a lover's gift. And the note, the damning note. *For those beautiful tresses of spun gold.*

"Stop crying, Mother, please."

"He's ruined you, hasn't he?" she whispered through choked sobs. "You can tell me, child. I know about—a mother knows about these things. A mother knows."

"Hush," Leydi said, kneeling down before her mother, hugging her. Hating herself for those moments she'd thought the gift genuine rather than an ingenious device to hurt her. She couldn't be sure, but her heart told her she was right. Oh, he'd warned her. He'd told her to beware.

"I wish I could explain, Mother. He's a complicated man. We had a terrible fight over business and the gift—it's just his way to . . . to . . ."

To hurt Leydi. To cause pain. To manipulate her mother into believing a lie. She knew Quentin Rutherford had a genius for maneuvering men on matters of finance. And now he'd focused all that intuition and skill into Leydi's life.

"I don't believe you," Elaine whispered, barely able to speak the words. She pulled Leydi's braid through her fingers almost painfully. "I told you to cut it. You should have cut it!"

"Mother, don't," she whispered. "Please don't do this."

"He loves your hair—admit it. I see such horrible images of the two of you together. You should have cut it."

"I'm nothing to him, Mother! I swear to you. For once, can't you believe me?"

"If not now, then when?" her mother asked desperately, wringing Leydi's hands between hers. "It's just a matter of time before he lures you down dark paths, if he hasn't already. I told Kincaid no good would come of your gaining an occupation. A girl should marry. You should have married long ago, damn him. You could have had a simple but happy life."

"I do have a simple, happy life! I'm no man's mistress!"

Her mother watched her with a cold steady stare that belied the tears pooling in her eyes. She picked up Leydi's long braid of hair. "Then cut it now," she whispered. "Cut it and show me it's not special to him."

With her mother's request, Leydi remembered the words she'd spoken foolishly to Quentin. Urging him to make amends with his father, she'd given him the very weapon he'd needed to prove her wrong. *I'd forgive any wrong;* she'd practically boasted it to him. She'd been sure at the time that she could.

And he wanted to prove to her that she could not.

She stared down at the braid in her mother's fingers. She'd grown her hair without cutting it for eight years. It was the one thing she'd refused to change for her mother. Her one vanity.

And he'd guessed. Oh, yes, he guessed. That moment he'd untied her braid and spread her hair over her shoulders in his receiving chamber, she'd thought he'd been acting like some knight-errant—urging her to defy her mother. But he'd just been gathering information, sensing her attachment to her hair, testing his theory—seeing if he'd guessed right. He was such an observant man.

Forgive any wrong.

Her certainty surprised her. The jeweled combs had been so subtle. But she knew. In the same manner that he'd made a fortune from Gellman's coffee, Quentin was conducting another negotiation here. He'd thought her mother was behind her decision not to wear the green gown. He would know what reaction the jeweled combs would effect. He was too brilliant not to—too angry with her not to want to teach her a lesson.

Leydi ground her teeth, pressing her lips together in a bloodless line. Damn him. Did he really think he knew anything about her, about her life or the hardships she'd suffered? Did he really believe her so shallow that her hair would finally break her? Well, he was wrong. He had no notion of the things she'd forgiven her parents. The brown clothes, the constant criticism . . . the fear that they didn't really love her. That the money was what counted most.

"Yes Mother. We'll cut it. It's a nuisance. You were right all along."

And Quentin was wrong. He may have made a fortune surmising people's weaknesses and using them to further his goals, but not this time. She would prove that in this one matter he was wrong.

Never in her life had she thought herself unfeeling, but she felt nothing as her mother sat her down in the cane chair. There were no ready daydreams to take away the pain of the moment— she didn't want them. She merely sat in the chair, undid her braid, and waited.

The scissors were sharp and her mother thankfully quick. When she finished, Leydi's hair bobbed fashionably just to her ears. It surprised her how little she seemed to care. She'd expected something, some wave of emotion to strike with the loss. But she merely glanced down at the shorn curls piled at her feet dispassionately. It was only hair. He'd been wrong to think it mattered. She wouldn't cry.

Instead, she went to her room and nestled in her bed. It was late afternoon, too early and too hot to go to sleep, so she lay above the covers on the counterpane, wearing only her petticoat and chemise. She opened a favorite book, Defoe's *Robinson Crusoe*. It was a book that allowed her to forget where she was, who she was . . . a book that propelled her to another world.

But somehow she couldn't be distracted. The curls brushed against her ears, tickling her. Her head felt unusually light. The hours inched by, torturously slow. She refused supper when her mother knocked on the door. When it grew dark, she rose to light a candle.

She battled to finish reading, to concentrate on the great dangers Crusoe faced, telling herself that the little dramas of her life were nothing in comparison. But when she finally turned the last page, she found she was no more sleepy than when she'd gone to bed hours before.

She stared at the canopy of mosquito netting covering the tent bed. The starlight was bright enough to seep into the chamber, the frogs and monkeys, a symphony. The wind beat the palm fronds outside her window. She thought there might be a storm coming. Waiting in the silence of the room, Quentin's words repeated over and over in a sullen refrain. *Some things, you can never forgive.*

She reached up and touched her hair. It barely grazed her ears.

The tears came then, so quickly and violently she actually

laughed. He was ingenious, a brilliant tactician. Able to sense, even when she had not, that so simple a thing could matter to her.

Hatred for her mother crept into her heart like a thief. She'd told herself she wouldn't give Lord Ruthless the satisfaction. Damn him, she'd weathered worse. Christmas without presents. Brown, drab clothes and shoes that pinched. Corsets her mother tied so tight, at times Leydi thought she should be ashamed of her body—the secret fear that her mother had accepted money from Kincaid, letting him purchase her fourteen-year-old daughter. That money could make Elaine forget the impropriety and danger of her daughter working for a pirate.

And Leydi had believed she'd forgiven every wrong.

But this night, in a rare moment of insight, a deeper knowledge leaked through her carefully crafted defenses. She realized she hadn't forgiven. As the night grew darker and her dreams wouldn't come to rescue her, she could think of nothing but the hate in her mother's face, hear only the snip of the scissors.

She'd thought herself the good daughter, accepting of all her parents' little flaws—that Argus ignored her, that her mother at times seemed to despise her. But the simple truth was Quentin was right. Some things a person can never forgive. All that meanness had just festered inside her, waiting for the day that she could ship them off to their own plantation and buy her freedom.

It was near morning when she admitted she didn't like her parents. She hated them.

She watched the room grow pink with dawn. Quentin had planned so craftily to place this final wedge between her mother and herself, but that wasn't the only emotion he'd engendered. Some of her hatred was for him, a man who thought to teach her such a stinging lesson.

He didn't have a heart, damn him.

She knew her hate made her less of a person. It ate at her. For years she'd accepted brown clothes and tight braids just to prove it wasn't there. But now it blazed full in her heart.

If she had courage, she would turn her back on them all— Quentin, her parents. Every one of them. But she didn't know how to sever ties that meant so much to her. She knew only how to be Leydianna Carstair, the daughter of Argus and Elaine Carstair, and the bookkeeper to a pirate. And her only escape had been her dreams.

Tonight, with his calculated meanness, Quentin had robbed her of even that.

He hadn't seen her in two days. The sight of her now was just a bit shocking.

She was wearing a brown dress propped by petticoats and a dull-colored apron. On her head was the familiar mobcap, its lappets pinned back up into folds. Her hair had been clipped to her ears. Very modern, very fashionable. And very plain.

There'd been two times in his life when Quentin had truly despised himself. When Clarice had died. And now.

She walked around him as primly as always, not saying a word. He looked for signs of the struggle that had kept her absent these past two days, but he found nothing obvious. His own nights were plagued by fitful sleep, now haunted not only by Clarice's ghost, but by his conscience as he wondered how the Mouse had fared with his ploy.

Still, there seemed just as much bounce to her step, just as much starch to her posture. With familiar energy she plopped down in the chair before the desk and laid out his papers. The soft mink curls bobbed around her cheeks. She thrust them back behind her ears before she reached for a quill.

He could see that she planned to ignore the entire incident. He, however, could not.

"Should I offer you up a pair of scissors?" he asked. He leaned over the rosewood desk and wagged his queued hair before her face. "You could have a go at my head."

He wished she would cut it. He yearned for her to yank his queue with all her might and saw it off with a dull knife. She could shave his head. But somehow he knew his cruel deed couldn't be so easily appeased.

He assumed she realized it was his gift of the combs that had brought about the haircut. And if she didn't, he knew he must pay the price by giving her that knowledge. He'd always been quick-witted, able to perceive most every weakness in his opponents. But just this once he wished he could have been wrong—that the Mouse would have waltzed into this receiving chamber wearing a fortune in jewels in her hair, no more the wiser for his dastardly intent.

"Shall I call George, then? Tell him to bring the shears?" he asked, teasing her, testing his reception. Trying desperately to make light of his misdeed.

The Mouse kept her eyes carefully on the papers on the desk. She straightened them, keeping all her considerable concentration on the task. "I harbor no ill feelings toward your hair, Lord Belfour. You can stuff it in a wig, for all it matters."

He liked the way she'd put that little emphasis on "stuff it." She didn't sound the least downtrodden. Why should he feel so base for the loss of her curls, when she appeared unscathed by the event?

But he knew better. She hadn't looked him in the eye once since coming into the room. That wasn't like the Mouse.

He continued around the desk, wishing suddenly he'd left her alone. God damn him and his temper. She was a mere child in her innocence. An inept spy. A daydreamer. He shouldn't have given her meddling a second thought. He shouldn't have played his vile trick to check it. Who was he to teach her anything? Even the need to protect herself from that bitch of a mother.

"I suppose it will grow back," he said from across the room.

There came no response. She merely scribbled the inked nib across the vellum and reached for the pounce pot.

He found it extremely unsettling that she continued to work while ignoring the fact she looked like a sheared lamb. Her obsessive energy as she breezed through the morning's correspondence reminded him of himself, of the years he'd spent concentrating on making his fortune, working to forget Clarice, his father, and London. The words and numbers on those papers mesmerized her, she hovered so close to each.

He plucked a calfskin-bound book off a shelf. Giving himself something to do rather than stare at the Mouse, he opened the tome. When he realized he'd turned to Locke's essay debating the validity of Original Sin, he slammed the book shut.

He wondered if she would ever look him in the eye again. Before, she'd always watched him as if he were an intriguing puzzle. Perhaps from now on she would look right through him.

In a slow circle he ranged closer to the desk and its captive, his eyes on those stern little shoulders, that dainty little cap. The curls swayed with the rhythm of her scribbles. She was such a tiny thing. He stopped right behind her and reached for her mink-colored ringlets. For an instant he wavered, thinking better of touching her. And then he cursed softly and snatched off her mobcap, tossing it to the desk. He placed both palms on her head, digging his fingers into the thick, soft curls.

She stopped what she was doing, freezing like a doe scenting hunters.

"It will grow back," he said gently, trailing his hands through her hair to her neck, his fingers coming to rest on her shoulders. Sending the combs, he told himself, wasn't as heinous as he was making it in his mind. It had been her decision to allow the haircut, after all.

"It really doesn't matter," she said. But as he watched, her fingers curled around the quill, tightening until her fingertips turned white.

"Leydianna . . . I . . ."

But he couldn't seem to find the words that would grant forgiveness. He dropped his hands to his side and stepped away. He told himself he was being ridiculous. He wasn't averse to putting down competitors. It was she who'd meddled first, taking that note from the fire where he'd set it to burn. Going to spy on the earl. Bringing back tales. Surely, what he'd done was no different.

And yet . . .

He leaned across the desk. With his hand under her chin, he tipped her face up to his. "You're still a beautiful woman." And he meant every word.

Her lips pursed together; her eyes narrowed just a fraction. He thought she was trying her damnedest not to tell him to go to hell. He could almost see her choking on the need to say it.

"I've work to do," she said, twisting away, returning to her ciphering. Dismissing him.

Some devil inside him refused to be dismissed, not this easily. Or perhaps he just didn't have the courage to walk away with his guilt intact, its black weight dragging down his heart and soul. He needed her to confront him. To fight. He shoved aside the correspondence and propped his hip up on the desk. "Why don't you tell me to go to hell, Miss Carstair?"

"I need this position," she said, not contradicting her desire to do just that. She stared at the paper as she scribbled across the vellum. "As you pointed out; you pay quite well."

Quentin's mouth twisted into a not-so-nice smile. He suspected her pirate and not the admirable wages he paid kept her glued to that seat. More and more he'd begun to agree with Bishop. She was Kincaid's spy. Harmless, perhaps. Inept—certainly. But a spy just the same. The very thought made his temper swell. Good God, why should he feel the least bit sorry for his Mouse and her shorn fleece?

Because what you did was wrong. So very wrong, a little voice whispered.

He swatted both hands on the desk so his fingers splayed across her cherished correspondence, obscuring her view. He couldn't listen to that voice damning him inside his head. He wanted to hear the Mouse say it. He needed to hear her tell him to go to blazes. Her temper seemed the only forgiveness he could allow himself.

"Perhaps I'm giving you more credit than I ought to," he said, fighting his sense of guilt with anger. "Perhaps you didn't realize I did it on purpose?" he added, trying to goad her from this businesslike stupor. "The expensive combs—asking Stevenson to give your mother the box. The note. It was all carefully orchestrated so she'd beg you to cut your hair! I wanted to see what you'd do when she shed those persuasive tears of hers."

"And now you know," she said almost placidly.

He surprised himself by pounding his fist on the desk, causing a ringing boom, making the Mouse jump in her chair.

"Do you know," he whispered, his voice ominously low, astonishing himself at the lengths he would go to force her to confront him, "that a very small part of me actually thought you'd have the gumption to stand up to her?"

She ignored him, refusing to say a word. It was too much, this pathetic lack of spirit. He jumped to his feet and walked behind her. He couldn't seem to stop himself. He picked up the chair—Mouse and all—and turned it so she was forced to face him, her back to the desk and the bloody correspondence. He couldn't quite believe what he was about to do. He put one hand on each arm of the chair and leaned very close.

"I thought . . ." He let the words hang for a moment, making her wait. "Never mind. I see now I was wrong. You could never do anything to surprise me."

He saw her stiffen. Finally, his words had scored a response. It was what he wanted from her—the cleansing heat of anger. He saw it brewing like a storm in those beautiful gray eyes. And he intended to fan the flames. Needed to. He wanted them to be opponents. He wanted to erase the image of the Mouse as his victim.

"What say you, Mouse?" He took her by the hand, forcing her to her feet. "If you're not too angry with me—if it really doesn't matter"—he closed one arm around her waist, bringing her flush against him—"shall we set aside these books and find other pursuits?"

She looked at him as if he were mad. "Quite frankly, I'd sooner go through the cane presses."

"Oh-ho!" he said with a smile, letting her go as she backed away. This is what he'd wanted from her, this final show of anger. When her lovely backside hit the chair, he took a step toward her, forcing her to sit down when the backs of her knees caught the seat. "All brown and plain and conscious of her duties to mother, work, and country. But not without some spirit. One day, I'll persuade you," he whispered, hovering over her, her wrath granting just a touch of solace, enough to make him goad her more. His lips almost brushed hers. For an instant he was tempted to steal that kiss, throw the last bit of fuel to the fire. Instead, he stared at her mouth, letting her know with his lingering gaze how much he wanted to kiss her. And then, at the last possible moment, he stepped away. "I'll hear 'Sweet Prince' from you yet."

As he walked away, he thought he heard her murmur, "More like warty toad."

He twisted back, smiling. "What was that?" His grin spread. He was delighted to see her mother had sliced off only her hair and not her spirit. "I didn't quite hear you, Mouse."

"I said hardy road, Lord Belfour," she answered, not batting a lash. "I saw you were leaving. It's a parting of sorts. Welsh, I believe."

"Those Welshmen. So inspiring."

"My thoughts exactly."

"Then you wish me well, Mouse?"

"Could I desire anything else?"

He saluted her, relieved to see she no longer avoided his gaze. Her gray eyes blasted him like two cocked pistols.

"By the bye," he said at the door, going for the final blow, stepping back into the less intimate game they were playing. She was Kincaid's spy and he would yet push her to make a mistake. "I spoke to Bishop yesterday. I thought you'd like to know that you were wrong in predicting our venture doomed. I should have Kincaid soon. By month's end, in fact. I thought you would like to know that you needn't have worried for me. When I put my mind to something, I make certain I succeed. Perhaps we'll even have him before you leave St. Kitts. I imagine his hanging will be a spectacular event. Don't you?"

He stepped into the hall, calling over his shoulder, "Stevenson will be in shortly for the accounts. Do get on with it, Mouse. You've a lot to make up for the past two days."

Chapter Twelve

Leydi had moped for two days.

For two days she'd skulked about the chamber in a bed gown and bare feet, pulling on a strand of hair at the back of her neck as if she might magically make it grow. For two days she refused to answer the summons of either dear Mr. Stevenson or her mother, her not-so-civil commands to leave her be obeyed by both. For two days she'd stalked about the room, infinitely familiar with every crack in the Spanish walling, every dusty corner and cobweb, leaving the room for only the occasional food or drink.

And two days of sulking had been all she could stand.

On the third day she'd marched into the front room. She'd peered into the gilt gesso mirror and said hello to this new Leydianna Carstair. She'd studied the short curls, decided the style made her look sophisticated—more mature. It brought attention to her face, and it wasn't such a bad face. Her lips weren't full and pouty like Gabby's, but she had large gray eyes, a tiny cleft in her chin, and a rather nice nose. It was very narrow, very distinguished. She'd clamped her teeth together and smiled. White, straight—and not a single one missing despite her advanced age of two and twenty.

Looking into the glass, she'd vowed that with her shorn curls would be born a better, stronger Leydi. One who didn't daydream. One who wouldn't be bullied by the likes of Quentin Alexander Rutherford, Lord Who-Cares-What.

That day she'd dressed herself from head to toe in brown—brown buckled shoes, brown mobcap, brown cotton dress with brown laced bodice. Even the apron had been off-white. The color no longer represented her mother's wishes but Leydi's challenge to Lord Ruthless. Armored in brown, she'd marched off to face the dragon in his den.

She'd thought he'd be a tiny bit repentant.

Leydi plumped up her pillow of feathers and switched to her left side. It was the middle of the night and she hoped, despite the horrid day, to manage a good night's sleep. But thoughts of the daunting Lord Ruthless made that possibility remote.

Oh, he'd been contrite when she first walked into his receiving chamber after her two-day absence. Leydi had even sensed the sweet taste of revenge as she ignored his tender overtures.

But the arrogant beast hadn't allowed her the pleasure of seeing him grovel. Soon enough, his light banter had gained an almost vicious edge. He practically boasted of his misdeed with the combs, silencing any doubts that might have lingered about his intent, taunting *her* because she'd fallen into his trap.

You could never do anything to surprise me, Miss Carstair.

Indeed. As if she cared to—as if he and his opinion mattered one whit!

Leydi flipped to her back. She threw an arm over her brow and sighed. Her neck ached from hovering over two days of correspondence. She had to squint to see clearly, her eyes were so tired. Quentin had come back later that afternoon, disrupting what was turning into a most profitable day. Ruining her rhythm. Her lips twisted into a grimace as she remembered how he'd taken her hand and examined her bitten fingernails. He'd stroked her palm with his thumb, pretending to be so solicitous, so gallant. So devious.

"Anxious, Mouse?" She heard again those whispered words, spoken with that devilish grin she was beginning to detest.

Lying in her bed, she almost snatched back her hand as she'd done in the receiving chamber. Refusing to show how he affected her, she'd tapped her quill against the tablet and told him tartly, "Anxious about these figures, yes."

"Such a diligent little worker." He'd walked behind her, a habit of his that was beginning to grate. It gave a person the impression of being stalked. Soon enough he leaned close, so close his breath whispered against her cheek. "I don't deserve you."

"You have *that* right," Leydi answered out loud, her voice echoing across her empty bedchamber.

The beast. She could see he enjoyed her heated blushes. *I try so hard to be distracting,* he'd told her, letting his fingers brush against the curve of her cheek as if by accident. *But the Mouse will not be diverted.*

Leydi flipped onto her stomach, turned, and thumped the pillow into a round ball. She plopped her head back and grabbed the ends of the bolster, pushing them up against her ears. Oh, he was distracting, all right.

Her eyes had strayed to his muscled shoulders beneath the lawn shirt, had lingered on the rather charming dimple near his mouth. Despite the anger brewing inside her, she'd worried about those red-rimmed eyes that looked almost fevered from lack of sleep.

Leydi expelled a long, slow breath. She glanced at the pier table at bedside, wondering if whatever Lord Ruthless had was catching. Perhaps if she read another chapter of Esquemelen's book she might find sleep. She sighed, reaching for a candle and the tome. At least one good thing had come of Quentin's wicked vexing. She felt not a modicum of guilt for the planned kidnapping.

"It might just do the arrogant beast some good," she said, propping herself up on her pillow, the leather-bound book open on her lap.

Perhaps she should tell Gabby to instruct the men to give Quentin a tiny jab or two with the cutlass. Nothing to hurt him, mind you, just a little—

Leydi heard soft tapping. Someone was tossing stones at her window. Dropping her book, she threw back the counterpane and swung her legs over the rail of her bed. She stood on tiptoe and peered out the window into the dark. She saw nothing, but there was only one person who would come to find her this late at night—the day before Rutherford's planned abduction.

She grabbed her wrap from a hook on the wall and tossed it over her head. She peeked into the front room. Argus's drinking had relegated him to the horsehair chair, where he snored loudly while Mother slept undisturbed in the back bedroom. Leydi crept past her father's supine figure and inched the front door open.

Outside, she found Gabriela pacing under Leydi's window. Even with the meager light from the stars and the full-crescent moon, she could see enough of Gabby's face to know something was terribly wrong. She held her finger to her lips and pulled Gabby a safe distance from the bungalow.

"What happened?"

"Disaster, *caro*. They're gone. The men I hired. They never showed up at the shop. Leydi, we've been had. They took our money and ran."

"Good Lord, Gabby. Now we're done for," Leydi cried. "This is worse than you know." She remembered all the things Quentin had threatened that day. *I should have Kincaid soon. I imagine his hanging a spectacular event.* Her hand crept to her neck. "Bishop is closing in on Kincaid. We've not a day to spare."

"And Cy coming with the *Fortune* tomorrow night. All for naught."

Leydi racked her brain for some way to salvage matters. Their whole plan hinged on presenting Cy with a fait accompli. If they asked Kincaid's second-in-command to kidnap Quentin and Lieutenant Bishop, Cy might have an idea or two of his own on how best to dispose of the men who threatened Kincaid. Someone could get hurt, even killed. No, it was best to have the lieutenant and Quentin trussed up and harmless, making Cy understand Kincaid had little to fear from the two. But between them, Leydi and Gabby didn't have enough coin to hire more men, even if they could find trustworthy ones to do the deed before the following night.

Leydi shook her head, desperately thinking. With the movement, the wrap she wore over her head slipped back, pooling over her shoulders. Gabriela sucked in a breath, seeing the shortened curls for the first time.

She reached out to touch the tendrils brushing Leydi's cheek. *"Caro,"* she whispered, a wealth of regret in the word.

The two friends shared a moment of silence, their heads drawing together in sympathy. Leydi didn't need to explain to Gabriela how the haircut had come about. Gabby was only too ready to blame Leydi's mother for everything; she would guess what had happened. But Gabby did need to know the whole truth. Not just for Leydi's solace, but to let her know how truly savage Quentin could be.

"Rutherford sent the combs to make my mother jealous of my hair," she said, meeting Gabby's eyes. "He told me so himself. He was angry because I pressed him on a matter that he thought none of my business. In retribution, he sent the combs."

"Lord Ruthless," Gabriela whispered.

"Exactly. And now he's set his sights on Kincaid. I was actually relishing the thought of him facing those brigands we hired. Why, if I could—"

Leydi stopped. She blinked. An incredible idea formed in her head. She saw herself wielding that scabbard before a gagged and bound Quentin, giving him a tiny nudge or two with the sword point.

Out of habit, she reached for the end of her braid . . . and grasped only air. It was a poignant reminder of how dangerous Quentin could be. Her eyes narrowed as she heard those fateful words: *You could never do anything to surprise me, Mouse.*

"I can do it," Leydi said. She turned to Gabby. "We can do it, Gabby. You and I. We'll be like Mary Reed and Anne Bonny."

"Lady pirates?" Gabby dropped her hands from Leydi's shoulders and took a step back.

Leydi nodded, her plan taking shape as she spoke. "Why not? We'll dress like men. Disguise ourselves. Oh, Gabby, do you think you can take Bishop at gunpoint? Do you think you can truss him up and deliver him to the inlet all on your own?"

Gabby hesitated. "Is that what you plan to do with Rutherford?"

"Yes," Leydi answered, reminding herself that she was a new woman now. She would save Kincaid. She wouldn't let him fall into Quentin's hands. "I've a key to the house. I'll sneak in through the servants' quarters, steal inside his room. I'll be disguised. We'll keep to the same plan—tie them up and take them to the inlet. Then meet with Cy at Old Town Road. With Cy and his men and the *Fortune* just offshore threatening, we'll wave our cutlass and pistols and let Rutherford and Bishop know Kincaid is one step ahead of them. When he sees Kincaid's spies can outwit them, Quentin will think twice before he goes after Daniel again. We'll warn them in particular that any trouble in the future will go far worse for them than being dragged from their beds in the middle of the night."

"But won't Rutherford suspect you?"

You could never do anything to surprise me. "No," she said, certain that he wouldn't. "He thinks I'm capable of only adding up the numbers in his books. He'll never see it's me if the disguise is right." Her heart pounding in her ears like an eighteen-gunner, she grasped both Gabby's hands. "We can do this. We can save Kincaid."

"It just might work," Gabby said, smiling slowly. "It just might." She stared hard at Leydi, her green eyes very intent. "And if it doesn't, *caro?* What then?"

"There are few people I would give my life for. You're one of them." Her earnest gaze met Gabriela's. "Kincaid is another."

Gabby nodded solemnly, her eyes focusing off in the distance. Leydi knew Gabriela cared for Kincaid—despite her friend's constant carping against the pirate. She would never have asked Bertie to intervene otherwise. Now she must see just how much Gabriela cared.

Gabby nodded with a sigh, the simple gesture speaking volumes of her regard for Kincaid.

"George's boy is my size," Leydi said. "I know where the laundry is kept for tomorrow's washing. And Argus has a pistol. I can use one of his old hats and a cutlass he keeps under the bed."

"Tomorrow, then," Gabriela said, hugging her friend. "Good luck, *caro.*"

"Have a care, Gabby," Leydi said, squeezing her friend tight.

* * *

The pounding on the door woke Bertie from a sound sleep. Startled, she grabbed up her wrapper and tied it around her waist as she slipped on her mules. Passing Gabby's door, she knocked gently and whispered that her daughter stay put. Then with the utmost care she took the wheel-lock pistol from the walnut bureau in the hall and made her way down the back steps.

The pounding was coming from the shop. Easing the back door open, she stepped inside.

She recognized Hugh's pleading voice almost instantly. Lighting a candle, she glanced at the basket clock and cursed softly. It was near midnight. With no little disgust she heard his voice slurring as he called out her name in a bellow, then belched.

Bertie marched to the front door, tempted to use the pistol to whack Hugh's beautifully formed head. It still stung to hear him call her name like that, like a lover. There were many things Bertie could tolerate, but infidelity was not one of them. Kincaid had taught her that painful lesson the years they'd been together. That damned pirate had never been faithful to anyone but Consuelo.

Her cheek resting against the shuttered window, she allowed herself the luxury of listening to Hugh beckon to her. He was really nothing more than a boy—she should never have taken notice of his advances, much less encouraged them. But he'd fanned the flames of her lagging vanity. He'd made her feel young.

With a sigh she dropped the hand holding the wheel lock to her side. Though she knew Hugh was a no-good lothario, she still missed him at times.

"Go home, Hugh!" she said, very tired. "I've a pistol and I'm not averse to using it on your cheating heart!"

"Madonna, my love. I must see you! Bertie, stop this torture." More pounding. "Open this door!"

"*Basta!* Enough! I'll give you to the count of ten before I open and shoot. One, two, three . . ."

"If you'd just let me explain—"

"Seven, eight," she continued, skipping a few numbers to hurry up this farce.

"Bertie. Bertie! All right, if not for us—for our love—then for your daughter. For Gabriela's sake, *mon coeur*, you must hear me out. I've important news for you, Bertie. Concerning Gabriela."

Bertie stopped counting. Her daughter was the most precious thing in her world; Hugh knew that. Would he stoop so low as to use Gabriela in his plight?

"Go upstairs, Bertie," he urged through the door. "Bring Gabriela down. If what I heard is true, you should speak to her this very night! Let her hear what I have to say and deny it if she can."

Bertie dropped the gun on the counter. Her breath catching in her throat, she dashed out to the back stairs. In a glance she noticed the wagon was gone. That in itself was not so startling; Bertie had friends who used the wagon late at night with her blessings. But a prickly sense of unease tingled through her as she remembered that last evening Gabriela had ridden out late to the Rutherford Estate to speak to Leydianna. She'd asked Bertie's permission to use the wagon then, taking a friend Bertie trusted to guard her. Not so this evening.

In a gasping rush Bertie ran up the steps and down the planked-wood corridor to her daughter's room. After a single knock, she opened the door. The chamber was dark, too dark to see. Quickly, she ran to the bed. It was empty.

"Meu Deus," she whispered.

Her heart lodged in her throat, she raced back to the shop. At the counter she picked up the pistol and checked that it was primed to fire. When she opened the door and Hugh stepped inside to embrace her, she ducked under his arms and aimed the pistol at his heart.

"Tell me where my daughter is!"

"She's gone?" His whole demeanor changed. His charming-boy's face clouded; his shoulders slumped as if weighed with despair. The coil that was Bertie's stomach twisted tighter. *"Sacrebleu.* Then I am too late," he told her.

She jammed the gun barrel to his chest. "By all that's holy, tell me where my daughter is."

Hugh let out a long, slow breath, then carefully turned the gun away from him. "That, I don't know. I was at the Stone Elephant when I overheard two men in their cups bragging of how they'd taken money—from the ice princess herself, Gabriela de Sousa. They said she was foolish enough to believe they would abduct two men for her." His sweet eyes stilled on Bertie, his expression very sober and very serious. "Two very important men."

Bertie sat down on the stool near the counter. She cradled the pistol in her lap. "Dear God. Rutherford and Bishop."

Hugh nodded. "My guess is she's out trying to hire more men now."

Bertie shook her head. *"Não."* Suddenly the past three days of her daughter's odd comings and goings began shifting into a pattern. "She is hiring no one else—she has not the money nor the patience. But we will find out where she is." She grabbed Hugh's hand, needing for a moment his strength. "We will find these men, get them to tell us this plan she concocted. I'll know what to do then."

Hugh dropped to his knees before her. "You will let me help you, Bertie." He kissed her hand. "Together we will find her."

Bertie nodded, stroking Hugh's cheek. "Yes, Hugh. Together. You come with me to the Stone Elephant. Just give me a moment to get dressed."

Gabriela had trailed Bishop since he'd left the harbor. Now, as they neared the outskirts of town, she knew it was time to make her move.

She was wearing what she'd presumed were Hugh's clothes, having found them in the laundry at the shop. The striped waistcoat and trousers fit her—though well proportioned, the Frenchman was on the small side. She wore a scarf around her neck, ready to lift it to just below her eyes when the time came. She'd stuffed her shoulder-length curls inside a woolen cap. In her hand she carried a loaded pistol, cocked and primed.

It hadn't taken long to find Bishop. The lieutenant was making the rounds of the grog shops and taverns on the waterfront almost as if he were looking for something—or someone, more like. Each time he'd gone inside for a drink, Gabriela had waited in a darkened corner, no one recognizing her as a woman in her disguise. She imagined he'd drunk a great deal. The rum they served was potent brew. But her hope that drink might make the lieutenant easier prey died when he ducked out the final door and walked down the planked colonnade, his step as steady as a soldier's on a march.

Now, as he neared the deserted streets beyond the hub of the waterfront, Gabby tucked up the handkerchief to cover her face. Her hand clasped the pistol to her side and she ran up behind Felix. Jamming the barrel into his ribs, she said in her deepest voice, "That's far enough, mate."

He froze. "I've not much money."

"Turns out it's not money I'm after," she said, feigning a sharp accent unlike her own. "Into that alley and be quick about it."

Together they backed into a black hole of a street that dead-ended in a pile of rubbish. The stench was almost unbearable; the faint rustling, surely rats. Gabriela tried to quell her misgivings as she led Felix deep into the darkest shadows of the narrow lane.

"Now," she whispered hoarsely, "stand real quiet and put your hands behind your back. Together like."

He did what he was told. Gabby silently cursed, realizing she'd need both hands to tie the ropes she'd hitched to her belt. She could feel the sweat forming between her breasts as she remembered the night he'd kicked the knife out of her hands. He was a dangerous man, and very quick; things wouldn't go well if she let her guard down.

She tightened the ropes, twisting hard. "There now," she hissed into his ear. "I want ye to—"

He slammed his shoulder against her; the pistol flew from her hands. It landed in the dirt, discharging in a shower of sparks. Bishop elbowed her stomach. In a loud whoosh of air she hit the alley wall. *Thwack!* His fist struck her jaw, making her see stars. She swallowed her groan as the night went from black to nothingness.

She fought for consciousness. If she blacked out now, all was lost. *Hold on!*

Battling for her life, she crawled backward, just managing to duck the next blow. She landed in a sprawled heap at his feet. He jumped, reaching for her. They wrestled, rolling in the dirt. His hand brushed against her breast.

"What the . . ."

He had her pinned in an instant. Straddling her hips, Felix leaned over her, his breath coming in harsh, uneven pants. Their eyes met in the moonlight. His hand circled her breast, then he yanked the scarf off her face.

"Gabriela?" he asked.

His stunned tone made her feel infinitely sad. He was watching her as if he couldn't quite believe what he was seeing—as if, despite all his suspicions and threats, he couldn't believe she would do him harm.

"Let me up, please," she begged, stalling for time. "I can explain."

He shook his head. His eyes grew darker, dangerously so. There was a twist to his lips that spoke of more than mere anger.

"I think not." His hand closed around her breast, squeezing lightly, seductively. "I believe I have you exactly where I want you."

As he continued to caress her, Gabriela's fingers latched around the rock she'd been groping for in the dark. Felix leaned close, as if to kiss her. With all her might Gabriela smashed the rock on his head.

A soft oath breached the silence. Felix collapsed on top of her in a dead weight.

Gabby wriggled out from under him, feeling violently ill. She checked his breathing. The reassuring puffs against her cheek brought back some semblance of sanity. Panting, she finished tying the rope around his wrists and put a gag in his mouth. She checked the abandoned street, then dragged him to the alley wall and propped him up against the damp brick. She stared at his slumped shape.

"Dear God," she said to herself. "What do I do now?"

Chapter Thirteen

Bookkeeper turned buccaneer. At best it was a preposterous plan.

Leydi prowled up the stairs of Rutherford's mausoleum home to the landing. One hand cradled a pistol, the other moored a sword at her side. She adjusted the mask and tricorn of her pirate garb, brushing back the hat's ostrich plume before it made her sneeze.

I must be mad, she thought. The Mouse kidnapping Lord Ruthless? But she dismissed the disparaging titles, names that made her sound weak and Rutherford strong. She couldn't afford the luxury of weakness. Not now. Not this night.

Her fingers closed around the cold enamel of the doorknob. She listened carefully, knowing Quentin didn't sleep well. But the sound of his soft, even breathing let her know the time was ripe for action. She didn't wait the span of a breath before she eased the door open and slipped inside.

The chamber was a study of light and shadow. The windows had been left open, allowing the trade winds whispering past Mount Misery to cool the room. From every corner, walnut furniture sprouted vines and flowers. Gauzy curtains floated like pale hands fluttering on the breeze, allowing a spectral luminescence. Her mouth suddenly too dry, her palms a torrent of sweat against the sword and pistol, she searched the chamber for its occupant.

There. The tester bed. Leydi peered through the filmy cover of mosquito netting draped from a canopy of wooden vines, trying to make out the shadowed figure beyond. Her breath caught in her throat.

Quentin lay in the middle of the feather mattress. He'd kicked the silk sheets to the footboard; the moon bathed his body in silvery light. He was perfectly naked.

"Perfect" was the word that echoed in her head as she stared. His dark hair, now loosed from its queue, feathered across the pillow in rich ebony waves. Strands brushed past his muscular shoulders, leading her eyes to the planes of his chest and flat stomach. He looked like some fairy-tale prince trapped in the enchantment of sleep in his wooded bower. Bared of all clothing, Quentin Alexander Rutherford was most impressive, reminding her of the alabaster statues gracing the manor gardens. Transfixed, she followed the arrow of dark hair trailing past his navel before she realized what she gaped at. Hastily, she backed out of the room, managing not to trip on the cutlass by sheer stroke of luck.

Leydi braced her shoulders against the silk-covered walls of the corridor, shutting her eyes against the image of Quentin. In that room she'd forgotten her purpose. And not merely because of the provocative view. He seemed so innocent, almost vulnerable in his sleep. She glanced down at the pistol in her hand, admitting that her feelings for Quentin had become dangerously confused.

Viciously, she reminded herself of his softly spoken innuendos the past week. She forced herself to think of how sweetly he called her "Mouse," saying it like a pet name—the bookish secretary he claimed could never step beyond her practical, sensible world of letters and numbers.

You could never do anything to surprise me.

His words still smarted, perhaps because she feared they might be true—that she was all her mother had made her. Not the new

Leydi born of Quentin's misdeed, but a dreamer who would always let others live her adventures.

She scolded herself that now was not the time to battle with such questions. Mercilessly, she squelched her self-doubt. She must find the courage to be more than the dutiful daughter and the obedient bookkeeper. To save Kincaid, she could no longer play Quentin's mouse.

Leydi swallowed back the tightness in her throat and opened her eyes. She clutched the handle of her pistol, recalling everything she'd told Gabby.

Tonight the Mouse would turn the tables on Lord Ruthless.

She crept back into Quentin's room. This time she stared precisely at the vined headboard of the enormous tester and worked her way down to the pillows.

The mattress lay empty.

"A little late for guests, isn't it?"

Leydi spun toward the window in the direction of that cool, masculine voice. Beside a cascade of crewelwork chintz, Quentin stood, still quite naked, his magnificent body half in shadow, half in light.

His gaze flitted over the pistol in her hand. A crooked smile graced his lips. "Or does the lady have something more interesting in mind?"

It startled her how quickly he'd guessed her sex. Nor did it help much that he waited cool-as-you-please naked before her, while she—fully clothed and holding a gun—shook like a leaf. But she took heart in the fact he'd not recognized his "Mouse," and hoped that the pistol put them on an even footing despite her sex.

"I've something interesting, all right, mate," she said, coming up with a fair imitation of Cy's brogue. "Now get into your slops. We're going for a wee ride."

"I never argue with a beautiful woman."

"Or a loaded pistol, I'll wager," she added, wagging the barrel back and forth.

His smile deepened. "As you say."

Leydi caught her breath when he stepped out of the shadows. The same sculpted muscles that had enthralled her scant seconds before caught the light of the quarter moon. A feathery stroking wrapped around her ankle as if his very sensuality had gathered shape to touch her. She almost jumped out of her shoes before she realized it was only Aloysius, begging to be petted. She sighed, doing her best to ignore the cat, almost not having the presence of mind to stop Quentin before he reached the flowering wardrobe.

"A moment there, gent," she said, stepping lightly over the orange tom. She motioned for Quentin to back away from the clothespress. He could very well have a weapon hidden in the walnut cabinets. "Happens I'll find the clothes fer ye."

"By all means," he said, motioning for her to precede him.

Quentin watched as his captor backed toward the wardrobe. The menace of the pistol was somewhat tarnished by her flamboyant attire. The tight breeches molded every delicious curve of her charming derrière; the stockings exposed the slim turn of her legs. The billowing linen shirt tucked into the pants did little to hide her voluptuous breasts—breasts he could clearly see were no longer restrained by stays. The sword at her side weighed enough to make her list starboard. She needn't have bothered with the slitted mask; her face was engulfed by the tricorn's ridiculous plume.

In his wildest dreams he couldn't have imagined this scene. Naked, with the Mouse, in his bedroom—now, that combination he'd thought up countless times. But never with a gun trained on him.

She made an enchanting pirate, enough so that he stepped back into shadows, hiding his very physical reaction to her. The enormity of her attraction surprised him. It seemed that with time the Mouse only gained appeal. He'd been dreaming of Clarice and the baby, and nothing made him happier than to wake from those images of death. Yet passion was hardly the response that followed his nightmares. Bless the Mouse for at least changing the character of these sweaty awakenings, whatever her plans for the night might be.

He caught the shirt and breeches she tossed at him. "What? Not the silk with the frilled cuffs?"

She seemed to catch herself just as she turned to reach for

the requested shirt. Her lovely mouth crimped into a look of utter disgust. She trained the pistol back on Quentin. "Ye put on those clothes or leave wearing only what God gave ye, man. It's a mild night and I've little patience for yer fashion sense."

Quentin stepped into the breeches with a grin. He had the bizarre sense he'd just walked into one of the Mouse's daydreams. He wondered whom he had to thank for this midnight visit? Was this retribution for the combs or some enfeebled attempt to stop him from capturing Kincaid, as he'd threatened? He had no idea how this strange scene would play out, but he thought he'd pay good money to find out.

He knew who'd entered his bedchamber the instant he smelled her lavender scent. The fact she thought she'd fooled him with her half-cocked disguise and broken accent spoke eloquently of the Mouse's naiveté and her chances of succeeding tonight.

"Might I ask where we're off to?"

" 'Tisn't far. Ye'll be back safe in your bed come morning if ye behave yerself," she said in her atrocious brogue, throwing him his jackboots one at a time.

"And the reason for this midnight toilet?"

"Seems ye've run afoul of some important sorts."

"Ah. Kincaid, I presume."

With her nod, the tricorn flipped forward, the plume and brim half covering her face. She propped up the mass with the back of one hand, peeking out from the enormous feather to steady her aim. "Aye. Kincaid's on to you and your wee plots."

"And I suppose I have my charming bookkeeper to thank for all this?"

He watched her flinch. "I've not a blasted clue who yer speakin' of, love."

He grinned as he stomped his foot into his boot. "It's her all right." He stepped into the other boot. "There's no one else who could have told you about my plans for the pirate."

"Kincaid has his spies. Ye can't think to hide such grand schemes from him. I heard about it meself from one of the navy men bragging in a grog shop, as it so happens."

Quentin shook his head. "No navy men were involved . . . not yet. I told no one else but my bookkeeper. You see, I thought she could be trusted. More fool me," he added.

"I'd say yer a fool," she answered with some heat. "If ye thought yer cold-hearted tricks could buy her loyalty—"

Her teeth snapped shut on the last. She looked like she wished she could call back each and every word, knowing how well her anger gave her away.

"So you do know my Mouse?" he said, making most of the slip. He found he liked this side of the normally restrained Miss Carstair. It seemed his misdeed with the combs had coaxed her to show more spirit than he'd bargained for. "Yes, I suppose I've been less than kind. But then, she meddled in what was none of her business." He folded his arms across his chest and leaned back against the window sash. "I did some meddling of my own."

"Here." She threw him a coat. "Perhaps after this night ye'll think twice before interfering with the Brethren of the Coast."

He shrugged on the velvet jacket. "Does Kincaid always have women to do his dirty deeds?" It was his opinion that Daniel "Heartless" Kincaid, scourge of the seven seas and no little menace to Quentin's own ships, was smart enough not to send one lone female bookkeeper to kidnap him. No, this whole fiasco smelled rightly of the Mouse's own fertile brain. "I suppose kidnapping and sundry can be such a burden for a pirate."

The Mouse bit her lip. He could see she was thinking furiously. She held the gun steady as she backed up against the door and reached for the knob behind her. "Happens I'm his daughter."

Quentin raised his brow, thinking this bit of improvisation quite ingenious. "And Miss Carstair? Is she of any . . . special interest to Kincaid?"

He spoke with enough nuance that even the Mouse's pristine imagination would get scent of what he implied.

"Best damned bookkeeper in the seven seas!" she barked out defensively, letting Quentin know what he'd suspected all along: The Mouse wasn't Kincaid's woman, not in any carnal sense.

"Made him a bloody fortune over the years," she added, her lips puckered in almost mulish defense.

"What a shame it wasn't enough to keep him from my cargo."

"Aye, well—she's tried her best to bring ol' Da around to new times. But ye ken pirates. They're a greedy lot."

He finished putting on his coat and executed a flawless bow, his hand practically sweeping the French carpet in exaggeration. "I'm all yours, Madame Pirate. To do with as you please."

"We'll just see about that" was all she said, motioning him toward the door.

Gabriela waited in misery, hoping to God she'd not killed poor Lieutenant Bishop.

The rock had cut the skin at his temple. He'd bled badly, but after she had him bound and gagged, she managed to stop the bleeding. She'd probed the wound a bit; it wasn't too deep and did well enough bandaged with the strip of linen she'd ripped from her shirt.

He hadn't woken once, only moaned a bit when she'd pushed him up into the back of the wagon. That worried her. During the long trip to the inlet, he'd been as quiet as the dead.

Now, sitting in the sand directly in front of him, the surf a pounding rhythm behind her, she took heart in the steady rise and fall of his chest. She'd sat him up against a palm and tied his hands behind him. She removed the gag, thinking no one would hear him on this stretch of deserted beach outside Old Town Road. But the fact that he'd not woken was beginning to take its toll on her conscience.

"Please God. Please! Don't let me have killed him," she whispered.

As if in answer to her prayer, his eyes flickered open. Myriad emotions washed over her as she saw him come fully awake. She'd been careful to tie him to the tree. Still, she backed away, checking that her mask was still in place as his eyes focused on her, no longer dull.

"Gabriela. Why?"

She thought of a million answers, but then sighed, knowing it was useless to deny her identity. Now she'd have to leave St. Kitts—perhaps even Bertie would be forced to close the shop. But she supposed it was not so high a price to pay to save Kincaid.

"You shouldn't have crossed Kincaid," she said, pulling down the handkerchief masking her face. She hoped to keep as close to the original plan as possible. "As you can see, he has spies aplenty. He knows of your paltry plans to capture him with the patrol."

For an instant he looked puzzled. "And what paltry plan might that be?"

"Don't play ignorant with me; Kincaid heard it all, how you and Rutherford discovered his favored route and planned to intercept him. Don't you see," she said with true feeling, "it's useless to go against Kincaid."

This time he didn't bother to deny his scheming. Instead, he whispered, "You speak from experience?" His eyes glittered with the moonlight. "Have you tried to go against him, Gabriela?"

His gentleness surprised her. She hadn't realized the emotion in her voice had given so much away. But the night's ordeal had caught up to her, making her less than discreet. "Yes," she said, happy somehow to tell him this bit of truth. "I tried. And failed. Same as you."

"I could help you," he said, his voice low and persuasive. "I want to help you."

She closed her eyes, her fingers still on the gun. She wanted to cry. In the sympathy he offered, she saw a final trap snap shut.

For more than a decade she'd waited for true love—the love of her grandparents. She knew she would settle for nothing less. But what if love wasn't always fostered by kindness, as she'd believed had happened with her grandparents? What if it wasn't seeing Soltan's face hovering over her, offering solace, that had made her grandmother fall in love with a slave? What if it was a force inside you that said simply, *this is the one!* For good or bad—this is the man you will always love.

She put the gun down in the sand. On her hands and knees she crawled the few feet separating them. When she was close, close enough to see those intense brown eyes in the moonlight and that guileless spray of freckles, she brushed back the russet hair from his face.

"Gabriela, I want to help you," he whispered again. "Whatever he has threatened, I can protect you from Kincaid."

Gabriela closed his eyes with her fingertips. It was easier, with his eyes closed, to lean toward him. He seemed to understand, and kept his eyes closed as she lowered her mouth to kiss him.

It was nothing like the searing kisses he'd given her before. This time he was gentle. Tied against the tree, he was still able to put a wealth of feeling into the kiss, letting her know that what she'd feared was right. She'd found true love at last.

Biting back her tears, she looked away, raising the handkerchief once more. She felt safer behind the mask somehow.

She supposed it hadn't been terribly convenient for her grandmother to love a slave, but Maria had done so just the same. Gabriela always hoped to repeat their grand passion—and now it seemed as if she had. She'd felt its lure in those soulful brown eyes, its plea in Felix's kiss.

Anger swelled inside her with her sadness. Here was yet another happiness Kincaid would deny her. Because no matter how sure she was about love, Kincaid, damn him, had to come first. She owed him too much.

"You don't believe me," she heard Felix whisper. "You think he's more powerful. You're choosing him," he said, anger rising in his voice.

Slowly, Gabriela backed away. She picked up the pistol and aimed back at Felix. "You would never understand. That choice was taken from me long ago."

Chapter Fourteen

Leydi steadied her pistol on Quentin and tried to dismiss her sense of impending doom.

Under her instructions, Quentin guided the gig down the moon-drenched road. Shadows from palm fronds striped across the dash and rail. The air seemed heavy with sea salt and the perfume of orchids. An unnatural quiet lulled the night, like the hush of a jungle when a predator walks abroad.

Leydi held the pistol with both hands, trying to squelch her overactive imagination. She assured herself that all progressed well. Thus far, nothing untoward had happened. It was only Rutherford's complacency that gave her the sense she was walking the plank over shark-infested waters.

He didn't seem the kind of man to go down without a fight.

She held back a sigh. At least, he hadn't guessed who she was. Apparently, he couldn't imagine his bookkeeper doing anything as intrepid as an abduction.

"How long have you known my Mouse?" he asked almost as if prompted by her thoughts.

Leydi bit back an instant retort she'd surely regret. In a single breath, he had managed to sound both possessive and patronizing.

Keeping her grip on the pistol, she wondered what the Lady Constance would do in her situation. She imagined the bold heroine of the adventure novel would take this opportunity to gather intelligence of some sort. Couldn't she do the same?

Sitting straighter against the leather squabs, she swatted the feather of her hat aside and tugged at the cutlass where the hilt pinched into her side. Rutherford had already guessed Leydianna Carstair was involved in his kidnapping—though not the extent of her participation. Most likely, she would have to leave St. Kitts tonight and never return. And she didn't mind. Perhaps she was even ready to abandon Elaine and Argus, to leave them her money and not her person. Her pirate employer had earned her devotion these past eight years. She wouldn't let him down. Not ever.

Leydi nibbled on her bottom lip and narrowed her eyes on Quentin. The shadows danced across his handsome face, making the austere planes even more pronounced. Yes, indeed. Why not use this opportunity to do a bit of prying?

"Shows how much you know about Leydianna Carstair," she said in her feigned brogue, quite proud of how well she'd pulled off this disguise. "Calling *her* a mouse!" She rolled her eyes and gave a snort for effect, shaking her head as though the very thought of disparaging one so daring as Leydianna Carstair were laughable.

"Oh, do tell," he said with that same condescending tone.

"Are ye daft? She works for pirates. The Brethren of the Coast. That in itself should tell ye what she's made of."

"It does bring up a few interesting possibilities."

"Aye, ye've misjudged her, and that's a fact. Why, she has Heartless Kincaid eating out of her hand." *Sometimes.* "And his men follow her orders like it's Kincaid himself who's given them." If she phrased it just right, gave the proper incentive. Yes, they'd listened to her once. Perhaps even twice. "She's a leader of men."

"Imagine that," he said with enough astonishment to be insulting. "And all along I thought she was merely a feckless female browbeaten by a jealous mother and prone to daydreaming."

Leydi pressed her lips together, then barked, "Well, there's them that's taken in by the simple look of things. Then there's others who look beyond the obvious for a deeper truth, eh?"

"A pirate who spouts philosophy?" He clicked his tongue to the horses, looking as if he were enjoying himself on a ride around St. James's Park rather than fearing for his life. "Are you familiar with Descartes? I'm somewhat partial to his writings."

"She spoke a great deal about ye," Leydi said, refusing to let him get the best of her when *she* held *him* at gunpoint. "Oh, aye, she did. She called ye Lord Ruthless."

He laughed, the sound deep and clear and startlingly joyous. He glanced down at Leydi. He hadn't tied his hair back, and it brushed across his shoulders, blue-black in the moonlight. She could swear there was a merry glint in those midnight eyes. "And here I was hoping she spoke of my unending charm and how difficult it was to ignore my seductive advances. Ruthless?" His mouth curled into a smile that could be termed only smug. "Yes, I suppose I can be a real son of a bitch."

"Ye've the right of it there," Leydi said, gaining steam. "She mentioned some bad business with yer father."

That sobered his expression quickly enough. Now it was Leydi who smiled beneath her mask as she added, "Can't imagine anyone turning their back on their own. Kincaid's not always a saint, mind ye, but he's me da just the same. I wouldn't let much come between us."

"No. I see you've quite willingly followed in his illustrious footsteps." His gaze flitted over her pirate garb. "Perhaps my father's boots weren't so tempting to fill."

"Oh, aye. I adore the buccaneer life," Leydi said, getting into the spirit of her role. "But 'tis more than that. A family, even a bad one, can be a valuable asset."

"Now you're beginning to sound like the Mouse."

Leydi flushed, realizing she'd said too much. "We share a view or two. Over there," she said, pointing off the road, no longer comfortable with her ruse. "We'll go the rest of the way on foot."

Without a word Quentin steered the horses off the path and reined them to a halt. He held out his hand to the Mouse—which she ignored, jumping down to the sandy ground on her own. Her cutlass teetered off its precarious hold on her belt and clattered to the ground. She scrambled to pick it up, twisting help-lessly to strap the enormous sword back to her side.

He couldn't help smiling; she looked utterly ridiculous and twice as charming as she managed to anchor the cutlass in place, then cursed the absurd ostrich feather engulfing her face, bat-ting it aside. He crossed his arms and waited for her to get control of her disguise. So far, he'd counted eight opportunities she'd given him to disarm her. But he found he was enjoying their little adventure too much to cut it short prematurely. And per-haps he'd earned this bit of retribution. Let the Mouse have this moment to make up for her shorn curls. He wasn't too worried. She'd mentioned something about having him back in bed be-fore dawn, and he took Leydianna as a woman of her word.

Still, as she motioned him with the barrel of the wheel lock to walk toward the beach, he knew it was time to take some precautions. Before the Mouse could spring whatever calamity she'd come up with for a trap.

He did the simplest thing possible; he pretended to stumble. Landing in the soft sand, he let out a convincing groan of pain and clutched his ankle. Just as he expected, the Mouse imme-diately dropped down beside him. It was an easy thing to take the gun from her. He tossed the weapon aside. It discharged harmlessly in the sand. Grabbing both her hands, he pulled her to her feet and pressed her up against a coconut palm.

"I think this is far enough," he whispered. "At least for what I have in mind."

Before he knew it was his intention, he kissed her. He found himself savoring the sweetness of her breath, stealing the inno-cence there for the sampling. He told himself this was enough, this simple taste. He must release her now—but he couldn't seem to pull away from the warmth of her. He could only caress her further, capturing the delicious essence of this woman with his mouth and his hands.

As his lips coaxed hers to open, he began to suspect this kiss was part of the reason he'd allowed the abduction. Here, with the moon and soft sand beckoning, he could finally put aside his conscience and give in to the desire firing inside him. With every touch, each stroke, Leydi alternately battled him, then returned his kiss.

He wanted her. Oh, yes, indeed. The need to press against her delightful body, presented in all its soft and gentle splendor by her disguise, was powerful. Overwhelming. And incredibly surprising for its strength.

He hadn't known he'd longed for the Mouse this much.

She stopped kissing him. She turned her head, trying to move away from him. But she was incredibly small, not so strong. Without the gun she was quite powerless against him.

He kept trying to persuade her with his mouth, ignoring her pounding fists on his back. For an instant it frightened him that here was a weapon he'd not counted on. Her gun and cutlass he'd dismissed immediately. But what if she should turn lax in his arms, become suddenly receptive to his lovemaking? What then? The intoxicating play of her body against his made him just a bit mindless. He told himself he mustn't hurt her. He argued it was enough—that it was well past time for retreat.

"Come now, Lady Pirate. Don't I tempt you just a little?" he whispered, trying to keep to the spirit of the game—telling himself there was nothing more to these fevered kisses he gave her.

"No," she said, still struggling. "I'd sooner go through the cane presses!"

She stilled. Her mouth opened and she gasped in a small breath, realizing the enormity of her mistake. She recalled saying those same words as his bookkeeper a few days back.

Her slip brought back a touch of sanity. This time when he tested the softness of her lower lip and she waited frozen by her fear, he felt in control. He cupped her cheek in his palm. "I wonder why that sounds so familiar?" he whispered, toying with her, happy to be back in the sport of her abduction.

He took off her hat with its flamboyant plume and flung it. It sailed through the air and plunked to the sand as he yanked out the pins that had restrained her short hair. Keeping her trapped between the tree and his body, he twined his fingers through curls the color of dark honey, granting himself this one last luxury. Her hair was soft, irresistible really. Like the woman. "I find your distaste of me insulting in the extreme, madam."

She didn't fight his gentle teasing kisses, though she tensed like a rabbit waiting to flee at the first opportunity. He took her lack of response as a challenge. For one wild moment he thought to make her respond to him.

He caressed her cheek with his lips, struggling to keep his touch light. He stroked the side of her delicious mouth, thinking to tempt her with sweet, soft licks. "So what was the plan, dearest heart? A secret rendezvous?" The kiss that followed became less controlled. "Cohorts waiting at the beach?" The brush of his mouth across that plump lower lip seduced to seek a deeper touch. "Or did you plan to be my only menace?" he whispered, knowing instinctively that this was her plan all along. Poor little Mouse, so harmless. "When were your compatriots planning to make their appearance, I wonder?"

"I'd say right now would be ideal," she said breathlessly.

He laughed, and then stopped. Her gaze flickered behind him, fixed there. The fine hairs stood at the back of his neck. For a moment he forgot their kisses. She was either pulling a hell of a bluff, or someone was standing directly behind him.

Her gaze turned up to his in the moonlight. Those lovely gray eyes beyond the mask shone with laughter. A smile bloomed across her mouth, showing white, even teeth. And then the muzzle of a gun poked between his shoulder blades.

"Two steps back, ye scurvy dog," came an accented voice from behind him. "And be careful to turn around slowly. I'd hate to shoot a man in the back."

The Mouse didn't wait for him to comply, but slipped under his grasp. Quentin turned, hands outstretched to show he wasn't armed. Leydi stepped beside a taller pirate, this one masked by a handkerchief. But from the voice and figure, Quentin knew this, too, was a woman.

He realized immediately he'd miscalculated badly. He almost laughed as he realized how much he'd underestimated the Mouse. An odd thing, that. Though he took many chances, he wasn't often wrong. He couldn't actually believe anyone else was involved in her harebrained scheme to steal him from his bed in the middle of the night, even as he stared down the muzzle of the woman's very real gun.

"Not a step farther, mate," said the wool-capped woman.

"Will you let her shoot me, Mouse?" he asked Leydi, his eyes on hers alone. He took a step toward the two women, making this final gambit. He tested the compassion he knew she possessed—the same sweetness that had let him disarm her minutes before, when he'd faked his fall. He took another step, thankful when he saw both women retreat a pace rather than shoot him.

"Don't be a fool," the taller pirate shouted. But her voice shook, as did the hand holding the gun. Quentin lowered his arms, continuing to walk forward. Before the pirate masked with the scarf could shoot, Leydi stayed her hand, veering the gun away from Quentin.

"I thought not," he said quietly with a smile.

"Perhaps the gels won't shoot ye," called a man's voice from behind him, the deep voice buzzing with a distinctly genuine Scottish burr, "but mind ye, sir, I'd nae hesitate a breath."

Surprise registered on both women's faces. A cold knot twisted Quentin's stomach, telling him he was in a great deal of trouble. Both lady pirates disbanded, running past him toward that voice. Quentin turned around very slowly, holding his hands high.

A whole gaggle of pirates faced him, pistols strapped to their chests, swords and knives tucked at their sides. They were led by a towering figure with an impressive red beard shot with gray. Cradled between the scoundrels was Bishop. One of the brigands held a pistol aimed at the lieutenant's chest.

Leydi ran into the red-bearded pirate's embrace with a familiarity that turned the blood in Quentin's veins white-hot. Was this Kincaid? The fiend who'd not shown his face this past decade was making an appearance now? Almost dispassionately, he registered he was jealous. He reined in the emotion and concentrated on how the hell he was going to get out of this predicament alive.

Leydi bear-hugged Cy, smelling the familiar scent of his pipe tobacco. "Thank heavens you're here," she whispered, thinking now everything would be all right.

"Are ye now?" Cy pushed her back to arm's length. "One wouldn't think it from the letter I received. *Old Town Road,* the missive said. When the quarter moon rose full in the sky. By my calculations, that was near two hours ago." He narrowed his eyes on Gabby. "And the letter was signed by yer fair mother, though I'm beginning to suspect how genuine that signature might be. I was searchin' the beach, when I came across this lovely bunch of coconuts." He jogged his head toward poor Lieutenant Bishop. "And don't the two of ye make a fine sight," he said, staring at their costumes, picking up a strand of Leydi's short hair and shaking his head.

"The letter said to wait for me," Gabriela whispered harshly, so only Leydi and Cy would hear. "And where's the ship? I asked—"

"Yes, yes, that I wave the Black Flag grandly in the moonlight from the bowsprit. Jesus Christ, gel. We had trouble enough evading the patrol to make ground here. Have ye nae sense? Now save yer breath and tell me what all this is about."

But Gabriela's eyes were fixed on Bishop. A stone's throw away, Jack and Randy held him between them, Jack pressing a pistol to the lieutenant's ribs. Leydi's relief at Cy's very opportune appearance vanished at the sight of those determined faces. Kincaid's men didn't look at all pleased.

Leydi racked her brain to try and decide how best to broach the topic of Quentin and Bishop's plans for Kincaid—without tempting Cy to feed both men to the fishes. In the waning light of the moon, shadows struck each of Kincaid's men, catching knife scars, shimmering off gun barrels and knife blades. Leydi frowned. Over the years she'd counted these very fellows as friends. Yet, by some trick of the moonlight, their dirty faces and scraggly beards made them appear more villainous than endearing.

"All right, mates," Cy said. "Take these two blokes to the skiff. We'll row them to the *Fortune* and decide what to do with them there."

"That won't be at all necessary." Leydi stepped in front of Cy. She told herself she just had to get matters back on the proper path, take the right tack with Cy and the men. She needed to make them understand Quentin and the lieutenant had been taught their lesson; in the future, they'd leave Kincaid be.

She licked her lips, getting a glimpse of Gabriela's anxious expression. "These gentlemen are our prisoners," Leydi began. She tried a smile. No one smiled back. She noticed Randy was twirling a knife in one hand, every so often testing the edge with his thumb. "Gabby and I just thought to set them straight on a few matters. Now, why don't you just leave them tied up for us and row back to the ship and Gabby and I will be about our business."

"I'll just bet you will, imp," Cy said, not moving an inch.

"We've everything to rights now," Gabby said, pushing Leydi aside. "So be on your way before you cause us trouble."

Leydi groaned, wishing Gabby could be just a tad more conciliatory. About to launch into a second salvo of explanations, she snapped her mouth shut when she heard the distinct thunder of horses and a carriage over the pounding crash of the surf. She turned, straining to see behind her.

Up over the ridge of sand, a cabriolet led by a team of two horses came to a steaming halt. She could just make out Bertie's turbaned head in the moonlight. The woman stood on the short step of the two-wheeled carriage, waving her arms like a sailor sighting land. She shouted, *"Basta, meninas! Meu Deus!"*

"God preserve us," Cy said, watching Bertie step down into Hugh's arms from the cabriolet. "Now, if this isn't all that was missing."

Her wide skirts flying, Bertie stumbled down the sand bank to Gabriela. In a barrage of Portuguese, mother and daughter exploded into a heated argument. Despite the foreign tongue, Bertie's extravagant arm gestures left little to the imagination as she blistered her daughter's ears.

Cy stepped between the two, pushing mother and daughter apart. "Speak English, fer the love of God!"

"These are the men I warned you about in my letter. They're after Kincaid," Bertie said in a rush of breath, pointing to Quentin and Lieutenant Bishop a few feet away like a barrister singling out the accused on the stand. "And these two . . . *idiotas,*" she said, switching back to Leydi and Gabby, "hired men in Basse Terre to pose as pirates and kidnap these fellows. They were to scare them into leaving Kincaid alone. Only the men Gabriela pays, they do the smart thing—"

"Mother!"

"They take the money, laughing to any who will listen about this stupid plan of Gabriela's. Now I find the girls playing pirates—" she gasped, for the first time in her hysterics noticing Leydi's hair. *"Mãe de Deus,* she cuts her hair to look like a pirate! *Que crime."* She shook her head, threading her fingers through the curls. "A crime! And what do you do here?" she asked, blinking up at Cy, calming down enough to realize Cy's presence was unprecedented. She turned to look at Kincaid's men surrounding them, completely mystified. "What do you all here?"

"Oh, I got a special missive, all right, Bertland, my love," Cy said, glaring at Gabriela and Leydi, "but it didn't mention these fine gents—only that I was desperately needed here, me and the *Fortune."*

Leydi pulled on Cy's arm, getting his attention from the fray. "Our plan can still work," she whispered feverishly. She pointed to her half mask. "They don't know who we are," she lied, suspecting that Quentin knew exactly who she was but thinking that knowledge would condemn him in Cy's eyes. "Just tie them up and leave them here. Now they know how Kincaid deals with those who cross him; they won't be so eager to challenge him again. Why, any reasonable man can see—"

"Shut up, gel. I can't think!"

"Leave them here to us," Leydi continued, lowering her voice so the two in question couldn't hear. "Aboard the ships they'll be nothing but trouble. Bertie can even take credit for liberating them. Why, she can plead for their lives now and play the heroine."

"Leydi's right," Gabby seconded, coming up behind Cy. "It's the only way."

"And who the hell is he?" Cy shouted, eyeing Hugh as the man shamelessly listened to the entire conversation, his eyes growing wider by the second.

"He is of no importance," Bertie said, stepping forward, waving her hand as if dismissing a fly.

"Bertie, my love," Hugh protested. "Just a few days ago you said I was the light in your soul. Can you forget what we shared so easily?"

Bertie turned on Hugh, her dark eyes smoldering. "At the time I didn't know just how much sharing you were doing, Hugh. Don't think for a moment your help tonight has made me forget that! And how dare you use my daughter to gain entrance to my home, much less my heart? I should let Cy take you as well, teach you a lesson or two."

Leydi was shaking her head, not liking the turn the conversation was taking. She was about to interrupt, when the sound of cannon fire roared through the still night. The tableau of pirates and captives turned toward the beach. A second blast exploded.

Cy whispered under his breath, "The patrol."

A gun boomed its response. The thunderclap speared through Leydi's heart as surely as if it had been aimed there.

"And if I don't miss my guess," Cy said, "that's the *Fortune* answering."

Quentin pulled his arms from the grasp of the man holding him. He stepped up to Leydi and ripped the mask from her face. "What the hell is going on, Mouse?"

Leydi's eyes met Quentin's. She heard another blow of cannon fire, then another. The blast ripped through her dreams and plans. Everything was a mess. All was lost. This was no harmless make-believe, and she had just lost control of her adventure.

The men grabbed Quentin from behind. They pushed him past Leydi toward the beach, where two boats waited.

"Have I misjudged you, Mouse?" he shouted back as the men latched onto each arm and dragged him through the sand.

The moon flared its light on Quentin like a torch singling out an actor onstage for the grand finale. The sound of his voice tugged at her heart. Though she hadn't realized it, the name he'd given her had become a pet name, an endearment, and no longer a jibe used to goad her.

"Will you let them take me?" he asked as they forced him down to shore.

Knowing there was nothing she could do to stop them, she answered simply, "Yes."

* * *

Quentin leaned back against the moist wood of a crate marked *round shot* and watched Lieutenant Felix Bishop pace the close quarters of the *Fortune*'s hold. The dank room smelled of fish oil. Lit by the faint glimmer of a single smoky oil lamp, it was packed full of odd crates and barrels, coils of hemp rope and dismantled guns—as cold and cramped as a dungeon. Seated on a rolled-up jib sail, the Frenchman called Hugh Piton muttered softly to the cadence of Lieutenant Bishop's boots thumping against the boards.

Quentin gave the Frenchman a quick glance; Piton nodded to himself as if running through a silent discourse, gesturing with his hands. Quentin shook his head. He estimated the *Fortune*'s guns hadn't fired in the past hour. Kincaid's ship had evaded the patrol with little effort.

"How can you just sit there," Lieutenant Bishop snapped, "with that . . . that half-smile on your face! We are prisoners of the biggest butcher of the seven seas, for God's sake. Have you no sense of self-preservation?"

"Butcher?" Quentin asked, stretching one leg before him while propping his elbow on the bent knee of the other. "It's Kincaid you speak of, not Blackbeard. I've had the pleasure of having three of my ships boarded by his men without so much as a bullet fired over the heads of the crew. The fiend may be robbing me blind, but he's shown some restraint for a pirate. Besides, I heard one of the men speak about a ransom. I imagine once it's paid, we'll all be on our merry way."

"His reputation—"

"It's been my experience that a man's reputation can be greatly exaggerated," Quentin answered, thinking of the gossip surrounding his own past. "Now, you heard them say Kincaid is out on the Pacific, not expected back until the end of the season. We'll be well out of his way by then. Don't make this any worse than it is, my friend."

Felix squinted against the smoke of the lamp, staring at Quentin as if he'd grown a second head. "I don't see that I'm being overdramatic. We are, if I'm not mistaken, on our way to some pirate hideout, at the mercy of his men until Heartless returns and decides how to dispose of what's left of our hides."

A ringing moan rose from the Frenchman.

Quentin almost laughed. He couldn't believe his luck. The whole situation was a farce. One moment he was fulfilling every fevered fantasy he'd had with Leydianna. The next instant he was tucked up in the hold of a pirate ship. Snagged by a mouse.

"I don't share your fears," he told both men. "Good hard coin will pave our way to freedom. That and perhaps something more."

He kept seeing the Mouse's face when she'd reasoned with the man who'd introduced himself gallantly as Kincaid's second-in-command. The red-bearded pirate had listened to her every word. For reasons Quentin couldn't divine, Leydianna held some sway over these men.

"I'd wager we're more at the mercy of the pirate's women than anything else." He gave Bishop another half-grin. "Which puts a very different light on this kidnapping indeed."

Felix shook his head. "You don't know Kincaid. He'll not listen to Gabriela or your friend."

"He might," Hugh Piton whispered from his corner, the first sign of anything other than despair from the Frenchman. "The women, they argued well for our release." And then he frowned, his expression drawing inward. "I mean, *your* women argued well for *your* release." His hand strayed to his collar. He tugged at the scarf he'd tied around his neck. "Bertie, she begged them to take me."

"Precisely." Quentin wrapped his arms behind his head and leaned back. "It's the women who have brought us here. And my money's on them that we're released without more than a bad crossing. I blame myself for this mess." He chuckled. "It seems I got caught in my own mousetrap."

Felix shook his head, still disbelieving how lightly Quentin took their capture. He'd always thought Quentin Rutherford was too sure of himself. "And why are you here?" he asked the Frenchman.

The younger fellow, no older than twenty, shook his head. "A woman scorned." He shrugged his shoulders in a Gallic gesture of defeat. "*Sacrebleu.* I still cannot believe that the love of my life,

the woman whose voice is the music of my soul, has brought me
to . . . to"—he glared about the dingy quarters—" . . . to this."

Quentin studied the two bedraggled men. The lieutenant's
shirt was torn at his shoulder. There was a ragged bandage
around his head, stained brown with dried blood. The Frenchman needed a shave and stank of rum. They made a sorry sight.
But then his thoughts turned to that final kiss in the moonlight,
and he sighed. He could still smell her lavender scent.

Even if it cost a good coffer of gold, he was glad to have witnessed this final show of spirit from his prim bookkeeper. He'd
actually enjoyed himself on that moonlit beach before things
had turned sour. Her shorn curls no longer made her look the
victim. Even in that silly pirate garb, she'd appeared more like
Joan of Arc leading her troops when she'd debated for his freedom with Kincaid's man. He was beginning to believe she might
not lead a lackluster life after all.

He nestled back against the wet crate. Soon enough he would
explain there had been no plots or plans to capture Kincaid.
The game had been between only himself and the Mouse. The
pirates would send a ransom demand for the men to Stevenson,
who would pay without question, and this charming adventure
would come to an end. He smiled, realizing for the first time he
would miss his Mouse.

He wondered about the odd sense of relief that touched him.
He was, as Bishop had so heatedly pointed out, at the mercy of
pirates. And yet an almost calm had befallen him, as if—at last—
he had made up for his mistake of sending those combs.

Or perhaps he merely thought himself safe here. Perhaps he
believed Clarice's ghost couldn't find him in this dark hold.

He gave a short chuckle at his colorful imaginings. It seemed
he'd imprisoned himself too long in his receiving chamber worrying about inconsequential investments if an abduction were
enough to lift his spirits. He was actually pleased to think that
for the next few days there would be no missive from the earl to
turn away. His smile turned inward. By the time Stevenson arranged for whatever ransom the pirates demanded, the earl
might even have returned to England.

"I think your optimism is wrong," Bishop said, hovering now

with the shadows playing across his face. "I can't imagine what awaits us at the end of this trip, but I can't take it lightly. Kincaid has murdered before. I just pray to God we're not his next victims."

Part Three
Dead Men Tell No Tales

Chapter Fifteen

Devil's Gate, island hideout of Daniel Kincaid

Leydi's shoes clicked across the satinwood floor as she paced. She stared at the toes of her slippers, nibbling on her fingernail as the late morning sun bronzed the polished floor. The Lady Consuelo's sitting room was all an elegant woman could wish. There was a Japan chest, a pair of indigo mohair chairs, now occupied by Gabriela and her mother. An enormous glass in a gilt frame peered grandly above a marble-top table, granting the illusion of space. The room's ample windows—it sported four, triple hung—allowed the trade winds to cool the heat of the tropics.

But the lovely breeze tugging at the nape of Leydi's neck beneath her mobcap did little to ease her heated worries. Her concern for Quentin, now jailed in the compound's brig, was like a fever she could douse only with this ceaseless pacing. Over and over she relived that moment when he'd called her name above the thunder of the surf. *Will you let them take me?*

She shot a glance at Gabriela. Her friend was dressed in an embroidered cream silk, the color giving Gabby's golden skin a mellow warmth that belied the bruised circles beneath her eyes. Gabby's fierce frown and the fine lines above the bridge of her nose showed she, too, felt the burden of their inadvertent kidnapping. Seated near the pier table, Gabby gave an occasional crank to the planetarium, dispassionately watching the sun, moon, and planets revolve around the gilded case.

Leydi reached for her braid—but her fingers twined around only the brown muslin of her gown. Almost a week had passed since her mother had taken the shears to her curls, and still she fumbled for her braid like a soldier seeking some phantom limb lost in battle.

Have I misjudged you, Mouse?

She closed her eyes. Good heavens, the man was beginning to haunt her.

She peered across the sun-swept room, searching for Consuelo. Kincaid's lady sat in the carver chair, an embroidery hoop balanced on a frame before her. As always, she was dressed in black—a color she'd sworn to wear until the day the fat merchant the Church called her husband died and she could marry Kincaid. From her ear, Kincaid's gold hoop gleamed above a square-cut emerald. Leydi grappled for some miraculous plea that would sway Consuelo to her cause—but found none better then the odd two dozen she'd spouted since her arrival at Devil's Gate two days before.

Leydi threw up her hands and doubled her pace. "You simply don't understand, Consuelo! We weren't suppose to *really* kidnap them!"

"Sit down, Leydianna," Consuelo said, keeping her eyes on the embroidery hoop. "You make a woman dizzy pacing like that. You remind me too well of Kincaid. And you know how I miss him."

But Leydi couldn't sit still. She kept seeing the accusation in Quentin's blue eyes as he studied her through the bars in the cell door. Let Bertie and Consuelo perch in their chairs sipping coffee, acting for all the world as if they always had the brig full of men awaiting Kincaid's judgment. Let Gabriela daze away, playing with the planetarium.

In her estimation, Leydi had ample reason to pace. Three

days had passed since they'd stolen their infamous cargo from the shores of St. Kitts. And Leydi had failed miserably in her attempts to convince Cy that Quentin and the other men should be released.

"God in heaven, I will never wish for adventure again," she vowed, crossing the room a fifth time. "Why won't Cy listen to reason!"

"*Mi cielo,*" Consuelo said in her soft dulcet tones and softly accented voice. "Cy *is* listening to reason. These men, they are a threat to Kincaid. It is best to keep them here, until Kincaid can decide if they should be released."

The skirts of Leydi's brown muslin wrapped close to her ankles as she turned to face Consuelo. Fear like a deadly fruit lodged in her throat. If she couldn't convince Consuelo to release Quentin, she didn't have a prayer of swaying the more pigheaded Cy.

"These are honest men with lives back on St. Kitts. Families." The specter of Quentin's father, his shoulders shaking with his silent tears, danced before her eyes like a haunt. Had she stolen even the possibility of a reconciliation?

In three steps Leydi reached Consuelo. She dropped down beside the lady's chair, not too proud to beg. She squeezed Consuelo's hands with entreaty, reassuring herself that here was a woman she thought of as a mother. Surely Consuelo would understand.

"All we need is their parole that they'll leave Kincaid alone," Leydi whispered, "and then someone can take them back to Dominica or any other island. Please. Talk to Cy," she begged. "He'll listen to you."

Not a flicker of compassion sparked in those calm dark eyes the color of sweet chocolate. Not for Quentin. Certainly not for the lieutenant or the hapless Hugh.

"*Mi cielo,*" Consuelo said gently, "you are being naive."

Leydi stood. She shook her head, fighting the sense of helplessness that threatened to immobilize her. Consuelo was right—she was naive, utterly and decidedly without the guile necessary to make right what was surely the product of that naiveté. She remembered how merrily she'd played the role of pirate on that trip from Rutherford Estate to the sea—how frightened yet exhilarated she'd been with Quentin's kisses. Was this the price she must pay for playing at adventure?

"I feel so utterly responsible for this mess."

"Caro—" Gabriela began to say, willing as always to take her share of the blame.

"And what about your Hugh?" Leydi asked Bertie, marching to her side. "Will you serve him up to Kincaid's wrath as well?"

Bertie reached up and patted Leydi's cheek. "Trust Kincaid to do what's best, *menina.*"

"What will he do to them, *Mãe?*" Gabriela asked, looking as though she were contemplating a hanging rather than the men's eventual release.

Consuelo and Bertie glanced at each other. The two women shared a silent exchange that chilled Leydi's blood.

"What are these men to you that you plead so for their release?" Consuelo asked.

Now it was Gabby and Leydi's turn to remain quiet. Both carefully avoided the eyes of the two older women. Their silence rang ominously of secrets and regrets.

Bertie sighed. She put down her bone-china cup. "I am beginning to wonder how blind I have been these past weeks, sulking over my Hugh."

Leydi sank down in the chair beside Bertie, dropping her face to her hands. "Can't you understand? I don't want the responsibility of their capture."

"We did what we thought was right," Gabby said, commiserating.

She peered up at Gabby. In her friend's green eyes she saw the misery that burdened her own conscience. Suspicions twisted around her heart, whispering teasingly that her motives for this kidnapping might have been less than laudable.

She argued she'd never meant to cage Quentin on Devil's Gate, but subtle doubts challenged her, reaching even into her dreams these past three nights. *Wasn't this what you wanted all along? To have Quentin at your mercy?* She peeked up at the curtain rod above Gabby's head, where Nigel slept, a discordant fixture nestled among the expensive silk drapes. Had she plotted in the darkest depths of her heart to keep Quentin, like Nigel, a pet chained to her side?

She reached up and twined her finger through a swag of hair slipping past her mobcap. She pictured Quentin in the compound's small jail. He was indeed very much at her mercy. *Isn't that what you secretly wished?*

She bit her lip, twisting her hair painfully, recalling how she'd joked about giving him a prick or two with the point of her cutlass. The questions lingered . . .

Lady Consuelo de Garcia glanced up from the hunting scene stretched across her embroidery hoop. From beneath the fringe of her lowered lashes she studied the faces of the two young women she loved like daughters. Both Gabriela and Leydi looked utterly miserable.

She sighed, poking the needle through the pattern of the hoop. It wasn't in her nature to deny these two women anything. Nor was she a hypocrite. Twenty years ago she'd left the security of that fat old merchant her father had picked out as her husband. She'd turned her back on the sisters and mother she loved so well, choosing to live in exile with Kincaid—and she'd never regretted her decision, not for a moment.

But if her suspicions proved correct, the choices Leydi and Gabriela faced were difficult ones, not to be treated lightly. She wouldn't make matters too easy for them.

"Until Daniel returns," she said, hoping to at least placate the girls on this one matter, "I don't suppose these men need to be at too great a discomfort. That brig can be a furnace during the day, drafty at night. And those cots are miserable for sleep."

Leydi shook her head. "Cy won't let them out . . . I even offered to give up my tobacco fields. He won't speak to Gabby because she threatened to poison the meals if he didn't release them."

"He's been cooking his own food these past two days." Gabby's smile showed she wasn't averse to exacting her measure of revenge. "I can hear him cursing both our names from the kitchen."

"Well, it's not as if these men you've brought here are dangerous," Consuelo said sensibly.

"Hugh?" Bertie gave a delicate sniff and took a sip of her coffee. "Only to every woman on the island above the age of twelve and below the age of seventy."

"Of course they're not dangerous," Leydi quickly added, seeing her chance to bring Consuelo to their cause. "The compound is closely guarded. They have no weapons . . . only the clothes on their backs."

Consuelo rose, placing the embroidery hoop on the seat of her chair. Picking up the train of her gown, she walked to Leydi's side and placed a delicate hand on her shoulder. "I'll talk to Cy. See what can be done."

Leydi looked up with a weary smile. "Thank you," she said, standing. She gave Consuelo a quick hug. But when she stepped back, Consuelo thought her lovely face looked twice as weary. "I suppose I should go check on them now. The last time I went to the brig, they didn't seem too pleased to see me."

"Three days and nights . . ." Gabby murmured, counting the days since the men had been captured on the beach.

"I'm sure they'll be in a better frame of mind if you can at least offer the freedom of the compound," Consuelo said, looping one arm through the elbow of each girl, guiding them both to the door. "Now run along and see how your prisoners fare. I promise to speak to Cy very soon."

As the paneled door shut behind Leydi, Consuelo turned to face Bertie, the only other person in the sitting room. She took a deep breath. She had not been alone with Bertie these past twenty years. Perhaps now, for the sake of the girls, it was time to speak a few truths.

"There's more going on than those two are telling us," Consuelo said.

"*Sim,*" Bertie agreed. "More is the pity. When Kincaid returns, I would not give two pesos for his mercy for those men."

"I'm afraid you are right," Consuelo said, pacing closer to Bertie, noting with just a touch of envy that despite the years, Kincaid's first love was still a beautiful woman. "The best they can expect is marooning."

Bertie nodded. "Though I plan to plead Hugh's case, there is nothing I can do for the others—a British naval officer and

Quentin Rutherford, of all people. You know how Kincaid feels about Rutherford."

The two women's eyes met. Tension filled the air as they contemplated the secret knowledge they held. But eventually their silence spoke of more than what they shared, veering to the things that kept them apart—years of jealousy and competition for Kincaid's affections.

After a moment, Consuelo spoke. "I love those two as if they were my own children. They have been a blessing to me—allowing me to mother them when I could have no babies of my own. For them, for Leydianna and Gabriela, can't we work together?"

"It was never my intention that there should be bad blood between us," Bertie said sadly.

Consuelo laughed delicately, even as tears welled in her eyes. "Yes. I take all the blame. It really was all mine, the jealousy. The hate." She turned, staring at Bertie with a daring light in her eyes. "I forced him to send you to St. Kitts."

Bertie took a drink of her coffee and set the cup on the pier table. "I know."

"Oh, I was very subtle about it. I told him how sad you were cooped up here. How much you would be admired with your own shop—a free woman of color. How he could protect you with his name and money. And I knew you valued your independence. I thought perhaps, just perhaps, if he sent you away, you might start a new family and be happy. But you never did, did you?" she finished, her voice heavy with regret.

"I wanted to leave," Bertie said, holding up her chin, her gold hoops brushing against her neck. "That was my choice. Though I don't mean to challenge Kincaid's love for you, if I had fought his decision . . ."

"Perhaps you're right," Consuelo said with a begrudging smile. "Still, you gave him what I could not." She crossed her arms in front of her. "And I could never forgive you for it. Or myself."

"And now?" Bertie asked.

Consuelo smiled. She held out her hand to Bertie. Bertie stared at the outstretched fingers covered with gems that were love gifts from Kincaid. Slowly, she placed her hand in Consuelo's.

"I've known I was wrong for a very long time, Bertie. Please. Let this be something we can do together. For the girls, and for the love we hold for them, can we be friends and work to save these men from Kincaid's wrath?"

Bertie returned her smile. "For the girls, then. And for Kincaid. That big lout can be brought around every once in a while if a woman is smart."

Consuelo's eyes brightened. "And we are very smart women, Bertie, you and I."

The sound of a tin cup grating against the bars filled the daub and wattle cell with a sound like mortar fire.

"Let me out!" Hugh banged the cup against the bars. "*Sacrebleu*, I am not English. I am French. I fought men such as these—they stole our very lands on St. Kitts. For the love of God. Let me out! Take me from these English dogs."

"Would you shut up!" Quentin said, pacing the small cell. God, it was bloody hot; and by his estimation, not even near the noon hour. They had hours to roast like hens in a coop.

Two days they'd been caged inside this hellhole. Two days the men had shared a small bowl of water and a cloth to wipe their hands and faces. Two days and there'd been no more talk of a ransom—no possibility of escape.

He glanced over at Hugh prying his nose through the bars in the door. And now the Frenchman had gone dotty on them.

Hugh looked over his shoulder at Quentin. His gaze swept to Felix Bishop lounging in one of two cots that took up half the space in the cell. "I am sorry about the dog part, but you see, I must convince them that I am not one of you. There has been a terrible mistake. I never planned to capture Kincaid." Turning back to the door, he scraped the tin cup across the bars.

"Oh, for the love of—" Quentin yanked the cup away and hurled it across the room. It clattered against the wall, bouncing off the empty cot and falling to the hard-packed earth. The Frenchman stared at the cup longingly.

"There was no plan to capture Kincaid, you fool," Quentin snapped. "I made it all up. I hadn't a notion of Kincaid's whereabouts, much less how to trap him."

Hugh squared his shoulder beneath the ragged linen shirt and patched coat. He lifted his bristled chin an inch before he answered, "Well, next time you try to trick a woman into your bed, *monsieur,* I would suggest you choose one not under a pirate's protection."

"I wasn't trying to—" But Quentin bit back his defense, wondering if the Frenchman hadn't hit on a truth. He turned away in disgust and continued to pace the cell.

"Oui, mon ami," Hugh continued, dogging Quentin's steps, finding his lagging courage. "You listen to this son of France. There are better ways to seduce a woman. Now, poetry, I find very useful."

At that bit of advice, Felix burst into laughter.

"Oh, yes," Quentin said to Bishop, close to losing his slim hold on his temper and sanity. "This is all so bloody funny."

Felix propped himself up on his arm and stared up at Quentin from the cot. "Two days ago, in that hold, I believe it was you who were laughing, Rutherford."

"Yes, well, that was two stinking, bloody days ago," Quentin said, dropping down to the cot opposite Felix.

Two days of cramped quarters and no bath or shave. Two days of waiting for a ransom request that wouldn't be coming—of watching his little game of cat and mouse become a desperate bid for freedom. Two days of this black sense of betrayal sinking its claws into his heart, of thinking surely—*surely* the Mouse would break him out of this cell.

Two days of sleeping like the dead.

Quentin rested his head back against the Spanish walling, wondering about that little anomaly. Each night since he'd left St. Kitts, he'd fallen into a deep sleep. There'd been no nightmares to disturb him. No haunting images of death.

"It's this bloody heat," he told himself. The air seemed more tropical here, twice as dense. Difficult to breathe. "Thick enough to smother you into sleep."

He reached for an orange, taking it from the basket of fruit on the floor. The food, at least, was sound—what little he could stomach of it.

He turned the orange slowly in his hand. Thinking better of eating, he tossed it back to the basket. Bishop was right; he had completely and utterly misjudged the Mouse's intentions. Leydianna, the woman who had kissed him, battled over his books, and urged him to reconcile with his father, would serve him up to her pirate without so much as a by-your-leave. And if Quentin didn't find a way off this island before Kincaid reached shore, it might be the last mistake he made.

"No, I'm not laughing anymore," he told Felix as he stared straight ahead, seeing the Mouse's galling expression of innocence. He remembered those sweet kisses he'd coaxed from her—how he'd practically handed himself over to her and her pirates, thinking to make up for the loss of her curls. Every time Leydi stuck that lovely kittenish face up to the grate built into the wooden door and asked him how he fared—choosing her pirate over him—he wanted to reach through those bars and strangle her. But he could do nothing, just sit there in the stinking cell and watch as she left him to rot!

"We have to get off this island," Quentin said almost to himself.

"Of that I am in total agreement," Felix said.

"Open up!" Again the grating of metal against the bars. "I am one of you. Let me out before the English dogs string me up!"

Quentin rose with a curse and dragged the Frenchman back to the corner. Hugh stumbled back against the wall, hitting the daub and wattle with a satisfying thud and a whoosh of breath.

Leaning close, Quentin smiled a not-so-nice smile. "How many Frenchmen do you think are out there, hmm? I'd wager Kincaid's band is made up of an English dog or two."

Hugh swallowed, perspiration dripping down his perfect brow. "You may be right, *monsieur.* But these buccaneers, they are a democratic lot, eh? Perhaps I should distinguish myself as a common man, while the two of you are most probably landed and wealthy?"

With one hand pressed to the middle of the Frenchman's

chest, Quentin shoved Hugh to the blankets on the floor, where a very democratic vote by Bishop and himself had relegated the Frenchman to sleep. Quentin signaled the lieutenant to come closer.

"I suggest otherwise," he whispered to the Frenchman. "Like it or not, you are stuck with these two English dogs. And if we want to get out of this hellhole in one piece, I suggest we start working together."

"Thank God," Felix whispered under his breath. "What are you planning?" he asked, anticipation in his eyes.

Quentin darted a glance at Bishop. So, the lieutenant had been waiting for Quentin to realize the Mouse would not come to his rescue. He thought of the precious days he'd lost relying on her compassion—on the special bond he'd sensed between them. Now, wasn't that rich! Well, he wouldn't delude himself any longer. He knew from past experience women couldn't be trusted. Now he understood even sweet little innocents like the Mouse had their claws.

Quentin grinned, recalling the Mouse's comment that he smiled when he was the most angry. "Gentlemen, I believe three women got us into this cell." He looked each man in the eye. "And three women will get us out."

"How?" Bishop asked, frowning.

"What have men always done to sway women to their cause?" Quentin asked, feeling not the least prick of conscience for his plan. When Bishop and the Frenchman remained silent, Quentin added in a low voice, "Why, seduce them, of course."

A long, slow whistle sounded from the Frenchman's lips.

Bishop shook his head. "You're mad. We exchange no more than a few words with that little brown hen you goaded into kidnapping us in the first place. Do you plan to seduce her through the bars?"

"That will be our first task," Quentin said, undeterred by Bishop's skepticism. "To get out of this cell. We must convince them we need some measure of freedom. And then we show no mercy."

"And Kincaid?" This from Hugh, with an expression that showed he didn't much care to come face-to-face with the pirate.

"Is off on the account, searching for Spanish booty in the Pacific," Quentin said, resting his forearm on his knee as he leaned closer and lowered his voice. "I estimate we have some time before he shows up. And, gentlemen, I suggest we be well off this island by then."

"Of that," Bishop said, "we are in total agreement. But how do you suggest we accomplish it?"

"Hugh here seems our best bet," Quentin said, though he hated to rely on the Frenchman for escape. "He's in this cell only because of a lover's tiff with the fair Madame de Sousa. Surely, with your more than abundant charms," he said, watching the Frenchman almost preen under his compliments, "you can talk her into releasing you from this crypt?"

Hugh seemed to think a moment. His full lips curled in a dreamy half-smile as if he contemplated success—then he shook his head. "Perhaps not, *mes amis*. I forgot to mention a small detail. The lover's tiff. You see, though Bertie holds my heart in her hands, though she is the love of my life, my *raison d'être*—" He cleared his throat, looking a bit anxious as he glanced away from Quentin and Bishop. "Though we made such wonderful love—a brush with heaven, really—"

Bishop rolled his eyes and gestured for Hugh to get on with it.

"—the reason she's a bit . . . displeased with me . . ." Hugh sighed. "We made love, and afterward she found me with another woman."

Quentin studied the younger man, not quite believing the images that were coming to mind with the Frenchman's peculiar wording. "Let me see if I understand. You made love—and a day or so later she found you with another woman?"

"Not a day . . . or so." Hugh waved his hand in a circular motion as if trying to surmise the exact measure of time. Then he stopped and stared at both men. "She was actually still warm from my embrace, peeking out the window above my bed, when she caught me kissing Monique."

Both Quentin and Felix gaped at Hugh in complete and utter disbelief.

"The French" was all Quentin could think to say.

"She'll hang him by the balls," Felix whispered.

"It was a cousin," Hugh stated primly, as if this explained everything. "A distant cousin . . . but family just the same."

"But I gather this wasn't the kind of kiss one gives a family member?" Quentin clarified.

Hugh shook his head. "You see, while Bertie is the love of my life, the woman who holds my heart in her hands, my—"

"*Raison d'être,*" Quentin supplied, hoping to get to the point.

"My Monique." Hugh whispered the name as if he'd just pronounced a great delicacy. He sucked a breath between his teeth. "She is quite . . . *extraordinaire.*"

Bishop met Quentin's gaze, then fell back against the wall as if shot through the heart. "So much for true love."

"Do you think you can convince her to forgive you?" Quentin asked.

"It has been my quest these last days. But Bertie. She is not so forgiving, you see. It has broken my heart," Hugh finished dispiritedly.

Bishop gave him a jaundiced look before saying to Quentin, "Now what?"

But Quentin would not give up so easily, already plotting ways to strip the Mouse's loyalty from Kincaid. He remembered all those lovely blushes when he'd whispered teasingly in her ear. How her gray eyes would grow dark when he caressed her cheek. He recalled the taste of her kisses. Yes, there'd been a spark there . . . and he planned to use it to his advantage in this war between them.

"As I said," he told the men, "there's three of us, and three of them. One of us is bound to succeed."

Chapter Sixteen

"What do you think Kincaid will do to them?" Leydi asked, walking beside Gabriela on the crushed-shell path. Bertie's ominous silence to the same question tolled like a death knell between the two women, ringing a distressing counterpoint to the *crunch, crunch, crunch* of their shoes on the path.

Gabriela's green eyes fixed on the daub and wattle hut in the middle of the compound. Several sheep grazed near the barred wooden door as a group of children played bear leader in the grassy courtyard, stomping around the blindfolded boy leading another on hands and knees by a cord. A pair of girls capped in lace pinnets toyed with a rattle Leydi had devised to scare the parrots from devouring her experimental fields and the vegetable gardens. They screamed and danced with delight at the rattle's discordant clapping. A buccaneer in a short coat and trousers carrying a hoe doffed his hat in good morn to an aproned matron loaded with sun-dried sheets as each crossed the square. Just another day at Devil's Gate.

"Marooning them is about the best we can hope," Gabby said with a sigh. "They might actually live long enough for someone to find them."

Leydi's steps slowed as she approached the guardhouse. She didn't have firsthand knowledge of how Kincaid dealt with his enemies, but pirates weren't gentlefolk. A particular passage from Esquemelen's book about pirate torture came to mind in vivid, ghastly detail.

"Do you think Consuelo can talk Cy into giving them some measure of freedom until then?"

Gabriela shook her head. "They were planning to hang Kincaid, *caro*. That's why we kidnapped them in the first place. There's little chance for leniency."

For a instant, Leydi tried to think of Quentin as the enemy—the man who would destroy Kincaid. But instead, she remembered his kisses, some rough, others gentle in their teasing. She heard again that almost boyish excitement in his voice when he charted yet another financial coup—and how he called her Mouse. Only, in her memory, the name wasn't mean or goading. It held instead a gentle sweetness.

"So we do nothing?" she asked Gabby. She pictured Quentin watching her through the barred door of his cell. *You betrayed me, Mouse.* "We just let Kincaid do his worst—torture them to death if he must." She stopped and threw up her hands. "Gabby, I've studied Rutherford's estate books, read his correspondence, shared his supper . . ."

"Kissed him," Gabriela added, tugging Leydi's sleeve to coax her along the path. "Though it looked more like he was doing the kissing and you the fighting-off."

"It wasn't always like that between us," she said, meeting Gabby's eyes in confession. "I wasn't always fighting him."

"That much I gathered," Gabby said, tugging Leydi onward. "It doesn't change a thing. We owe Kincaid."

Gabriela's avowal was singular enough to be startling. Over the years, Leydi couldn't think of a single time Gabriela had been on good terms with their pirate employer. Their fragile truce seemed bandaged together by the spit and string of Bertie's hopes and wishes. Yet, it was Gabby now who'd put Kincaid's interests first. And she was right—they did owe Kincaid their loyalty. Still . . .

"Sometimes he made me laugh, Gabby," Leydi whispered.

"And cry. He made me feel things. You can't let a man die after that."

Rather than answer, Gabby stopped abruptly and pointed toward the hut. *"Caro,* isn't that Nigel? Up on the window."

Leydi glanced up with a smile for her dear pet. She'd missed him terribly when she'd been on St. Kitts, but Cy had indeed taken good care of him in her absence. Her smile vanished when she realized her pet's intentions.

She was just in time to see Nigel's tail disappear as he slipped through the bars of the brig's single window.

Right into Quentin's cell.

"Dieu," Hugh said with whispered horror. "What is it?"

All three men stood with their backs to the door of the cell, watching in morbid fascination as the green scaly creature dropped to the clay floor. There was a thorny frill at the top of its head. The face looked like a mosaic sculpture of white, gold, and green scales. From the tip of its brown and yellow striped tail to its horny nose, Quentin estimated the beast was at least four feet long.

"It looks like a dragon," Bishop whispered, standing beside Quentin, taking a step back as the animal inched forward in a wobbly, serpentine gait.

"I'm not sure," Quentin said. His eyes narrowed on the beast. "But whatever it is, if I'm not mistaken, that *is* a red satin ribbon around its neck."

As the other two men peered closer, indeed catching sight of the gay ribbon carefully tied around the creature's thick neck in a merry bow, a woman's voice called from the door. "Hello? Hello there!"

The voice sounded breathy, as if the speaker—whom Quentin immediately identified as Leydi—had just arrived at a fast clip.

"Don't be afraid," she said. "It's only Nigel. He won't hurt anyone. Well, actually, he's only bitten Randy, and he was teasing him horribly. I'll just get Cy, and he'll fetch him out right away."

"I don't think that will be necessary," Quentin said, seeing an opportunity as he stared at the beast's ribboned neck.

He pushed Hugh aside and gazed down at a pair of familiar gray eyes outside his cell. Even with the barred door between them, he was struck by a shock of connection between them, as if his body hadn't quite caught up with the fact she was the enemy. She wore her same brown uniform, but there was a spark to her eyes that he'd never seen on Rutherford Estate, a presence—as if she were finally home. The rich brown of her hair caught the morning light; the curls framed her face beneath the mobcap, making him wonder why he'd ever thought the haircut unattractive.

He shoved away the treacherous thoughts, getting to the business at hand. "Nigel," he said with a certain relish, "will be staying on a bit—as our guest. Until we can come to some agreement about our release."

There was a stunned silence outside the door. And then, "You're holding my iguana hostage?"

Quentin turned away and leaned up against the Spanish walling. He winked at the two men now watching him as if he'd finally lost his fragile grip on what was left of his sanity. "Exactly."

Worried gray eyes appeared through the bars then narrowed on the beast making his way unerringly to the basket of fruit. For an instant those lovely eyes widened, showing their thin band of green, then Leydi vanished. A wash of frantic whispers followed, bringing a smile to Quentin's lips. He raised his eyebrows at Bishop, giving him a we-have-them-now grin. The lieutenant turned to study the animal thoughtfully. Even Hugh looked a bit pensive as he watched the beast gnaw on an orange peel.

"This doesn't seem a particularly good negotiation tactic," came Leydi's distinct soprano through the bars. "I'd advise against it."

"I must disagree, Mouse. Nigel is looking more and more like the golden goose fallen into my lap."

She cleared her throat. "Nigel is of no importance to anyone but me."

"Well, then," he said, his voice growing soft. "I suppose you'll do your merry best to see our demands are met, won't you?"

"Don't you think I've tried to help?" she said, sounding a bit desperate. "I don't happen to have much leverage in the matter, as it happens."

"Poor Nigel."

"You would hurt a defenseless animal!"

"As it happens," he said, repeating her words with a smile as his gaze blasted her through the bars, "yes. The fact that it's an overgrown lizard helps a bit, I admit." He glanced back at the iguana. "Yes, I do believe between the three of us, we could make things very unhealthy for Nigel."

Leydi stepped back from the cell, her heart pelting against the wall of her chest. She wondered if any man in the world would ever make her feel this way, as if she'd just been run over by a runaway carriage but lived to tell what a wonderful experience it had been to be crushed beneath its wheels. She motioned Gabriela away from the door and spoke in whispered tones, "Now what do we do?"

"Do you think he'll really hurt Nigel?" Gabriela asked, quite attached to the iguana herself. He had an unnerving sense of time, seeming to know the exact moment to come begging for scraps in the kitchen. You could almost set the table clock by him.

Leydi bit her lip. "I don't know. He's desperate—I'm not sure we can depend on his good graces." She turned to Gabby, making up her mind. "But this may be just the excuse I need to get some concession from Cy."

Leydi stepped back to the door. "I have a deal to make with you, Rutherford."

Inside the cell, Quentin crossed his arms and yelled up to the grate in the door. "I'm listening."

"Release Nigel unharmed and I'll try to gain you the freedom of the compound." That much, at least, Consuelo had promised to help with.

"You'll have to do better than that, Mouse."

"Be reasonable . . . he's my pet, and I'm only the bookkeeper here. Isn't time outside of this cell worth Nigel's freedom?"

Quentin looked at Bishop, who nodded. Hugh, too, seemed eager to agree, looking with yearning at the patch of blue sky and fluffy clouds just beyond the bars of the room's only window.

"How do we know that once you have Nigel we won't find ourselves back in the brig?" Quentin asked.

"You have my word on the matter."

"Well, that's a relief," he said with more sarcasm than he'd intended. He sighed, knowing he really didn't have much choice. "All right, Mouse. But Nigel will stay here as our guest—until our release."

When he heard the footsteps fall away, Quentin smiled. "Well, my friends, if I'm not mistaken, we're one step closer to getting off this island."

"That . . . that thing is eating our breakfast," Hugh said, pointing a shaking finger at the iguana. Curled up in the basket of fruit, the lizard was happily devouring a mango, the red bow gaily bobbing up and down with the rhythm of its jaws.

"Do you think she can manage our release from this cell?" Bishop asked, ignoring the Frenchman now inching closer to the basket.

Quentin dropped down to his cot. He picked up the orange, whose thick skin had proven too bitter for Nigel. Peeling a section, he offered a slice of the juicy fruit to the iguana. Nigel left his mango, reaching out with his pink tongue for the orange.

"Haven't you wondered, Bishop," Quentin asked, watching Nigel chew on the orange slice, "who these women *really* are? They work for Kincaid, visit St. Kitts at leisure, enjoy the protection of his name. The Mouse, I know, is extremely well educated, with a certain naiveté that shows she's led a protected life for a pirate's cohort."

Bishop met his eyes. "What are you thinking?"

Quentin reached out and stroked the side of Nigel's head. The skin was smooth, like pebbled glass, not at all unpleasant to touch. Quentin smiled as the iguana reached up for another slice of orange, taking it from Quentin's fingers. Nigel chomped happily as Quentin schemed against its mistress. "I think, my friends, that Miss Carstair, bookkeeper to pirates, might wield a bit more power on this island than she's leading us to believe."

* * *

"He can roast the thing alive—he can strangle it with his bare hands. He can eat it raw, fer all I care," Cy shouted, shaking the rafters of his quarters. "Those three stay right where they are until Kincaid arrives."

"But—" Leydi said.

"I'm telling ye, gel, don't pester me over this." He was leaning over a washbasin, trimming the growth of beard from his neck. He cursed when he managed to nick the skin. "I'm Kincaid's man and I'll put his interest before all, as well ye should, I'm thinking."

"But the compound is walled and gated," Leydi said, handing him a towel, finally managing a word through his tirade. "It's practically a fortress here. What harm can they do in the compound?"

"We'd have to keep track of all the weapons," Cy ticked off on his fingers. "I'd need a man on each, day and night. Maybe even two—"

"What harm can it do to let them roam a bit?" Bertie asked. She reached up and retied Cy's cravat, giving his cheek an affectionate pat when she was done.

But Cy grabbed her wrist before Bertie could draw away. "Joining in with them, are ye?" he said, a dangerous gleam in his blue eyes. He crossed his thick arms before a chest the size of a twenty-gallon barrel and peered down at Bertie. "And why are ye so fired hot to release them, Bertland? Might it be that young boy ye have hangin' on yer skirts ye want roaming about?"

"Because I say they should be released," Consuelo said firmly as she entered the room.

The train of her gold-shot black gown trailed behind her grandly as Consuelo glided across the chamber. "I'll take responsibility for the captives, Cy. On my wishes, you shall release the prisoners, and there will be no more questions about the matter."

Cy looked first confused, then disapproving. He tossed the towel to the washstand and eased Bertie aside. "So ye've turned against him, too? Ye'd let his enemies have full run of the place?"

"I would give my life for Kincaid, as well you know, you silly man," Consuelo said. "Don't you dare question my loyalties."

Cy had the good graces to blush beneath his red beard. "Aye, Consuelo. 'Tis just my fine temper speaking. But still, yer not thinking straight trying to please these hoydens."

With a smile, Consuelo pardoned the insult. "I think between the four of us," she said, gesturing to the women in the room, "we can keep a few men in line. But to be safe, you shall assign them each a guard. I think Randy, Brody, and Martin will do nicely. And put them in separate sleeping quarters. Now, stop sulking, Cy." She glanced over at Gabby and Leydianna, watching both women with the benevolence of a doting mother. "I think Daniel would approve."

Quentin stared into the two beady eyes, one fixed on each side of Nigel's head. They seemed to work independent of each other, one veering left, the other peering right. He took another piece of mango and held it out for Nigel to chew on.

"You, know," Hugh said to Felix beside him, "I do believe the thing likes him."

Nigel was perched squarely on Quentin's chest—exactly where he'd found him when he'd woken from his catnap. He'd used Bishop's cravat to tether the animal by its ribbon collar at the foot of the bed, not wanting his captive to escape. When he'd found Nigel sitting atop his chest, his colorful horny toad face fixed on Quentin, he'd almost jumped out of bed and thrown the iguana across the room. Now he was coaxing it to eat some fruit from his fingers, thinking Nigel wasn't as fearsome as he looked. Quentin had to admit, he'd never gotten this much attention from Aloysius.

He tried to incorporate this new knowledge of the Mouse into his vision of her. An iguana was rather an exotic pet—not particularly endearing. "Did she come to your rescue, I wonder?" he asked Nigel. "What made her think to give you a home and such a proper English name, old boy?"

He planned to find out the answer to these questions and many more. He wanted to know everything about the Mouse. A proper seduction always required knowledge.

A small part of him whispered this was what he'd waited for

all along, an excuse to seduce her. The same wicked voice that taunted his desire for her had driven him to tempt fate, had lulled him into this trap so he could fight back—do his worst against the Mouse without a touch of conscience. His mouth twisted into a frown as he pondered the possibility. Hadn't he wanted the Mouse from the first time he'd seen that sweet face peer up to him with an expression that begged, "How might I please?"

"What kind of a woman keeps a dragon for a pet?" Hugh asked out loud, still gaping at the iguana in rapt horror.

"Probably the same kind that would dress up like a pirate, kidnap a man, then come visit him three times a day to ask how he fares," Felix supplied from where he stood by the window.

"*Oui.* She does seem very concerned about you, Rutherford." Hugh pouted, his full bottom lip making him look particularly boyish. "Not my Bertie. She hasn't come to see me once."

"If we ever get out of here, you'll have to remedy that," Quentin said, dismissing the scruples that warned against his plans. He handed the iguana another piece of fruit. He'd be damned if he'd worry about the Mouse's fragile heart while he was still behind bars. "You are our best hope of getting off this pirate's island."

"This plan of yours, to seduce the women," Felix said, staring moodily out the window. "I'm not sure I like it."

Quentin watched Nigel languidly chewing as he sat on his chest, the iguana's triple chin swaying with the motion. "Is the fair Gabriela not to your liking?" he asked, thinking that possibility doubtful. There was a beautiful sensuality about the tall quadroon that would draw any man.

"My battle isn't with Gabriela." Felix shrugged. "When I fight, I like to do it face-to-face, not hiding behind the skirts of a woman."

Quentin threw his feet over the bunk and wrapped Nigel's tail around his neck so the iguana perched on his shoulder. He stood and walked up to the lieutenant. Bishop's misgivings echoed too well that small voice of conscience still chiming inside him— enough that he needed to silence the man's qualms.

"When I fight, be it in business or in life, I do what is expedient. And getting off this island before Kincaid arrives is extremely expedient," Quentin reminded Bishop.

Felix shook his head. "I know the difference between right and wrong. I doubt Gabriela would be involved if you hadn't threatened Kincaid by making up those stories about our plan to capture him. You forced her to act. I won't hold that against her." Bishop turned to face Quentin squarely. The sun outside burned his hair a fiery red; his brown eyes grew darker with some deep emotion. "I don't feel right, tricking her," he said, apparently coming to some decision.

"The end justifying the means, my friend," Quentin said sharply, not intending to let Bishop's too-fine conscience hamper their chances of leaving this prison. "Good Lord, is this the man who lectured me for hours about Kincaid the murderer? Kincaid the fiend? Will you really let some foolish sense of propriety stop you from eventually bringing the pirate to justice?" Quentin asked, remembering the fanatical energy with which Bishop had argued his case against Kincaid. "If I'm not mistaken, Gabriela gave you this fine memento fighting for her pirate," he said, pointing to the healing scar on Bishop's head. "Will you let her keep you from your goal?"

Bishop's mouth thinned. He reached up and touched the bruise on his head, wincing when he pressed too hard. Though the cut had healed, it would most likely leave a scar. "Perhaps you're right. Yes. We'll do as you say."

Chapter Seventeen

The towering Scotsman tossed the limp sack of goods. It sailed across the bedchamber, landing with a soft *thump* in Quentin's hands.

"Fresh clothes," the Scotsman pronounced with his soft burr. "And there's water in the washbasin. By the smell of ye, ye'll be needin' both."

Quentin scanned the small chamber. A chest of drawers with fine oyster veneers and cross-banding perched opposite a tester bed. There was a stool, and, near the door, a William and Mary walnut chair with cane backing and a frivolous fringed seat that looked out of place in the masculine setting. He noted someone had already taken the precaution of hammering the wooden shutters closed. The louvers were open, striping the bed and its swaths of mosquito netting in the afternoon light.

"I'll be staying close by," the Scotsman said with an edgy grin. "To keep an eye on ye. It was a whim of the ladies to let ye have the run of the place. The idea don't set too well on me, ye ken?"

"Forewarned," Quentin answered, dropping the sack of clothes to the lively canary-yellow counterpane. The room was furnished sparsely but handsomely; apparently Kincaid catered to fine tastes. Quentin had been told by Cy Cuthbert that he'd landed a berth in the pirate's grand cottage-style home. The others were being housed in separate quarters in the compound.

"Ye look like a man with a fondness fer games of chance," the Scotsman said, giving Quentin an appraising stare. "Ye play cards, mate?"

"As often as I can," Quentin answered, this time returning the man's grin.

"Ye can learn a lot about a man by the way he plays cards," Cuthbert reasoned, already making a study of Quentin from beneath his bushy copper brows. "The boys and I have a friendly game most evenings, if ye care to join in a bit before I lock ye up fer the night."

Quentin held out his empty hands. "I'm afraid I'm a bit light in the pocket these days."

"Well then, maybe we'll have to play fer something other than blunt. Something more interesting—like a few fair truths."

"Just tell me the time and the day," Quentin answered, not the least intimidated by the Scotsman's play for answers.

The door shut behind Cuthbert. Quentin could well imagine the Scotsman was curious about Quentin's relationship with the Mouse. She'd kidnapped him at gunpoint, then tried to protect Quentin from Cuthbert's own plans. Certainly, this new plea to give him freedom of the compound would inspire a few questions.

Quentin heard the key turning in the lock, the bolt slamming home. His eyes focused on the locked door of his newest cell.

"Run of the place, indeed," he muttered to himself.

He turned to the bed and dug through the sack of clean clothes. At least he'd gotten away from the ripe smell of men perspiring in too close quarters. After three days a bit of privacy wouldn't go amiss. Felix was all right in a quiet, morose sort of way, but Hugh had him almost mad with his unceasing mutterings and laments over Bertie de Sousa.

He shook out a shirt and breeches. The clothes were plain fare, but the material was a fine worsted cotton. Not bad considering his circumstances on this pirate island. The short walk from the brig, too, had been surprising. The compound was almost as large—and certainly cleaner—than the city of Basse Terre itself.

With a linen towel in hand, Quentin shrugged off his waistcoat and shirt and walked to the washbasin. They'd reached the island in a day, so he imagined the hideout was well hidden among the riddle of islands that made up the Antilles, making Kincaid's choice of home rather sound. It seemed that while other pirates had been driven from these waters by the Royal Navy, Kincaid had managed a comfortable nest.

With a tired sigh he looked at his reflection in the small mirror hanging above the basin. His beard had grown thick and itchy, and he'd stopped tying back his hair when he'd lost the bit of twine Hugh had given him. It hung in coal-black hanks to his shoulders. He felt caked in dust and sweat. He grimaced in the mirror.

He thought he might actually frighten a small child.

He looked through the drawer and cabinet of the marble-top washstand and found a wooden cup, brush, soap, and blade. With a bit of water he beat up a good foam. Leaning closer to the mirror, he reached to brush on the soap, then stopped.

"Boo," he said softly.

It didn't take long to remove the beard stubble. Afterward he sat down on the bed and used the towel to wipe his face and neck. He looked longingly at the mountain of feather pillows piled against the bedstead, tempted to take another nap. But instead, he put on his shirt and the new breeches and shrugged on his old waistcoat.

He lay back on the moss-and-horsehair mattress. The air seemed moist and thick in his lungs, and he shifted on the counterpane, fighting to stay awake. He wondered about this strange bout of somnolence, wondered if he wasn't making up for seven years of sleeplessness.

"Or perhaps Clarice's ghost, like the Royal Navy, just can't find this deuced place," he muttered to himself.

Lying back on the pillow of his arm, he knew it wasn't just his dreamless nights that he found so odd. He had a sense he'd somehow left the dreary reality of his world. In one night he'd been spirited away from his father and his many financial responsibilities to fall right smack in the middle of some strange fantasy.

The adventure was almost too wild to be real. Kidnapped by beautiful women, held captive by pirates on some tropical paradise dipped in cotton clouds and swathed in an emerald cloak of mountains. And now, long restful nights of languid sleep—as if he'd never battled his nightmares, never spent endless hours contemplating the waste his life had become and the lackluster future he'd chosen.

He grimaced. Perhaps all he'd needed was for someone to threaten his life before he could come to appreciate it.

The soft knock at the door stopped his musings. He heard the *snap click* of a key turning, the bolt sliding. The door opened, parting like a curtain to reveal the Mouse in all her brown splendor. Mobcap securely in place, she waited in the doorway.

His first instinct was for vengeance. It was almost too tempting to see her standing eagerly without a weapon, her gray eyes shining with that deceptive innocence. He could take her now, drag her from the door, have her at his mercy—if only for a scant second or two. God, it would almost be worth it.

But he restrained himself, keeping an eye on the greater goal: escape for him and the two others he'd come to think of as his cohorts in this farce.

"Welcome to my humble home," he said, standing, sweeping a bow. He sat back on the bed and patted the counterpane beside him, giving her his best smile. "Come for a visit? Have you missed me, Mouse?"

She granted him a jaundiced look that said she wasn't the least taken in by this show of civility. She plunked the key in the pocket of her apron, gave it a pat, and plopped down in the William and Mary chair. The door remained open. "I thought it was time we talk."

"More than time." He sat up on the bed. "Tell me the rules to my cage."

She kept her gaze steady, looking more in command and less apologetic. "You'll be locked in at night . . . and during the day, if no one is available to escort you places. Otherwise, you can go most anywhere."

"With an escort."

"Yes."

"I suppose it will have to do." He leaned back on his elbows and propped his jackboot on the footboard. He patted the bed once more. "Won't you come closer, Mouse? I promise not to bite—though I might be tempted to take a small nibble."

She sniffed, crossing her arms over the laced bodice. "Brody is just outside the door, standing guard."

"Oh, dear," he said. "I suppose that means you don't trust me?"

"Let me get to the point," she said with uncharacteristic acerbity. "I never intended for this to happen—the kidnapping, I mean. I planned only to frighten you into leaving off your plans for Kincaid. But now I'm quite stuck with you, you see, so I'm going to promise to do my best to get you home in one piece."

He didn't say anything. Enough had happened to make him guess she'd never intended her ruse to go this far—her promise that night that he'd be back abed before dawn, her argument with Cy to leave him on the beach. But the fact of the matter was, she'd botched his abduction, and he didn't have much faith in the Mouse's ability to gain his release. Not unless she was willing to do anything to help him—even go against her darling Kincaid's interests.

He lay back on the counterpane, glancing up at the plain ceiling beyond the canopy of netting. He planned to make certain that soon, very soon, he would have the Mouse's complete and undivided loyalty.

"I miss my angels," he whispered, launching into what he'd already decided would be his best tactic. He looked back at the Mouse, watching her gray eyes for her reaction as he asked, "Will you take their place for me?"

She looked puzzled. He'd managed to shock her out of that little admiral's pose. For a fraction of a second he was almost sorry for it, that she was such easy prey. But he warned himself not to be taken in by her innocence. He knew the Mouse was a worthy opponent, and the stakes they played for were all too high.

He sat up and propped a shoulder against a bedpost. "I told

you I talked to them. My angels," he said, presenting to her all that was helpless and vulnerable. The tarnished hero of one of the adventure books he'd seen her reading as she walked about the estate in a daze. "And sometimes, if I listened very carefully, I thought they might just answer me." He allowed the pathos of the statement to sink in, giving her the hidden message: *I was that lonely, you see.* "What do you think, Mouse? Will you play their role? Give me the counsel I seek to see me through this ordeal?"

His confession had its desired effect. The Mouse responded with her whole body. Her lips turned soft in sympathy. Her silver eyes sparkled with silent distress. She even leaned forward just a bit, worrying the pocket of her gown for the key inside.

The true brilliance of his plan was its simplicity. He knew she was infinitely curious about him. Good God, she'd meddled enough in his life to prove that much. Now he would reveal all those lovely secrets she hungered for. He'd give her the truth, show his real self—a lonely man who'd banished himself these many years, suffering from a profound guilt. Do-gooders like the Mouse wouldn't resist. He and his miserable past were the finest cheese for the trap.

"Are you a good listener, Mouse?" he asked.

"Yes," she said, her voice cracking just a touch on the single word.

"Will you listen for me, then?" he asked. "Be my angels while I'm so far from home?"

For a moment he thought she hesitated, perhaps even getting a whiff of his rotten deception. But then she sat back into the chair and nodded.

"I have my own confession, then," he began simply. "There was never any plan against Kincaid. Oh, Bishop wanted him, sure enough. And I was willing . . . until . . ." He let the sentence fade like a question.

"Until what?" she asked, no longer plunking at that key in her pocket, now looking very involved in his tale.

He pushed off the bed and paced toward her. "Until I discovered you were part of the catch," he said softly. "You see, Bishop made the connection between you and Kincaid," he told her, taking the next step in his gambit. "Apparently, he's known for some time that Gabriela's mother sells pirate booty. Not many care about the connection—Kincaid's greased enough palms to make certain of that. A real gentleman pirate, your man. But Bishop seems to have a personal dislike for the Brethren. He made it his mission to fell the grand Heartless Kincaid."

He stopped at just the right moment to make an impression. His gaze searched hers imploringly. "Only, I couldn't go through with his plans when I heard he'd seen you at the shop. He told me you were one of them—in Kincaid's pay. I wouldn't believe it at first. But Bishop said I should consider that Kincaid's interest in my ships and your coming to work for me were no coincidence."

"I'm only his bookkeeper," she said firmly, her fingers now curled on the arms of the chair, pressing against the wood. "I have nothing to do with pirating other than trying to convince Kincaid to give it up. And neither does Gabriela. She works for him keeping house. Nothing more, nothing less. I took the job you offered for money. I would never give Kincaid information on your shipments."

"But I wasn't sure." He stepped closer, laying out his bait. "I didn't want Bishop to trap you as well as Kincaid, so I refused to cooperate," he said, realizing as he spoke that it was the truth. He'd been trying in his own deluded fashion to protect her. "But my mistake was, I couldn't help baiting you—just a bit— with our supposed plan to capture Heartless." Slowly, so as not to frighten her, he placed his hand over hers on the chair. "More fool me, given the outcome."

Leydi blinked her eyes as if waking from the lovely rhythm of his words. Suddenly, she snatched her hand back. "You're saying you were trying to protect me?" One amber brow shot upward in a look of suspicion. "I'm supposed to believe that?"

"Let's just say I didn't want to do anything until I knew the exact ramifications. Bishop was after blood, you know."

"And the plan to trap Kincaid?"

"As I said; I made it up. I wanted to goad you into revealing your exact connection to the pirate. I knew sooner or later you'd tip your hand." He picked up a curl and twined it around his finger. "Just as I knew what would happen when I sent the combs."

He knelt down beside her, the soft spiral still laced between his fingers. Her hair peeked out from the frilly edge of the cap in a riot of gold-tipped curls. He used the tendril to feather a caress across her cheek and over her ear. "I'm sorry about your hair."

And he meant it. That was the beauty of his plan. Everything he presented to the Mouse was heartfelt. All too real. She wouldn't be able to resist. But he knew the game he played was dangerous. Despite his own ready anger and need for freedom, those soft eyes tempted only too well. He warned himself not to forget how seductive she could be.

She took the curl of hair from his finger slowly, thoughtfully, not snatching it away as she might have before his little confession. "I don't care about my hair," she told him. "Not anymore." She seemed to think a moment, as if it were important that he understand what she said. "I think I learned *not* to need that long braid." And then she laughed, looking up at him. "If truth be told, it doesn't make us near even. After the mess I got you in."

"Things might not be so bad," he said softly. He cupped his hand around her cheek. His fingers strayed to the heat of her supple neck, making him wish for a mad instant that it were all true. That he and Leydianna were lovers, hidden away from Kincaid and the reality of his imprisonment. "No. It wouldn't be at all bad to be here with you."

"Don't," she said, turning her face away.

He grabbed her shoulder, forcing her to look back at him, not so gentle anymore. "I'm not playing games, Mouse." He bit the words out, giving her this much truth. "Not now. I want you. I think I have from the first. That's why I agreed to Stevenson's ridiculous suggestion to offer you employment. Well, I'm going to be just like our good lieutenant. I have my mission," he warned her. He tipped up her face to his. "And my mission is you."

"You don't need a mission. I want Kincaid to release you,"

she whispered. "I'll do my best to convince him; I just can't promise he'll listen."

"And escape?" he whispered, leaning down until only she could hear, his breath brushing against her cheek. "Will you help me escape?"

She closed her eyes, looking miserable. "I can't."

"Then I have a bit more persuading to do," he said, brushing his mouth across hers in a kiss that was all too real for the desire it promised.

She ducked under his arm and jumped out of the chair. She stood near the door, her shoulders shaking from her ragged breathing. She stared at him with luminous gray eyes. "You must think I'm a fool."

"Not hardly," he said, standing, his own breath as labored as hers from the aborted kiss. "Sometimes what I think is that you're absolutely irresistible," he allowed himself to say, not surprised that it was the truth.

He found he liked speaking to her like this. He wanted her; he was letting her know just how much. The circumstances gave him permission—forced his hand.

"I don't know how you do that," she said, shaking her head, perplexed. "Act so sincere. You must seduce a lot of women that way."

"I want to seduce only you, Mouse," he warned. "Given enough time, I'll succeed."

She crossed her arms over her chest, looking once again so endearingly prim. "Well, we shall just see about that. As I recall, your efforts were less than successful on St. Kitts."

He smiled. "I wasn't trying to seduce you then," he said almost gently. At the time he'd been trying to force her away before she drove him completely and utterly mad with her alluring innocence.

She frowned. "I'm not the silly nitwit you think I am."

"Just be my angel," he said, stepping back from the door, granting himself some distance. He'd delivered enough in this first volley—enough to challenge both of them. "You took me from them, after all. Just listen to me when I get lonely."

She stepped around Quentin, giving him a wide berth. As she

reached the door, she stopped, almost tripping. She peered down at the floor, then scooped up Nigel from the corridor, where she'd nearly stepped on him.

"I don't know how he got here. He never wanders into this house." She glanced over to Quentin, then down at the iguana. "You know, I think he actually likes you. How odd. He doesn't take to people often," she said, turning to go.

Quentin stopped her. "Leave him. Nigel and I understand each other," he said, taking the iguana from her with a smile, "Cold-blooded creatures that we are."

It wasn't right, what he was doing.

Felix sat on the edge of the bed, staring at the bare white-washed wall of the single-room hut. There was a guard outside the door. Peering through the slats of the louvered window, Felix had seen the man lounging in a cane chair, polishing his gun. Now, nearly an hour later, Felix waited on the quilted bedspread, mulling over his plots and plans for Gabriela.

It was one thing to kiss her, to acknowledge the honest emotion he'd experienced with her in his arms that dark night in the alley, to allow her image to fire his dreams at night. But to try to seduce her in order to escape, to use her in such a fashion, making her the brunt of the pirate's ill will—that sat none too well with him.

From the beginning there had been something between them, an attraction, a fire—enough to make him follow her that night and steal his kiss in the shadows of the colonnade. He imagined it had been the same for her. When he'd been tied on the beach, she'd kissed him as if she, too, were testing the limits of their attraction, wondering if it was there or imagined—feeling it burn between them. But those heated exchanges were different from what Quentin had asked of him.

He was to seduce her, trick her. Hide his true intentions to manipulate her into helping him.

It wasn't right.

Felix stood, beginning to pace the hard-packed clay floor. Reaching the wooden chest strapped with iron bands at the foot of the bed, he doubled back. He stared up at the beams of the thatched roof.

He knew only how to confront people with the truth. *What you do is bad, I'm here to stop you. I stand for good.* Even that first time, when she'd given him the rose, he'd left it behind, letting her know that her belief he was some smitten swain was false. It had been a warning. *I know what you're about, you and your mother. You can't hide from the consequences much longer.*

But now he was to hide everything, pretend it didn't matter that she was one of Kincaid's. He was to make her believe they could be close despite her connection to the pirate—when Kincaid made anything between them impossible.

There came the sound of the key turning. The door swung open on its hinges. Gabriela stepped inside and pocketed the key. She leaned back against the closed door, her arms crossed behind her.

"You asked for me?" she said.

He nodded, taking her in with one look. Despite everything, or perhaps because of it, the sight of her still took his breath away. She was dressed in a lime-green silk, the bodice and skirt trimmed with embroidered yellow daisies. Her hair was pinned back with pearl combs and the tight chestnut curls brushed against her shoulders. She was possibly the most beautiful woman he had ever seen.

On St. Kitts there were many women of color, and Felix found he had liked that. With their bright-hued kerchiefs turbaned around their heads, they'd sauntered down the streets with more assurance than the white settler women. They wore less packaging, were more honest with their womanly attributes. He liked the color of their skin, their full lips, and rounded shape, not hidden by a mountain of petticoats and ridiculous panniers.

But Gabriela was different. Different from the white settlers and the black women, free or slave. She dressed like the privileged class, but she wore her clothes as if the finery meant nothing to her. She had the airs of a queen. And looked it.

Felix sat back on the bed, drinking in the sight of her. He liked her color; she was all soft shades of the sweetest chocolate.

When he'd kissed her, he hadn't wanted to stop. He wanted to kiss her now.

Their eyes met in the soft light streaming in through the opened louvers of the windows. He questioned then if he was capable of anything other than honest emotions. He didn't know if he could pull off this charade and its calculated guile.

"Come here, Gabriela."

Gabriela ventured closer, keeping her head high, not wanting him to know how hard her heart pounded in her chest. The attraction between them was so powerful, it scared her. Forbidden passion.

So this is love. It wasn't what she'd thought. She hadn't opened her eyes one morning to find her knight hovering over her, as her grandmother had, but the emotion was no less powerful. The truth was, the forbidden love between a slave and his owner's niece had certain parallels with her own situation.

"You must know, I didn't mean to have you brought here," she told him.

"To Kincaid's den? To drop me into the hands of the man who would most likely destroy me?" *Even as he slaughtered my family?* "No," he said, shaking his head. "I don't think you intended my kidnapping here. Just as there was no plan to attack Kincaid," he said, holding her gaze, beguiled by those fantastic green eyes, "not yet, anyway. It was all a story concocted by Rutherford to impress your friend. But you weren't so far off in your suspicions. I plan to destroy Kincaid. I just haven't found the method."

There, he told himself. At least he could give her that much honesty. He was after Kincaid. *Beware.*

She nodded, taking it all in, saying nothing. She didn't even register surprise, just smiled. "I suppose I looked ridiculous, dressed up like a pirate." Instinctively, she raised her hand to brush the bruise on her cheek where he'd hit her.

"Does it still hurt?" He couldn't stand the thought that he'd actually struck her, even if he hadn't known it was Gabriela at the time. "Come closer," he said, gesturing toward the bed. "Let me touch you."

The same irresistible force drew Gabriela toward him, making her answer his summons. When she stopped within his reach, he took her hand and drew her so close that she stood between his legs, her knees beneath her gown resting against the bed rail.

Felix stayed seated on the edge of the bed with Gabriela nestled between his legs. Her muscles felt rigid with fear. She was staring straight ahead, over him, not daring to meet his eyes— but he didn't mind. He could see her chest rise and fall with each breath. He raised his hands and rested both on her hips, drawing her even closer, so they touched. She didn't try to pull away; he wouldn't allow it. Her breath grew labored. Like his.

His hands traveled up her hips, testing the softness of skin and bone beneath the fine silk of her skirt. She had wide hips; he liked that. One hand traveled across her stomach, delicately concave. His own breath came rushing through him as he caressed her. He stared up at her breasts, temptingly displayed in the neckline of her bodice. He wanted this woman more than anything. But he couldn't want her; he had to use her.

He buried his face against her breasts, wrapping his arms around her to her buttocks, pulling her against his body, embracing her. He felt her fingers dip into his hair, then brush it gently back.

"Will you let him kill me?" he asked, whispering against her warmth, pressing his cheek against the softness of her.

Gabriela wove her fingers through the thick red curls and brushed the tips across the spray of freckles on his nose. She knew then with a certainty that she'd had her deepest wish come true. Here, then, was her forbidden love. She traced the small scab where she'd struck him with the rock, sorry for that hurt.

True love. Hers for the taking. She just didn't think she had her grandmother's courage to embrace it.

"You would have hanged him," she said, continuing to stroke his hair, her fingers feathering across the puckered skin of the cut at his temple in apology.

"What hold does he have on you, Gabriela?"

She closed her eyes, wishing for the hundredth time that Kincaid had no hold on her at all. That he hadn't spent a lifetime caring for Bertie's physical needs as he broke both her and Gabriela's hearts. "It doesn't matter. I won't betray him for you."

"Will you let him kill me, then?" he asked again, this time meeting her eyes.

She cupped his face in her hands. "I won't have a say in the matter. I'm just his housekeeper."

"I'm not so easily deceived, Gabriela. Why would a servant dress up like a pirate and kidnap an officer of the navy to save a pirate's life?"

She pushed him away, breaking their embrace. "Because she's a fool."

He grabbed her hand before she could leave him. "I'll keep asking. I'll force you to choose between us, to choose me." And he meant it.

"Don't," she whispered, pulling her hand free and moving to the door. Just before she stepped outside, she whispered, "Don't make that mistake."

"But *why* can't you forgive me?"

Bertie looked into Hugh's handsome face. His pale blue eyes were fringed in dark black lashes so long and thick, they were wasted on a man. She sighed deeply. For the last ten minutes he'd begged for her forgiveness. The damned fool hadn't figured out his life was at stake, and it was well past time to stop his laments over the small loss of her love.

She almost told him as much, but caught her breath as he reached out and stroked her hand. His long, tapered fingers fluttered over her wrist, bringing her hand to his lips as he kissed her with that talented mouth. Hugh, quite unfortunately, continued to be utterly adorable and deceptively beautiful.

"Bertie, do you remember the night we met?"

"Oh, Hugh. *Basta*. Please stop this nonsense."

But he pulled her back into his arms before she could leave him and his pleas. They were inside the cottage where Hugh was being held prisoner. He'd washed and shaved and smelled endearingly of soap. She regretted answering his summons—it might prove too big a test to be alone with Hugh for so long.

With familiar intimacy he stroked the side of her breast just where she'd tucked her kerchief into the laces of the linen bodice. She slapped back his hand, the tantalizing gesture bringing back her sanity. Undeterred, he tugged her toward the tent bed—she pushed him away, giving him a long-suffering look.

Ever persistent, Hugh walked up behind her and kissed her neck. He whispered into her ear, "I'll never forget seeing you that first time at the Stone Elephant. Do you remember, *mon coeur?* You were seated in the corner, laughing that wonderful laugh of yours." His mouth brushed across her cheek; his hand wrapped around to her stomach. "I wanted you then, Bertie, just hearing you laugh. Just like I want you now." He kissed her ear, blowing gently.

Bertie gave him a good shove back with her elbow. Hugh landed with a thud and a curse against a sea chest at the foot of the bed.

"That is the *problema,* Hugh," she said tartly. "You hear a woman laugh, and you want her. You want everyone."

He stood and brushed off his jacket, restoring some dignity to his pose. "That is not true, my heart." For the first time, there was some force to his voice—enough to get Bertie's attention. "Be fair. I was faithful to you, Bertie. So I kissed a lady . . . or two. No one shared my bed those months we had together!"

Bertie looked at him wryly. "You are so serious. I almost believe you."

"Because it is true. Were we apart for even one night?" he demanded. "So Monique might turn my head for a bit. I'm a man, *non?* It did not mean I stopped loving you, Bertie."

Bertie sighed, disbelieving that she could actually forgive this scoundrel. Still, she wondered if she wasn't entirely to blame for her own heartbreak. Hugh was young, much younger than she. She really had no business loving him in the first place.

She reached up and stroked his cheek with a wistful smile. He grabbed her hand and kissed her wrist tenderly.

"Is all forgiven, then, *ma chérie?*" he asked.

"We shall see," she whispered. "Now, be a good boy and stay out of trouble before Kincaid gets back. Your Bertie will do her best to keep you safe, whether she forgives you or not."

"And the others, Bertie," he asked, now trailing kisses up her arm to the lace cuff at her elbow. "Rutherford and Bishop. Can you help them as well?"

Bertie frowned, then slowly extricated her hand from Hugh's loving kisses. "That, I cannot say. Watch yourself, Hugh. Do not link your fate to theirs," she warned.

Bertie stepped into the light of the courtyard and locked the door behind her. She smiled at Randy, who'd been assigned to guard Hugh, thanks to Consuelo's tinkering. Bertie and Consuelo together had decided the wardens chosen should be a bit on the lax side—perhaps allow the girls an opportunity to seek out their men in private. Walking down the crushed-shell path, she sighed, shaking her head at this nonsense. It was ridiculous that poor Hugh had landed in the middle of this mess.

She veered left, intending to stop by the kitchens to see how her daughter fared. She nodded a greeting to a passing group of men, then frowned. She hadn't any idea why Cy had taken Hugh in the first place, much less kept him prisoner. Still, as she snatched a blossom of white ginger and breathed in its spicy scent, she had to admit there was a naughty part of her that enjoyed his punishment. Serves him right for cheating on her.

In her musing, Bertie didn't see Cy step out from behind a vine-covered laurel. She almost collided into his substantial chest. "Cy, *querido*. Where did you come from?" she asked with a smile.

There was no answering grin from beneath Cy's red and gray beard. He stood glowering, his blue eyes narrowed on her, his arms crossed over his striped waistcoat. "I'm not sure 'tis the wisest course fer ye to be spending time with that fellow, Bertland. Don't ye be getting yer heart set on him. His fate is in Kincaid's hands."

"Bah! My Hugh is no threat," she said, taking the blossom of white ginger and tucking it behind Cy's ear. He snatched off the flower. His scowl deepened.

"Admit it, Cy. It is the other two who plotted against Daniel, *sim?*" Bertie twiddled her fingers in good-bye, continuing down the path to the kitchens. "Kincaid will release Hugh soon enough."

"The man's too young fer ye, Bertland," Cy said in a booming voice that echoed across the courtyard.

Bertie turned, surprised that her gentle Cy would stir himself so much against the harmless Frenchman. After a moment she merely shrugged her shoulders. "Most certainly he's too young. Still, one can't control one's heart." She kissed her fingertips and blew a kiss.

Cy remained on the path, watching Bertie's backside sway deliciously with her swing-hipped gait. He could hear her humming softly to herself. The enormous gold hoops in her ears flashed with a spark of sunlight.

"My Hugh." He said the name under his breath like a curse. He glanced back at the flower he still held and tucked it into the buttonhole of his waistcoat. "Damned woman."

Chapter Eighteen

Quentin broke off a piece of banana and handed the bit of fruit to Nigel. It was a blistering afternoon, the wind just enough to jostle the humid air around the courtyard in the semblance of a breeze. Quentin lounged beside Bishop and the Frenchman Piton under the shade of a banyan. The men used the enormous tree roots as seats, lying boneless against the smooth bark.

A gaggle of guards played dice nearby on a hard-packed patch of clay. Presumably, this troupe of sentries was carefully supervising Kincaid's precious cargo of prisoners. By the way the men roared with each roll of the dice, and the speed with which money exchanged hands, Quentin doubted if even a volley of cannon fire from an eighty-four gunner could wrest their attention from the game.

Quentin fed Nigel another chunk of fruit. The iguana sat perched on his shoulder, two dainty clawed paws of distinctive lime green visible where they hooked into the linen shirt at his collar. The iguana chewed languidly, the up and down motion of his jaws the beast's only movement. Today Nigel sported a forest-green ribbon, the same ribbon he'd dragged into Quentin's chamber that morning. Quentin had taken one look at the long band of satin dangling from Nigel's mouth and shrugged his shoulders. He'd tied the ribbon in a jaunty bow, happy to oblige the lizard's toilet, and then sat down to share his breakfast.

"If I ever get my hands on a gun," Hugh muttered in his lilting French accent, "I'm going to shoot me one of those parrots."

Quentin finished off the banana, tossing the peel to the basket of fruit at his feet. The soupy air of late afternoon misted over the hills beyond, threatening rain, keeping a constant crown of clouds surrounding the island's central peak. He peered at the drove of birds squawking discordantly from a vine-covered laurel. A week had passed since he'd been abducted to Kincaid's island and the Frenchman still complained about parrots.

"Every morning, *cawk cawk cawk!*" Hugh mimicked. "With the sun barely over the horizon."

"Must be a toil to wake up before the noon hour," Bishop said, goading Hugh, his habit of late.

Shooting the lieutenant a quelling look, Quentin told the Frenchman, "I'd think you'd be used to the noise by now."

"One shot . . ." Hugh pretended to aim down the sights of his finger. "One miserable shot, and I'd have them all gone."

Unhooking each of Nigel's claws, Quentin transferred the beast to his lap and leaned back against a tree root, one booted foot stretched out before him. He closed his eyes and took in a weary breath, wondering if the moist heat wasn't sapping every bit of strength from him as it fired Bishop's short fuse of a temper and dampened whatever dull senses the Frenchman had left. "How go things with Madame de Sousa?" he asked, stroking the spiny frill at the top of Nigel's head.

"*Comme ci, comme ça.* I think, with a bit more work, I am safe from Kincaid. But the two of you—" He shook his head, clucking his tongue. He graced Quentin and Bishop with a look he might save for a man destined for the gallows. "It does not look good, *mes amis.*"

"Listen to me, you French Casanova," Bishop spat out under his breath. "We're in this together. Don't try to make a deal for yourself."

"I take offense. I have done nothing but speak of your plight while romancing the woman I love—the woman I have loved from before this stupidity of yours landed me in Kincaid's sights."

"Both of you, be quiet," Quentin snapped, glancing up at the guards.

"No, he's right," Bishop said, bucking his shoulders up against a root. He dropped his head back as he turned a mango in his hands. "It's this damned heat that has me in such a foul mood. God, a man could boil in his own juices on this blasted island."

Quentin studied Bishop as the man peered listlessly at the mango he held. Quentin thought he would do well to take a bite instead of examining the fruit. The lieutenant was beginning to look rangy. The shirt and waistcoat he no longer bothered to button hung loose off his trim body, as if he'd lost weight through their ordeal. Even his hair seemed duller, now the shade of a dirty copper ha'penny.

"I can't help thinking it's not right, what we're doing," Bishop whispered, the lament a ballad repeated often the past four days.

"I'd rather break a few hearts than serve up my neck to that pirate," Quentin said. But his justifications were growing thinner with each passing day of the Mouse's smiles. "It's them or us, my fine friend," he said sharply, losing his patience with Bishop's tender conscience and its constant nudging of his own. "And I choose my own hide, thank you," he said, wondering even as he spoke how long that would hold true.

Bishop shook his head. "I wish I could be so certain."

"What could be more simple?" Hugh asked, not understanding Bishop's reluctance. "You make love to her—she helps you escape; to honor the love you share. *Voilà!* Everyone is happy, *non?*"

Bishop steeled his eyes on the piece of fruit as if the mango were a crystal ball holding vast secrets to their future success. "I make love to her. I use her love to gain my release. Then I leave her to face the consequences with Kincaid—a man who will most likely kill her for betraying him. Yes, everyone's happy indeed—"

"No one said you had to make love to her, for God's sake," Quentin said, cutting him off. "Be friendly. Is that too much to ask your puritan conscience?"

Bishop said nothing, just tossed the fruit again, catching it in one hand.

"What about you, *monsieur,*" Hugh asked. "How goes your pursuit?"

"Fine," Quentin barked out, stirring uncomfortably. Of late, his own qualms about seducing the Mouse had become a grating murmur he could not silence. He hadn't bloody well asked to be kidnapped, damn her!

Quentin crossed one jackboot over the other, trying to staunch the misgivings Bishop had managed to fire up despite Quentin's vigilance. For the love of God, he'd had enough jousts with his conscience to bear the burden of putting Bishop's at ease. When Kincaid showed up—oh, ho!—then all of Bishop's sentimental claptrap would disappear soon enough under that menace. Only, it would be too late.

Quentin glanced through slitted eyes at the kitchens where the women worked. Oh, yes, it was a simple thing to grow complacent with those fine ladies coddling them, bringing them oysters and tea with their bread and butter each morning or silver trays laden with fruit, touring them around the grounds of the compound on bended elbow—and Cy Cuthbert going along with this absurd farce like a doting uncle. But Quentin would not let down his guard.

This past week he had used every opportunity to get close to the Mouse, executing his plans with the finesse of an artist composing an aria. But too many times he found himself wondering who'd set the trap and who would step in its iron jaws.

He hadn't touched her—not since that first day when he'd tried to kiss her in Kincaid's house. He'd decided that given his own predilection to forget his plots and plans when he cuddled her warm in his arms, friendship was the best tool to seduce the Mouse. No need to share those kisses that threatened his sanity, whispering teasingly to forget escape. He knew the Mouse craved heart-searching truths. She wanted to dig inside his soul and make a home for herself there. And he planned to accommodate her wishes. In a day or so he'd display his past miseries for her to pore over like the pages of an insipid adventure novel. Only once she thought she'd secured her niche in his heart would she hand him the keys to this prison.

One thing threatened his plans: The Mouse wanted love. He could see that much from the way her eager eyes followed him. Quentin hoped the semblance of it would be enough. Yet, each day he played at their courtship, it became a bit more difficult not to return her soft looks—a little more enticing to make the emotion he played at real. The Mouse made him want to forget his own daunting past with love and its consequences.

Just this morning she'd sat across the table in her brown finery, detailing her secret plan to turn Kincaid and his men into planters—an enterprise whose success Quentin sincerely doubted. But he found it intoxicating to watch her chatter of her hopes and dreams for her island of pirates. Over tea she'd immersed herself in analyzing those silly drawings he'd played with during moments of boredom on St. Kitts. The progressive Miss Carstair seemed entranced by the idea that some magic machine might harvest the cane that now took the blood and sweat of so many slaves.

Oh, yes, his little Mouse and her pleasing attentions could be addictive.

"I'm setting my traps," he said to Hugh, knowing he must keep a tight rein on the Mouse's ability to twist reality into her make-believe. He must watch himself, be careful not to look forward so eagerly to their mornings of yarning over tea. After he left the Mouse's company, the loneliness of the past must be enough. "I plan to be well off this island before that pirate shows up." He watched Nigel scamper off toward the kitchens, green ribbon bobbing through the grass. He was probably bored with fruit and looking for better fare. "Tonight I might even do a bit of exploring."

"Don't they lock your room at night?" Bishop asked, tossing the uneaten mango back to the fruit basket.

"I'm trying out a new talent." Quentin took out a single hairpin from his pocket, careful that the guards not see it. He'd found it on the floor of his room beneath the bed. "I thought I might try a hand at the fine art of lock picking."

"Any success?" Bishop asked.

"Not yet. But I've time."

"And the guard?" Hugh whispered, leaning closer.

"Brody likes his rum," Quentin answered softly. "One way or another, I plan to get free of Kincaid—with or without the Mouse's help." He glanced away from Bishop, not quite able to meet the man's earnest gaze. "And I have no preference as to which. The end justifies the means, my friend."

"I don't suppose we can help them escape, or something like that?" Leydi asked, looking hopefully at the other women in the kitchen.

"Trust Daniel to do what's best," Consuelo said, helping Gabriela pour goat milk into a pine vat, where it would sit until it separated. Both women were dressed in simple wrap gowns draped with aprons, their hair protected by scarves. The task of making cheese was one they enjoyed doing together. Consuelo claimed her goat cheese the best to be had in the islands, the recipe she used of mysterious Greek origins.

"Trust Kincaid to do what's best for Kincaid," Gabby said, wiping her hands on her apron.

"What's best for all of us," Consuelo corrected her, "including the families who live on this island, for whom he is responsible. And what's best for you, my dear."

Gabriela turned away, checking on the whey that cooked over the kitchen fire in a black kettle hanging from a crane.

"Quentin's been so utterly wonderful these past days," Leydi said. She and Bertie were loading the thickened squares of cheese from the draining table into wooden barrels filled with brine. Fresh cheese already hung in cheesecloth in the pantry shed, the product of the morning's labors. "There's been no sign of Lord Ruthless. I'm certain it means he's up to something. It's not as if he would suddenly want to be my friend."

But she wished in her heart it could be otherwise. Over the past days, bringing him breakfast, showing him the grounds, she'd discovered a man she wished she could call friend. Gone were the red-rimmed eyes of sleeplessness, the cutting slice of his sarcasm. The new Quentin laughed and told charming stories about his boyhood in the country. He listened and asked questions as if his entire day revolved around her visits. There seemed no sign of the cynical sensualist hiding behind his vicious silences when you dared to pry into his secrets. A man who would fashion a gift in vengeance for some imagined wrong.

But Leydi warned herself not to be gulled by these mysterious changes. She was through daydreaming. She brushed aside a sweaty curl from her forehead with her sleeve and sighed. "I almost wish he did try to coax me into helping him escape. Then at least I would know what was going on in that devious head of his."

"He will ask," Consuelo said sagely. "You are all that stands between him and Kincaid. It is not wise to believe his motives are other than self-serving."

Leydi dropped into a cane chair at the draining table. She puffed out her cheeks in a long, slow breath. "I feel like the farmer fattening the goose for Michaelmas. I'm making them comfortable—but for what?"

"Kincaid will not kill them, *menina,*" Bertie said, shaking her head so her gold hoops swung against her cheeks. "Not if Consuelo and I have anything to say about it."

All four women remained quiet, the silent *marooning* hanging in the air with the salty-sour scent of warming goat milk and brine.

Leydi stood. She scooped up the last squares of cheese ready to be barreled. "Nigel loves him. He can't be all bad. Perhaps we can try a compromise of sorts," she said, suddenly coming up with an idea. "We could convince all three to swear fealty to Kincaid. They could become one of his men! Then Kincaid wouldn't have to do anything to them."

From her place at the hearth, Gabriela looked unconvinced. "Bishop has a personal vendetta against Kincaid; I'm sure of it. And your Rutherford is too rich to turn his back on his island kingdom."

"There are not enough women on this island for Hugh," Bertie said with a sigh.

"There must be something," Leydi said, turning imploringly

to each woman. "Something we can do. And soon. We can't just sit here like silly geese waiting for Kincaid to do his worst."

But no one had an answer to her silent plea. The lone strategy seemed to wait . . . wait for Kincaid and his questionable wisdom. Only Leydi knew how close she was to falling prey to Quentin's overwhelming niceness.

The past days she admitted she'd let her guard down. If he'd tried to seduce her, playing his sensual games as he'd done on St. Kitts, she could have fought that. But what he'd done was much more subtle, more devious. So much more effective.

Leydi remembered just that morning watching him share his breakfast with Nigel when she'd come hunting the culprit down. Gabriela's drawer had been pilfered through, a ribbon stolen. From past experience, both women recognized the iguana's handiwork. But when she'd stopped at Quentin's door, about to ask if he'd sighted the iguana, she'd found Quentin tying on the green satin bow, telling Nigel how handsome he looked.

Leydi had stayed in the shadow of the open door, feeling as if a gentle hand had taken her heart and squeezed. For a moment she'd watched silently as Quentin tempted the iguana with a bit of biscuit slathered with cream. Both had looked absolutely endearing.

She didn't want him to be so likable. It made her want to believe these changes weren't so much out of character. She'd seen the seeds of this man during her hours of working beside him on St. Kitts. It was such a simple matter to believe he'd merely found peace on Devil's Gate, as she had these many years—so tempting to think the old Lord Ruthless wouldn't return.

She touched her hair, forcing herself to remember the missing braid.

"I hope Kincaid comes soon," she said, almost voicing her concerns that despite all her effort to the contrary, she was slowly but surely being lulled from her vigilance against Quentin.

Quentin scooped the small hoard of gold and silver coins to his side of the walnut table. In the past three nights he'd been able to win enough money to pay back the stake Cy had given him, and then some. But the game was winding down now, it being well past midnight. The four remaining players huddled around the card table, drinking rum. Some lay tipped back in their chairs, balancing on two legs—others fiddled with the coins heaped before them. Each showed signs of growing restless as their eyes shifted lazily around the confines of the single-room hut.

Quentin began stacking his coins methodically, thinking he could grow fond of the nightly games. It almost felt like the old days in London, when his greatest worry in the world was whether to visit the Mermaid Tavern or some other gaming hell. Back home on St. Kitts, most all the entertaining he did involved business—the company boring and with little talent for any game other than whist.

"Ye've the devil's own luck," Cy said, taking a puff from his long pipe.

Brody, the young towheaded buccaneer who normally guarded Quentin, stuffed a hand inside his waistcoat and scratched his stomach. He tossed the cards on the table. "I'll say."

"There's only one other that does this well at the table," Cy said.

The door creaked open on its iron hinges, capturing the attention of those in the room. Leydi stood framed in the doorway, the moonlight silhouetting her delicate features. A low groan swelled from the men.

Cy laughed. "Speak of the devil . . . Leydi, me darling. Come in, gel. But yer too late to fleece us this night. Rutherford has picked us clean, I'm afraid."

Leydi strolled in almost hesitantly and rounded the table. Her fingers dusted across the scarred walnut as she smiled a greeting to each man. She was dressed in her typical brown. The curls of her hair peeked out from the frill of her mobcap, sweeping in tendrils to brush her cheeks. The flickering tallow candle cast tempting shadows across her mouth, catching the dimple in her chin.

Quentin wondered if he didn't perhaps like her better with

her hair short, all soft and flowing. When it was long, she kept it tied up in a braid. The free curls made her look more a woman and less the child. In the candlelight she seemed like some romantic Titian painting come to life to tempt him.

"Will you join us?" Quentin asked, the blood rushing through him, his body already anticipating having her near.

"No," she said, shaking her head. "I just came to say good night."

With a wave to all, she turned to leave. Immediately, Quentin stood, tossing his cards to the table. "I'll call it a night as well, then."

"Brody," Cy said, nodding to the man who usually guarded Quentin.

"I think Miss Carstair could do an admirable job of putting me to bed," Quentin said with a grin.

His joke failed miserably. All four players seated around the table—the very men who just minutes earlier had joked affably, treating him as if he were one of them—suddenly looked like dogs with their hackles up. Hostile expressions steamed from every corner. Ethan, a singularly tall black who wore only a waistcoat to display his admirable musculature, picked his large white teeth with the blade of his knife.

"Then again," Quentin added with a shrug, "Brody has a certain flair for the task. Come along, then," he said, gesturing to the man.

The tension in the air evaporated. A few men actually grinned as they, too, tossed down their cards. Quentin took in this new piece of information. Whatever Leydi was to Kincaid, every man in that room gave her importance beyond that of a bookkeeper.

As all three walked across the courtyard, the night filled with the music of frogs accompanied by the percussion of insects. The grass was still wet from a late evening shower, sparkling like diamonds dusted with moonlight. Quentin watched Leydi walking beside him. He tried to dissect the reaction of Kincaid's men, a reaction of which she seemed completely unaware. There was something heartfelt about the men's loyalty to her, a protective air that had come from each and every tar in that room.

God knew she was a likable thing, he thought, not without

some anger, because right now he didn't want to like her. He wanted to be cold and calculating, able to forget Bishop's warnings of what doom his plans could bring her.

They continued down the crushed-shell path toward the main house. Quentin hadn't known he was frowning until he chanced to see Leydi giving him a tentative smile. She arched her delicate brows in a questioning glance. He grinned back, telling himself he needed to be more careful.

When she turned to follow the fork in the path leading to her own cottage, Quentin grabbed her hand. He gave her fingers a quick squeeze and tugged her to his side, motioning with his head that she should follow.

In the dark Brody noticed nothing. Nor did he object to Leydi's decision to help deliver Quentin to his room. Exceedingly glad she'd followed, Quentin marched silently beside her. It seemed that when his conscience pinched, he became his most devious, as if he were warning himself it was time to tell his nobler side to be damned.

It didn't take long to reach the sprawling cottage-style home. As far as Quentin could figure, the three prisoners were being housed as far apart from one another as possible. As he'd told the others, he planned to make use of his particularly prime location. He'd thought at first to pick the lock. But now he had quite another plan.

As they neared his chamber, snaking down the narrow hall, Leydi fell into step beside him. Brody walked a few steps back, whistling tunelessly. Quentin glanced down at the Mouse. Catching her eye, he whispered just loud enough for only her ears, "I'm getting lonely again; I miss my angels."

As they reached the door, Quentin spun her around. Bracing her up against the door, he whispered in her ear, "You have the key to my heart, and Brody snores—very loudly."

He kissed her soundly on the cheek, making a loud smacking noise.

"Hey now!" Brody shouted.

Quentin stepped back, whispering, "Hit me."

The Mouse stared at him blankly. She blinked her eyes, reaching to touch her cheek where he'd kissed her. She looked adorably like a sleeping damsel waking from her long vigil of waiting for her knight. He mouthed the words *hit me* again, trying with his eyes to show his urgency.

She seemed to catch on. Biting her lip, she swung her hand back and let loose. She slapped him hard, belting him across the cheek with a resounding *crack!*

The strength of the blow took him by surprise. He actually took a step back, nearly colliding with Brody, now rushing to Leydi's side.

Quentin stroked his burning cheek and grinned. "You must have wanted to do that for some time."

"Serves ye right," Brody said from behind Leydi, his hand falling protectively on her shoulder.

"You can't blame a man for trying," he told Brody with a wink. To Leydi he granted one lingering glance, hoping he'd set the bait. "Good night, then."

Brody closed the door behind him. Hearing the key grind in the lock, Quentin propped a shoulder against the door and smiled.

Chapter Nineteen

Leydi listened to Brody's rhythmic snores tunneling down the corridor. She pressed her cheek to the gooseneck of the stair's railing, still disbelieving that she had come. But she found she couldn't deny Quentin his simple request for company. She opened her hand and stared down at the key in her palm.

The key to his heart, indeed! She grimaced. She knew exactly what key he'd wanted.

She closed her fingers around the cold bit of iron. Its skeletal edges bit into her palm. Perhaps she was just fooling herself claiming it was for Quentin's sake that she was there. The truth could be that she enjoyed too well the thought that she was special—that she could make herself indispensable to him. *Be my angel.* She sighed, clutching the key to her chest. Yes, the task was too tempting to resist.

Taking a deep breath, she hiked up the remaining steps and skirted the corner, checking first to see if the coast was clear. Only Cy stayed in Kincaid's house while the pirate was out on the account. Consuelo had her own house elsewhere on the compound. And Cy's quarters were safely ensconced in the opposite wing on the first floor. The snoring Brody would be her only challenge in this gauntlet.

Leydi inched down the Chinese runner toward the guard's slumbering figure. Brody's arms crossed over his wrinkled waist-coat. He smelled of rum and tobacco and sat deep in the cane chair, his head buried to his chin in the collar of his shirt. Leydi tiptoed around him and stabbed the key into the lock. Twisting the key slowly, she winced when it made a soft *click*.

Brody remained asleep, the satisfied smile of a child wreathing his face.

Leydi opened the door and slipped inside. She eased the door shut behind her and crossed her arms behind her back. Quentin sat on the bed, propped against the headboard on a mountain of pillows. He wore only his shirt and breeches. His waistcoat lay abandoned at the footboard; he'd opened his collar far enough to display the shadowed planes of his chest. His ebony hair remained tied in its queue and one booted ankle hooked over the other in repose. With the light of a single candle flickering across his face, he looked like an enticing satyr.

"I expected you much earlier than this," he said.

Leydi grimaced. And then she bit back a laugh. Rutherford looked so sure of himself, like an arrogant king on his throne instead of a prisoner locked in for the night. Sometimes his bra-zenness actually struck her as funny.

"Well, I'm here now," she said. "But only for a short while, so get on with this confession that couldn't wait until morning."

He patted the spot next to him on the mattress. The gesture seemed out of place after four days of friendly smiles and casual conversation—teasing, like the old Quentin. There was a still-ness to him, too, like a predator making ready to pounce. She searched his eyes. In the dim light they looked quite black, with-out a hint of redeeming blue.

A hollowness pitted her stomach. Perhaps her musings of the morning had been answered, then. Lord Ruthless was back.

He patted the bed again, smiling almost playfully this time. She sat down on the chair near the door, plucking at the fringe of the seat.

Quentin arched a single brow, then glanced at the empty space beside him on the yellow counterpane. "How . . . disappointing."

"I'm listening," she prompted. "You said you needed your angels?"

His eyes seemed to study her for a moment, his gaze growing impossibly darker with some deep emotion. Any semblance of humor vanished. The change was compelling enough that she sat forward in the chair, wanting suddenly to comfort him even before she knew what was amiss.

"It's Bishop. I'm concerned about him." He kept his voice low, evenly paced, yet she sensed a pulse of distress underlying the words. "He doesn't eat. I'd say he doesn't sleep much either, by the looks of him. And . . . I think it might be my fault."

She slipped the key in her pocket and wet her lips. "And why would you think that?"

"Because I've asked him to do something displeasing to him. Something that grates against his good character—his sense of right and wrong. I think it's . . . affecting him."

She told herself not to ask, to keep quiet and not challenge him. She didn't want to be reminded they were at odds on this island. But the question came out just the same. "What did you ask him to do, Quentin?"

The glimmer of candlelight played over the stern planes of his face. There was no other movement in the room. The chamber was so utterly quiet; only the dim hum of insects and swaying palms invaded the silence. And then he smiled. "I'm afraid I must keep that small confession to myself."

"You're up to something," she charged.

The smile turned into a full-fledged cocky grin. "But of course."

Leydi flopped back into the depths of the chair and stretched her hands along the cool walnut arms. She knew that look—the tactician at work. She wouldn't get anything more from him.

It made her sad, this struggle between them. But then she reminded herself of her purpose there. "If you're truly worried, why not let him do as he pleases?"

Quentin shook his head. "I can't."

There came no other clarification—just that. *I can't.*

The silence implied so much. I can't. *I need his cooperation for my dastardly plan of escape to work. I can't care about a man's conscience.*

Leydi shook her head, trying to silence her fanciful thoughts. She pulled at the fringe of the seat, telling herself to be sensible; she could read silence no better than she could read Quentin's mind. She took a moment to study him. He looked troubled, sitting there in the darkness of his bed as if he were waiting for her to condemn him. As if he condemned himself. She wanted to reach out and smooth those lines bracketing his mouth, rub away the deep grooves between his eyes that spoke of pain and regret.

Leydi bit back a sigh, losing the battle inside her that said *beware!* She couldn't help but want to give solace despite the fact she suspected it might not be in her best interest.

"Gabriela seems to have taken a liking to him. Perhaps I can ask her to try and cheer him up?"

He seemed to think over her suggestion, his azure eyes glittering in the candlelight. "I think that would be an excellent idea." And then he smiled, the gesture sweet and simple, bringing a dimple to the corner of his mouth. The cynicism of the past no longer tainted his face. His boyish grin charmed. "You're better than my angels, Mouse. They seldom talk back. They leave me to interpret their somber painted faces for my answers."

Mouse. The way he said it, almost like a caress, the name no longer sounded silly or disparaging. He spoke it intimately—as if marking her his with the special sobriquet.

"Anything else?" she asked, standing, feeling suddenly too warm.

"Don't leave," he whispered, the sound itself seductive. "Not yet."

"I really must."

But she didn't move, didn't breathe. She only waited, the entreaty in his voice acting as an anchor. It was then that her worst misgivings were confirmed. She'd known it was a mistake to come. Four days now she'd thought of this man as a friend. Four days, and she'd let down her guard.

"Come here." He held his hand out to her, still lounging back on his throne of pillows. "Come closer."

She stood perfectly still, unable to move. She'd never had a moment of indecision in her life. A reasonable person needed only look at the alternatives to determine a sensible course of action. So why was she paralyzed with indecision? Her head told her to leave; her heart to walk to the bed. Instead of doing either, she remained rooted to her place next to the chair.

He kicked his feet over the bed and stood. One slow step after another, he came toward her. He seemed to be giving her time to change her mind, to shoot for the door and lock them apart. But she stayed exactly where she was, like the scared little mouse he'd named her, waiting for the trap to snap shut.

Quentin stopped beside her, standing close, so very close. Leydi shut her eyes against her fears. She bit her lips to stop her protest. She waited, waited for his touch, knowing deep in her heart that no matter what the cost, it was what she wanted.

When it came, it wasn't what she expected. The gentle stroke of his fingers on her cheek wasn't lightning burning her to a crisp where she stood. It was warm and respectful and a little familiar.

"Should I try to persuade you? Is that what you want from me, Mouse? God, I see it so clearly in your eyes," he said against her cheek as if he, too, were fighting the attraction. Both his hands fell warmly to her shoulders. She heard him curse softly and murmur something like "So much for good intentions."

He eased her closer to his body. His breath was warm against her face and smelled sweetly of rum. "If you wish it. I can make you want to stay. But only if you wish it, Mouse," he whispered like a lament. "Only if you think it's right."

Leydi pressed her eyes closed, fisting her hands against her sides. She thought of all her knight-in-shining-armor dreams. That once-faceless man now wore Quentin's aristocratic features, granted only his arrogant smiles.

Suddenly, she could remember only the good times. Going over his books, the many instances he'd asked for her opinions, making her feel he respected her. Making her feel an equal. It was probably the most seductive thing he'd done her entire stay at Rutherford Hall. Not seductive in the sense of this night, or his kisses. But to earn the respect of a man she so admired was something very powerful indeed. Something she'd forgotten to shield herself against.

A new tension sprang to life between them. It was as if she couldn't find the strength to lift her hand and take his fingers from her cheek. And her passivity had nothing to do with the safety of Kincaid's house, or Brody sleeping in the hall. She felt not the least bit safe.

"What are you thinking, Mouse?" he asked softly, his eyes on her mouth.

"That I should leave. That I'm no match for you and I was wrong to think I was. That you frighten me."

"No," he shook his head, his thumb brushing across her bottom lip. "Don't be frightened, my intrepid little soul. You're more than a match for me." He leaned forward, closer still, his breath brushing her mouth. "And it's only a kiss."

She murmured a protest, taking a step back.

"Shhh," he said, settling his lips over hers, holding her gently but firmly by her chin. "I'll be quick." He caressed her mouth with his. "I'll be nice."

Everything inside Leydi stilled, her breath, her pulse, her heart. It felt so delicious, the warmth of him against her, his mouth touching hers. He was so *solid,* a wall of heat she wanted to embrace. But she didn't move, just waited, feeling the tingling radiate from her stomach to the rest of her body.

"Is it nice?" he whispered, his mouth still brushing lightly against hers. "Am I being good?" he asked, slanting to give a much more intimate kiss, coaxing her to open her mouth for him. And she did, dying just a little as she felt his tongue smoothly kiss hers. "Put your arms around me, Mouse. Touch me."

She wanted to, but a lead-shot heaviness stayed her hands. She barely inched her fingers up his chest, resting her palms on the hard muscle beneath the linen as her breath came in heavy pants. The feel of him beneath her fingers tempted her to explore; she wanted to touch him there, where the collar of his shirt parted to expose his skin. And that's what truly frightened her.

With a strangled groan she pushed him away. She spun around and stared at the toes of her shoes, catching her galloping breath. They were the same sensible brown shoes she'd always thought so fitting for a bookkeeper. But now they pinched her toes and looked terribly out of place next to Quentin's fine polished boots.

Dear Lord, what can I say to him? How could she explain without sounding like a total fool?

"Enough, is it?" he asked, seeming to read her very thoughts. When she didn't answer, he turned her back to him and tipped up her face. "I said I'd be nice." He spoke the words softly and with a smile.

"I came here only to be your angel," she told him, knowing in her heart she'd just betrayed Kincaid in some awful, awful way. That things could never be the same and she could never trust herself to have Kincaid's best interest in her heart. She'd wanted that kiss, and now Quentin knew it. "I came only to talk, so you wouldn't feel lonely. I can't help you escape from here no matter what happens between us. So you can just stop trying to seduce me—"

He placed a finger across her lips. He looped a curl around her ear. "When you come tomorrow," he said. "Bring a deck of cards."

She snapped her eyes open. She craned her head up to his. She tried to register his words, running through them in her head. *Cards? Cards!* He'd just honed in for the kill. She stood before him, wood for the fire, virgin to be sacrificed—she'd just made her terrible confession by allowing his kiss. And he wanted to play cards?

"W-what?"

"When you come tomorrow," he said slowly, steering her toward the door, "bring a deck of cards."

And that was all he said before he opened the door and scooted her out into the hall, shutting the door behind her.

Gabriela stood in the shadow of the vines covering the majestic laurel. By the light of the moon she could just make out the thatched roof and daub and wattle walls of Samuel and Ken's cabin. Both men were gone to the Pacific, seeking booty with Kincaid. But the cabin wasn't empty. Felix was locked inside.

It wasn't the first time she'd stood hidden in the night, smelling the orchids and fresh rain. Outside the cabin, leaning back in his chair, Martin—the man guarding Felix—had fallen asleep. *Too much rum, no doubt.* And Gabriela should know. She'd brought him the bottle now lying empty beside his chair.

She leaned back, deeper into the shadows. *Be careful what you wish for*—no truer words had ever been spoken. Inside that hut Martin guarded what was surely the end of her dreams.

The past days she'd tried to convince herself she was being ridiculous. You couldn't just look into a man's face and know you loved him. There had to be more.

Perhaps it wasn't love at all that brought her there, but hate. Perhaps in some horrible way she was trying to get even with Kincaid for what he'd done to her and her mother. It could be revenge that made her fall for a man sworn to see Kincaid hanged. Maybe now, after all the years of swallowing angry words, she was too filled up with bitterness. She might actually try to hurt Kincaid.

But she knew that wasn't true. What she felt for Felix was like the breeze on your cheek, the rhythm of music inside your heart. It wasn't something devised, rather something that just existed. Like the color of her skin. At last she'd found what her mother had always called the "missing half."

Martin shifted, snorting in the moonlight. Gabriela stilled, but he fell back into a contented sleep. She took a breath and stepped forward, telling herself it was now or never.

Quickly, Gabriela raced to the cabin. She jammed the key she'd taken into the lock, turned it with a quick prayer. When she'd opened the door, she threw herself inside and shut it. She pressed against the door, waiting for Martin to sound the alarm, for sounds of discovery. Nothing.

The room was lit by a single tallow candle. Felix was in bed, propped up against the headboard, reading a book. He looked tired. And she knew why. Unlike Gabriela, he was fighting this attraction between them.

He shut the book and swung his legs over the bed. He didn't look the least bit surprised to see her. She walked toward him slowly, now suddenly afraid of the choices she'd made. Perhaps if Leydi hadn't sneaked out before her—if her friend had stayed behind to give her strength not to come.

But then Felix opened his arms, as resigned as she to the inevitable. Seeing the desire in his eyes, she knew nothing Leydi could have done would have made a difference. She flew across the room into his embrace.

They kissed as if the touch of their mouths were air for breathing. They touched as if they were old lovers who'd finally come together after too many years apart. As he slowly leaned back into the bed, Gabriela followed, no longer afraid, knowing that she had made the right choice after all.

"I'll make you forget him," Felix whispered harshly as he pushed the sleeves of her gown off her shoulders. "Whatever hold he has on you, I'll break it."

Gabriela shut out his words with her kisses, pushing his shirt off his body. She blinked back the tears, knowing he was speaking of Kincaid. As he kissed her, he stroked her breast with a possession that burned like fire. But she knew no matter how much she loved Felix, no one could ever break Kincaid's hold on her. She'd tried for years and failed.

The day was fair; the sun was bright. As far as Hugh Piton was concerned—in spite of capture and captivity—all was right in the world.

He whistled as he made his way to the kitchens, his guard but a few steps behind him speaking amiably to a comrade. Every tree, flowering bush, and blade of grass sparkled with morning dew in the courtyard. To Hugh, his step seemed lighter than air. He thought he might just float away in his happiness. He didn't even mind the shrieks of the parrots.

Last night, just after walking him back to the cabin where he was locked in for the night, Bertie had kissed him.

Grâce a Dieu, she'd forgiven him.

Oh, she hadn't quite realized it yet, but it was just a matter of time before she was back in his arms—and in his bed—for good. And this time he wouldn't ruin things. He wouldn't so much as look at another woman. Bertie and he belonged together. She was the love of his life. He knew that now, after almost losing her. No other woman would do. He just needed to convince Bertie that he could be true.

He frowned. He'd best get to the convincing part fast. If he wanted to help Rutherford and Bishop, that was. Certainly, once he had Bertie in hand, she could convince these pirates to let the men go. They were good sorts, those two. Hardly any threat to Heartless Kincaid.

Hugh crossed his arms behind him and smiled grandly. Why, they were all as good as free now that he had the love of his life back. Perhaps he would even ask her to marry. Yes, that's what he'd do, Hugh thought, already thinking of Bertie dressed in white with orange blossoms in her curls. He'd get her to marry him and then—

"Ah!"

The blow was quick and unexpected. A body slammed into his. Oranges flew everywhere. But it wasn't fruit he felt against his chest. He recognized the enticingly soft shape of two breasts immediately.

A high-pitched squeal sounded like a whisper in his ear. He removed his hands instantly, as if he'd just touched red-hot coals and not delicious ripe flesh. A delightful giggle followed, floating like music in the air.

"Pardon, Mademoiselle."

He didn't so much as look at her, sensing the danger. He quickly dropped to his knees and helped the young woman pick up the oranges, scrambling alongside her for the fruit. Quite by accident he turned, catching sight of the most incredibly luscious backside surrounded by a calico skirt.

He took a gulp of air, steadying himself as the lovely blonde turned around. Her blouse dipped enticingly, revealing two beautiful breasts. They were the most exquisite breasts he had ever seen. Globes of milk-white perfection.

The air caught in his throat. Two dark green eyes like jewels blinked up at him, surrounded by thick golden lashes. Her lips, rosy like the petals of a flower, curved in an impish smile. She giggled again, a sound that traveled up his spine to the tip of his head.

The image of Eve held out an orange and whispered, "Hello."

He couldn't speak. He couldn't breathe. Perfection stood before him in all her radiant female glory.

A horrible sense of doom flooded Hugh as he stood and watched Eve walk away, her hips swinging, the curls of blond silk bobbing beneath the lace pinnet. He watched all his wonderful plans of the morning shimmering like a mirage, slowly disappearing.

He wasn't going to rescue his newfound friends.

He wasn't going to help Rutherford and Bishop at all.

He wasn't going to help himself.

They were doomed by the beautiful beguiling smile of the wench sashaying away from him, blowing him a kiss over her shoulder as she balanced a basket of oranges on her oh-so-lovely hip.

Chapter Twenty

Quentin watched Leydi shuffle the cards. The stack glided from one palm to the other in a perfect stream. Using one hand, she cut the deck, cut it again, each time folding the stacks into each other without so much as a stutter in her rhythm.

"Play often, do you?" he asked, his tone dry.

She slowed her shuffling, looking down at her fingers as if just realizing what she was doing. "Yes . . . I suppose I do, actually."

"Well. That should make things interesting." Quentin pushed back the walnut chair from the chest of drawers they were using as a table, the chair's fanciful fringe swinging with the movement. He stood and walked to the washstand next to the bed. He reached into the cabinet below the drawer and brought out his own little surprise, a bottle of rum and a dram glass. "I'm glad you're familiar with the game. I never enjoy an easy win."

"So sure of yourself?" she asked, watching the bottle.

"Of course." He placed the bottle on the chest of drawers. Shards of light shone off the green glass with thc candlelight dancing over the oyster veneer. "A little concession I won from Cy in a game myself," he said with a wink. "I hope you'll join me?" He wagged the tumbler before her eyes. "Though I have only the one glass."

"Do you plan to get me drunk?"

He grinned. "Most certainly."

He could almost see the wheels turning in her head, calculating what she should do about this new turn of events. She wanted to stay—he guessed that much from the way she bit her lip and gripped the cards—but she also knew it would be more prudent to leave him and his rum alone.

He allowed her to think about it a moment longer before he tipped the scales in his favor. In planning the events of this night, he'd managed to allay his fears about the misstep of the previous night's kiss. That tiny loss of control had not cost either him or the Mouse too dearly. And he had himself well in hand now. Within two glasses of rum, the Mouse would be sleeping in the chair while he explored Kincaid's house, using the key now in her pocket.

"Come now," he coaxed her, "Cy says you enjoy brag. Perhaps I might convince you to stay . . . if the stakes are right."

He could see he'd captured her interest. She lay the deck facedown on the chest of drawers, sitting back on the stool she'd pulled over.

"The winner of each hand," he said, "can ask the loser one question, and the loser must answer truthfully. Now, does that intrigue you enough to risk me and my rum," he said, pulling the cork and pouring a drink.

He knew he'd dangled a rather large carrot before her curious eyes. In the past she'd studied him as if he were a nice puzzle box she'd like to unlock. He gambled she wouldn't be able to resist the temptation of asking her questions.

The trick, of course, was not to let the Mouse become the puzzle, and he, the intrigued.

Too often he'd found himself pondering about this woman, and his curiosity had nothing to do with getting off Kincaid's island. Her occupation. Her connection with the infamous pirate. Her obvious influence—as well as how ignorant she seemed of that power—made her deceptively intriguing. He admitted he'd become fascinated. It made him want to ask a few questions of his own, a temptation he must arm himself against.

He rocked the bottle back and forth as he waited for her answer. She bit her lip, the gesture making her look quite adorable.

"All right," she said with a nod, beginning to pass out the cards. "But I warn you. I'm rather good."

"I love a challenge." He held the dram glass out for her. "Ladies first."

Leydi drank a sip as Quentin arranged his cards. "Of course," he said, "we could always play for kisses."

Leydi choked on the rum, making him smile. He enjoyed the teasing. He thought if he could make fun of the attraction between them, he could certainly control it.

"If I lose," he said with a straight face, "you kiss me. If you lose, I kiss you."

She had to laugh, he was so outrageous. She continued to drink the rum slowly. "I think that sounds all to your benefit."

"Not at all, Mouse. I'm rather good at kissing."

They way he spoke made Leydi entirely too warm. She knew she was blushing. To cover up, she belted back the rum and handed him the empty glass.

"I'll take the former stakes," she said with as much sophistication as she could muster. "I have some excellent questions."

Quentin barely managed to keep his bland expression as he watched her toss back the rum. No choking, no gasping. Just a smooth, even swallow. But he didn't say a word. Instead, he filled the glass again and drank a bit himself, thinking his plans wouldn't take long. Yes, indeed. Soon enough he'd have the Mouse snuggled in the chair, her sweet snores sounding like the finest music.

"You won't cheat, will you?" she asked, her brow arched.

She waited for her answer, quite sincere and expecting an honest response. Quentin bit back a smile, her question was so naive.

He planned to cheat all right, but not the way she thought.

He already knew how to steal her loyalty from Kincaid. He'd calculated it like a formula. She wanted to get to know him, to find out all his hidden truths and unearth the secrets of the intriguing drama her fertile imagination had cooked up for him. He would play this card game and offer her the real Quentin. A man the Mouse would need to help and rescue.

The rum, of course, would help ease out those hurtful truths—and a few other things. He'd keep her drinking, letting her win game after game as he satisfied her curiosity. Once he had her good and soused, he'd take the key and have a look around Kincaid's lair while she slept.

Oh, he planned to cheat all right.

"A gentleman never cheats," he said.

The first round progressed smoothly enough. She unfortunately dealt him a rather good hand, but Quentin was able to discard the pair of kings and was gratified to receive a set of mismatched low numbers. She beat him handily with a pair of tens.

Leydi glanced up, her excitement and the rum shining in her eyes. She nibbled on her plump bottom lip, a habit Quentin was finding quite charming.

He drank slowly from the glass. "Well, well. I believe the game is yours."

"Your father," she said breathlessly. "Why are you estranged?"

He raised his brows, feigning surprise. "Allow us to warm up to the game a bit, please."

"You didn't set any limits on the questions."

"No, I did not." Because he hadn't wanted any. He'd wanted to dish himself up before her, tell her all those ugly truths that she would no doubt twist in her hero's heart to be something warm and sympathetic.

He sighed, knowing he'd gotten what he'd wanted. And still, it was difficult to speak about Clarice, the baby—his father—even as he guessed it was the sort of sordid tale that would win Leydi's heart. If he told it right. If he told it all.

He watched the clear liquid swirl in the glass, almost frowning. He'd been so angry when he'd hatched his plans against the Mouse. It was a funny thing, that anger. So real, making him feel alive. Making him care. He hadn't realized how invigorating his scheming would feel after the past listless years of making only money.

How odd that the thought of Clarice could bring back the guilt-ridden heaviness of the past so easily. He seemed to feel it like a shroud clouding over him. Even as he tried to launch into the story, the words seem to back up in his throat. *Ah, the truth. The god-awful truth of his past.*

"Pick another," he said, surprising himself.

She shook her head, pressing him. "I won. I want my answer."

He leaned forward. "Are you sure you won't settle for a kiss?" He puckered up.

She clasped his hand, firmly locking her fingers around his. Her eyes were steady and not without sympathy. It actually surprised him the way she gripped his palm in so strong a gesture. At the moment she didn't seem the least afraid of him. And she showed no hesitation when she shook her head.

Quentin played with her fingers, forcing her to withdraw her hand when he tried to kiss it. He sighed playfully, then glanced back at his glass. "I haven't drunk enough yet," he stalled, convincing himself it would be best to save his story until the Mouse had drunk more, become a bit more pliable. His reluctance had nothing to do with his own fears about facing the past. "You'll have to wait for the hard truths." He toasted her and pitched back the rum. He thumped the empty glass on the chest. "Pick another."

He assured himself he'd done right to make her wait. It only whetted her appetite if he delayed.

She worried her lip, seeming to calculate as he pulled the cork and poured another glass of rum. He handed her the drink. She finished it quickly. He tried not to show his dismay at how much she drank. Two glasses of the strong brew, and he was beginning to feel the first effects—the warmth, the lightness. Leydi was possibly half his weight. He couldn't imagine her drinking much more. He filled the tumbler and sipped.

"All right," she said, "we'll leave the hard ones for now." She straightened in her chair and shuffled the cards. She cleared her throat, then slanted him a glance. "Have you ever been in love?"

He smiled. "But of course, Mouse. Haven't you guessed I love you true?"

His teasing remark missed its mark—badly. Longing sprang in her eyes, then disappointment as she realized he was joking.

"I once *thought* I was in love," he said more gently.

"How can you *think* you're in love? Love is an emotion. It . . . it happens. You feel it—like fear or happiness. You can't *think* you're in love."

"That sounds like someone who's never been in love," he said with some bite because the subject of Clarice and love was a difficult one. He handed her back the glass, watching her sip the rum this time. They were halfway through the bottle and he was beginning to think he might have miscalculated. Her eyes looked too sharp and clear under the candlelight. She was far from snoring in the chair, while his focus was beginning to swim a bit on the edges.

"I was in love with an idea. Not a person," he told her trying, as he always did, to keep the fine distinction.

"The woman you loved turned out not to be the person you thought?"

He shook his head. He could feel the liquor doing its work, easing the path of the words. "She was just as I thought her to be. She never tried to hide her true nature or what she wanted from me. It wasn't so much she that I loved—but what I thought she might give me."

"And what was that?" she asked, anticipation in her voice.

He smiled. "That's another question."

"So it's to be that way, is it?" Frowning, Leydi flicked the cards smartly and passed out the next round. "I should have guessed you wouldn't play fair."

He smiled to himself as he filled the glass once more and pushed it across the table to her, happy suddenly not to give the very answers he'd schemed to press on her. When he picked up his cards, he saw he had a strong hand. It hadn't been his intention to win—but he thought not to make things too easy for her.

When he beat her pair of twos with three sevens, he settled back into his chair with a sense of relief. He found his curiosity for the Mouse difficult to control with the rum warming his veins. He knew instinctively she would be more forthcoming than he with her answers.

"Kincaid." He finished his drink and poured another glass for Leydi. They had almost finished the bottle. "What's he to you?"

She looked puzzled. He hoped it was the liquor at work. This time she took a long pull of the glass and mulled over his question.

"Well, that's a wasted question," she said. "He's my employer. You know that. I've worked for him these past eight years, keeping his records."

"Nothing more? You seem so at ease here, among pirates. I wondered if there might be some other . . . connection?"

She knew immediately what he was fishing at and waved the suggestion away. "The man's old enough to be my father." She frowned again, looking at the bottle. This time she took up the rum and pulled the cork. She poured a glass and handed it to Quentin. "Sometimes I almost wish he were."

"A pirate for a father? Now, wouldn't that just suit," he said, chuckling.

"He's always treated me better than my own." She took the dram glass from his hand even though he hadn't finished the rum in it. She took a sip. "He and the Lady Consuelo."

"Well," he said carefully, setting the cards aside. "I imagine Argus and Elaine aren't the most attentive of parents. But replacing them with a pirate?"

"Argus is . . ." She shook her head, giving him back the drink and shuffling the cards. "Argus is Argus. A man of few words. He hasn't spared me more than ten since the day I was born. And my mother . . . she's led a difficult life. First indentured, now only a kitchen servant."

"And that excuses everything?"

"They did their best—sometimes that's all a person has a right to expect."

"No," he said, shaking his head, angry for her. "That's not near good enough."

"He and my mother paid for my schooling with dear Mr. Stevenson." She shuffled with a vengeance, pitching the cards against each other. "They were planning to use the money to buy their papers of indenture from your grandfather, but instead they used every penny they had to educate me. Oh, perhaps they never tucked me into bed or read me stories . . . but if not for their hard work and sacrifice, I would never have what I do today."

Quentin said nothing. He stared at the cards she shuffled, too surprised by the anger that had so instantly flared inside him for her. Certainly he'd never been tucked into bed—a little thing she seemed to think any child would merit—but at least his parents' neglect hadn't involved such a vile deception.

He remembered only too well the day Stevenson had told the tale of Leydi's mother haggling over the coin to pay him to tutor Leydi—and how Stevenson had refused even a shilling. Apparently, her parents had used her gratitude to their advantage just the same.

"Oh, yes, dear old mama and papa," he said. "So self-sacrificing."

"Don't say it that way," she whispered, suddenly very serious. "They try to be good people."

He reached across the table and pulled at a curl hard enough to hurt. "No. They do not."

She looked deep into his eyes, hiding nothing. "She didn't cut my hair for the reasons you thought. She wasn't jealous. She was *afraid* for me," she said. "She thought I'd caught your eye and you would seduce me. In her own way she was trying to protect me."

He laughed, a sharp bark that filled the room. "Dear Lord, that's rich. Next you'll be saying she did you a service." He leaned forward over the chest of drawers, trailing a finger across her cheek. "She can't trim off your beauty with shears. She can't make a man stop wanting you by changing your hairstyle. Look at how you're dressed, for God's sake. You look like you could suffocate in those stays. She tried to flatten everything that made you a woman, while she used your money to buy herself beautiful gowns and lavish panniers, giving herself the color and curves she robbed from you."

She continued to shuffle, staring hard at the cards. "Believe what you will."

"Listen to yourself. You just told me you wished Kincaid were your father. I imagine that's a bit like saying anyone would have been better than the parents God gave you."

She dealt the cards, her lips in a grim line, and set to playing. It didn't take long for her to win the next hand. She looked up and pinned him with a stare. "My mother said you killed your mistress. That she was with child and tried to trick you into marriage—so you had them both killed." She shot the words out. "Is that true?"

He smiled at her vehemence. He'd gotten her goat with his questions about her parents.

He glanced down at the empty glass, then picked up the empty bottle. "I need another drink."

She seemed to see the empty bottle for the first time. She blinked. He hoped she was drunk. And then he realized he wasn't far behind.

He tapped the bottle on the chest of drawers, thinking he *needed* another drink. "How about it, Mouse? You could dash out there and get us more rum. Then I'll answer your question."

She didn't even think it over, just rose and left the room—but he'd noticed it had taken her a couple of tries before she'd gotten the key in the lock. For a moment he thought of calling her back. Another bottle of rum might be too big a risk with Brody snoring in the hall. But he told himself he wouldn't get what he wanted without it. An entire bottle lay disposed of, glowing with candlelight on the oyster veneer, and still she was far from asleep.

It didn't take long before he heard the door open once more. Mildly, he realized she hadn't locked him in when she'd dashed out for her bottle. It didn't matter. His escape would have to be better planned than a drunken race for the shore in the middle of the night.

She brought a new bottle and set it carefully on the table, her movements the well-orchestrated dance of someone who'd drunk too much but didn't want it to show. When she finished filling the glass, she looked up at him.

"Did you kill her? Her and the baby?"

He drank the liquor slowly, letting the menace build between them before he said, "Yes, I killed them. Both."

She seemed stunned by his response, her eyes growing just a bit wider, showing that elusive band of green he found so charming. The rum slowed her responses. She shook her head. "I don't believe you."

"Ah, but it's true," he said honestly.

"No. No, it's not. You want me to think something awful about you—just like you want me to hate my mother," she said almost angrily, leaning forward over the chest. "Well, I won't hate like that. No matter what you say. I know people, and their character. You didn't kill them."

"You little fool," he said, leaning forward himself, meeting her face-to-face, the liquor and her vehemence making him angry as well. "You don't know a damn thing about me."

"Yes. Yes, I do," she said, lowering her voice. "Enough to know that you're kindhearted even when you want to be mean. I know it here," she said, pointing to her heart. "You've been torturing yourself ever since you sent me those combs, you're so sorry for what you did. I see the way you watch my hair, the way you touch it. You acted out of anger and you regret it. No, you wouldn't kill a woman. Oh, you might try to make me think you're horrible and unloving. But I don't believe it. I don't."

He stared at her, hating her belief in him, battling it. "Then you, my dear Mouse, are even more foolish than I thought."

They remained silent. She stared at him, her belief in his goodness burning between them.

"You didn't kill them," she said softly. "But they died just the same. How?"

He kept staring down at her, his breath coming in deep harsh bursts. He couldn't understand why he was so angry. He thought it could be the liquor. Or the fact that she could be so gullible, so easily duped. And then he fell back in his seat, knowing he had no right to his anger. "That, Mouse, is another question."

She seemed to hesitate, looking as if she might complain. But instead, she sipped the next drink, then passed out the cards with her lovely precision.

He was near a boiling point of sorts; her blind faith made it that much more difficult to betray her. That and the alcohol at times made him forget the point of the game. So much so that he planned to win the next round and his schemes be damned for the moment!

He picked up his cards, shifted through them, more determined with each passing minute to beat her. And so, as the game progressed, he did what he had to do to win. He cheated.

He was quite good at it, of course. Even drunk as he was, he could save the cards he needed, turning the odds in his favor. When he was fairly sure he'd gotten as best as he could without tipping his hand, he stopped.

It came as a damned shock when she won the round just the same.

She fanned out the cards before him, a triumphant smile on her pixie face. Two queens and two knaves. For a moment he stared nonplussed at her hand. She'd won. But that wasn't possible. He'd made certain she couldn't win. She shouldn't be holding the cards she'd laid out before him.

The cards began to blur, a combination of rum and disbelief. And then he realized the truth.

"You cheated," he said, so surprised that his words slurred.

She smiled. "You did it first."

He gathered up the cards. "It doesn't count."

She slapped her hand over his, stopping him from picking up the cards. "Of course it does. We both cheated, that makes us even. I cheated better. That makes me the winner. Now I want my question answered."

He stood, knocking the chair to the carpeted floor. He turned away from her with a curse. He had indeed drunk too much. It was this damned island. Everything seemed to affect him more here. The room swirled around him, making him unsteady. He almost had to reach for the bedpost to stop from stumbling. He glanced back at the chest, peered at the second bottle of rum. Had they really downed half?

He felt her hand on his shoulder. She turned him around to face her. "How did they die?"

He shook his head, disbelieving of how his little trap was spinning out of his control. He seemed more drunk than she. And he was unwilling to dish up the truths he'd thought to use against her, to lure her to his side.

He told himself he was being ridiculous. She stood before him, waiting for her answer, already binding herself to him in the way he'd hoped, that he'd calculated. He tried to shake off his foggy sense of disorientation. He picked up a tendril of hair near her ear, twisting it through his fingers.

"I killed them, Mouse. I'm not lying to you." His tongue felt slightly thick, as if he were having trouble forming his confession. "But I lied about Clarice. I loved her. More than I care to admit. That's why I came to St. Kitts. And why I won't have anything to do with the earl. I killed her. I killed the woman I loved and our child."

But the undying faith didn't waver from her eyes. She didn't bother to try to contradict him this time, just waited, knowing there would be more. And there was. A lifetime of it.

He sat down on the bed and leaned back on his elbows until he could see only the canopy. "Where are those damned angels?" he whispered, not as a ploy, but because he actually wanted them. He'd had them painted for these moments, when the past came too close.

"Here," she said, lying down beside him, curling up to him with absolute faith. She took his hand and held it between her two. "I'm listening."

He stroked Leydi's hair, lacing his fingers through its silkiness. He sighed, wondering why he was fighting this. He knew what came next just as well as he knew the steps to a quadrille. All his battles to stop this attraction from taking over his schemes had been for naught. His foolish assurances against last night's kiss had been just that—foolish indeed. He knew what would happen with Leydi in his bed, snuggling against him, waiting for her truths. And then he didn't fight it anymore.

"Clarice was a woman of the world. She was everything you're not," he said cruelly. "Sophisticated. Knowing in the ways of men and love. Nothing about her was average. Brown."

He wanted to push her away with his mean-spirited words. He didn't want her to stay in his arms. But she kept stroking his fingers just as gently, even as the lines appeared between her eyes saying that yes, he'd hurt her. He smoothed them back with his thumb, sorry he'd spoken so harshly.

"Clarice was a whore," he said simply.

When she looked miserable at his wording, he said, "She was my mistress. And the mistress of many men before me. That's how she made her living. And she was very good at it. She wanted only one thing. Money, lots of it. And she would stay by your side only as long as you could pay her price. But I was young. I fooled myself into thinking I could capture her heart."

Even as a saner part protested, he settled back, placing his head on Leydi's lap. She didn't hesitate, but sat up against the pillows to make him comfortable. She stroked his hair in a gentle rhythm that made him want to close his eyes and groan from the sheer pleasure of it.

"I was young and so very infatuated. I was in my rebellious stage. I'd tried for years to get my father to notice me, but it seemed only misdeeds caught his attention. For a long time I was very, very bad. I gambled and whored what money he gave me. I left notes when he stopped giving me coin directly, knowing he'd be embarrassed enough to pay my debts. Clarice was merely the culmination of all that rebellion."

The rhythm of her hands made him fall into a bit of a sleep. He could see Clarice again, her vibrant red hair and unbelievable violet eyes. A woman like her, poor but with such arresting looks and startling beauty, what chance did she have but to play the courtesan? Her parents had nothing, mere servants. It was a simple thing for her to get more than what life had offered her by using her body.

He opened his eyes. Leydi leaned over him, her hair falling forward in a beautiful confusion of curls. The candlelight made the tendrils only more exquisite, highlighting them with honey. Her eyes were dark, but he knew they carried glimmers of silver and green. She was beautiful. More beautiful than Clarice.

He remembered Stevenson's story about Leydi in his grandfather's library, trying to teach herself to read. Her facility with numbers, her eagerness to please. Leydi seemed by her very existence to denounce the choices Clarice had made with her life.

He sighed. *God. If he weren't careful . . .*

He kissed her hand, then kissed each of her fingers, not being the least bit careful. He found he liked the feel of them against his mouth, all warm and soft. Oh, yes. The Mouse could be so easy to love. . . .

"Go on," she whispered.

He played with her fingers, kissing each again slowly, gently, as if holding on to her made his story safe. "Clarice was my mistress for many months. Then one day she came to me and told me she carried my child." He grinned, still able to remember the day with a whisper of joy. "She'd thought to trap me, you see. She thought I was young, only twenty-three to her near thirty. And in love. She'd probably waited years for this chance— to trap a gentleman of wealth and title into marriage. I may not even have been her first attempt." He shook his head. "But she didn't know, she couldn't know, how happy I was with her news. I wanted that baby. I thought it might bring me her love. And if not, then at least I would have the child to love."

Unbelievably, his throat tightened. His chest clenched. He waited a moment, letting it pass, telling himself that the rum made him maudlin.

Clarice and the baby. He hadn't allowed himself to want anything other than revenge since.

"She made me very happy that day."

The room seemed to grow darker, warmer. He could hear the palm fronds swaying in the wind outside. He closed his eyes, wondering if he wouldn't just fall asleep there, forget his grand schemes for escape and just rest in Leydi's arms. She and this island had given him so many lovely nights of sleep. Let Kincaid and his men do with him what they pleased. He'd stopped living a long time before. Weren't these days of captivity the closest to life he'd come yet?

"How did they die?"

Her voice woke him. He didn't know how long he'd dozed, but he knew he had in fact fallen asleep. The nightmare of Clarice had been waiting for him in the darkness just behind his eyelids, as it always was, mocking him.

You didn't get there in time. Why hadn't he gotten there in time! Clarice. God, Clarice.

He closed his eyes again, drifting, then falling into the memories. He recalled how happy he'd been that day. He'd challenged the earl the very night before. He'd told his father exactly what he planned—to marry Clarice and raise their child. His father had ranted and raved, pacing before Quentin, screaming how he would ruin his life falling into that age-old trap. Did he even know the baby was his, for God's sake? He was the son of an earl. He couldn't marry his mistress, a woman known for her exploits in the bedroom. Had he no common sense?

But Quentin had merely smiled and shut out his father's screaming. How many times had he heard the same warning? *You're ruining your life, gambling. You're ruining your life, drinking and whoring. You're ruining your life* . . .

All Quentin could think was that at last he would have a life.

The baby. It was all he really wanted. A real family. The kind that hugged and gave kisses. A family who held hands and showed affection. Clarice might deny him all that; he wasn't foolish enough to count on her love. But the baby. The baby would. Children did that. They couldn't help themselves. They didn't know better but to love.

Quentin grabbed Leydi's hand, gripping her fingers. She seemed like a lifeline—*don't let me fall into this nightmare.* But he'd brought back the memories himself. And they were there, waiting for him.

He could see himself that day, so young. God, so young. Foolish enough to dream about the future and plan where he and Clarice would live and how he would support them. He'd even brought her roses that day.

He squeezed Leydi's hand tighter. Tighter yet. But there was no help for him. No help . . .

He was there again, walking down the street to Clarice's town house, dressed his dapper best, powdered bagwig and all. He'd practically danced down the pavement, even tipped his tricorn to a nurse walking a babe, thinking of his own child growing in Clarice's womb.

Of course the earl would disown him. Quentin didn't care. There had never been a strong enough connection between them to feel he was severing himself from anything. And as for the money, he had a flare for knowing where a profit could be made. He'd inherited that much from his ancestors, one of whom had more or less bought himself a title to pass down through the years.

Oh, yes, he could support his family. Quentin had advised enough friends on business ventures to be certain of that much. Sutherland and Webster would help him get a new start in thanks for his few words on the Exchange. And he didn't much care if he had to sell shoes to get free of the earl and put food on the table.

He'd arrived at the front step of the house full of hope, smelling the roses he carried. Clarice loved roses. She always had. Bloodred roses. When the door opened, he looked up with a smile at the little maid whose wages he paid.

She wasn't smiling. Her face was deathly white, her eyes filled with tears.

"The mistress . . ." She couldn't finish the sentence, just waved her hand toward the stairs.

Quentin dropped the flowers. He climbed the steps two at a time. His breath came in loud, frightened bursts. All he could think about was Clarice and the baby. It was so early in her pregnancy. Had she lost the child? *Please, God, no. Keep the baby safe. Please!*

He found Clarice in bed. The sheets were soaked in blood. Her face had no color—her eyes looked lifeless. Her auburn curls were black with sweat, tendrils sticking to her cheeks and temples.

He knew then there would be no baby. There would be no one at all.

The doctor at her bedside shook his head and closed his bag. He gave Quentin a scathing look, letting him know where the fault lay.

"A botched abortion," the man said crisply. "She shouldn't have done it. It's going to cost her life. There's nothing I can do."

Quentin didn't even notice as the man left, he just kept staring at the bed. She looked so small in that enormous canopy bed covered in blood, so white and frail. Her breath was shallow. He realized he was breathing in a rhythm with her, so much so that he'd grown light-headed.

He fell on his knees and grabbed up her cold white hand. "Don't die," he whispered. "Please, Clarice, don't die."

He didn't know how long he knelt there before he felt her hand on his head. He looked up. Her eyes barely focused on him.

He squeezed her hand between his. He could feel his tears wetting their fingers. "Wasn't my love enough to tempt you even a little? Why, Clarice? Why!"

"Because I am a coward." She took another gasping breath, and he thought she wouldn't speak again. A moment passed. The mantel clock was the only sound in the room. And then she whispered, "Your father came to see me last night. He said if we married, the money would all disappear."

She turned her head to look at him. Those lovely violet eyes beseeched him, asking for forgiveness. "He said he could take it all away. That we would find ourselves on the streets." A tear streamed down her cheek, dripping past her pale mouth. "I've lived on the streets, Quentin." She shut her eyes for a moment, seeming to gather her strength. Finally, she whispered, "Nothing, not you, not the baby, will send me back there."

And then she died.

Quentin opened his eyes. He stared up at the canopy of mosquito netting, no longer in that opulent town house he'd let for his mistress, but in Kincaid's simple tent bed. He still dreamed of Clarice that way, dying in that enormous, ostentatious bed she'd begged him to buy for her, telling him she wouldn't live on the streets.

"That's so terribly sad," Leydi whispered.

He hadn't even realized he'd spoken the story aloud. Still groggy with rum, he focused on Leydi above him. Tears pooled in her soft gray eyes.

"That's why the money is so important to you," she whispered. "I always wondered why someone with so much wealth would want more. She didn't have faith in you. She believed your father, that you'd be out on the streets without his money."

He took her hand and laced their fingers together. She was

so very tiny. Her fingers barely reached his knuckles. God, she gave so much. He wanted to give her something in return.

He stroked a tear from her cheek. "Such a clever little mouse you are," he whispered. "I wonder if you can be so insightful about your own situation."

"My parents?" She sighed, the sound deep and thoughtful. "Yes. I suppose you're right. I suppose you really can't buy love, can you?"

"No," he said, pulling her down to him, holding her close.

"Will you never make up with him—with your father?"

"He disowned me."

"It seems he's had a change of heart," she whispered, her tears once more filling her eyes.

"But I haven't."

He drew her into his arms, kissing her. This time there was no struggle, no hesitation. He didn't question his actions; he hadn't the strength. He wanted what she offered too much.

She opened her mouth to him, folding her body into his caress on the bed. She loved like she did everything else, wholeheartedly and without reservation.

"You should leave," he warned her, knowing she wouldn't listen. He'd given her exactly what she'd wanted all along, the puzzle, the tarnished hero of her books. And he'd done it better than any actor, because he'd meant every word. Even as he kissed her, he knew he'd just doomed them both. There was no retreat from this. Still, he warned, "I'm only going to hurt you."

"Shhh." She lay her fingers across his mouth, then kissed him. "It's all right. I trust you."

"You shouldn't," he said, returning her kisses, wanting her as he'd never wanted anyone before. "I'm after one thing, escape from this bloody island."

But she welcomed him with the press of her body, her mouth beneath his lips. "I'm willing to gamble you want more than that."

"It's a hell of a risk."

"I have a good instinct about these matters."

"But I don't always play fair, Mouse."

"I know how to deal with cheaters," she whispered, twining her arms around his neck.

He kissed her as if she were air to breathe, needing her with the same urgency. He tugged at her clothes with a lack of finesse that bordered on something elemental. But she wasn't frightened. She kept her mouth close as she helped him undress her, then reached for his own clothes. As he took in her scent, a mixture of lavender and a wonderful womanly smell, she gathered him to her, welcoming him with a force that held nothing back.

"You're a virgin," he said, kissing her just the same, kneading her breast with his palm, caressing her bared hip.

"I don't care," she answered, rounding the muscles of his shoulders. "I want you to banish those horrible memories. I want you to believe again in love."

"So self-sacrificing, Mouse?" He lowered his mouth down her neck, kissing her collarbone, brushing his mouth across the flesh above her breasts. "And if I take what you offer and give nothing in return?" he whispered, voicing his greatest fear.

She stilled his hand and cupped his face in her palms. Her eyes were large, dark with desire. "You'll give me what I want, Quentin, because you know deep inside"—she lay her palm on his chest where his heart lay—"deep where it counts, that I can give you all the love you have ever wanted."

"God, you've read too many books."

"I've read enough for both of us," she said, kissing him lightly on his mouth. "And I know the way to the happy ending."

Quentin crushed her to him, kissing her again with that same urgent need. He knew she'd beaten him, beaten them both, because she gave so goddamn much. She held nothing back. There was no avarice in her eyes as she lay back on the bed sheets, pulling him down to her. There wasn't even need in her kisses. Just simply giving and love. And no man, certainly not Quentin, could turn his back on her.

He cupped her breasts, stroking the nipples with his thumbs as he watched her. She seemed to almost curl up as she smiled, sliding her hands down his arms to his wrists. She was a sensual woman, parting her lips, enjoying his touch as her nipples pebbled beneath his fingers, not the least shy as she reached up and pulled his mouth back to hers.

But he wanted more than the taste of her mouth. He lavished her breasts, circling the nipples, sucking them into his mouth. In that moment of need, and desire, and recklessness, he wanted everything. Her soft whimpers made him groan. He wished suddenly he hadn't drunk so much rum. He wanted no gentle haze to their lovemaking. He wanted to feel every inch of her.

His mouth explored downward, reaching her navel. His tongue dipped inside and she sighed, seeming to stretch as if reaching for the pleasure. He couldn't imagine what she would be like after years of lovemaking, when she would be free with her knowledge and experience to search out new heights. For now his kisses trailed lower. His hand stroked the insides of her thighs, smooth and warm.

"I think I'm on fire," she whispered.

"Hush. This is just a warm glow," he told her, his mouth kissing a path from her hip to the top of her thigh. He reached down with his fingers, stroking the folds of her sex, now moist with her desire. "Here," he whispered, easing his finger inside her, testing the tightness there, then pressing another finger inside her. He continued to kiss the inside of her thigh. "I can show you pleasure."

She sighed, her hands fluttering above his shoulders. As he replaced his fingers with his mouth, her hands kneaded against the muscle of his arms, encouraging him—then suddenly pulling him up to her, as if she'd changed her mind.

"I want you to feel this, too."

"I do," he said, tasting her, caressing her with his tongue. "I feel it."

She shook her head, still plucking at his arms. "No, I want you to feel as much." She bent down, determined. She wrapped her arms around his neck, clutching him. "Tell me what to do."

"All right. Yes," he agreed, his own desire catching up with him. "Lay back," he whispered, pressing her back to the bed with his body.

"Should I kiss you? Should I touch you?"

"Shhh." He cupped his hand over her breast as he eased her

knees apart. "Don't ask so many questions." He feathered his fingers across the opening to her, fitting himself to her as he caressed her, making her flow for him. "Love can be a quiet thing." He kissed her mouth once, twice. He stroked her open with his fingers. "It can be patient and soft and wonderful," he said, licking her lips. He pressed himself inside her, feeling her tightness, wanting it but holding back just the same. "It can also be painful."

"Gabriela told me," she said, kissing him back with a frenzy that was not the least bit quiet or soft, but utterly wonderful. "I don't care." She pushed up with her hips, placing him deeper inside her. "I don't care—ah!"

It was just a soft gasp, but it conveyed pain just the same. He pulled back just a bit so he was still inside her but not quite as deep. He focused on her mouth with his lips while his fingers cherished the petal folds of skin and their treasure pebbled inside, making her gasp again, but not with pain.

"Mouse," he whispered. "Let me teach you this one thing; don't try so hard to guess."

She held his face in her hands, watching him with soft eyes. "I can't help myself."

He smiled, easing farther inside her. "I know. But just the same"—he changed the rhythm of his stroking, making her close her eyes, making her catch her breath—"just the same, let me do this for you." He kissed her lightly, playing with her mouth. "Let me do this for us."

While his hand circled and explored, his mouth and tongue tasted her lips and the soft inside of her mouth. He pressed deeper. He'd never done anything like this, waited so long, tried so hard to make it magic. He felt the rhythm beating inside her, building as he continued to bring them together, and still he held back, wanting the perfection of it, the union. He knew what he was doing, binding her to him in a way she could never forget. And he knew the cost: He, too would be bound. Yet he did it. When her breath caught and she reached a climax, pulsing around him in gentle waves, he plunged the final step, making them one.

She didn't cry out, but he cried out for her, that much they were in harmony. He knew there had been pain, but the pleasure had been there as well. And he knew there would be more.

Though everything inside him screamed for his own release, he let it build. He kept with his strokes and with his kisses, sensing that like the tide, her ebbing passion would rise again. He couldn't even think of himself as Quentin, a man who'd vowed not to father a child, not to let the lure of love hurt him again. He was someone else, someone who wanted desperately to make this woman his.

He worked himself inside her, watching her moist lips open once again as her eyes watched him in wonder. There. It was coming again. And he would wait for it, for her climax. It hadn't been enough for her to reach her pleasure with the pain of her breach. He wanted her to have just the pleasure.

He perspired above her, his breath like hers coming in deep, heavy pants. A voice inside told him he had never worked this hard to capture a woman's love, but he shut off the warning and its implication. He didn't want to know why he pressed her, bringing her closer and closer to that edge of fulfillment. He knew only he would do it. Now. Yes, now.

She released a soft moan. The gentle squeezing waves throbbed around him. He reached for his own release. It flowed over him, swallowing him, making him know he'd accomplished what he'd wanted.

In that moment he'd tied them together in a way neither she nor he would forget. For that instant, just as she'd asked him to, he believed again in love.

Chapter Twenty-one

Felix stroked the dark curls of hair flowing across the pillow to the tips of Gabriela's bared shoulders. She lay asleep beside him. He wished her sweet dreams. He could find none.

He'd never done anything he was ashamed of in his life. He lived by a code of proper rules, of right and wrong—just as his foster mother had taught him. He tried to tell himself that Kincaid deserved to be destroyed. But he knew in his soul it should not be at the cost of Gabriela's happiness. That was wrong. Very wrong.

She turned on the bed, sighing in her sleep. Alight with moonlight, her face was perfection. Wide-spaced eyes, high cheekbones, high-arched brows. Very full, very kissable lips. He leaned over and stroked the warm skin of her cheek with his mouth. She moaned softly.

Kincaid had some hold on her—that much he knew. Whenever she spoke of the pirate, he could sense that her feelings against the villain were as strong as his. But he didn't know how to help her, how to sever the ties that kept her prisoner and cohort to Heartless. That made her Felix's enemy.

"Go to sleep, Felix," she whispered.

Hearing her voice, he smiled. "You're awake."

Gabriela cuddled alongside him, hooking one long limb over his. Holding her close, he returned her embrace, hoping that he could allow himself that much honesty. What he felt for Gabriela, this desire, was real. He twined her hair in his fingers, loving the feel of it.

"Come away with me, Gabriela," he whispered in the dark. "Help me leave this island."

She groaned against his chest. "So you can come back and destroy Kincaid?" she said in a tired voice, the conversation old territory. "I can't do that."

"He'll kill me."

She hugged him fiercely. "I won't let him."

"And how do you plan to stop him?"

She leaned up on her elbows, looking at him. Her beautiful green eyes beseeched him. "You could join him. Or we could get married. He won't hurt you if you're mine."

He stroked her hair silently, infinitely sad as he told her, "Eve holding the apple out to Adam. I'm afraid I must refuse."

Gabriela collapsed on top of his chest. She hugged him with all her strength.

"So," he said after a moment of silence. "You really are one of them?"

Gabriela pulled away. For an instant he held her gaze, but then she turned and scooted off the bed. In the dark he could just make out the shadow of her gathering her clothes and dressing. When she finished, she leaned over him on the bed. A sliver of moonlight fell across her face.

"Yes, Felix," she whispered, kissing his brow. "I really am one of them."

He heard the door click shut behind her. The key turned in the lock. He rested his head in the crook of his arm, watching the shadows.

She was choosing Kincaid.

He shouldn't have made love to her.

Quentin knew it with the certainty not often allowed a man.

Holding Leydi's warm body naked against him, he sensed his mistake to the marrow of his bones.

He wouldn't be able to walk away from this.

He'd fallen into his own trap.

Still woozy from the rum, he tried to convince himself it was the liquor that made his mind such a muddle. He must concentrate on the other men and escape. He hadn't just had a brush with heaven with Leydi in his arms. He reminded himself of his situation: captive on some pirate kingdom, waiting for Heartless to arrive and do his worst.

But then she snuggled closer, her breast brushing up against his bare chest. A profusion of curls swept across his shoulder. The moonlight sparkled the shadowed tendrils with fairy dust. She was dead asleep, finally succumbing to the rum. He looked down the length of the bodies; their limbs were twined together among the bed sheets. It was the first time in seven years he'd stayed in bed with a woman after they'd made love.

They'd made love several times, as if both feared it might be the last as well as their first time together. For a while he thought she actually might outlast him. The very thought brought a smile to his lips. She was just a slip of a girl really.

And I am an utter fool, he told himself.

He worked on clearing the fog of rum and satisfaction from his head. He thought of Clarice—of his father. The past. He felt something knot up inside him and lodge in his heart. He thought it might be fear. He was afraid he would fail the others, allow Leydi to lull him into making a mistake . . . as he had last night.

In the past his fantasies had guided him down a path that from the first had promised only disaster. His father had been right all along—Clarice would never love him. And yet he'd shut out those warnings, convincing himself he could make a family with his mistress. He'd closed his eyes to the obvious until it had been thrust up in a bloody scene of Clarice dying in that bed.

He must not let that happen again.

He was a prisoner. Two men depended on his plans for escape. He couldn't make a happy ending with Leydi, as she'd promised.

Heartless Kincaid wouldn't arrive to bless their union and set him and the others free. *Don't forget Bishop and Piton.*

Gently, he unwrapped her arm from his chest. He didn't know what had driven him to make love to her with such finesse, and he didn't much want to analyze his motives. The feelings she invoked were too powerful, too seductive. When he managed to wriggle free of the covers and Leydi, he dressed quickly. He picked up her gown and apron from the floorboards and searched the pocket.

Slipping the key into his hand, he reminded himself that more than his life was at risk on this island. He had Felix and Hugh to think about. It was all fine and well for him to give up, to tell Leydi that at last he'd found a slice of happiness, but his brief encounter with bliss would do little to help the other two men.

He continued down the hall, telling himself he couldn't worry about Leydi and the love he'd seen in her eyes. But in the shadows, as he slipped past Brody snoring in his chair, he saw only Leydi's smiles, remembering her touch and charming faith in him.

He felt like a first class son of a bitch.

He armed himself with the knowledge from his past. *Don't delude yourself. Don't fall for the dream.* He would remember Clarice, remind himself that love could be treacherous. Steeled against her, he didn't take long to find Kincaid's study. He wound a path around the heavy oak furniture, careful not to disturb anything. He opened the velvet curtains a sliver and scanned the moonlit room, trying to find something that might be of use in an escape attempt. Tonight he wouldn't take anything, fearing it might be missed.

In the few minutes he allowed himself, he came across a wheel-lock—no powder—a compass, and what looked to be Kincaid's logbooks. He recognized Leydi's handwriting on many of the papers littering the seaweed marquetry of the rolltop desk. Apparently she really did work for the pirate in the capacity of a bookkeeper. From what he could see, she'd made sure the culprit had enough money in legitimate holdings that Kincaid could retire comfortably from his life of crime.

He kept coming back to the logbooks in the breakfront bookcase. Finding a tinderbox, he closed the curtains and lit a candle, shielding the dim light with his body and hand. At first he wasn't sure what use the logs might be, but then he realized it was curiosity more than anything that drove him to open the glass door of the bookcase and thumb through a few of the volumes.

In the glimmering candlelight he could see the books dated back many years. Unconsciously, he'd been searching for a particular date—eight years ago, when Leydi had told him she'd first started working for Kincaid. Her connection to Heartless, the years she'd lived under his protection, still struck Quentin as odd. Odd enough that he was driven to try to read the chicken-scratch scrawls of ink.

It didn't take long to discover a mention of Leydi, but the entries following her name were strange—only money amounts. Apparently paid to one Elaine Carstair, Leydi's mother.

The chilling thought came that the woman had sold her daughter to Kincaid.

He brought the book closer to the candlelight, trying to read as quickly as possible through what appeared insignificant entries on Kincaid's exploits. He found Leydi's name again, followed by the same mysterious sums of money.

> Monday, June 12, 1720—10 pieces of eight:
> *Went to the plantation again. Got to make Elaine see reason—*

Quentin jumped back, almost dropping the candle when he sensed a faint scratching on his bare leg. He peered down to see Nigel, one clawed paw now perched daintily on Quentin's toes. He picked up the iguana.

"Snooping in the shadows at this hour?" He put the candle on the desk, thinking Nigel's amber eye had a bit of a jaundiced glint. "Know I'm up to no good, do you?"

The sound of a door opening downstairs warned Quentin. Quickly, he put Nigel down and pinched out the candle. He slipped the book back onto the shelf and closed the glass door. Careful to avoid detection, he left the room as he'd found it, confident that he'd get his hands on the key again. With that damning thought came the knowledge that he didn't intend Leydi's stay in his bed to be for just one night.

Back inside the room, Leydi lay snuggled on the bedclothes, her legs entangled in the sheets. He sighed and shrugged out of his clothes. After seven years of loneliness, he was no match for the longing she stirred inside him. The Mouse, and not he, must hold her fate in her hands.

Cy whistled a ditty as he walked down the oyster-shell path, thinking it would be a fine day. The sun was just peeking over the treetops, the hour still early. The parrots cawed in the distance. He had a day's work ahead of him and a purpose to his step. It was all he ever asked of life.

And then he saw Bertie.

Damn that woman.

She was staring ahead at that fool Frenchman. Hugh was flirting with the Ramsey girl, a flighty young thing destined to cause trouble on the island if Kincaid didn't marry her off soon. Bertie was watching the coquettish exchange with a dull look in her eye. Obviously, that young pup and his opinions still mattered.

He was beginning to sorely regret bringing the Frenchman to Devil's Gate. But at the time he'd been jealous as hell, and wanting to string the idiot up by his thumbs. When he thought of his Bertland making a fool of herself over the lad—well, it made him so furious, it had stolen his better senses clean away.

Taking a deep breath, Cy continued down the path to where Bertie watched Hugh. A begrudging smile came to his lips as he saw what a sight she made, dressed in a golden gown that gave a special glow to her skin. Cy thought Bertie was the color of rich dark coffee, making him wish he could take a sip. Her raven curls were tied up in a colorful scarf, and she wore the familiar hoops in her earlobes. If it weren't for Kincaid, Cy would have charted his course years ago. He glared across the courtyard at the effeminate piece of fluff Bertie had set her sights on. As things were looking, perhaps he'd waited too late.

He placed his hand on her shoulder and turned her around

slowly. "Now, Bertland," he said in his most reasonable tone. "The boy could be yer get."

She shrugged off his touch. "Speak for yerself. He might be young enough to be your son, Cy. Not mine."

"Ye want him that bad, do ye, gel?" he asked.

In answer, Bertie stared off into the distance, as if giving the question real thought. "I don't know what I want anymore, *querido.* "She sighed, her shoulders rising and falling. She looked up at Cy, her jet eyes sparkling, making his heart catch in his throat. "Perhaps what I don't want is to be spurned. You could be right, Cy," she said, brushing her fingers across his cheek. "I am a foolish old woman."

He took her hand by her wrist, then held it between his two. Her ebony fingers almost disappeared in the grip of his sun-tanned hands. "Hush, now. Don't ye be saying such about yerself. If ye want the boy, I've a plan, if you'll listen." He hadn't wanted to go to these extremes, to trick Bertland, but he knew his chance was now, and he might not get another.

"Fools like that Frenchman there, they value only what they cannot have. They don't got the sense to see what's before their eyes." Looking at Bertland's dear, familiar face, wanting her as he did, Cy knew he'd been just as big a fool to wait so long. "They need a little push to show them what's what. You should try to make him jealous, Bertland. And I'm volunteering for the job."

She looked genuinely confused, which did him little good. But then with a sigh he realized that just like men, some women needed to be shown what's what.

He leaned forward and kissed her. Soundly. He kept at it until he felt her melt into his arms, then open her mouth and return his kiss. When he thought she had the rhythm of the thing, that he'd made his point, he pulled away. Looking over her shoulder, he nodded his head to where the Frenchman was now staring at them.

"Ye see what I mean?" he told her softly.

Bertie turned toward the boy, looking a bit confused. She seemed to think a moment, then turned back to Cy. *"Sim,"* she said, watching him intently. "I think I do." And then she stepped up on her tiptoes and kissed him until he forgot all about the Frenchman watching them.

When she finished, Cy stepped away with no little regret. "Well. I'm at yer disposal, Bertland." He doffed his woolen cap. "Top of the morning to ye, darlin'."

He walked away whistling as he tossed the key to Rutherford's room into the air, catching it in one hand. Now that he had his plans for Bertland progressing in the right direction, it was time to check on that other matter.

Chapter Twenty-two

Thank the good Lord, the knocking woke her.

Everything that had happened the night before roared over Leydi with the force of her headache. So did the fact that the sun was shining merrily through the shutters and that Quentin was in bed beside her, pressing his naked body to hers.

The very possibility of discovery jolted in her veins with the surge of a tidal wave. Despite a headache, a roiling stomach, and weak knees, she jumped out of bed and grabbed her corset and what clothes she could get her hands on. She was just scooting under the bed, Quentin tossing her petticoats and chemise behind her and kicking the fringed chair back to its place by the wall, when she heard the key turning, the door creaking open, and Cy's greeting from the hall.

She couldn't see anything, nor did she want to. She closed her eyes like an ostrich. She could feel Cy's boots stomp across the floorboards, making the floor bounce until his steps became muffled by the carpet. The squeaking of the bed ropes followed as Quentin sat on the mattress above her.

As the horror of discovery faded and the sheer precariousness of her position settled in, Leydi actually had to clamp both hands over her mouth to stop from laughing. She'd read this very scene in a book, or something just as ridiculous. And then the odious effects of too much rum sailed over her. She collapsed against the floor, resting her cheek on the cool boards as she listened.

Though she couldn't make out too many words, she settled for the melody of Quentin's deep voice. She still tingled in all the magic places he'd shown her last night. Even the memory of his touch made her shiver, as if her body were readying itself for him again. And then she remembered the story of his father—his mistress, Clarice, and the baby.

She shut her eyes and prayed, prayed hard that she could give Quentin that child. And then she sighed, counseling herself that he might not give her that chance.

She thought over the discoveries of the night. Quentin needed her love so much—and she wanted to give it all to him. She wanted to be there every day to soothe away the memories of his awful past, a past that had driven him to his desolate plantation in the shadow of Mount Misery. She longed to ease the heartache that had made him hoard money and swear off love. But there was a fierceness to Quentin that pushed her away, almost as if he refused to allow himself that much happiness. So often he wanted only to portray himself as mean-spirited, even allowing the gossip of murder to hover over him unchallenged. Perhaps it wasn't just his father he wanted to punish for Clarice's and the baby's deaths.

Nor was Quentin's obstinacy her only problem. Clutching her clothes to her naked body, Leydi reminded herself that soon Kincaid would return to Devil's Gate, breaking this idealistic rhythm to her days. Myriad thoughts spun round and round in her head—Kincaid, Quentin, the earl—all making her very dizzy, very tired.

Halfway through her silent disputes, she fell asleep.

Seated on the bed above Leydi, Quentin listened to Cuthbert as the man paced the room, recounting for his prisoner the day's agenda. At one point he thought Cuthbert stared at the William and Mary chair suspiciously. The fringed chair was at an odd angle where Quentin had kicked it up against the wall and away from the chest of drawers. The cards were thankfully out of sight; Quentin had just managed to dump the deck into the first drawer. When Cuthbert continued his litany of the day's events, appearing none the wiser of the night's happenings or Leydi's presence beneath the bed, Quentin released the breath he'd been holding.

Through sheer force of will Quentin held back a groan of pain. After consuming nearly two bottles of rum with the Mouse, he hadn't been up for the charge of blood thundering through his veins with Cuthbert's impromptu visit. As his pulse continued its hammer-and-anvil pounding inside his head, Quentin waited for Kincaid's second-in-command to have his say and leave.

"Had a nip, did ye?" Cuthbert said, nodding his head toward the two bottles, one empty, the other half full. "I'd say ye should have stopped at one, lad."

"No truer words have been spoken," Quentin answered, instantly on guard for Cuthbert's questions about the second bottle. He'd given Quentin only the one.

"Perhaps Brody can show ye the mineral baths." Cuthbert winked, seeming not the least bit interested in the mysterious second bottle. "That hot steam helps clear the head sometimes."

Apparently having said his piece, Cuthbert stomped to the door. He gave the two bottles another glance in passing and shook his head as he chuckled.

Opening the door, Cy peered over his shoulder at Quentin. "Just remember what I told ye; if ye do yer best to keep from trouble, I'll promise to put in a good word fer ye with Daniel. Well, I'll leave ye to it, then. I'll send Brody down for your breakfast since the gels haven't been by with it. Oh, I almost forgot," he added, turning back. "Kincaid's ship's been sighted. Seems he's come back earlier than expected. Ye've not long to wait now—perhaps no more than two days or three. Well, it's best for you and the men that we settle this thing, aye?"

With those prophetic words, Cy stepped out of the room and closed the door.

Quentin stared at the paneled wood. The shock of Cuthbert's words ripped through him, pulsing with the rhythm of his aching head. For an instant the room seemed to dim, then tilt on its axis.

Kincaid was due back in only a few days.

He had just run out of time.

Leydianna was dreaming. In her dream she was safely ensconced in Quentin's arms, receiving his kisses . . . and more. With every breath she whispered her promises to keep Quentin safe from Kincaid, to fight anyone who might harm him. Returning his caresses, she vowed to make him feel loved and cherished.

But then Quentin's soothing touches grew stronger, more desperate. His grip settled on her wrist, squeezing—too tight—bringing pain. She locked her eyes on his midnight gaze, pleading that he not hold her so. But he only smiled and whispered, "I told you I'd hurt you, Mouse."

Leydi woke from the dream with a start, finding that indeed Quentin's fingers were locked around her wrist. He was kneeling down, crouching beside the bed, trying to wake her. He pulled on her arm gently, coaxing her out from under the bed.

Leydi brushed off the disturbing tendrils of her dream, smiling as she wiggled from the bed. The sight of Quentin, even scowling at her, brought her instant joy. Two days ago, after she'd allowed that first damning kiss in this room, she knew he'd managed to wrest her trust from her. But last night all her fears over that choice had been vanquished. What she did now was not a betrayal of Kincaid. She would accept Quentin—Lord Ruthless and all—because she could do nothing else. She loved him.

Fearlessly, she launched herself in his arms, sending them both crashing against the carpeted floor, raining kisses over his face. She thought if God could just let her have this one happiness, she would never miss her daydreams again. She didn't know exactly when it had happened, when she'd fallen in love, but she suspected it could have been the first time he'd saved her from her mother's sharp tongue. Yes, even then he'd sown the seeds inside her heart, seeds that had grown and blossomed with the enormous attention he'd given her over these weeks. Even the painful moments they'd shared had nourished that love in the shower of the strong emotions between them.

She huddled closer, squeezing his arms around her, happy at last to admit the feelings she'd been battling. Love was everything she'd imagined it to be, exciting, adventurous, exhilarating. Sneaking into his room at night, making love on Devil's Gate—the only place where she'd known happiness—it was all so perfect. Better than her books.

She laughed, twisting around in his arms and kissing him again, forgetting her disturbing dream and Quentin's thunderous expression. She allowed herself the perfection of this first brush with love, no longer afraid he would ask too much of her—she wanted to give him everything.

Despite his better sense, Quentin finally succumbed to Leydi's ardent kisses and smiles, grinning, too, as he captured her mouth in a breathless kiss. Cuthbert's warning should have acted like a pail of cold water, but he found it had not. Now that he knew what it meant to hold her, to kiss her, to make love to her, it seemed he wanted her all the more.

What surprised him was the genuine happiness that flared inside him as they stood, and she pushed him back onto the bed, giggling as she nestled against him on the counterpane. He held his finger across her lips to keep her quiet, then kissed her mouth twice. With a nod she cuddled closer. They stayed on the bed, just holding each other.

Quentin closed his eyes, allowing himself this fantasy she wove around them like a protective cocoon. For these short minutes he wanted to believe they belonged together in this room. He wanted to enjoy the touch of the sun coming through the shutters, making him feel good. For an instant, optimism for life and love flowered around them like the scent of orchids on the breeze.

But his pounding headache would not go away, nor would the doubts it started. Kincaid was due back in just mere days. Leydi had been compromised—a mouse he'd once sworn to protect against those who sought to take advantage of her.

You shouldn't have made love to her; you'll never let go of her now—and you must! They were enemies, not lovers.

Even holding her, he remembered her damning words: *I wish Kincaid were my father.* He knew she would hand him up to her pirate, naive enough to think she could stop the man from harming Quentin and the others. *Don't mistake that light in her eyes for freedom.* Kincaid still had her loyalty.

With the cacophony of doubts storming inside his head, Quentin pulled Leydi from his arms. He gave her a quick buss on the lips, then kissed the tip of her freckled nose to soothe the disappointment in her eyes.

"You'd better go. Brody will be back with my breakfast soon."

She nodded, then bit her lip. "I can show you the mineral baths later today. It's a good remedy for the rum—as good as any I know of."

Quentin studied her earnest gray eyes. She was handing him yet another opportunity. And though he hated himself for using her, he knew he had no choice.

"So Cy was kind enough to mention." He tipped up her chin and kissed her gently. He put every ounce of feeling he possessed into that kiss—betraying them both and the love they'd shared the night before. He must let her show him her island. He must explore it for a means of escape. "I'd like that. Very much. If you can convince Cuthbert I can be trusted with you."

She jumped out of bed and began to dress. "That won't be a problem. I'll just ask to take Samuel with us."

He pulled her back against him, his hands cupping her breasts because he couldn't seem to help himself around her. It still amazed him how full they were. And angered him, because he knew how tight her corset must be to hide them. He kissed her neck, lingering over a warm spot that smelled richly of lavender. "And will you be able to get rid of Samuel, give us some privacy?"

She turned and kissed his chin. "That's why I picked him, silly. He has a terrible sense of direction."

Lacing her hands around his neck, she gave him another lingering kiss on the mouth, this time twining their tongues together, moaning when she had to pull away or risk another bout on the bed. There was so much hope in her embrace, it almost hurt to feel it. Still, as he watched her finish dressing, he said nothing. He only smiled as she peeked out the door, then turned and blew him a kiss. A smile that faded as she stepped into the hall and closed the door behind her.

He had to get off this island.

And everything else be damned.

Cy stomped down the crushed-shell path, wondering not for the first time how Quentin had gotten two bottles of rum when he'd given the man only one.

Tucking his hand in his waistcoat, Cy made his way to Bishop's cabin. Rutherford deserved watching, and that was a fact. Over the past nights he'd made a study of how the man played cards. Though he'd never cheated, Rutherford played with a vengeance to win. And he wasn't lenient with those who got in his way. Cy had seen him play along the unsuspecting until the poor cull gave his last twopence.

He sighed, crunching down the path as he thought of what Daniel would make of this mess. Well, it was Kincaid's choice what to do with the men, not Cy's.

Nearing Bishop's cabin, Cy wondered how he'd find the gent this morning. Unlike the others, Bishop didn't seem to be doing too well. Cy was afraid the lieutenant might be taking ill, and the man would need his strength when Kincaid came back. He'd ask Gabby to tend to him, the gel being good with herbs and such.

With a shake of his head, Cy looked out to the horizon. Any day now Kincaid would return. And if Cy knew Daniel, no matter what Consuelo thought, all the loving care these gents were getting would be for naught.

They didn't call him Heartless for nothing.

Chapter Twenty-three

"I won't do it," Hugh announced, strutting before Quentin in his patched trousers and faded striped waistcoat like a molting peacock.

It was past the noon hour and all three prisoners stood under the shade of the banyan, their guards playing dice a stone throw's away. Quentin was angry enough to become foolhardy in his censure against the blithering Romeo of a Frenchman. He unhooked Nigel's claws from his shirt and put the iguana down on the ground next to the coveted basket of fruit. With the threat of Kincaid bearing down on them, the last thing they needed was Hugh to mutiny.

"Bertie is not stupid," Hugh added doggedly. "She will know I am no longer sincere in my love for her." He stopped his pacing and waved his hands with the drama of Hamlet delivering a soliloquy. "I cannot go on with this farce of a romance. I believed Bertie was the love of my life, but this is no longer so. I tell you, I have lost my heart!"

"Well, then find it again, you idiot," Quentin barked. "That woman is your best chance of getting off this island alive—and ours as well, by the bye. If she even suspects your interest lies elsewhere, my guess is she'll do her damnedest to see we hang high. Good God, man. Can any woman turn your head so easily? Have you no sense of self-preservation?"

"When the arrow of love strikes . . ." Hugh said with a Gaelic shrug.

"The arrow of love?" Quentin echoed, disbelieving. "The arrow of—" He'd been willing to betray Leydi to gain their freedom, and now this blithering fool was blithely speaking of cupid's arrow? "I'll tell you what arrow is going to strike, you—"

Felix stayed Quentin's hands just as Hugh danced out of reach.

"Non, monsieur. It is impossible for me to carry on this charade. Molly has completely eclipsed my feelings for Bertie."

The palm fronds rattled like distant sabers; the air grew moist and thick with menace. Quentin shrugged off Felix's hold, taking two steps toward Hugh. "This isn't a game," he whispered. "Bertie de Sousa could very well hold our lives in her hands. If I see you anywhere near another woman, I'll kill you myself."

With his threat cloying the air between them, Quentin sat down on a tree root and picked up the orange Nigel had culled out of the basket. He peeled a slice and offered it to the iguana, giving Nigel's spiky frill a stroke.

"Do you have anything to say here?" he asked Felix, completely exasperated by both men. Last night Quentin had damned himself and Leydi by taking that key after they made love—and these fools couldn't stir themselves enough to stop from sabotaging his plans to save them?

"I'm not sure he's wrong," Felix said. "I told you; I, too, have questions about your tactics."

"Oh, yes," Quentin said, anger and venom flowing through him with the night's liquor curdling in his stomach. He tipped up Nigel's head, speaking as if the iguana were his sole audience. "Only I, bastard that I am, would stoop so low as to use these poor ladies. We should all sit quietly and wait for Kincaid's good humor and hospitality to choose our doom."

He darted a glance at the guards. A shout rippled through their ranks as the dice landed in the clay patch, announcing the victors. Quentin shook his head. They weren't treated like prisoners, more like cherished guests. In these honeyed surroundings it would be easy to grow lax, to forget escape.

Nigel nosed at his hand, begging for another slice of fruit. Today he wore a bright yellow ribbon. But even the iguana's antics hadn't nudged Quentin from his foul mood. He couldn't understand Bishop's and Piton's reaction to his news of Kincaid's impeding arrival. Romeo was planning his next courtship. Felix looked ready to face the gallows, apparently willing to die to keep in Gabriela's good graces.

Quentin broke off another slice of orange for Nigel. Cuthbert's warning and Leydi's smiles struck his head like hammers against an anvil. *Don't be a fool,* he told himself. *Don't fall so easily into this trap as they have.*

He clung to those words of self-preservation with the familiarity of old times. Like a cherished friend, the voice inside him gave strength. *You're not one to sit by and let others beat you. Remember the lessons of Clarice.* He wouldn't let soft kisses and scented promises from the Mouse wipe away the hard-won knowledge of the past.

But somehow he couldn't do the deed under Nigel's watchful eyes. Taking the iguana from his lap, where the animal had crawled up to enjoy his meal, Quentin set him on the ground again, leaving the peeled orange for him to feast on.

He pulled each man down beside him, careful not to step on Nigel's tail. "You two have lulled yourselves into a fantasy on this enchanted isle," he said, crouching low beside Piton and Bishop, thinking of Clarice and how quickly dreams became nightmares. "Do you plan to stretch your neck out on the chopping block, too? You think that because we are given rooms, free reign of the place, that all is well? Lest you forget, we are now privy to the identity of several women who Kincaid has strategically placed on St. Kitts. I don't believe we'll see our homes ever again." Catching their gazes, he lowered his voice and added, "Unless we escape first. Something I plan to do soon—tonight, if possible."

"Tonight?" Hugh asked, plucking at the scarf tied around his neck as if already sensing the danger.

"Have you succeeded in picking the lock, then?" Felix asked.

"Or do you plan to take the key from her pocket as she sleeps in your bed?" he added, damning Quentin with his all-too-knowing gaze.

Quentin swallowed his retort. It was for these fools he fought, to make sure they were far away from the menace of Kincaid before the pirate arrived—a menace Quentin himself had brought upon them with his machinations. Dammit, they were running out of time!

"I'll do whatever I have to do to get off this island," he told Felix, knowing that he would. He was no longer that young man letting thoughts of love lead him to make mistakes that could cost others their lives. He kept seeing Clarice's dead face. "Now, are you with me?"

Bishop watched him with those haunted eyes. For an instant Quentin saw in their depths his own perfidy—his tactics against Leydianna, the fact that they'd made love. That he wanted to make love to her always. Oh, how easy it would be to throw his lot in with these two fools, to believe he could stay in Leydi's arms forever and Kincaid be damned.

But he shook off the charming image that Leydi incited of love and children. All the sweetness the Mouse had to offer wouldn't change the past, or the fact that he was responsible for these men's lives. He wouldn't let them die like Clarice for his mistakes. He'd told Leydi as much. He'd warned her fairly. If she came to his bed again, she did so at her own peril. She'd made her choice.

Studying the naval officer, now thin from days of too little eating and too much sulking, Quentin could see that Bishop still had doubts. For Bishop's own sake, Quentin had to change that. Sensing as he often did a man's desires and motives and how they could be exploited, Quentin used his instincts to his advantage.

"Where is all that grand hate you held for pirates?" Quentin whispered in Bishop's ear. "Have you really been able to swallow it all? You spoke so eloquently about the horrors they've committed," he added like a man used to outwitting opponents. "What of the innocent planters and their families tortured and murdered—all for a few pigs and a hen or two? Are you going to let Kincaid, the man you painted as the demon of the seas, escape? Just because you have some scruples against hurting his housekeeper's feelings?" He inched closer when Felix would turn away. "A woman who kidnapped you? Who chose Kincaid over you? Who continues to choose Kincaid over you?" he asked, knowing as he spoke that his words were meant for himself as much as Bishop.

"He has some hold on her," Bishop said, staring in the distance, battling Quentin's logic. "When I know what it is, I can help her."

"And who's helping you in the meantime, hmm? Who's helping us?" Quentin asked, including Piton in his plea.

He knew he'd struck a spark. He saw it kindle inside the depths of Bishop's dark brown eyes. Knowing he was a government man, Quentin fed the flames. "Are we to let Kincaid get away with murder and mayhem against the very people you've sworn to protect? Isn't it your duty to see Kincaid stopped—by any means necessary?"

Bishop looked up at him. In his eyes Quentin saw the old hatred, the fever to destroy he'd heard in the man's voice so many times when he'd come to Rutherford Hall to recruit Quentin for his campaign against the pirate. "No. No, we can't allow him to continue to kill any more people."

"What about you?" Quentin said, turning to the weak link.

Hugh sighed heavily. "All right. I will try." He shivered. "But I think it is a mistake, *mes amis*. Yes. A big mistake."

Quentin pressed his lips together, not knowing whether he should feel relieved or damned. But he'd made his decision long ago, and he would stand by it—he needed to get off this island of dreams, and fast. Before he forgot the hard truths reality could teach the unwary.

He sat down on the tree root. To distract himself until Leydi came to find him, he reached for the orange Nigel battled over, thinking to finish peeling it for him. But when his hand neared the iguana, Nigel skittered back, his jaws dropping in a silent hiss.

"Well, what do you know," Felix said, watching the exchange. He raised his eyes to Quentin's. "A perceptive beast, isn't he?"

* * *

"This way," Leydi said, waving Quentin forward. "Quickly. Before Samuel catches us."

Quentin watched Leydi climb over the black lava rocks, her skirts hitched enticingly up to her knees. They were deep in a heaven of giant ferns, colorful succulent shrubs, and majestic trees cloaked in vines and climbing orchids. The sound of rushing water blended with the music of thrushes warbling and parrots crooning. If possible, the air was thicker here, smelling faintly of sulfur. This, then, was paradise, as wild and new as the Garden of Eden.

Quentin trekked up behind Leydi. The entire afternoon had passed with haunting slowness, reaching this point. The latent images of Leydi smiling in his arms, Felix's and Hugh's expressions of distaste, even Nigel hissing, brought forth emotions that one month earlier he would have staked his entire fortune he would never experience again.

Good God, he was too old to feel contrite, too jaded to care about a young woman's splintered heart. This was a matter of survival. Those idiots needed him to show some sense, even if they could not.

But as he climbed over the moss-embedded pumice in Leydi's wake, brushing aside the dewy fan of vines and ferns to catch sight of her lovely backside wiggling up a questionable incline, he felt so weak of will. The seductive question seemed to hover: *Why bother?* Why not just give in and play her mad game of make-believe?

If he were honest, even now with everything at stake, he'd admit he'd never been this close to happiness. Here at last, he'd banished his nightmares. Running after Leydi through a path cleared of its tangle of jungle forest by a buccaneer's cutlass, laughing and playing catch me if you can among the vine-covered palms and tree ferns of this elysium, he could almost forget the danger and act as if this were one of her fantasies, and the ending was certain to be a happy one.

He watched her grin from her perch atop an enormous lava rock. She tore off her mobcap and flung it in the air, watching as it caught the breeze and sailed into the emerald carpet of vegetation behind her, never to be seen again. She shook loose her curls, the movement lush and sensual. *Oh, how she tempted.* But he wasn't a man to let go of sanity like that, he told himself. He had once, with Clarice, imagining happiness in his grasp. And it had all fallen to disaster.

Leydi threatened the same. Disaster.

"Up there," she pointed. "Over that rise. Come on—it's well worth the climb. And I want us to see it before Samuel catches up."

He let her pull him along, returning her smiles, lying with every breath, every move, because he had to. "Samuel went back to get water, just as you asked." He tugged her to a stop. Of their own volition, his arms twined around her waist, inching her toward him. "I thought you said he couldn't find us out here."

She laughed, a spirited, joyful sound. "With my 'shortcut,' it will be a good hour before he discovers us. Still," she said, twining her arms around his neck. "I don't want him to come too soon." She lowered her lips to his.

He allowed her to kiss him, to wrap him up in her warmth and joy. He played along with the dream, telling himself it was necessary, this ruse. And then, as her mouth moved over his and she tugged him down to a flat plateau of rocks, it stopped being a ruse.

Last night he'd told himself it was the rum that had allowed the choices he'd made. That he was on his guard. But he could see it wasn't true. Even sober and with only the scent of lavender intoxicating him, he was making the same choices, allowing himself this little bit of magic she granted.

When their kiss grew too heated, it was Leydi who danced away, shaking her head. "Not here. It's just a bit more. Come on."

The pool was everything she promised. Carved out of black lava rock by the bubbling stream beneath the surface, it was surrounded by the vines and shrubs of the jungle forest. A pagan paradise. Hummingbirds with blue and scarlet throats drank nectar from blossoms the size of Quentin's two fists. The hint of sulfur mingled with the perfume of orchids. Blue parrots roosted among laurels and evergreens draped in succulent vines and trumpet flowers. Despite the warm air, a thin cloud of steam hovered over the indigo water.

Leydi turned to him. Her eyes on his, she unbuttoned her bodice and slipped it off her shoulders. Her petticoat followed as she stepped out of the skirts and kicked them aside. She no longer wore offending stays. She stood displayed before him in only pale pink stockings and a shift so sheer, he could see the coral outline of her nipples and the dark thatch of curls at the apex of her legs.

"I wish we could stay here forever," she whispered, a hint of longing in her voice. As she unlaced her shift and let it pool at her feet, there was a shine to her gray-green eyes, as if she, too, knew this moment couldn't last. "I love you, Quentin."

She stood naked in Eden, wearing only her stockings, the sight more perfect, more erotic than anything he'd ever seen. Botticelli could not have done her justice, the image was so lush and rich. She was a gift—one he could not turn his back on, no matter how he damned himself for loving her.

Two steps, and he held her in his arms. He dropped down to his knees, unrolling the rosy silk of her stockings, kissing every inch of calf, caressing her toes until she melted down beside him, utterly beautiful. She stroked his cheek with her fingertips and a breeze rustled the curls around her pixie face. He pressed his lips against her breasts. God, he wanted this dream to go on forever.

The specter of Kincaid melted under to the heat of his blood. He tugged her down to the carpet of moss, smelling the sweet orchids and Leydi's lavender until he was as drunk with those scents as with the rum. All his plans for deception slipped away with the last of his clothes. They dipped into the steaming water of the mineral springs she had found for them. But he was on fire already, had been for some time.

He kissed her neck, her face, until she laughed, kissing him back. He opened his mouth over hers as he dropped them both into the shoulder-deep pool, until she laughed no more, just held on to him with the same desperation pulsing through him.

He wanted her. He wanted this vision of happiness. And for

the moment, he thought he could have it. Here, in paradise, he was free to love her true.

For Leydi, holding Quentin in her arms again was a dream. She told herself she wouldn't let doubt mar an instant of it, wouldn't let Kincaid's threat cloud its perfection. Returning his kisses, sucking in a breath as the churning waters of the pool splashed their faces, she grasped to the spiderweb fragility of the moment, hoping all her hopes and dreams could keep the cracks from showing too glaringly.

She stopped kissing Quentin just long enough to tug him down under the sulfurous water. They both submerged, then laughed when they surfaced, gasping for air. She told herself God would let her have this one happiness—that despite the hesitation she saw in Quentin's eyes, she could make him love her. She wouldn't listen to the taunting voice that warned she hadn't given up her daydreams, merely brought them all together to create this myth of love.

Quentin pressed her against the rocks, his midnight eyes suddenly so focused on her, it stole her fears away. *He doesn't even know how much he needs me,* she thought, reaching up to brush the wet curl of hair from his face.

He laced their fingers together, then kissed her breasts where the water skimmed the heated skin. She gasped as he took a nipple in his mouth, sucking sweetly until she thought she would die from the pleasure of it.

"The way you touch me—" She moaned, sliding her fingers through his hair. "I didn't know it could be like this, making love." She buried her face against his neck, her hands brushing up and down the muscles of his back as she told her doubts to hush. "Is it always so magical? A pleasure so deep, it's a little like dying?"

He picked up her legs beneath the water and twined them around his hips. Pressing her against the water-polished rocks, he drove himself inside her, making her gasp from the sheer pleasure of it.

"I don't know," he whispered, kissing her neck, cupping her breasts. "It's never been like this for me."

Leydi smiled, pressing closer to him. His words were like a

declaration of love. She let the magic of it dispel all her fears as he cupped her buttocks and brought her closer, rubbing himself against her even as he plunged deeper inside her. She didn't care anymore if this, too, were a lie—a daydream—she would take what she could.

The special sorcery of his touch swirled around her like the bubbling water. With anticipation she waited for the building, the sweetness, that made her moan. She bit her lip, vowing that this time she would be silent, but he kissed her mouth open, making her groan once more with pleasure.

"Don't hide from me," he whispered. "Give me everything. Everything."

And she did. She couldn't help but give everything, especially when he asked it of her with his beautiful touch and kisses, bringing them nearer and nearer to that edge. With the rhythm he had set inside her, she pressed herself closer, closer . . . until the pleasure of the lovemaking flowed over her, making her smile and catch her breath.

For the longest moment they stayed in each other's arms, letting the fire inside them dwindle to a pulse beat. She cradled him against her as she kissed his shoulder and tasted his warmth with her mouth. She had never experienced anything so binding. She knew at that instant why a man and woman married for life.

The thought of marriage startled her from her blissful state. She hugged him with almost desperate strength, as if the sheer force of her embrace could make him hers.

But she knew she couldn't. Given the choice, Quentin would leave her today and make his bid for freedom. And she sensed it wasn't so much Kincaid he ran from—the pirate she'd sworn to protect him from—but rather his past. He was afraid to love. And time was running out for her to change his mind. To make him believe they could be happy together.

Quentin hugged her back, then pushed away, splashing her playfully before he leaned against the rock, leaving her alone. Even though he smiled with a special warmth in his eyes, she felt cold where they no longer touched. She told herself to dismiss the nagging sense to protect herself from heartbreak. What he gave her now was so utterly wonderful; surely it was worth any risk.

She dipped lower into the water so it covered her to her neck. Whatever happened between them, she would take the chance to make Quentin happy. If she told herself often enough that the future didn't matter, with time she might even come to believe it was true.

"I don't know if that helped or hurt," he said, laughing softly.

"It helped," Leydi said with a small smile. She blew him a kiss.

In response, he stroked through the water back to her side, holding her again. He pressed his cheek against her hair. "It's probably not good for Samuel to see us like this."

She sighed. "You're right." Slowly, every touch showing regret, they released each other and stepped out of the pool. She had time to don only her shift before Quentin came up behind her, hugging her to him.

He kissed the side of her mouth and she turned in his arms so he could kiss her fully.

"Will you show me your island?" he asked between kisses.

She had a moment's hesitation, thinking of Samuel coming to look for them. Perhaps it wasn't such a good idea to completely disappear and leave the poor man to return to the compound empty-handed. But then Quentin kissed her again, and she forgot her misgivings. She had no weapons against him.

She stepped back, holding her fingers to her mouth as if to seal the taste of him there. Then she nodded. Perhaps just one special place and they'd double back, before Samuel found them.

It didn't take long till they reached the encampment of Caribs. Leydi held her finger to her lips and pulled apart the fronds of an enormous banana plant. She stood back to let Quentin see the Indian village.

He was quiet for a moment, taking in the thatch huts and the near-naked figures walking past fire pits. He whispered, "I understand they're cannibals."

Leydi frowned. "Perhaps in times of war. Kincaid keeps a truce between our two camps. He thinks the fact the Caribs are here helps keep others away. There's even some trade between us."

He turned back to Leydi. "They travel freely to other islands?"

"In canoes," she said. "Hollowed out from trunks."

He leaned close and whispered in her ear. "That, I would most certainly like to see."

She smiled and grabbed up his hand, glad to be able to indulge him. "Come along. I can show you one I discovered not too far from here." And the harbor kept by the Indians would lead back to Samuel and the mineral baths. She skipped forward, smiling back at Quentin over her shoulder. If she hurried, they would return before Samuel worried too much and set out to find them.

Felix heard the key before the door opened. He waited in the shadows, knowing she would come, as she had last night. He'd been thinking all day of what Rutherford had argued, realizing he'd let himself become entangled with a woman who worked for Kincaid. The man who had murdered his family.

She walked in slowly, as if she already sensed danger from his stance. Before, she'd always run into his arms. Tonight she stopped, not touching him.

"You told me you were one of them," he said very carefully. "Did you think I would still welcome you after that?"

She dropped her head. She wore no cap, and the curls fell forward like a veil to hide her face. He tried to tell himself she was Kincaid's; he tried to hate her. He could find an excuse for everything she'd done thus far, but her loyalty to that heartless pirate went too far. It was the one thing that didn't fit his image of the loving and caring woman he wanted so much to believe she was.

She tossed her hair back, her eyes meeting his without the least bit of contrition. She stepped toward him, slowly reaching up as if to brush his cheek. But at the last minute she dropped her hand back to her side. "I came because I couldn't stay away, Felix."

He grabbed both wrists and pulled her flush against him, kissing her with punishing strength. She kissed him back, even as he knew he must be hurting her.

"I can't be your enemy, Gabriela," he whispered. "Don't make me your enemy."

She shook her head, clutching at him. "You don't have to be. I love you."

"Then come away with me. Tonight. Before the bastard comes back and stops us. I have to know that you choose me."

"You don't know what you're asking of me—"

He pushed her away, angry. "Then tell me, damn you," he whispered softly. "No more mystery between us. For the love of God, I want the truth. What is this man to you that you would come to my room each night but leave me here knowing he and not I holds your loyalty?"

She shook her head, as if she feared to tell him. Then in a very small voice she said, "Kincaid. I love him, too. In a different way than I love you. Don't ask me to choose."

"He's a murderer of women and children."

"No. I can put many things at his doorstep, but that's not one of his crimes."

He sneered, looking at her as if she were too gullible. "I know different." He turned his back to her. "You've made your choice. Get out of here, Gabriela."

He heard the door open on its hinges, then Gabriela's voice whisper back, "I love you, Felix. I won't let him hurt you. Please believe me. I'll keep you safe."

Chapter Twenty-four

Quentin sat on the bed, his legs stretched out before him, his arms laced behind his neck. One bare foot perched over the other. The moonlight from the open louvers of the window banded the yellow lace pattern of the counterpane and the swags of netting dripping from the tent bed. Nigel, his majestic tail draped over the footboard, watched from his place at Quentin's feet, waiting.

Whether it was a figment of his imagination or delusions of his guilty conscience, Quentin thought the iguana studied him with not-so-friendly eyes.

It *was* odd how Nigel sat so still and far away. Quentin was used to the iguana seeking his company, often crawling up around his neck as if he sought a better perch from which to view the world around him. The distance Nigel kept between them seemed a silent message: *All is not well.*

"Good Lord, even a demon lizard takes the high road," he muttered.

It was the middle of the night; he expected Leydi to arrive soon. Tonight he must lull her into giving him her key. Only this time he had no rum to subdue her.

He reached to the nightstand, where he kept a supply of fruit to appease Nigel. After breaking off a bite of banana, he held it out to the iguana, wagging the fruit temptingly in his hand.

Nigel remained unmoved.

"So you'll not be bribed?" Quentin dropped the banana back to the nightstand. He slipped down to the foot of the bed, coming face-to-face with the enormous dragonlike creature. "You want me to believe in her—to trust she can protect me from her pirate? You think I should face the truth that it's not so much Kincaid I fear but that charming mistress of yours and how she twists my heart in her hands?"

Nigel didn't bat a lash—which, of course, he didn't possess. He merely returned Quentin's glare for golden glare.

"But that choice isn't mine to make," Quentin said softly. "I can't just hand up my hide and Bishop and Piton be damned. They'll be waiting in the jungle tonight for me to make my move. And I must, whether it hurts our sweet Leydi or not."

The sound of the key turning brought his attention back to the room's entrance. In a moment Leydi swept into the chamber, a whimsical swirl of brown skirts and gold-tipped curls. Her hands behind her and a smile on her face, she shut the door.

"Brody?" he asked.

She held up her hand for him to be quiet. "Listen. Do you hear that horrible wheezing?" She grinned, the smile making her look painfully young. "That's him snoring down the hall. I don't know how he manages to stay in his chair. He must get an awful crick in his neck come morning."

She stopped halfway to the bed, seeing Nigel for the first time. "There you are, you silly." She glanced up at Quentin. "It seems he cares to spend more time with you than he does with me."

"I told you," Quentin said, reaching for the iguana to take him off the bed, "we're kindred—ah!"

He snatched back his hand with a sharp intake of breath. He stared down at his finger where it bled. Where Nigel had bitten him.

Leydi ran forward, taking a look at the damage. Just as she reached for Nigel, he scurried down the bedclothes and darted under the bed. Only the yellow and brown striped tip of his tail still peeked out from under the rail.

Leydi grabbed the towel next to the chipped porcelain bowl on the washstand and dipped it into the water. She gently dabbed away the blood. "He's never done that before," she said, pressing the moist cloth to the bite.

"Perhaps he thought I deserved it."

"Now who's being silly? Besides, what could you do to make Nigel angry with you?"

"I could think of a thing or two. Seduce you," Quentin said, his voice all too serious. "Use you to get off this island."

For an instant they stared at each other, the spoken words too honest to be ignored. Leydi broke off her gaze first, concentrating on her ministration to his finger.

"You don't need to use me," she said softly. "I'll help you. Which I'm sure you've guessed by now." Their eyes met once more, but she quickly looked away, the moment too intense. "There," she said with a final pat. "All better."

He grabbed her wrist before she could walk away. "Will you help me get to that canoe?" he asked. "Me and the men? To escape this island tonight?"

She wriggled out of his grasp and folded the towel neatly, then replaced it on the washstand next to the porcelain bowl. "Kincaid isn't going to hurt you; I'm going to make sure of that."

"But you won't help me leave before the choice is his instead of mine?"

She closed her eyes, appearing for an instant to feel pain. When she looked up at him again, all the love and desire he could ask for shone from her eyes. "God help me, Quentin. I'll do anything you ask."

And then she waited, waited for him to ask.

Instead, he took her in his arms, folding her into his embrace because he had seen her love too clearly. No one had ever looked at him like that, with so much adoration he could drown in it. He closed his eyes, cherishing the memory of it, allowing himself this one instant to return it. He recalled the years he'd wanted only one thing from life, for someone to love him without reserve or hesitation.

"We'll do it your way, Mouse," he whispered into her hair. He found it was better to trick her. He wouldn't make her choose. Or perhaps he was too great a coward to crush her dreams. "We'll wait for Heartless to come, shall we?" He kissed her temple and cupped her face in his hands, turning it up to his. "And then you'll protect me, hmmm?"

Tears welled in her eyes. Her lips quivered as she smiled, damning him all the more with her tender display of emotion. "Oh, Quentin, thank you. I thought . . . I thought you didn't believe me. Your trust—it means everything to me." She hugged him fiercely. "I love you, Quentin. I love you with all my heart."

"I know, Mouse," he said, holding her gently. Hating himself. Hating the power she had over him. "I know."

He turned her in his arms and kissed her, not thinking of the key or escape. He wanted only to find some way to make up for his lies. She returned his kisses sweetly, putting all her longing in each brush of her lips, every caress, seducing him with her mouth. He found his hands reaching for the buttons of her bodice, unlacing her shift, giving her with his hands what his words had denied her.

He parted the cotton shift. The lacy edges fell back to reveal the lovely offering of her breasts. They filled his hands with her warmth, tempting him to want more. He stroked her neck with his mouth, tasting every curve, breathing in the scent of lavender. But it wasn't enough—not nearly enough.

He circled each nipple with his tongue, thinking only of this moment, wiping his conscious mind of all plots and plans. He wanted his hands to love her, even as he knew he couldn't give her what she wanted. The whole dream. He tugged off her skirts and knelt down before her, entranced by the beauty of the simple curve of her thigh, the delicious sweep of her buttocks. He rolled back her stockings with ritual slowness, kissing a path his fingers eagerly followed. She plucked at his shirt, protesting her nakedness before him, until he stood and hushed her with his mouth. Lifting her in his arms, he lay her on the counterpane, taking a moment to see the pearl-pink perfection of her body in the moonlight.

"Quentin?" She held her hands out to him, Venus in all her glory.

He undressed quickly and climbed up on the bed beside her, completely mindless in his pursuit of her, not daring for a moment to weigh the cost. She was too necessary to him; what she offered, too essential to them both. He kissed her stomach, nibbling on each delectable curve, dipping his tongue into her navel as his hands swept up to cherish her breasts. Her fingers trembled on his shoulders. She tried to pull him up to her, to her lips. But he wouldn't allow it, and so she took his hands and kissed each fingertip instead.

Inch by enticing inch, he savored her body with his mouth, molding his lips over the softness of her breasts, the scented warmth of her wrists. Reaching its goal, his mouth settled over hers in familiar greeting. Slowly, he lowered his body, pressing against the welcoming heat of her.

Their gazes met, hers lusciously dark, as if she were lost in the sensations he'd created. He guided her hands to the corners of the pillow where her head rested and curled her fingers around the opposite corners of the pillowcase. He made her grasp the linen cloth on each side of her head and whispered, "Hold this, tight."

When she would protest, he kissed her silent, wrapping his two hands around her fingers, forcing her grip on the pillowcase. He dipped down to kiss her neck, his hands slowly releasing hers to circle her wrists, pinning her for a instant to the bed as if to tell her, *stay.*

His mouth lowered to the enticement of her breasts. He laved each nipple, then reached down to stroke and pebble one luscious point with his fingers. He sucked the other deep into his mouth. She moaned, twisting her hips beneath him.

"I don't know if I can do this," she whispered, just a little afraid. "Let me hold you."

"No," he warned, nibbling on the sweet skin of her nipple, then blowing on that moistened tender point. "No, I want to do this. I don't want you to forget . . ." He stumbled over the words, thinking that he'd meant to say he didn't want her to forget *him.* "Never to forget this night," he said instead.

He reached down to open her legs for him. Already she was wet. It was a simple thing to dip his finger inside her, to tease her. But he wanted so much more.

On the bed he knelt between her legs, his hands caressing her parted thighs to keep her from moving and sitting up to hold him. He glanced up at her face. Leydi held her eyes closed. She bit her bottom lip as he feathered his fingers up and down her thighs, then touched his thumb to the heart of her. She clutched the pillow as he slipped the tip of his thumb inside her, then eased back to stroke the pearl of skin that held all her desires.

With Leydi it was always like this. He made love to her almost desperately, as if it were vital that they never forget the experience. It seemed this was the only part of the dream he could allow himself. He lowered his mouth to the mound of lovely curls the same honeyed color as her hair, wanting to brand her with his memory. Never wanting either of them to forget. This was theirs, this special moment. Even if they never had another together, he wanted this memory to be enough for all their tomorrows.

He kissed her there, between her legs, as he held her parted for him. Her whimpered cries of passion made his own desire rise and flow over him, overwhelming him until he couldn't decide whom he'd branded by this kiss. And when her muffled pleas against the pillow heralded the pulsing against his mouth, he knew he would never forget this woman.

He continued to stroke her with his lips, tasting her, cherishing her with his tongue so that she would ride the last wave of pleasure to its end. When that, too, subsided, and she lay boneless on the counterpane, her hands opened against the linen covers. He inched up over her, slowly letting his weight settle to cover her body. But she didn't wait. She pulled him down to her, clutching his hair, his shoulders, twining her legs around his hips, taking all of him.

This time it was Leydi who brought them together, lifting herself to join them. Leydi who set the rhythm as he kissed her mouth, her neck, her warm shoulders . . . Leydi who cherished his mouth with hers, making the moment memorable as she pulsed around him, making him shut his eyes and grip the sheets as he found his pleasure. Found his heart.

When they lay sprawled on the counterpane, legs and arms circling each other's so that it was difficult to find where one began and the other ended, the very intensity of their lovemaking startled him. He knew he should roll away, should run from this bed and this woman. But instead, he held her only closer, thinking he could never get enough of her. In the silence he heard her even breathing. There came a soft patter against the shutters.

"It's raining," she whispered.

He scooped her closer to him, spooning her up against his chest.

"It will stop soon."

She turned in his arms and took his face in her hands. He smiled, knowing how she felt. Feeling the same.

"You're going to marry me," she whispered. There was just a touch of awe in her voice as she said it. "That is what this is all about, isn't it? You wouldn't have done this if it weren't forever?"

It was so lovely, the way she spoke. Too wonderful. "You're right," he said, stroking her bottom lip with his finger, wanting to give them more of the dream. "It's forever."

He told himself he hadn't completely lied. He did want her forever. If the choice were possible, if the choice were his. He would marry her now, give her all the children she could spoil with her loving kindness and patience. He closed his eyes and listened to the rain, thinking this time it was he who had spun the dream, learning from her how to cheat reality. Needing her "forever" as much as she did.

"I want to thank you," she whispered.

"Hush." He kissed her nose. "Go back to sleep," he said, drifting off a bit himself.

"No. Not about this." She stroked his chest, her fingers brushing the hair in a languid rhythm. "The combs. I want to thank you for the combs."

He frowned, not wanting reality to intrude so quickly into this vision they'd made, wanting to pretend just a bit longer. The combs reminded him that he could be a bastard. That he could hurt. "I don't want to talk about the combs."

"Well, I do," she whispered. She climbed up on her elbows, looking down on him with those soft eyes, making him realize gray was entirely too giving a color. "You were right to send them. Those combs made me realize I was just hiding all my hate, letting it fester inside me. After she cut my hair, I finally accepted how angry I was at my mother. And Argus. It helped." She plucked at his chest hair playfully. "It's not good to lock up all those ugly feelings inside yourself. It's better to face them."

He groaned, rolling over. "Why do I feel you're leading to something."

"Because you're a brilliant strategist," she teased in his ear, hooking her arm and leg around him. "You can see my ploy long before I launch my attack."

He flipped over and placed his finger across her lovely mouth. "I don't want to talk about the past. About my father."

She kissed his finger, then his palm. "All right." She cradled his hand against her breast, kissing his mouth in quick butterfly brushes. "You're right. I must show patience." And then she glanced up, hope turning her eyes dark with just a slim wedge of green and silver. "But someday you'll let me help you?"

He didn't speak, unable to voice that lie out loud. He simply nodded.

When she fell asleep, she lay curled in his arms, breathing softly against his chest. It must have been hours he lay there, thinking, trying to make this impossible choice. The moonlight streamed through the window, glowing in her hair. She looked like one of his angels. Deliciously innocent.

He knew it was her innocence he hadn't been able to resist. He threaded his fingers through those curls of golden brown, hating that she was silly enough to love him—and such a poor negotiator, to have given him all her heart, not even saving a small sliver for herself.

For the longest time he battled the obvious, trying to keep alive the visions they had spun. He could love her; he wasn't tainted by his memories. Here, in her arms, he'd been re-deemed. Perhaps she was right and she could save them all from

Kincaid. But as the minutes flowed into hours, the gilded edges of the dream began to tarnish and the past crept back into his heart, shoving away his lovely fantasy. In his arms he no longer held the woman who would be his wife; he held only the young innocent who had kidnapped him and held him as if all her love could make dreams come true.

His fingers twisted from her hair. Nigel had been right to bite him.

Careful not to wake her, he crept off the bed and gathered his clothes. He told himself nothing had changed; she couldn't be a part of his life. He didn't need another blood-soaked bed to haunt his dreams or Leydi's lifeless eyes to keep him awake at night. He couldn't allow her precious longing to manipulate him into making mistakes. Better to hide. Better to escape. Despite all her hopes for a happy ending, he didn't have the love he'd promised her. It had died too many years ago to be revived now.

For an instant he became angry with her, watching her on that bed in the moonlight. Why did she make it so easy, damn her? Why was she so gullible, so easily duped? But in the middle of his tirade he realized the truth behind his anger. She'd touched him in a way he'd promised himself no one would ever touch him again, not his father, not a woman, not a child. Leydi, damn her, was no different from the earl, sneaking in, trying to make him feel things—succeeding.

He needed to escape, and he allowed that it wasn't just Kincaid he ran from. He thought he'd made love to her to give them both a memory. But his motives might not be so noble. In a moment of insight, he realized that if he broke her heart, she would never come back to find him on St. Kitts.

He stared at her in the bed. The bedclothes tangled where his body had lain. She sighed in her sleep and turned over.

He stayed only until she settled down, and then he found the key.

This time he didn't hesitate when he reached Kincaid's study. He grabbed up the compass and headed for the seaweed marquetry of the desk, where he'd found the gun. It was still there. He searched a bit more and was rewarded by a horn of powder.

He tucked the loaded pistol into the waistband of his trousers at the small of his back, preparing to leave Leydi's island of dreams.

And then his eyes fell on the logbooks.

Leave, you fool, the voice in his head told him. *Stop wasting time.* But he couldn't move.

He told himself he no longer cared to know what secrets lay between Leydi and Kincaid. He argued that the mystery of their relationship no longer mattered; he was well on his way to escape. Still, he kept staring at those journals behind their pane of glass, thinking of Leydi, of the wistful tone she'd used when she'd spoken of her parents.

You're here to find weapons, a voice shouted in his head. His presence in Kincaid's den had nothing to do with Leydi. *Leave, you fool. Get out! Get out before it's too late!*

Quentin cursed under his breath and put down his booty. He opened the breakfront bookcase and yanked out the logbook he'd read last. Taking the calfskin journal back to the window, he opened the velvet curtain a crack and let the soft glow of moonlight fall on the pages. He searched furiously, knowing he'd stay there until he had his answers.

It almost astonished him how quickly he solved the puzzle. It was written so simply, he didn't know how he'd missed it before. That and the other truths the pirate had so carefully hidden.

Quentin read the words with a sense of the inevitable. He'd always known there was something special about her and the power she wielded on this island so effortlessly.

The slight creak of the floorboards warned him too late. He glanced up, for the first time catching sight of the man who stood in the doorway in total shadow. The flicker of a candle followed, carried into the room by Cy. Quentin had never seen the man standing in the entrance beside Cy—no one on St. Kitts had these many years. But the domineering planes of his sun-bronzed face and the bearded menace of his expression told him who he was.

"Kincaid," he said.

"Aye. And who the bloody hell might you be?" the deep voice blasted across the room.

"He's one of the men I told ye about," Cy said, entering the room behind Kincaid. "Rutherford. Quentin Rutherford."

Kincaid smiled, the wicked gleam of a predator in his eyes. In his elaborately laced velvet coat he swept a bow, brushing his tricorn to the tips of his black knee boots before tossing the hat to a chair. He crossed his arms over his embroidered waistcoat and studied Quentin. "Rutherford. Of Rutherford Estate."

"Where you once worked," Quentin said quietly.

The twinkle of mischief in Kincaid's eyes vanished. In its place was a chip of emerald ice. "Worked? I was no better than a slave."

"An indentured servant," Quentin corrected him, all the bits and pieces falling together. "That's why all the interest in my ships. Revenge. For the years you thought yourself mistreated."

"Your grandfather's overseer was a son of a bitch. He made the life of every manjack on that plantation an utter hell. Aye. There was a certain irony to stripping yer ships clean."

"I dismissed the man," Quentin said, remembering his own distaste for the overseer, a bull of man who thrived on useless cruelty. He thought it unfortunate his grandfather had turned a blind eye to the vicious abuse so many years. It had cost more than one man his life. "He didn't last the week when I took over the running of the plantation."

"Well, bully for you," Kincaid said, not the least placated.

"And that's where you met Leydi's mother. Both indentured servants on my grandfather's estate?"

For the first time, Kincaid noticed the logbook Quentin dropped to the desk. His face went perfectly still. He said nothing.

Quentin nodded toward the book. "I've read it all. Two daughters. And you made them your housekeeper and your bookkeeper. How . . . novel." Inside Quentin, a protective anger he had no control over seethed, goading him into saying, "Do you have any idea what Leydi's life has been like with that family you gave her?"

"Don't ye be judging me," Kincaid barked, his temper flaring. "I did my best fer the gel. It's cost me a bloody fortune to keep her here."

With a twist in his gut, Quentin realized that everyone Leydi

had admired and loved had betrayed her. "Did you know she
dreamed of you being her father . . . no, I don't suppose she
would tell you that. You being her employer and all. But you
know how eternally thankful she must be for all you've done for
her these past years. I wonder if she'd feel the same if she knew
you were really her father—the one who turned his back on her
pregnant mother, making her marry a drunkard like Argus Carstair. I can see now why the bitch is so bitter, why she takes her
anger out on Leydi—a decided reminder of your betrayal."

"Elaine was always a bitch if she'd the mind to be," Kincaid
said under his breath. "It wasn't my spurning her that made her
bitter."

"And that's the mother you left her to? Utterly thoughtful of
you, I must say."

"Ye bastard!" Kincaid lunged across the room, but Cy grabbed
him by his coat sleeve. Kincaid jerked his arm free, pushing Cy
aside, but he kept his distance from Quentin. "You sneaking
puppy, I brung the girl here as soon as I had the power to protect
her. I paid fer her schooling and gave Elaine enough gold to see
to even her greedy comforts. Though I've no need to make excuses to you, Rutherford." He spit out Quentin's name like the
lowest curse.

"But you never told her you were her father," Quentin said,
condemning him.

"We can take him right now," Cy said, coming up behind
Kincaid, setting the candle on the desk to free his hands. "He'll
never breathe a word of it to anyone."

"I'll tell her nothing," Quentin said bitterly, knowing how well
he belonged in this company—one more who would betray Leydianna. "Let me and the other two prisoners go, and we'll keep
your dirty little secret," he bargained.

"And I'll kill ye now and keep the secret just the same," Kincaid countered.

"There's no secret."

The simple words came from just beyond the door. The three
men turned, watching as a white-faced Leydi walked into the
room. She looked at Kincaid and then at Quentin. "No secret
to keep or bargain with."

For a moment no one moved. In the candlelight flickering from the desk, Leydi looked almost ethereal, a ghost.

"Everyone knows," she said, speaking to herself or Kincaid, it was difficult to say which. "That's why the men all treat me the way they do on this island. They know about me and Gabriela. Gabriela, my sister," she said softly, as if just realizing the relationship. She shook her head, looking mystified. "I always wanted her to be my sister, and all the while it was true."

"It's not like the yelp told it, gel. Let me explain," Kincaid said, walking toward her, holding his hands out to her.

She stepped back, not letting him touch her. She shook her head. "No. No, don't explain. I'm very bright, you see. I understand completely."

The heartbreak in her voice tore Quentin in two. He wanted to take her in his arms, to protect her from the years of hurt tumbling down around her. He wanted to tell her it didn't matter her father had rejected her, then hired her, keeping her on this island as a servant—shipping her back to endure her mother's bitterness.

Don't, a voice shouted inside him. *Don't try to make this right. They'll settle it later, among themselves.*

And it was true. She might feel betrayed now, but she finally had the father she'd prayed for. She didn't need him. All those tender moments they'd shared were just dreams. Reality was escape, for him and the others. He mustn't allow himself to help her, to fall prey to this tender scene—to become a part of it.

Slowly, Quentin pulled the gun from behind his back, where he'd tucked it in the waistband of his breeches. The gun felt heavy, unusually so. His movements were sluggish, almost hesitant. Still, he lifted the weapon, using the moment of disorientation to his advantage. He pointed the barrel at Kincaid.

"I hate to break up this charming scene, but I'm afraid I must be going." He motioned for the two men to step away from the door, but the movement seemed wrong. Stilted. He felt like a puppet playing a part he'd outgrown. He kept his eyes carefully off Leydi.

Kincaid only blocked his path, crossing his arms before his chest as if daring Quentin to shoot. "By the time ye kill one of us, the other will have ye good and proper. There's no escape for you, my man."

Quentin stared at the pirate. The soft *click* of the inverted bell clock on the desk pounded inside his head, slowing the rhythm of his heart. He gripped his fingers around the pistol, knowing there was another avenue of escape, even as Kincaid did not.

The air left Quentin's lungs. He couldn't breathe. It was as if he left his body, appearing to float above this scene as he watched himself turn to Leydi. In those precious moments of indecision, it seemed he had no choice. The same odd insentience washed over him as he beckoned her to his side. She just watched him, more misery dawning in her eyes.

"Come here, Mouse," he called softly.

She shook her head, turning from him to Kincaid, then back to Quentin. Her eyes begged him to leave her be, not to add this pain to her burden. Inside his chest his heart beat with suffocating force. He had to leave. *He must leave!*

"You said all I had to do was ask," he whispered, holding out his hand to her.

She closed her eyes, as if she couldn't bear this final betrayal. But when she looked at him again, it wasn't love or misery shining in her gaze, but a deep, burning anger. Her beautiful mouth pressed into a flat line as she took a step toward Quentin. When Kincaid tried to block her path, she pushed him away. She stopped only when she stood directly in front of Quentin, her little hands fisted to the sides of her simple brown gown.

She tilted back her head and looked him in the eye. He'd never seen more strength in her expression.

"Was this all you wanted?" she asked. "Telling me you trusted me, tricking me so you could steal the key?"

He wanted to tell her no. He wanted more—so much more. She'd made him want *her.* In just the few short weeks they had been together, she'd tempted him with her happily-ever-after. And yet . . . *and yet . . .*

He thought of Clarice. Of love, and death, and parting. And he knew, he knew he didn't have the courage to grab for love . . . only to find it slipping away into another nightmare.

"You want too much, Mouse," he said. "I can't give it to you. I told you to be careful. I warned you."

She retreated a half-step. But soon enough she blinked her eyes quickly and straightened her shoulders, rallying against her pain. "So it was all a lie, a ploy. You never trusted me. And I would have helped you. I would . . ." She caught her breath. She pressed her lips together, not meeting his gaze. When she had the strength, when she knew her voice wouldn't crack, she whispered, "I would have done anything for you."

He grabbed her and turned her around, no longer able to face her. "Gentlemen," he said to Kincaid and Cuthbert. "Your weapons, if you please."

Kincaid dropped his pistol, the only weapon between them. Quentin motioned them to step away from the door. He backed out of the room, choking on the scent of lavender. He continued down the hall, watching Kincaid and Cuthbert over Leydi's head, damned by the soft caress of her curls against his cheek as they stepped down the corridor. He forced himself to think of Bishop and Piton, of their safety.

He dragged her down the steps behind him, the gun now useless at his side. If all went as planned, the others would be waiting at the rendezvous point. He was almost too considerate as Leydi stumbled, supporting her when her foot caught on the carpet. His grasp was too tender as he urged her on, as if it were a kindness he did her instead of this dastardly betrayal.

Neither spoke a word. But when he reached the door, he pressed her up against the wall. He'd always thought her incapable of hate, but as she threw her head up to look at him, he could think of no better word to describe the storm in her eyes. He shook his head, sorry for everything. For so much. And then he kissed her hard and quick.

"You should never have loved me," he said. "Never."

They were his final words before he left.

Leydi stumbled into the courtyard, watching the dark shadow of Quentin disappear. She pressed her fisted hand against her mouth where he'd kissed her. She thought of all the things she'd learned this night, and for the first time she damned her agile mind. With a swipe of her hand she brushed aside her useless tears.

The sound of Kincaid and Cy thundering down the staircase ripped through her misery with the force of gale winds. An incredible anger swept through her, like none she'd ever experienced. She grabbed her skirts and raced back into the house, ignoring the men and their pleas as she darted past them. In Cy's room she found a gun and loaded it. With more strength than she'd ever been credited, she slipped out the back of the house toward the stables, bypassing the men Kincaid rounded up to capture his prisoners.

Unlike Kincaid, she knew where Quentin was going.

The three men ran until the air burned in their lungs. And then they ran harder. Through the wet loam of the path, over razor-sharp pumice, they battled the tangle of jungle. All three knew what they risked. If the pirate caught them, they were dead men.

"Up ahead," Quentin said, motioning through the darkness to the trail Leydi had shown him, the trail that led to the Indian canoe. "It's not far now."

Quentin raced on. The air choked in his lungs, the muscles of his legs screamed for rest. Visions of Leydi lunged at him from the black crevices of the forest surrounding him. There, behind the palmetto, her face crushed by pain. Beyond the vine-choked brush, her silver eyes bruised with anguish. *You betrayed me!* the jungle seemed to cry out.

He crashed past a thicket of seaside grape, motioning the men to pick up the pace. Damn it to hell, he'd told her not to trust him. He'd warned her.

Quentin twisted left, veered right. He thrashed past vines as thick as his wrist; limbs of palms snagged his shirt, their thorns slicing across his chest like sharp daggers. His boots beat against the black earth. But the scene in the study kept rising up to haunt him. He didn't see the stars overhead, only Leydi's eyes watching him, beseeching him.

He cursed, forcing himself onward. He'd always said he'd do

what was necessary to survive in this life. There would not be another Clarice to mourn over. But somehow it all felt so utterly wrong now, leaving her there in that house. As if he weren't running away from Kincaid at all, but from his last chance at happiness.

As they dragged the canoe into the surf, stumbling in the sand, gagging on the spray of seawater and blinking back the sting of salt, it was Leydi's face reflected in the indigo luminescence of the waves. He heard again the strength in her voice as she told him she would protect him—her joy when she'd thought he'd trusted her to keep him safe.

His steps faltered on the sandy ocean floor. The swells of water grew, as if the sea were sucking down at his feet, begging him like Leydi not to leave. He remembered her touching marriage proposal.

"Come on," Felix urged, pushing his weight against the canoe.

But Quentin had stopped, his legs knee-high in the breakers, his heart in his throat.

Both men stared at him. Hugh glanced at Felix, searching for guidance.

Felix grabbed Quentin by the shoulders. "Dammit, Rutherford! Now is not the time for regrets."

Over the crashing of the waves he heard a shout—someone calling his name. It echoed over the careening whitecaps like a siren's song, turning him toward shore.

The light of the moon shone on the sand like a beacon. Leydi stood beneath its halo, her skirts swirling with the wind against her knees. In her hand she held a wheel lock pointed at Quentin.

"You have to promise you won't hurt him," she shouted over the crash of the surf, wading through the waves to meet him with her threat. "Swear that you'll leave us all alone. That none of you will ever return here or harm us in any way!"

He cursed and shrugged off Felix's hold. He slugged through the water, stopping only when the pistol barrel was inches from his chest. The wind whipped around them, stinging sand and mist against the bare skin of his arms and face.

"And you'll still believe me if I give you my word?" He clutched her arms, shaking her like a doll. "How can you be so foolish? I've betrayed you over and over."

There were tears shining in her eyes. Her head slipped back and her eyes begged him. "Don't betray me now. Please," she said, the gun in her hands beginning to shake. "I couldn't bear it, Quentin. Please."

Her words tore at his soul. Her pain, so clear and cutting, smothered his breath in his throat. He shook his head, unable to bear the sight of her like this, so full of hurt, so anguished, yet still trusting in him. He could see himself reflected in her brimming eyes, could see the man he'd become mirrored in those silver depths. And he didn't like the image.

He'd told himself he must escape for the men now climbing into the canoe behind him. But that wasn't the whole truth. He'd clung to his nightmares of Clarice for so many years, he hadn't trusted Leydi and the love she offered. He hadn't trusted his own love for her.

God in heaven, everything he'd done was too contemptible. And despite it all she still believed in him. She still waited for him, the breakers crashing against her legs, sucking at her skirts—waited for him to give her his word and swear he would never betray her. And *she* would believe him, would believe in him always. The only person who would.

"Damn you," he said, realizing he couldn't leave her. She would yet make him face his devils.

"Come on!" Felix shouted.

A gun blast thundered across the sand. The shouts of men buffeted against the wind as several buccaneers careened out of the jungle onto the sand. A second bullet whizzed overhead.

"Stay right where you are, mates!" Kincaid shouted from the break in the trees. He stood in the moonlight with a pistol in each hand and two more strapped to his chest. Cy joined him, his face and body braced with equal menace.

"No!" Leydi yelled, shielding Quentin, the waves threatening to push her to the sand, making her cling to him for an instant before she found her footing. "I have their word they'll not come back or send trouble."

"And I'm not a fool girl to believe them," Kincaid shouted back.

"I want them gone!" Leydi kept herself between Quentin and the guns of the men onshore. "It's me he's hurt, and I want him gone."

"He'll be gone all right. When I'm through with him, he'll be gone to kingdom come!"

"For God's sake, Kincaid," she cried above the surf, "let them go!" She looked back at Quentin, her eyes dark and round. "You must promise," she whispered up to him.

He shook his head, a sort of calm easing over him. "Let Bishop and Piton go," Quentin told her. "I'm staying."

"You can't," she said miserably. "Oh, he may be sorry enough now that he'll listen as long as I'm standing before you, shielding you from his bullets, but afterward . . . I can't protect you . . . I . . . I don't know him anymore. I don't know . . ." She stepped away from him, holding her fingers over her mouth, the gun swaying dangerously loose in her grip. "Go! For the love of God, go!"

"Quentin?" Felix called out.

Quentin sloshed back to her side, grabbing her arms, ignoring the men behind him. "If they leave here now, you have my word no one will hurt you or Kincaid," Quentin vowed, meaning every word. "But I can't leave you, Leydi. What I did, what I said—"

"Stop it!" she begged, refusing to believe the wonderful promise of love she saw so feebly gleaming in his eyes. She pushed him away, waving the gun as if she meant to shoot. She realized now that the hurt she'd thought to heal was too deep in his spirit. He couldn't give her what she'd wanted—his love, a child to take away the nightmares of the family he'd lost.

With the waves beating at her knees, she battled to keep steady, not to let the misery of this moment lure her into making mistakes. She kept her hands on the pistol, as if it were some sort of link to sanity. Let him go to his black world of guilt, but he wouldn't drag her there. He'd showed her he would never trust her—that he couldn't. She was no longer foolish enough to think she was the woman to change him.

She met his eyes once more, blinking away the spray of seawater and tears. "I don't want to hear your declarations of love now," she told him, knowing how to make him get in that boat. Needing him to get in the boat, for her sake as well as his own. "I won't believe them. You wanted to make me strong; you wanted me not to be so gullible. Well, you've done your job well," she said, hurting as she hurt him. "I won't believe you ever again. You killed that faith inside me tonight; just as surely as you killed the love I pledged to you," she cried. "Go, damn you. You were right all along. You can't give me your love. Your past has beaten you, Quentin. It's beaten us both."

Her words slammed into him, pushing him back with more force than the waves or the guns of the men on shore. *Killed her love, her faith—just as he'd killed Clarice and their child.* But even as her words pounded against him, he couldn't seem to turn away. He wanted to argue, to fight her logic. He knew if he got into that boat, he would never see her again.

"I can't leave you like this, Mouse."

She shook her head. "Don't you see? I can't be your Mouse anymore, Quentin. I can't. You've taken that from me. Now go. Before I step aside and let Kincaid shoot you and the others." When he still hesitated, she aimed the gun she held at the boat instead of at him. "Go, damn you. Or I'll blast a hole in that canoe and strand you and the others here. *Go!*"

"Listen to her, Quentin," Felix called to him. "It's too late to change your mind now!"

"Leydi, don't," he begged, when he'd never begged anyone in his life.

"You wanted me to hate you," she said, the tears streaming down her cheeks. "Well, I do. I hate you, Quentin. Do you hear me? I hate you," she shouted. "Leave me. Don't make me more unhappy than you already have."

The last words seemed to pierce through him. The lines around his mouth deepened; his eyes grew dark. Quentin took a few steps back, then turned in the knee-deep water and sloshed to the boat. He jumped inside and the men pushed off, rowing hard against the surf.

On the beach Leydi collapsed to her knees. Her brown muslin gown belled pathetically around her, melting into the water as she sank back on her feet. She could hear the waves lapping against her, and the sound of Kincaid and the men splashing toward her. Before they reached her, she shrank down into the sandy water, her wet skirts clinging to her like a shroud as she watched the little canoe race away.

"I hate you, Quentin," she whispered, as if by saying the words she could make them true. "I hate you. Oh, please, God," she said, still clutching the pistol. "Let me hate him just a little."

Part Four
The Jolly Roger

Chapter Twenty-five

Two weeks later, Rutherford Estate, St. Kitts

Stevenson loped down the carpeted runner of the corridor, his buckled shoes stepping lively over the floral pattern of crimson and gold. The flanks of cornices nodding over each doorjamb, statued niches, and gilded wall sconces passed unnoticed as he glanced over his shoulder, checking to see if the gentleman following in his wake kept pace.

He grabbed his wig as it skittered off-kilter. Under his breath he muttered his reasoning for his outrageous strategy as if tallying the prayers on a rosary. He was still a bit disbelieving of what he'd done. Lord knows he'd tried everything else to bring the dragon out of his lair. Thus far, nothing, not threats of bankruptcy, not ruined crops—not even Mrs. Bailey's tonic had helped, landing as it had shattered against the wallpaper in a blossoming amber stain.

He shuffled forward, giving the gentleman behind him an encouraging nod. Since his return, Quentin had given no explanation for his mysterious absence, had exchanged no more than a few sentences with the staff, who had worried so passionately over his disappearance. Two weeks had passed since Quentin had arrived with his ragged clothes and red-rimmed eyes on the stone steps of Rutherford Hall. Each day the master of the house only seemed to fall into a darker sulk. Yesterday he hadn't even left the receiving chamber. Come morning, the tray George had brought remained untouched in the hall.

Yes, indeed, the staff was growing quite desperate. Stevenson was willing to try anything, even today's fantastic ploy, to nudge Quentin from this infernal despair.

Taking a deep breath, he stopped before the double doors and knocked. As expected, there came no response. With a sigh he opened the doors and motioned the older man forward. As the gentleman stepped toward the door, Stevenson whispered, "Good luck, my lord."

The earl stopped and nodded his regal head, a study in good breeding and confidence. But Stevenson thought the gentleman took a deep breath before he stepped across the threshold, pulling the door shut behind him.

Quentin stared at the edge of daylight bleeding past the crack in the curtains. Another day, he thought dispassionately.

He raised the tumbler of rum halfway to his lips, then lowered the glass to the table untouched, as if he couldn't be bothered. The first thing he'd learned when he'd returned to Rutherford Hall was that rum, no matter how much he drank, couldn't wipe away his regrets.

Another day.

He'd stopped counting the nights he'd sat in his bed, cold without Leydi in his arms, snatching bits and pieces of rest. He thought it possibly the longest he'd gone without sleep. Clarice no longer haunted him. At times he even prayed for her distracting specter. But it was another's face that pleaded with him from the dark now.

Another day.

He couldn't understand why Kincaid had allowed him to escape. Why hadn't the scoundrel come and found him, made him pay for his crimes against Leydianna? The first week, the anticipation of Kincaid and his men stealing into his room or besieging the manor house with the force of the pirate's rage was all that kept Quentin's hopes alive for seeing Leydi again.

But Kincaid hadn't come. No one had.

Quentin stared about the dawn-dusted room. His head dropped to the wilted linen of his shirt. He sunk deeper into the Turk chair. *Dear God, another day.*

He heard the door open. He waited, wondering why Stevenson had allowed him to sulk this long. By now he'd have thought his man would have attempted several forays into the room, no matter how fruitless his past efforts.

But it wasn't his steward who stepped into the darkened chamber. It was his father.

The earl said nothing, just stepped carefully to the center medallion of the wool carpet. Everything was blurry enough from lack of sleep that Quentin had no reaction to his father's arrival. Taking his silence as an invitation, the earl pulled up a hooped-back chair and sat down across from Quentin.

"Did Stevenson send for you?" Quentin asked. "Come to deliver me from the dark depths of despair?" He laughed, answering his own question. "Of course he did. They're all so concerned about me." He glanced at his father and picked up the tumbler of rum. He swirled the liquid in the glass, watching it catch the dawning rays of light. "A bit early for a call, wouldn't you say?"

"I was anxious."

Quentin smiled. "I thought you'd be long gone by now."

His father sighed and balanced both palms on the gold tip of his cane. "If you'd read any of the messages I'd sent you, you would know I wasn't going to leave without settling what's between us."

The words were on the tip of Quentin's tongue to tell him to be damned and leave. *Go back to England, where you belong, there's nothing for you here.* But he didn't speak, perhaps because he was so tired. Perhaps because for an instant he remembered Leydi sitting before him, telling him with heartfelt emotion the words she'd read in his father's note. *Come. Forgive.*

Quentin leaned back against the pillowed back of the armchair and studied the earl. There were lines around his father's eyes; age settling in at long last. Everything else about the man was tailored, pampered. The blue satin coat had stays at its skirts, granting the proper line. The red-heeled shoes and their shining buckle, the cuffed jacket and the lace of his shirtsleeves beneath, would be all the fashion. And yet for once the sight didn't fill Quentin with the sweeping anger that it had in the past.

He thought of Leydi, of what she would wish from this meeting. In their short time together, she had changed something inside Quentin, something basic to his soul. In her quiet manner she'd wiped away seven years of self-hate and ugly nightmares and replaced it with this numb regret . . . *if only.* If only he'd been able to make her understand on that beach. If only he'd made his realizations of what life would be like without her sooner. If only he'd grabbed for the happiness she offered so graciously.

Quentin scraped his fingertips across the wood of the armchair. He thought of that silly fringed chair in his chamber at Devil's Gate and pictured Leydi nestled against the elaborate cane back. She'd asked only one thing of him in her dogged determination to make him happy—that he forgive his father. Now, after everything that had happened, he should try. He could give her that much, at least.

He lifted his face, meeting those familiar blue eyes. "I'm listening," he told the earl.

Perhaps it was surprise over Quentin's mild acceptance after so long a battle between them—perhaps it was just the fact that old habits die hard—but the earl thumped his amber cane and attacked, "Well, young man, I'll have you know your little adventure cost me plenty in peace of mind," he blustered from his chair, his lecturing tone painfully familiar. "We had the authorities in quite a panic. If you've a mind to leave like that, you could at . . . least . . . tell . . ."

Like a sail that had lost its wind, the earl sputtered to a stop. His spine collapsed from its rigid pose and he slumped back into the chair, ruining the fashionable line of his coat. The blue satin sank into an unflattering ripple of wrinkles. He shook his wigged head and stared at the rings on his hand.

From beneath beetled white brows the earl glanced up at Quentin. "I thought I had lost you, boy," he whispered. "It was"—he seemed to search for the proper words—"it was too much, waiting like that, picturing you dead or hurt somewhere." He glanced away, as if he found the walnut paneling of sudden interest. "It frightened me."

Quentin tried to find the sympathy Leydi would wish of him. But his heart lay like a stone in his chest, unable to feel anger, or censure, or sympathy.

He frowned, wanting something to come from inside him. He didn't want to feel so dead. He grasped for the familiar patterns of the past, thinking of how to put that old wedge between him and the earl. Even the plotting of it felt right. He realized that yes, he wanted to keep the comfortable distance he'd managed over the years. He wanted his father gone.

It appeared that even for Leydi he wouldn't endure this reconciliation.

"I've done it again, Father," he said harshly, hearing that horrible edge to his voice, the tone he'd sworn he would never use again after he'd left Devil's Gate. His I-don't-give-a-damn voice. But he couldn't seem to help himself as he continued with self-derision. "I've fallen in love with a totally inappropriate woman. Once again I've forgotten my responsibilities as the heir to an earl."

He picked up the glass, gave his father a mock toast, and tossed back the rum. "She's the daughter of an indentured servant and a pirate, if you can believe that. Not much above Clarice and her machinations, wouldn't you say?"

His father remained silent, for once not voicing an opinion. It wasn't the proper reaction—it didn't fit those old patterns. The normally blustering earl looked to Quentin as if he might actually fear speaking, as if he thought the words might get him booted from the room.

"Go on," Quentin urged, trying to goad him. "Surely you have an opinion on the matter. You've never been shy before."

"Quentin, I don't know how to say this." Again the earl faltered. It was so odd to see his father so vulnerable . . . so old.

Strange enough to make Quentin sit up in his chair and take note.

"I wrote it so many times in those letters you sent back," the earl continued, focusing on something behind Quentin's head. "And it was damn hard to find the words then. Now . . ." He shrugged, then straightened in the chair. His dark blue eyes peered up at Quentin, as if asking him for help.

"Go on," Quentin repeated softly.

The earl nodded, then licked his lips in a thoughtful expression Quentin had never seen on his self-assured father. "Let me just say it plain, then. I'm sorry. I'm terribly, terribly sorry. And I take full responsibility for Clarice's death." He looked away, then, clearing his throat, he added, "Hers and the child's."

Quentin put down the rum glass. He thought of those words in the note. *Come. Forgive.*

"Perhaps if I explain the reasons behind my actions," the earl continued. "Perhaps then you can forgive me. It's really the only hope I have." Again there was silence . . . followed by a long sigh. "You may have noticed, your mother was not an affectionate woman."

Quentin barked a hollow laugh, thinking of just how distant his mother had been. To him, to his father, to anyone who wasn't a seamstress or an aficionado of society's hierarchy, a vital member of the *beau monde*.

"And I have never been a mild-mannered man. Not in my temper, certainly . . . and not in my passionate nature." The dark blue eyes held a mellowed edge of sadness as they met Quentin's. "I had a mistress, Quentin. A woman just like Clarice. She had twins."

The words speared Quentin into his chair. It was the last thing he'd expected his father to say. "Twins?"

The earl nodded. "A boy and a girl. My children. My illegitimate children." Quentin noticed for the first time how his father gripped the arm of the chair and the tip of his cane, the knuckles of each hand white from the pressure. "At the time that Clarice came to you, asking that you marry her, I didn't know why you couldn't just make the same choices I had. I loved my Mary very much, you see. But I had a responsibility to you. I couldn't just marry her, leave your mother. I thought you should do the same . . . I thought, later, when you were older, you would regret your rash choice. Good God, you were barely two and twenty."

"Twenty-three, Father," he said softly. "And old enough to know my own mind."

"Perhaps," the earl agreed, giving that much after so many years. "But I didn't think so at the time. After you left, I held on to my anger for what you'd done. I couldn't believe that you would give up so much. Your responsibilities were to the title, to your future children. I held on to my self-righteous anger. And then—"

The earl seemed to choke on the words. He shook his head again, the dark blue eyes, so much like Quentin's, shadowed with pain. He seemed deep in thought.

"I lost them," he whispered. "Mary and the children. A wretched fever."

The words, simply spoken, held a depth of emotion. Quentin studied his father's face, seeing there the marks of age, the polish now tarnished by a deep loss. And then he saw his father's tears.

Slowly, the silent drops wended down the lines of his face. Quentin could hear Leydi again, pleading with him: *He was crying, Quentin.*

The earl reached over and grasped Quentin's hand. He took a breath. "Be she the daughter of a pirate, a servant, a prostitute . . . though it's hard for me to say it, you have my blessing to take what happiness you can find."

"I wasn't asking for your blessing."

The earl laughed and let go of Quentin's hand. He wiped away his tears with the back of his hand. "No, you're not." He looked around the darkened room. "But you need someone to kick you out of this dour room and back into life."

It was incredible to see his father like this, so open, speaking to Quentin as an equal—treating him like one. The whole scene seemed so incredibly out of the context of his life, he sensed the bitterness inside him ebb like a tide. For a moment he feared it was just as likely to wash back over him if he waited long enough, tugged by the vital forces of the past. But it wasn't Clarice guiding him now. It was Leydi. *Forgive.*

Following the sweep of his father's hand, Quentin looked around the chamber. He glanced up at the ceiling. "I told her I came here to talk to my angels," he said, ready to exchange confidences. "But those paintings will never show me the magic they gave her. I thought perhaps if I were tired enough." He lifted the empty dram glass. "If I drank enough, I might have enough imagination to at least daydream an answer to getting her back."

The earl shook his head. "I don't understand. Does she not love you?"

All the dark gloom moved in closer, making the room seem even more harsh. The angels stayed stoic, unmoving, granting no answers. He twirled the tumbler between his fingers and wondered if the glass was a bit symbolic of his life—empty. What was left of the pathetic pattern of his days? Certainly, not his revenge against his father, a hollow goal if ever there had been one. Nor his money. That had lost its appeal long ago. But if he had Leydi's love . . .

He closed his eyes, the pain crashing into him as a series of images assailed him. Leydi laughing. Leydi kissing him. Leydi angry but still trying to help him. Yes, that's what he wanted. Her love. The very love he'd turned his back on and betrayed.

He remembered her final words to him. *Leave me. Don't make me more unhappy than you already have.*

He looked up at his father. He put the glass back on the table and folded his hands before him. "She said she loved me. But that was when she was foolish and naive. I set out to teach her how harsh life can be, how futile all her optimism." He smiled, a rather grim smile. "Does she love me still? I think not. I think I taught her too well how not to."

Leydi held Gabriela as her friend heaved over the basin. It was the second time that morning Gabby had been violently ill. Watching her friend barely recover, pressing the linen towel to her bloodless lips, Leydi felt none too steady herself.

She thought of Gabby looking tired these past few days. Gabby ill at ease in the kitchen, reacting to certain smells, as if any strong scent could turn her stomach. Gabby sick three mornings straight.

"Tell me you ate something that didn't agree with you," Leydi whispered. "Tell me you have a fever, a stomach ailment. Don't tell me you're—"

"Pregnant," Gabby finished. She dabbed the sweat beading on her brow with the linen cloth and reached for the support of the bedpost and Leydi's hand. "Yes. I'm expecting a child. Spring of next year, most likely."

"Oh, Gabby."

The two words hung like a lament. The silent *what now?* lulled behind, smoothing a chilling path through the warm air of the cottage they shared.

Leydi stroked back the sweaty curls from Gabby's face. *Her sister.*

"Come on," she said, guiding Gabby back to the bed. "You're in no condition to work."

Gabriela didn't protest. She lay back on the sky-blue counterpane the two women had sewn together the summer before, her head plumped up by an armada of pillows. She let Leydi tend to her, sighing with relief when she set a cool compress to Gabby's forehead.

"What about you, *caro?*" Gabby said, patting Leydi's arm. "You can't tell me all those nights you left me alone in our cottage you weren't about the same business."

Leydi shook her head, thinking of her monthly, which had come with daunting regularity. A hollow pang seized her chest, like a fist clutching around emptiness. Most likely it was the void where her heart should have been—before Quentin had stolen it from her.

"I'm not expecting a child," she said. And then, after a long silence. "I wish I were."

Gabby glanced up; her eyes filled with silent sympathy. "Then you won't feel too sorry for me, hmm? My mother showed the strength of character a woman needs to make a life for a child without a father." Her hand drifted to her stomach. "I'll not show my babe any less."

She took Gabby's hand between her two, grasping it tight. "And you have me, Gabby. Always."

"Yes, *caro,*" she said, giving her fingers a squeeze back. "Always."

The silence between them was filled with the comfort of familiarity, as if words were no longer necessary for compassion. More than two weeks had passed since they'd learned the truth about Kincaid. It had been an agonizing time for both women, filled with regrets and longings—painful enough that they'd waited this long to share the full grief of it.

Gabby turned away and pressed her eyes shut against another wave of nausea. She gritted her teeth. "It's the one thing I can't forgive him—that he didn't let me know you were my sister."

Leydi sighed. She'd avoided Kincaid these past weeks, allowing Consuelo and Bertie to act as a buffer between them. She couldn't seem to think straight. Her normally ordered mind was a tangle of that night—making love to Quentin, listening to him bargain with the hidden truths of her past for his freedom, then her own angry words on the beach to send him away. With her pain hoarded inside her, she'd cocooned herself against Kincaid and anyone else who might ask her to open her heart and forgive. She'd exchanged only enough words with her pirate father to ask that he not wreak the vengeance he constantly threatened against Quentin.

No, she hadn't wanted to confront Kincaid. Still, she could be more forgiving than Gabby.

She blotted Gabby's forehead with the compress, then turned back to dip the linen in the pitcher of water and wring it dry. "Does it really matter so much? Kincaid brought us together. Put us in this hut to live like sisters." She lay the cloth on Gabby's brow and stroked back the springy chestnut curls that had always been so becoming to that regal face, giving Gabby just a hint of mischief to challenge her air of sophistication. "And haven't we always looked after each other? You've been the sister of my heart all these years, goading me into finding life outside Kincaid's books. You gave me my adventures, Gabby. Did we really need Kincaid to put into words what we felt in our hearts?"

Gabby peered up at Leydi from beneath her lashes. Her green

eyes seemed suddenly so familiar in her beautiful tanned face—reminding Leydi poignantly of Kincaid. "You're right as always, *caro*. I would have treated you no differently had I known. You are and always have been my *irmã*. My sister," she translated. "And I like the way you said it—the sister of my heart." She patted Leydi's cheek with a thin smile, but her eyes showed her anger brewing against Kincaid just the same. "Still—"

"I know," Leydi said, wringing out the cloth once more. "I'm just so happy he didn't take it all from us. If not sisters all these years, he let us at least be the best of friends."

With a hug the two women communicated their love and trust for each other. Eight years they'd been together. From the beginning there had been this special bond between them. The words in Kincaid's journal had merely put a label on their unbroken devotion.

"Gabriela," Leydi began, knowing now they would have to broach the subject they'd avoided all these weeks. With the baby coming, it was time to make a decision about the future, decisions Leydi, too, had avoided. "I know you threatened to leave Devil's Gate, but is that so wise? I mean, with the baby and all. If we turn away from him now . . . well, it just won't be the same, being on our own. Whatever we might think of what he's done, the truth is, he's made our lives very comfortable these many years. He gave us a home, a place to call our own."

"Yes, *caro*," Gabriela whispered. "I suppose I'll have to swallow my pride, but I'm just angry enough at that jackass of a father to cut off my nose to spite my face—"

"But the baby," Leydi said gently, sitting at the foot of the bed, almost envious because she wouldn't have a child to give her comfort, to remind her that once she, too, had loved. "Whatever you wish, Gabby. I've saved quite a bit of money. Perhaps between the two of us? And with Consuelo and Bertie to help . . . ?"

Gabriela fell silent for a moment. Leydi could tell she was fighting a wave of nausea. When she opened her eyes again, the deep green shone strangely intent, as if she had something important to say.

"Leydi, my dearest friend. My newfound sister. I must confess . . . I knew Kincaid was my father—for many years. Bertie told me the truth, though she knew nothing about Elaine or your relationship with him."

"And you didn't tell him?" Leydi guessed, smiling sadly, knowing her friend and her pride too well.

"I made *Mãe* swear she wouldn't say a word." Gabby blinked back angry tears. "I kept waiting for him to acknowledge me, to say something." She picked at the stitching in the counterpane. "I thought he was ashamed of me, because of my mixed blood."

"Oh, Gabby," Leydi said in sympathy, finally understanding the tension between Kincaid and her friend and the sullen bitterness that tainted their volatile exchanges.

Gabby gazed up at Leydi, signaling her to sit closer on the bed. She held Leydi's hand between her long, elegant fingers. "But I don't understand why he wouldn't accept you. I was even jealous of you. I used to think, if it were Leydi—oh, then he would be quick enough to acknowledge his daughter." Gabby shook her head. "Now I don't know what to think."

Two sharp knocks rapped against the door. With a soft whistle of air the door swung open on its rusty hinges. Consuelo waited on the stoop. She was dressed in black silk, her hair swept up by combs. The breeze tugged at the lace mantilla around her shoulders. Her very stance bid the women to remain silent.

Consuelo gathered up the black train of her gown. Gliding into the room with familiar elegance, she made her way to a cane-backed chair in the corner and sat down. It seemed an odd distance to put between herself and the two women on the bed.

"I came to give you all your answers." She nodded her head to the open window. "I could hear the two of you outside. Since I wanted to speak about that very thing, I thought it was time I interrupted."

Leydi and Gabriela exchanged glances. Gabriela sat up on the bed. "Then tell us the truth. Was he ashamed of us?"

Consuelo shook her head, looking infinitely sad. "No father could be more proud. I can't tell you the times he would speak of your stubborn nature, Gabriela, and smile because you reminded him of himself. He loved the way you organized the compound, making it a home for so many. And, Leydi, he wanted nothing more than to quench that undying curiosity of yours.

To bring you books, and more books. To let you devise financial machinations to your heart's delight."

"Then why?" Leydi asked.

"Because of me. I asked him not to tell you." Her chin hitched up a notch. "Now"—she smoothed out her skirts, the strength back in her voice—"will you both stop this nonsense and speak to your father? If anyone deserves your censure, it is I, and not Kincaid. I can't imagine even another day of his ranting and raving about your betrayal and lack of gratitude." She pouted and held her hands out imploringly. "You know Kincaid."

"I don't understand," Leydi said, never in her dreams thinking that Kincaid's decision would involve Consuelo. "Why would you ask him to keep such a terrible secret?"

Consuelo met each woman's gaze almost wistfully. "You can't imagine the years I tried to have a child. I loved Kincaid. I left everything—my family, my fortune, my husband—to be with him. But I couldn't give him the one thing he wanted, a baby to inherit the kingdom he'd built for himself. When Bertie made her confession, that yes, as he'd suspected all those years, Gabriela was his child, I became insanely jealous. And fearful."

Consuelo stood and walked to the bed. She leaned forward and stroked Gabby's cheek. "I saw myself displaced—by you, Bertie, and Kincaid. The happy family. Your mother was so beautiful. And she and Kincaid had a long history of love and respect for more years than I'd known him."

"But it's always been you he loved," Gabby said, confused by this confession. "They were never happy together. Kincaid's eye wandered more than once. It was never like the love you share."

Consuelo shook her head. "You can't understand. I'd given up everything for Kincaid; there was no going back once I'd chosen to follow my pirate lover. No matter how much he claimed Bertie was a friend, I couldn't rest my fears. And so I did the unspeakable. I asked that, when Gabby was older, he bring her here, but never tell her the connection they shared. And I begged that Bertie stay on St. Kitts. He agreed to my conditions; he loved me that much." Her eyes turned to Leydi, dark with regret. "When he discovered he had another daughter, Leydianna, I asked the same."

She grabbed both girls and brought them together in a hug, her arms warm and familiar. "My jealousy and fears made me do the unthinkable. I told myself I could make it up to you both. I tried to be a mother to you," she said fiercely. "I fooled myself into believing it was enough. That you were *my* daughters. That I made us a family." She hugged them tighter. "But instead, I've hurt you all so much. You and Kincaid—the people I love. It's unpardonable."

Slowly, gently, each woman reached up. Gabriela's and Leydi's arms twined around Consuelo, returning her embrace. It was a silent acknowledgment of forgiveness, of going on.

Consuelo pulled away; she wiped her tears. Looking into each dear face, she whispered, "You are the only children I will ever have. I love you both. I think it's time I started acting like the mother I wanted to be. And so I'm here to make amends and make certain that this rift between you and your father is made right. Come, let us go and talk to Daniel, *sí?*" She stood, tugging at their hands. "It's long past time."

Felix sat in the ladderback chair. For the first time in two weeks, he seemed calm. He'd made his decision. It was right that he'd acted at last.

He glanced around the stark order of the government office, the sheets of paper neatly stacked on the herringbone pattern of the desk, the single cane chair and bookcase. Outside the window, he could hear a tinker hawking his wares. Just another day in Basse Terre.

But not so for Felix. Today would bring an end to the lonely war he'd waged these many years.

It seemed providence that a new member had been appointed to the Council—as if God were urging him to do what was right. He'd hesitated too long, dreaming of Gabriela in his arms, thinking of his promise to Rutherford to shelter Kincaid. The past nights his dreams had gained an agonizing fever, as if warning him he must speak or forever be damned. He could hear the screams of his parents in those nightmares. See his brothers being cut down, brutally murdered by Kincaid's men.

In those sleepless hours he knew protecting Kincaid was wrong. He no longer had a choice but to act.

"And you can tell us precisely where this hideout is?"

Felix looked up at the captain seated behind the enormous oak desk. From bagwig to buckled shoes, Captain Simpson was the epitome of proper naval decorum—a thin, hawkish nose, intense hazel eyes that even now studied Felix with a touch of suspicion. The man seemed rather young to have attained his exalted position. Felix assured himself he'd chosen right in coming here.

"Yes," Felix whispered, then clearing his throat, he added more forcefully, "Yes, I can."

"May I ask why have you waited this long?" Captain Simpson asked, steepling his fingers before his face.

"Kincaid. Sometimes I think he has half the government here in his pocket. No one would move against him. I was hoping—"

"I'm in no one's pocket," Simpson added in a voice that showed he was offended by the insinuation.

"You'll find you'll have problems just the same moving against the pirate."

The two men's eyes met, sharing a quiet understanding. Simpson smiled, showing crooked white teeth and a passion to succeed. He looked like a man who liked a challenge. "We shall see, my friend."

"One other thing." Felix stood, coming closer to the desk. "There are women and children on the island. I want your assurances they won't be harmed."

"The offspring of buccaneers—"

"My wife," Felix said without hesitation. "My wife is on that island."

The captain arched a dark brow. "Is she being held there against her will?"

"No."

Simpson picked up a quill, twirling it slowly in his fingers as he kept his steady gaze on Felix. "I'm not sure I understand."

"She and her family, her mother and good friends, they are house servants for the pirate. They are there of their own free will—but they have nothing to do with Kincaid's murdering ways.

We married during my captivity. I don't want anything to happen to any of them."

The man smiled. "You have my word on it." He shoved the map across the table to him and held out the quill. "Proceed."

Felix hesitated for a moment, holding the pen in his hand. Here, then, was the final step. At last he would make right his family's murder. It was something he'd spent a lifetime trying to accomplish, to silence those screams in his head.

Discordantly, the image of Gabriela appeared on the map, muddled by the lines of the sea and bodies of land. He frowned, thinking of how she'd always protected her pirate. He could almost hear her assurances that Kincaid couldn't possibly be responsible for the crimes Felix accused him of—

Felix frowned. Gabriela was too gentle-hearted. The man was a murderer by reputation and deed. She was just gullible enough to look for the good in anyone—even that fiend Kincaid.

With unwavering determination Felix dipped the pen into the ink pot. Slowly, methodically, he began marking the route from St. Kitts to Kincaid's island hideout.

Chapter Twenty-six

"Something awful is going to happen," Gabriela murmured. Gripping the olive plush of the settee where she sat next to Leydi, Gabby's fingers mangled the tasseled ends. The creamy tan of her face paled a chalky gold, as if she were fighting off another bout of sickness. "Felix," she whispered under her breath.

"Kincaid's heard the worst of it now," Leydi assured Gabby, glancing up at the pirate, a familiar sight in his knee boots and crimson jacket. "And we're still here to tell the tale."

Both women sat in the front room of Kincaid's cottage-style house, its louvered walls making the room breezy and bright in the late morning, a stunning contrast to the storm brewing in the vicinity of the pirate. Bertie, Cy, and Consuelo huddled around them like mother hens as Kincaid's boots thundered to the pace of his bellows.

"A baby!" Kincaid threw his arms up, the lace of his sleeves dripping back over his velvet cuffs. "Damn my blood, what's next?"

He stumbled, then pivoted back to see what had tripped him. His hand darted out. His finger stabbed like a sword point at his feet where Nigel lounged among the floorboards, a jolly pink bow flopping over the sides of his thick neck. "And why has yer monster taken up residence in my house? It's gotten so I'm afraid to take a step in my own rooms for fear of the beast underfoot."

Leydi picked up Nigel, crooning in his ear as she perched him on her shoulder. "Quentin stayed in the room upstairs." She kissed the top of Nigel's frilled head and murmured in the iguana's ear, "I miss him, too."

"Miss him—oh, for the love of God's little bodes," Kincaid shouted. "If that's not all that's needed in this farce. A lovesick iguana. If I'd known they were mates, I'd have dumped the beast in the sea to follow the sneaking pup home."

He pinned Leydi and Gabriela with another glower. Folding his hands behind the skirt of his jacket, he continued to rove the floorboards like a hungry tiger. His eyes flitted from one victim to the next, as if trying to decide who might make the tastiest morsel.

"Two weeks I've been treated like an outcast in me own home. Aye, bloody bastard that I am. Imagine me giving ye two a roof over yer heads, an education—and whatever else yer hearts desired? Whatever was I thinking of?" he asked, his voice oozing sarcasm. "Oh, aye, I've earned your censure, surely, for my fiendish regard for your well-being. It all makes sense that ye'd mope about the place with long faces, *longing* for the very men who plotted to stretch my neck!"

He swiveled about, his attention now on Consuelo. Cy and Bertie perched on either side of her black silk skirts. "And don't ye think I don't smell the reeking stench of yer plotting," he said, lancing each with his eyes. "You," he shouted at Cy. "And ye call yerself my man. Placing the weakest of the weak to guard the pack of crafty rascals. Were ye planning to keep them prisoners or matchmaking, pray tell?"

"Cy merely carried out my orders," Consuelo said, her face angled up in a provoking jut of chin only she would dare. She plucked at the lacy mantilla across her shoulders as if the speck of lint she found there were as important as Kincaid's tirade. She smiled sweetly. "You did say I was in command in your absence, *mi amor?*"

"And yer womanly touch is priceless here, Connie. Did ye

think to save these fine gents from the marooning they so richly deserved by having the girls aproned-up with their get?" He switched his gaze to Bertie. "Did ye?"

Bertie turned her dark eyes on her daughter. Her gold hoops swung against her neck as she shook her head. She reached out to grip Gabriela's hand in sympathy. *"Não,"* she whispered. "Maybe we did wrong. But we wanted to give their love a chance."

His pitch dark brows rose a notch. "Now, ain't that just poetic. Give love a chance," he said as if spouting a verse of a sonnet. He swung on Leydi. "Well? Will ye be giving love a chance come eight months, gel?" he asked, deliberately crude.

Leydi put Nigel down on her chair. He scrambled off the seat and scurried up the curtains to rest on the rod above, a ringside seat. She'd had all she could stand of the pirate's wasted anger. In the sweetest of dreams she would stand up and tell him she carried Quentin's child. The fact she could not only made her more angry. And lonely, so terribly lonely. Despite all her heated words on the beach, the truth was, if Quentin walked through that door today she could love him no less.

Her gaze flew over Kincaid's gray-tinged queue to his knee boots, searching for something familiar in the pirate other than his characteristic temper. Something she could reach out to and confront. No matter what Consuelo had confessed, it was Kincaid she'd heard barter away her happiness with Quentin, ripping away the fragile dreams she'd feebly woven as they bargained.

"And if I were with child?" she challenged, tilting her chin in a perfect imitation of Consuelo. "Are you concerned about my moral fiber? Well, they do say the leaf doesn't stray far from the tree."

Kincaid gave her a virulent stare, the kind of look that in the past would have set her heart to a wicked beating. Now it did nothing. All she saw was a man who'd allowed her to spend her life bullied by people who didn't love her. A pirate who for weeks had not addressed a single word to her other than to spout some mortal threat against Quentin.

The hard-won lessons of the past rose within her, counseling

Leydi not to turn her back on the dark emotions brewing inside. She realized that fair or not, she blamed Kincaid—for many things. Quentin's love, he could do nothing about; it was not Kincaid's to bring back. But her past, this one misery she would not hole up in her soul to fester.

She fisted her fingers at her sides and met Kincaid's icy glare. She might be small and dressed in deferential brown, but if there was ever a moment for Kincaid to show he cared one whit about her, the time was then.

As if sensing the changes in Leydi, Kincaid threw up his hands. He roamed the sun-drenched room, banging up and down the satinwood as if the very pounding of his boots could regain his advantage. But this time there was no cajoling Leydi, a woman who had always sought to keep others happy. Instead, she stood defiantly before him, fighting for no one but herself.

Kincaid took a deep breath. He paced three steps toward her, meeting her eyes for the first time with something other than anger. He reached out to her, then, thinking better of it, let his hand fall to his side.

"Ye can stop glaring at me," he said softly. "Oh, aye. I've wronged ye. Though I thought I did the proper thing by bringing you here to Devil's Gate. And perhaps I could have shown more patience with Rutherford." He nodded his head, a quiet retreat. "All right. Out with it. Ye look like ye want to spit in my face, so ye might as well have yer say."

Leydi studied Kincaid. She hadn't realized how much more silver there was in the dark queue of his hair. Despite time, he was still an inspiring figure, one she would have been only too proud to call father . . . if he'd given her that chance.

Employer. It had such a cold ring to it. Nothing like friend or family. *So you hired them to be your housekeeper and bookkeeper. How . . . novel.* She could still hear Quentin saying those awful words. And perhaps it was simply that which she held against Kincaid, that he'd never given her the chance to be something more special. That he'd given her only his books and papers to care for.

Leydi sat down and laced her hands before her, folding them neatly on the brown muslin of her lap. There wasn't a hint of ruffle, not a breath of lace to her gown. She reached up and yanked the mobcap from her curls. Recalling the years her mother had made her pay for Kincaid's betrayal, she could think of only one way to exorcise those spirits.

"When I was seven," she began, keeping her voice even, "Argus, the man I thought was my father, came home very drunk. It wasn't the first time, nor was it the last, but I remember that day very distinctly because he hit my mother."

She glanced up at Kincaid. She saw no apology in his gaze, just a haunting anticipation, as if he knew there would be more.

"He slapped her," she told him, "hard across the mouth. And the reason I remember that day so clearly is not because he hit her, though it was rare that he would, but because my mother turned to me and I knew—I knew—she blamed me." She shook her head. "As I grew older, I began to realize that in my mother's eyes, most bad things in her life were my fault. And I began to question why."

"Leydianna—" Kincaid began, stepping forward.

She held up her hand, stopping him. "I will have my say. You will give me this much."

He looked about to argue, but stepped back with a nod.

"Over the years I realized that if I bought her things, trinkets and the like, she seemed to look at me with just a little love. When my studies with Mr. Stevenson went well enough, I began my plan. I was going to buy Argus and my mother their own plantation."

She stared at her locked fingers around the frill of the mobcap. She could almost hear Quentin tell her she couldn't buy love.

"I thought perhaps it was our poverty she held against me. But it was more than that."

She blinked her eyes against her tears as the past washed over her, wave after wave crashing in her head. She could hear her mother shouting that she should wear her stays tighter. Her mother screaming that she keep her braid smoother. Tugging on a shorn curl, she twisted the tendril between her fingers. *Do you think I've never been young and foolish? Susceptible to men like Rutherford?* Her mother had struggled to snuff out anything beautiful about Leydi fearing a man would seduce her—as Kincaid most surely had seduced Elaine.

"I understand so much now," Leydi whispered.

"I don't know what to say," Kincaid pleaded. "What to do—how to make this right . . ."

Leydi shut her eyes against Kincaid's beseeching figure. Elaine had spent a lifetime lamenting the choices she'd made, making her daughter pay when fate had been unfair. Leydi didn't want a life of regrets. She didn't want to be haunted by lost love—or settle for less than what Quentin had given her so briefly. She wanted love here on Devil's Gate. A life that would give her something to fill the void Quentin had left behind—something to take away the emptiness.

"My question, to you, Kincaid, is this—" Her voice stopped, growing choked despite her resolve to do this in a businesslike manner. "My question is, can you, my father . . . can you show me some of that love I have missed?"

Kincaid stared at her for a moment. She watched him swallow, then turn away, as if he couldn't face her as he talked. "Have I ever shown you anything but respect and care in the years ye've known me?"

"When?" she whispered, wanting all the shadows gone. With her methodical mind she needed to leave no stone unturned. "When did you find out about me—and when did you come for me?"

He twisted around to look at her. For the first time, he touched her, bracing his hands on her shoulders. "Ye were eight, gel. I paid fer those fancy lessons yer Mr. Stevenson gave ye, though knowing yer spendthrift mother, I'm not sure he even saw the color of my coin. And I told her when ye turned fourteen, I'd come fer ye. That was our bargain, ye see. She made me wait that long."

Leydi pressed her eyes shut and smiled, her worst fears answered. He'd wanted her. He'd wanted her all along.

She took one of Kincaid's enormous hands in hers. It was odd to touch him like this—to acknowledge this incredible connection between them. It helped ease the gnawing ache inside her for Quentin. At last, that lonely little girl draped in brown, who'd fought so desperately to please a mother who would never be satisfied, had a home.

She glanced up. Kincaid was looking at her with that gentle expression she had never been able to put into words. Now she thought it could be only fatherly love.

"Gabriela," she whispered so only he could hear her, knowing he would understand.

He sighed and gave her hand a squeeze. He walked over to his other daughter. But Gabriela's eyes, the same beguiling shade of green as Kincaid's, seemed to pierce right through him.

"Now I imagine ye'll never forgive me, Gabriela," he said, kneeling down beside her. "That's because yer too much like me."

"I'm not tenderhearted like Leydi," she said, steel in her voice. I don't want your love. I just want your protection. For me and my child. And your word—your word, Kincaid, that you will never harm my baby's father."

He stood, looking as if she'd slapped him rather than spoken in a well-modulated voice. "The man's ruined ye, abandoned ye, and I'm still the hen-eared numskull behind all yer miseries? Oh, aye. I can see it in your eyes! So help me, Gabriela, I'll . . . I'll . . ."

And then he stopped. He closed his eyes and seemed to wait the count of ten. When he looked at Gabriela again, there was true regret in his eyes.

"I'm sorry." His voice was low and heartfelt. He clasped her shoulders. "Gabriela, this was all fer you," he said, waving his hand in a half-gesture to the treasures in the room. He glanced beside him at Leydi. "Fer you and your sister. Don't turn away from what I'm offering now. Don't turn away from *me,*" he said, clutching her hand to his chest. "Let me try a hand at this father business—let me be a grandfather to yer child. Give us that chance."

Gabriela stared hard at Kincaid. There was a suspicious sheen to her eyes. Her hand dipped to her stomach, covering the spot where her child grew. She kept looking at Kincaid, as if coming to some kind of decision, a peace. And then she nodded and whispered, "I'd like that. Very much."

Kincaid shook his head. He looked like a man who'd just stared down his greatest fears. He turned to the others in the room. Consuelo beamed with her happiness. Bertie blinked back tears as she gave Kincaid her approval.

Cy grinned widely. "What's life without a few challenges, eh, mate?"

"Indeed," Kincaid said gruffly. He stood and once again appeared the dangerous pirate, quickly putting behind him the odd moment of tenderness. "What are we to do about these scoundrels that have left my daughters, Cy? Shall we fetch them back fer ye, then?" he asked Leydi and Gabriela, deadly serious despite his smile.

The young women looked at each other, sharing a silent communication. Leydi reached out and clasped Gabby's hand. Speaking for them both, she said, "You can't plunder us husbands like Spanish booty. We want a family. Men who want to wake up beside us and hold our children in their arms." She squeezed Gabby's hand hard. "We brought them to this island and wrapped them up in all our dreams for a bit of time. If they want us, they'll come back to us. And God's truth, that's the only way we'll have them."

"You're absolutely miserable, Quentin. Anyone can see that," the earl sputtered across the gateleg table Stevenson had set out for tea in the garden. The older man's cheeks were red from the late afternoon sun and the exasperating conversation. "I don't understand why you simply can't get on one of those fine ships you own and fetch her back. She kidnapped you, for heaven's sake. What's sauce for the goose, and all that," he said, waving his hand.

"Because that's not the way it works. At least not for Leydi-anna." Quentin watched the flared tips of cane fronds in the fields sway with the breeze. "I betrayed her."

"Seems to me you're betraying her by not going back," the earl muttered under his breath. Getting no satisfactory answer from his son, the earl banged the cup back to its saucer. "Really, Quentin. What will you do now? Mope the rest of your days? Live off the nectar of regrets?"

Quentin stared down at the polished veneer of the table. His father had managed to pry him out of his dark room, but Quentin still donned his black mood like a hair shirt he dare not shed. He was plagued by memories of Leydi and their final night together. The awful, awful sight of her pale face when she'd discovered his plans to escape played over and over in his mind like a scene from some macabre play.

"Quentin?" the earl prompted.

He glanced up at his father. Dark blue eyes studied Quentin from across the table, eyes so like his own, he could be staring in a glass twenty years from now. Perhaps his father was right. Perhaps he was betraying Leydi with his fears. *Your past has beaten you, Quentin. It's beaten us both.* Had he merely traded the specter of Clarice for Leydi's ghost?

The French doors swung open, spilling Stevenson onto the garden of crepe myrtle and roses. Felix Bishop followed close at his heels. A smile of welcome came to Quentin's mouth as his chair scraped across the brick medallion set in the ground. He watched the men cross the grass path lined with pansies and anthemion. But as Felix drew nearer, Quentin's cheer vanished. He could see from the man's expression that something was terribly wrong.

The lieutenant doffed his hat and took the seat Stevenson pulled up to the table. His dark eyes met Quentin's in an unblinking gaze. "I came to tell you straight off—I owe you that much. Quentin, I've broken my word to you."

A feeling of dread spiked up Quentin's spine. He rose slowly. His chair crashed back against the brick as the back of his knees hit the seat. "Felix, what have you done?"

Those earnest brown eyes remained steady. "Kincaid is a murderer. I couldn't in good conscience let him go free to kill again. I have Captain Simpson's word that the women won't be harmed. I told him Gabriela is my wife and her family lives on the island— he'll make sure they're not hurt."

"You fool," Quentin whispered. "You damned idiot."

"I did what I had to do."

Quentin jumped across the table straight for Felix. Neither the earl nor Stevenson could stop his attack. He had Felix by the lapels of his waistcoat, shaking the breath out of him.

"Do you know what you've done, you fool?"

"I have made certain that Kincaid is called to pay for his crimes!"

Quentin shook his head, disbelieving that Felix could have betrayed them all in such a fashion. He pushed him away, watching as Felix stumbled to the brick.

"I thought I could hold you to your word as a gentleman. I thought you were a man of honor—that those weeks together on that island had bought me a modicum of your loyalty."

"I'm a government man." Felix pushed back a russet strand of hair from his eyes as he gained his feet. "You said yourself my first loyalty is to the innocent victims of that pirate."

"Gabriela," Quentin said, reminding him of other obligations.

"I know he has some hold on her! But this will finally put a stop to her misplaced loyalty." Getting no response from Quentin, just a condemning glare, he shouted, "He's a killer, dammit!"

"He's her father," Quentin answered.

Felix stared at Quentin, the pupils of his eyes growing wide. He took a step back, shaking his head.

Quentin picked up the chair and dropped back into the seat, raking his fingers through his hair. He should have never trusted Felix, and yet he couldn't believe the man had broken his word to him. Perhaps Quentin should have confessed Kincaid's relationship to Gabriela, but it had never been his secret to tell.

"Her father?" Felix stared down at the herringbone pattern of bricks laid in the grass, his voice filled with disbelief.

"Her loyalty to Kincaid isn't misplaced," Quentin said viciously, not sparing Felix. "Only her faith in you was a mistake. Do you think for a moment that if it comes to a battle, your Captain Simpson will hesitate to blast Kincaid's island into cannon rubble? You've put them all in danger. Not just Kincaid, but Leydianna, Gabriela . . . everyone."

The dawning dread in Felix's eyes came with a low groan of despair. He glanced up at Quentin. There was such raw misery in his eyes, it almost hurt to look at him. "He murdered my family," he whispered, "he and his men. Those fiends cut them down where they stood. I was only four, Quentin. All my life I thought of only one thing—tracking him down and making him pay." He shook his head, still disbelieving. "Dear God, her father."

Hearing Felix's confession, Quentin himself experienced a dawning revelation. He'd always thought Felix's fever to capture Kincaid merely the ambition of a young naval officer trying to make his mark. Now he realized it was so much more, a powerful force even Quentin would have trouble condemning.

Yes, he could well understand the man's motives. And yet, Felix's revenge had cut deeply, hurting the very woman he said he loved.

"What do we do?" the earl asked, coming to Quentin's side, ready to help.

Quentin turned to Felix, praying the man's love for Gabriela was stronger than his hate for Kincaid. "When does Simpson sail and what kind of force does he lead?"

"Tomorrow," he said without hesitation. "Two gunners."

Quentin stood, all the lazy fog of the past weeks vanishing in a single stroke of resolve. "Come," he said to all three men hovering at the table as he marched back toward the house. When they failed to fall into step quickly enough to please, he turned and shouted, "We don't have much time, dammit. Move!"

Chapter Twenty-seven

"I'm telling ye, Daniel, she's flying the Black Flag," Cy argued.

Standing next to Cy on the ridge, Leydi scanned the horizon, her hand blocking the sun high overhead. The breeze offshore tugged at the skirts of her dress, flapping the brown cotton against her stockinged legs. Any vessel in these waters was completely unheard of—yet a sloop, lazy and sleek, lolled on the waves. A strip of black silk sporting a white skull flew from the bowsprit.

"Damn my blood, yer right." Kincaid handed back the spyglass to Cy, his brow furrowed. "But who can it be? I'm practically the last filthy pirate left in these waters since they strung up Calico Jack Rackam. Nor do I recognize the ship or flag."

Cy fit the brass scope to his eye. He shook his head, his lips twisting in concentration in the russet nest of his beard. "Maybe not, but I'd not like to blast her if there's a question. Remember how we came across Avery and nearly had our mizzenmast split in two by his guns before he recognized us?" He perused the ship as it dropped anchor, examining its majestic open gallery and V-shaped hull. "She's a beauty and I—damn!"

Cy handed the spyglass over to Kincaid. "There's yer answer,

Daniel," he said, directing Kincaid toward the skids, where a launch was being lowered to the water.

"Blast the sneaking pup to hell," Kincaid muttered. He put down the spyglass and glimpsed nervously at Leydi.

The anxious glance from Kincaid unfurled a desperate hope inside her. "Who is it?" She grabbed for the spyglass even as Kincaid held it out of reach. "Who is it?"

" 'Tis that damned man of yers," Kincaid said. His sharp gaze centered on the longboat rowing toward shore. "No doubt come to fetch ye back."

From where she stood atop the ridge, the men inside the launch looked no bigger than a handful of ants. Grabbing two fistfuls of skirt, Leydi plunged down the steep path, stumbling, then gaining her footing to race faster to the lagoon below. She twisted toward the emerald waters, a cloud of red clay billowing around her, making her blink against the dust. The air seemed thick and hot as she gasped for breath, dashing around an elbow turn, teetering for an instant on the sandy brink before she propelled herself down the next path.

Quentin was back. He'd come back for her.

She watched the longboat maneuver into the inlet, the men throwing their backs into rowing up the mouth of the lagoon. As they closed the distance between them, she thought she could just make out the tall, dark figure of Quentin Rutherford at the boom. There was another man with him.

She grabbed the spyglass from Cy when he reached her side. Focusing the scope on the launch, her heart soared when she saw the beloved features of the man to whom she had given her heart. He looked so determined, his bronze face angled in bold lines of conviction, his eyes narrowed against the blazing sun. Tristan come for his Isolde. The thrill of seeing him flooded her heart, making her head swim. She searched for Felix, but saw no sign of him.

A deep longing for Gabriela clipped short her imaginings for a happy ending. Taking a breath, she told herself not to be too hopeful; experience warned she shouldn't be premature about Quentin's motives for returning.

She focused the spyglass on the older gentleman seated beside

Quentin and frowned. The features seemed familiar. She recognized the shape of the jaw, the slant of high cheekbones . . . the eyes.

"His father." She dropped her arm, cradling the glass in both hands. "He brought his father."

"A family reunion," Kincaid muttered under his breath. "How bloody thoughtful of him. Remind me to break out the good linen, Cy."

A million possibilities crammed into her head. Did this mean he'd made amends with his father? Was it a sign? Quentin's way of telling her that he'd found it in his heart to forgive and could she do the same? Or was he dragging the poor earl there merely to dump him on the island and be rid of the two people who'd made him most miserable in his life?

She shook off her pessimism, not allowing anything to darken the image of Quentin guiding the longboat to shore. He was back. She had him back.

Quentin jumped into the knee-deep water and began towing the launch toward the sandy beach. Leydi tossed off her shoes and sloshed through the water toward him, her skirts hiked up to her knees. But the smile that wanted to burst from her died when she saw he would not meet her eyes.

He couldn't look at her.

Something was wrong.

"I got here as quickly as I could," he told Kincaid, ignoring Leydi, acting as if she weren't there at all. "I may be too late. Two gunners are right behind me, unless Bishop and Piton have convinced the Royal Navy to turn about."

Kincaid didn't bat a lash at the threat laid out before him, while Leydi couldn't catch her breath from the fear pumping through her.

"Ye've a plan?" Kincaid asked.

Quentin nodded, motioning his father forward. The man came to stand at Quentin's side, his show of faith eloquently displayed by the hand he rested on his son's shoulder.

"We're going to try to bluff 'em," the older Rutherford told Kincaid. "It's chancy, but between the two of us, we'll make a good show of it."

"With your help," Quentin added.

Leydi caught tiny gasps of breath. The fact that the Royal Navy was at that very moment plowing the waters of the Caribbean for Devil's Gate froze the blood in her veins with the enormity of her mistake. She stared at Quentin, waiting for some sign, a denial. She'd been so sure. She'd staked not only her happiness, but the well-being of everyone on Devil's Gate on her faith that Quentin wouldn't betray her. Not in this fashion. Yet there seemed no other explanation.

As if sensing the tumult of emotions churning inside her, Quentin faced her for the first time, the water still lapping at his boots. She saw the infinite sadness in his eyes, sensed the apology coming. She closed her eyes against it. She shook her head, disbelieving of this final betrayal.

"You promised." The words were barely audible. "You gave me your word. I tr-trusted you."

"Perhaps, my dearest Leydi," he said, "that was your worst mistake."

Felix marched beside Captain Simpson, his boots digging into the soft sand. Hugh bobbed alongside, continuing the unceasing stream of complaints that Felix had hoped might drive Simpson mad enough to turn back for Basse Terre. No such luck. Ignoring the humid heat that pearled the sweat where his wig met his brow, the captain's smile fixed in place as he continued his campaign across the sand. A small party of the Crown's good soldiers paced behind them.

At the break in the trees, what appeared to be a small group of well-wishers waited in their Sunday best. Felix recognized a few of the men and the women sprinkled among them, all smiling jovially. And then he caught sight of Quentin, standing at the front of the crowd, the earl beside him. Felix gave a silent thanks that Rutherford's sloop had beaten the hunkering frigates to the island. His attempts to convince Simpson that he was mistaken about the location of Kincaid's hideout had been less than worthless.

Flanked by red-coated soldiers, Simpson stopped. Felix's eyes roamed the crowd of friendly faces until his gaze fell on the one unwelcoming countenance.

He recognized Kincaid instantly, though he'd seen him for only a brief moment the night of their escape. The sound of his pulse rushed through his ears like the roaring of the sea. He was a mere five steps from the man who had killed his family. In the company of the Royal Navy, all he needed to do was raise the alarm. *Point him out,* the voices of his dead siblings seemed to shout inside his head. *Point the bastard out!*

And then Gabriela stepped forward, standing alongside the man who was her father. Gently, the gesture filled with meaning, she placed her hand on Kincaid's sleeve and leveled her eyes on Felix.

"Is something wrong?"

Captain Simpson waited for an answer. Felix wanted to clamp his hands over his ears to stop the screams of the past rising inside his head.

"What's wrong with you, man?" the captain repeated, giving Felix a shake.

Gabriela's unwavering stare remained on Felix, not giving an inch. Not allowing betrayal.

"*This* is what's wrong," he heard himself saying. "This island. I told you on the ship it was the wrong island."

"He's right, *monsieur,*" Hugh said, scratching his head as if perplexed. "*Mais oui,* this is not at all familiar."

Felix pointed to the crowd of gentle townsfolk, obviously a welcoming committee and not a throng of cutthroats. "These— people. This place." He waved his hand around him, gesturing to the island in general, his eyes once more on Gabriela. "This is not the hideout of Heartless Kincaid."

"It was as I said all along," Hugh added, "the tiny island just west of Monserrat. Now, that looked quite familiar—"

"Enough!" the captain snarled, having had his fill of Hugh at long last. He took a handkerchief from his coat pocket and dabbed the sweat now inching down his face.

"Hideout?" The earl stepped forward, his hand extended, his expression that of the feudal lord welcoming guests. "For Heart- less Kincaid?" He chuckled. "Though I'm pleased for such distinguished company, I must protest its aim. The name's Ruther-ford," he said, speaking in one long breath, not allowing the captain a word. "Earl of Carrick and all the usual rigmarole I won't bore you with."

He laid his arm around the captain's shoulder and guided him toward the waiting crowd. "We sighted your ships, and I can tell you, it's quite a treat for the few of us living here to find ourselves in such grand company. But you must tell me about Kincaid. Has the rascal been sighted? I and my son have a bone to pick with Heartless. I hope you'll stay long enough for a par-ticularly delectable brandy—"

The captain dug his heels in the sand and very pointedly took the earl's arm from around him. He stared at the waiting dozen or so men and women, looking into the eye of each as if hunting for Kincaid himself—a pirate whose face had remained a mystery for more than a decade. He stared back at Felix, suspicion dawn-ing in his eyes.

"I told you," Felix said. "It's the wrong island." Beside him, Hugh gave a decided nod.

Quentin joined his father, holding his hand out to the captain. Simpson returned the gesture reluctantly, still trying to decide whom to trust.

"Quentin Alexander Rutherford," he said, shaking his hand. "Viscount Belfour. And I second my father's invitation. I, too, am quite familiar with Kincaid's antics and eager to find his whereabouts." He nodded to Felix. "Which I'm sure the good lieutenant has already discussed with you."

"Quentin Rutherford?" A light of recognition came to the captain's hazel eyes. He dabbed the sweat from his face and squinted up at Quentin, now more friendly in his stance. "Of Rutherford Estate?"

"Yes," Quentin said warmly. "I'm just here for a visit myself," he said, smiling at his father.

"Well, your lordship," the captain said, deferring to the men's titles as they'd all hoped he would. "Isn't this an odd bit of busi-ness? We're actually here pirate hunting." He shook his head at the gentlefolk waiting so courteously. "The lieutenant thought this the island hideout for Daniel Kincaid."

The earl laughed. He flicked out a kerchief and wiped his eyes, as if the joke were too funny by half. "I wasn't aware we were neighbors with the knave," he said with a wink to Quentin. "Good Lord, I believe my son said he's taken three of our ships just this year alone. Was it three, Quentin?"

"Since just spring," Quentin answered. "And I hope it won't be more with the navy tied up here and not on patrol." He turned to Felix. "Don't worry too much about your mistake, Lieutenant. It's easy enough to lose one's way in the Antilles."

The captain seemed fascinated by each and every face in the waiting flock. With a quick glance to Quentin, the earl stepped in front of Simpson, refusing to be ignored.

"I assure you, Captain," he said with a bit more starch to his voice. "I'm not hiding a pirate. And surely not Heartless Kincaid, who has cut half our profit this quarter alone, enough to make me want to see the scoundrel swing. Now, my son has made more than one complaint to the Council. Do come to your senses, man."

The captain shrugged past the wall of Quentin and his father. He paced before the assembly. It seemed as if not a bird stirred, not a man breathed. He glanced back at Felix. In the captain's gaze, Felix saw his mistake.

Unerringly, Captain Simpson stopped before Gabriela, who Felix had singled out with his eyes since they'd made shore.

"If I remember correctly," the captain said, "the lieutenant mentioned a wife on this pirate isle."

The soft gasp from Gabriela was all the confirmation the captain needed. The soldiers behind him tensed. A few drew their muskets.

Like a gentleman, the captain took up Gabriela's hand and touched it to his lips. "And who is this charming creature?" he asked the earl.

"May I present, Gabriela de Sousa," Quentin said, stepping in front of Felix before his face could give them all away. Just then Leydi pushed through the crowd to squeeze Kincaid back into the pack. She took his place beside Gabriela.

In the smooth motion of a dance, Quentin led her forward,

as if it had been his intention all along. "And this fair creature is my wife, the Lady Belfour. Sister to Mistress de Sousa."

The captain now exchanged Gabby's hand for Leydi's. He brushed his lips across her skin, lingering over her fingers a tad too long for propriety. "How charming. And though I've been but a short time on St. Kitts, I find it interesting that I hadn't heard of the nuptials."

"I'm a very private person," Quentin said.

"Now, that I had heard," the captain said with a smile.

"Let's put all this nonsense aside, old boy," the earl urged. "Won't you and your men have a look around? See if we're hiding pirates under the bed linens or some such nonsense?"

The captain kept his grin as he shook his head. Taking Gabriela and Leydi by the hand, he drew them forward, away from the others. "I must insist that you be *my* guests. It's not often I've a chance to entertain such gentle company. My wife says I'm becoming quite a boor. That I must increase my converse with polite society."

Quentin blocked Kincaid before the pirate could act. "My wife feels unwell on ships."

"Oh, yes," Leydi seconded. She gave the captain her most charming smile and tried her best to extricate her hand from his. "Truly. Even anchored, I simply die from that awful swaying."

In one quick move the captain swept her before him. He raised his pistol to her side and motioned for the guard behind him to take Gabriela. "I'm afraid I really must insist."

"This is outrageous," the earl shouted. "How dare you treat the viscountess in such a manner. I'll have your commission for this, man."

"I find the viscountess's dress interestingly quaint," the captain said, giving a glance to Leydi's familiar drab brown. "And I think the situation here quite strange. And until I discover the whereabouts of a certain Heartless Kincaid, I will continue to have both ladies as my guests."

"You're making a mistake," Quentin said, his eyes dark with deadly earnest.

"I think not. Have no fear, my lord. The . . . ah . . . viscountess and her sister will remain safe and sound aboard my ship."

The captain backed away, kicking up sand as two guards ushered Gabriela toward the waiting launch. He kept his gun trained on Leydi. He nodded his head toward Felix and Hugh. "These two men can stay here until their memories serve them wiser. In the meantime, all I want is Heartless. If he turns himself in, not a shot will be fired. He has until sunup tomorrow to meet my terms."

Chapter Twenty-eight

Two women stood on the upper deck of HMS *Excalibur* with not much more than the grinning moon to guard over them. Their elbows propped on the poop rail, their chins cupped in their palms, they watched the moonlight dapple across the black water like a dusting of diamonds and sapphires. The shadowed hump of island brooded before them as fingers of a breeze tugged at their curls.

Leydi sighed, a pensive sound that blended well with the night's somber rumblings. She nibbled her bottom lip. "It makes you wonder," she said to Gabriela beside her, "why they called us their wives?"

Gabby wagged her head back and forth, thinking. "Perhaps a lack of imagination, *caro?*"

Leydi sniffed. "Think again. Their plan to bluff Captain Simpson could inspire a novel."

"There speaks a woman who dressed like a pirate and kidnapped her employer at the point of a cutlass half again her size. I don't even think you could lift the thing properly, it weighed so much."

"Well, that's true enough."

The slap of waves beat a mild rhythm in the hush. Geese squawked from the coop tied to the side of the rail. A sailor walked across the quarter-deck, whistling as he carried a bucket belowdecks.

"Captain Simpson isn't a bad sort," Leydi said, picking at the cuff of her sleeve.

"He's been an admirable host," Gabby answered.

"He was so proud of those miniatures. Darling children."

"The boy especially," Gabby said, her hand brushing across the stomacher of her gown. She pouted in the moonlight. "Did you think it was wise to let him win at loo so often, *caro*? A bit obvious, weren't you?"

She shrugged. "It made him happy. That's as good a start as any for our plans tonight. The first mate hasn't warmed up to us yet."

"Tonight, after dinner, perhaps you should slip Lieutenant Thompson a card or two."

"It's a thought."

There came a short bark of laughter from the gallery below. The men had hoisted the main brace and the day's ration of rum had been doled out. The bell tolled, its haunting voice slipping across the water. It was eight o'clock.

"Still," Leydi said with a soft sigh, "it makes you wonder— their calling us their wives."

Gabby stared out over the water. "As if they could think of no better way to protect us than to make us their own."

"It makes a girl think."

Leydi folded her hands on the rail and leaned her cheek against her arms. The stars above winked in and out like an enormous diamond band. "When did you know, Gabby?" she asked in a low whisper. "When did you know you loved him?"

"I suppose when I first laid eyes on the fool, standing across the street from my mother's shop." She turned to Leydi. "And you?"

"I think Quentin's angels tried to tell me—I just wasn't ready to listen then."

Gabby shook her head. "Still daydreaming, *caro*? I thought you swore off such fancy?"

"I did. But I'm beginning to believe we need our dreams."

Gabriela patted Leydi's shoulder. "Concentrate on our plan and forget those idiots waiting for us onshore. There's nothing we can do about them now."

Leydi gave her a wan smile. "Are you going below?"

Gabriela nodded. "To rest a bit before dinner. I want to be ready for my performance." She gave a mock curtsy, the diva before her devoted admirers, then met Leydi's eyes. "You're sure you can convince this fellow, this captain?"

"In a breath," Leydi said, refusing to give in to uncertainty.

Leydi waited for Gabby to climb down the ladder to the quarter-deck. After watching the glittering black of the water, she decided to walk around a bit herself. She wound her way slowly across the ship to the forecastle, thinking their plan for freedom was worthy of the heroine in *Constant Constance,* spy extraordinaire. But Leydi thought it solid enough. Dear Mr. Stevenson had always taught her to use her head. This was no time to lose it, mulling over her doubts.

She smiled at a passing sailor, then gazed at the white patch of shore beyond the inky waters. She leaned back against the foremast, fingering the tip of the belaying pin racked there. Gabby was right that she'd given up daydreaming since her mother had cut her hair. It seemed that for once she'd been too busy with life to waste time on fantasy.

She thought of Gabby's suggestion, that the men had tried to protect them by calling them their wives. It seemed such a basic reaction, the act of men in love. She closed her eyes, allowing the gentle sway of the ship to lull her as she considered the possibility that Quentin truly loved her. She smiled. If she were to daydream an end to this adventure, it would most certainly be with Quentin declaring himself.

She sighed and pushed off from the mast, stepping closer to the rail. He'd never uttered such lovely words, and to be honest, she even had trouble imagining him as a lovestruck swain, falling to his knees before her. It seemed so much more like Quentin to blithely pronounce her wife to a stranger, making their love a fact that could be negotiated by such tactics, like the latest price of tea.

She closed her eyes and called up his face as he'd watched Captain Simpson carry her off to the waiting boat. It *was* love she'd seen in those dark blue eyes. And longing. As if the most cherished person in his life were being taken from him. She'd told him once his past had defeated them, but she wondered if coming here with his father, stepping into this adventure, he hadn't broken those ugly patterns that haunted him.

She stared out across the phantom water, biting her bottom lip as she gripped the rail. Would he always equate love with loss? Would Clarice's lack of faith always plague him, keep him from reaching for what he wanted most? Or could he change the litany of despair that marked his past?

A ripple of a shadow cut across the slick black glass of the sea. Leydi frowned, leaning closer over the edge. For a moment she thought she was again imagining things, picturing Quentin's sleek shape stroking across the water to her rescue.

As she watched, the dark figure climbed over the rail and dropped into a deep crouch. He scanned the ship's deck, then prowled behind one of the launches. Her heart lurched to her throat when a hand beckoned to her, all too real.

She glanced up at the guard pacing the upper deck. Making certain he wasn't watching too closely, she slipped toward the shadows of the boat. She squinted through the darkness and called out tentatively, "Quentin?"

It was the only word he allowed her before his lips fell on hers. There was so much yearning in that kiss, like a man finding a lost part of himself. She opened her mouth to him, not asking questions, answering his embrace with her own desperate touches and strokes as she pressed against his wet chest. It was a most wonderful way to say she was sorry for the past. That she loved him still and couldn't live without him.

He cupped her face in his hands and whispered, "I've wanted to do that since I saw you onshore this morning." He kissed her again.

"Oh, God, thank you," she whispered between kisses, knowing there would never be another love in her life. It had always been Quentin. Only Quentin. "Thank you. This is better than the sweetest dream of all—"

"It's not a dream, dammit." His mouth pressed over hers again, deliciously tasting her. "I'm here. I'm real."

"Now tell me you love me, that you can't live without me," she whispered just as urgently, taking advantage of the fact that he thought her dotty enough to believe she was daydreaming. "That would make it utterly perfect. I haven't dreamed those words from you in ever so long."

He pulled back with a soft curse. "Good Lord, the first time I tell a woman I love her and she thinks I'm some daft illusion."

He was drenched, his hair dripping to his shoulders. With his breeches molded to his thighs and not another stitch of clothing, he looked perfect, more handsome and desirable than ever. The man she loved.

"Then tell me again," she whispered, her eyes meeting his in a bold demand that could never belong to a dreamer. "And I'll believe you."

Instead, he kissed her, telling her with his mouth and hands of all the love that waited for them. She bit back her exasperation that he wouldn't utter the words, guessing that he was indeed afraid to say them out loud.

Of the two of them, she came to her senses first. She grabbed his hand and tugged him into the darkest corner in the shadow of the boat. "Dear Lord, Quentin. What are you doing here?"

"What's it look like I'm doing? I'm rescuing you."

She peeked out around the bow of the launch, checking for the guard. "You're going to ruin everything."

Just then another wet figure dropped down over the rail. At Quentin's hiss, the man crept over.

"Where's Gabriela?" Felix asked, shirtless and soaking wet like Quentin.

Leydi crossed her arms, staring at both men. "Is this the best you could do? Sneak up here to spirit us away? You'll start a bloody massacre—"

Quentin's fingers pressed against her lips. "There's no time to waste. Go bring your sister, before we have to fight our way off this deck."

Leydi yanked his hand from her mouth and shook her head. "What good would that do? If we leave now, the captain will just assume this is Kincaid's island. He'll come looking for my father. And this time he won't spare his powder."

"We're prepared," Felix said. "The women and children have been taken to the hills. Everyone is mobilized for a fight."

"No!" Leydi insisted, leaning close. "Gabriela and I won't risk everyone . . . Bertie and Consuelo—Cy and the men. Nor will we let Kincaid hand himself over. This very day, you and the earl talked him out of doing just that. Well, I agreed then, and I agree now. There's still another alternative."

"What alternative, damn you?" Quentin said, giving her a shake. "This is the best we can do—"

Leydi ducked under his reach and crawled away. Quentin grabbed her skirt and dragged her back to him. Before he could argue, she whispered urgently, "Your plan was a good one, Quentin. The bluff can still work. I can get Captain Simpson back to the island and willing to listen to you and the earl. Please! Trust me. Once he sees the proof we've prepared that your father owns this island, he'll be on his way."

"I can't take that chance."

"You must." She leaned forward and kissed away his response. "Trust me, Quentin," she whispered, raining kisses across his lips. "I'm not a noodle to risk Gabriela or myself. I can do this!"

She scooted away before either he or Felix could make a grab for her. Glancing back, she kept her eyes on the dark patch she knew hid both men. Her urgent gaze on them, she pleaded with her eyes and mouthed the words, "Trust me."

And then she turned and ran, not giving them the choice.

Chapter Twenty-nine

"What in blazes do you mean, you couldn't get her to come!" Kincaid's voice bellowed across the room, bouncing off the rafters. The two men stood before him, water dripping from their hair to puddle onto the polished floorboards. Cy leaned back against the shutters, his arms crossed over his striped waistcoat, his blue eyes narrowed with the same derision thundering in Kincaid's voice.

"Good God, man," Kincaid blared again, "are ye fools? The choice weren't up to those two gels how to settle things. How could ye leave them there after ye'd reached the ship clear?"

"I suppose I could have tossed her over my shoulder and jumped overboard," Quentin said, his voice mocking. "Stealth requires a bit of cooperation, if I may point out."

"I don't give a double damn what it requires. What was needed of you was a rescue." He turned to Cy. "Get a gun—get a sword. Get a damned rope! I'll kill him. I'll bloody kill him."

Quentin stepped in front of Kincaid, grabbing his arm. It was true that Leydi hadn't given him much choice in the matter. And yet, the gleam of confidence he'd seen shining in her eyes made him believe she knew what she was doing.

"Listen to me, Kincaid. Though I can hardly believe I'm saying this, at times she's shown a tactician's mind—one of the best I've come up against. Don't underestimate her."

"She's bloody good with numbers, that's all," Kincaid shouted. "It don't mean you're to leave her on that ship to her own devices!"

"It's more than that, and you know it. You've staked your entire fortune on her abilities for years. She knows Captain Simpson is playing for keeps—"

"I should have bloody gone to fetch the gels meself! Ye damned idiot," Kincaid whispered, facing Quentin. "Yer so in love with her, ye can't even see her failings."

Quentin met the pirate's glacial stare, allowing his accusation to settle over him, judging its fit. The past rose up with all its ghosts, taunting Quentin with the possibility of love and loss. *To actually marry Leydi, to raise their children together, and then lose her.* It would be a tragedy he could not survive. . . .

Quentin closed his eyes, biting back a soft curse. Hadn't his fears shaped his life long enough? Would he continue to allow Clarice and her lack of faith in him to manipulate him like a cunning competitor?

When he opened his eyes again, he didn't see Kincaid glaring at him. He saw another's gaze. Eyes the color of silver and emeralds—eyes that had shown him more love and faith than he'd ever dreamed possible.

"Yes, I love her. And if God sees fit to guide us through this fiasco with your sorry hide intact, Kincaid, I will make her my wife . . . if she'll have me."

"Oh, she'll have ye, all right," Kincaid said, never losing the gleam of rancor in his gaze. "More's the pity." He shrugged his arm from Quentin's grasp. "She's a dreamer, man! She's concocted some fancy tale where she risks her hide to save mine. And I'll not have it!"

But it wasn't a dreamer who had faced Quentin in the moonlight, daring him to speak of his love out loud. She was hostage aboard a naval battleship, and still she had challenged him—despite the fact that he'd led her to believe he'd brought the navy to her doorstep. Leydi had never given up on him. Perhaps it was time for him to give her the same trust.

"She's risking Gabriela as well," he reminded the pirate. "I wouldn't take that so lightly."

Cy pushed away from the wall, coming to Kincaid's side. He nodded his head toward Felix. "And you. What do ye think on the matter?"

Felix said nothing. His dark eyes fixed on Kincaid as if there lay the blame for the night's debacle. Instead of answering, he turned on his heel and slammed out of the room, spilling out into the black night.

All three men stared in shocked silence. It wasn't a good time for strife among the ranks. Kincaid stamped to the door, then glanced back at Quentin. "What the bloody hell was that about?"

Quentin stayed silent for a moment. When he spoke, he said simply, "If you want Gabriela to be happy, perhaps you should go out there and find out."

Felix stood beneath the pale moon shrouded in clouds, trying his damnedest not to march back into that room and put a bullet through Kincaid's black heart. The pirate's demise wouldn't bring back his mother and father. It wouldn't give him Gabriela, a woman he now knew carried his child. He leaned back against the trunk of an acacia. The thought of Gabriela hostage on that ship made him die just a little inside.

He'd given up everything for her—his revenge, even his peace of mind. He turned and pummeled his fist into the tree, wishing he'd drawn blood. Damn those women and their scheming! He didn't want to wait another night to see Gabriela safe. He didn't want to trade her life for her father's, no matter what her wishes on the matter.

He heard the door open behind him. Heavy booted steps that most surely belonged to Kincaid pounded down the stairs and trampled down the crushed-shell path. Felix braced himself, wondering if he could bear to see the man alive and free, day after day, even for Gabriela's sake.

"All right, out with it," Kincaid said. "What heinous crime have I committed against ye?"

Felix stared at the nubby bark in the moonlight, not gracing the remark with an answer. The sickly-sweet fragrance of the tree's blossoms threatened to choke him.

The sound of crunching bits of shell underfoot punctuated the rhythm of crickets and frogs. He sensed Kincaid directly behind him. Felix was still wet from his swim to the boat, though it mattered little in the mild night. What did matter was the knife still strapped to his leg. It would be such a simple thing to turn around, to attack.

"Ye think yer the only man who's looked at me with such hate in his eyes?" he heard Kincaid whisper behind him. "And yet, fer Gabriela, ye even turned against the government ye serve to keep me safe." There was a thoughtfulness threading through the pirate's voice. "Aye. Perhaps ye'll make her happy."

Felix fisted his hand against the bark. He didn't know how to break through this hatred firing inside him. He was almost afraid to voice the truth, charge Kincaid with his crimes—to hear out loud the heinous acts he'd committed against Felix's family.

"Say it, man," Kincaid challenged from behind him. "Be brave enough to face me, damn you!"

Felix whipped around, goaded into action. "Do I really need to give the bloody details? To you, it was just one more plantation pillaged. Just one more day of bloodshed to blend in with your many exploits," he said savagely. He grimaced as his gaze flitted up to Kincaid's. "How can you live with the burden of those murders? With the blood of innocents staining your conscience? Or do you even have a conscience?"

"And just whose blood did I shed?" Kincaid asked softly. "Because despite the fact yer very existence puts my neck at risk, I don't recall so much as a bruise on yer person."

Kincaid's words stopped Felix short. It was true that Kincaid had shown admirable restraint toward him and Quentin.

The pirate smiled, crossing his arms over his flamboyant red coat. "Aye, makes a man think, don't it? Seems to me, lad, the fiend ye believe me to be would have at least had the decency to pin ye up and skin ye alive." He *tsked,* looking disappointed.

"And imagine, not so much as a wee bullet through yer ungrateful heart."

Felix stepped around Kincaid, the man's questions nudging the subtle doubts Gabriela had planted so many weeks past. Though he'd been too angry to analyze Kincaid's patience with him, he could admit now the pirate hadn't lived up to his heartless reputation.

"Twenty-five years ago," Felix said softly, trying out the words he'd hidden inside for so long, "your men raided a plantation on Monserrat." He stopped when he stood directly behind Kincaid. "My family worked on that plantation. You and your men murdered every one of them. Except me. I was well hidden by my mother."

Kincaid nodded, as if he were only too familiar with his crimes. Then he turned, the moon striking his face in bold relief. "Twenty-five years ago?" He cocked his head and frowned, as if thinking. "How old were ye, lad, to remember me so clearly?"

Felix didn't move. Didn't breathe. He didn't know what he'd expected. A confession? Still, it surprised him that Kincaid would try to deny his acts. "The people who told me you were responsible had no reason to lie."

"And they were there, were they?" Kincaid asked, stepping closer to Felix. "They witnessed this slaughter? Such lucky bastards to have survived."

Felix shook his head, unable to answer Kincaid's challenges. "It was common knowledge—"

"Aye, 'tis always common knowledge that fuels the best gossip." Kincaid stopped only when he was nose to nose with Felix. "Happens I was very busy the summer that you speak of. Use your head and count, lad. Gabriela will be five and twenty. I spent that summer in the Brazils, enjoying my time romancing her mother. But don't take my word for it. Cy or Bertie can tell you as much."

Kincaid turned around and marched back up the path, leaving Felix speechless and wondering. Then he stopped. Still facing the house, Kincaid said, "I was a slave on a sugar plantation—Rutherford's, to be precise. I wouldn't turn against those poor souls who work the land so I might steal a few pigs and a jug of bad rum."

Kincaid slowly pivoted around, his face shadowed. But still, Felix could see his even white teeth parted in a smile.

"It appears I took nothing from you that summer, Felix Bishop. It appears I gave you something instead."

The room was a cloud of pipe smoke, the tobacco fragrance hanging in the air in a sweet fog. On the table bolted to the deck, six bottles of fine Madeira lay lined up like good soldiers— all empty. One lolled back and forth on its side with the roll of the ship.

Captain Simpson held both boots propped on the table, his pipe bit between his teeth as he fanned out his cards. He'd been entertained through dinner, cordials, and several rounds of loo. In the middle of the table was a pile of sweetmeats, used by the players to wager instead of coin.

The captain took his pipe stem from his mouth and leaned back in his chair, amazingly steady despite the amount of liquor he'd consumed. "Now, let me see if I understand you correctly, Miss Carstair." His eyes narrowed through the smoke weaving lacy trails around his face. "You and Miss de Sousa here dressed up like pirates and kidnapped Rutherford and Bishop? You held them captive—all part of some ruse to get them to marry you?"

Both Leydi and Gabby nodded dutifully. They'd hoped they'd given their story just enough truth to be convincing.

"And the deed was done *with* the earl's blessings?"

"It was his men who helped us bring Quentin and Lieutenant Bishop to the island, Captain," Leydi said, lining up her small store of sweets on the scarred table as if the candies held an inordinate amount of her interest. "On one of Quentin's ships no less," she added with a sheepish flutter of her lashes. "Poor man. Can't keep track of them all."

The captain dropped his booted feet to the deck and laid his cards on the table. The light of two lanterns flickered across his face. "And your plan was to kidnap the men, *pretending* you were cohorts of Kincaid, keeping them captive on the island until . . ."

"Until they fell in love with us," Leydi finished when the captain seemed reluctant. "So you see, Captain Simpson, you won't find the famed Heartless Kincaid here." She glanced at Gabby. "This is no hideout at all."

"And they did fall in love," said the first officer, now smiling dreamily from beside Gabby. The man had shed his jacket hours before. His hand lay tucked between the folds of his waistcoat where he'd unfastened two buttons. Leydi suspected his grin was fueled more by the Madeira he'd drunk than sympathy for the women's story. In a tidy pile before him, the lieutenant held a sizable treasure—the result of the evening's winnings and Leydi's quick hand with the cards. "I say, Captain. It's rather romantic."

"As a married man, I hope you can understand," Gabby said. "At times it is difficult for a woman to get herself to the altar."

Leydi met Gabby's eyes in what she hoped was the proper look of contrition.

The captain blinked. He reached for his Madeira, snatching at the glass once—and missed, his hand coming up empty. He frowned. With admirable concentration he slowly settled his fingers around the stem of the glass, smiling when he succeeded in nabbing his prize. He took a swig.

"I'm to understand the earl helped you because he wanted to secure an heir?" he said, recounting Leydi's tale.

"He was growing quite desperate with Quentin's determination not to marry," Leydi said. "As you can imagine, the man is getting on in years. And I'm afraid he's in rather poor health," she added for good measure.

The captain's expression gave nothing away. He bit down on the stem of his pipe. "I don't intend any offense, my dear. You and Miss de Sousa have been quite charming company, you understand. But I expect that when an earl seeks to marry off his son, he usually has"—he seemed to search for the proper words—"grander prospects."

"Perhaps. But how many of these charming ladies would stoop to kidnapping?" Leydi asked, meeting the captain's hazel eyes with a guileless smile. "You must understand the rift between father and son was enough to make Quentin quite ruthless in attempting to thwart his father's wishes. The earl was unable to get his heir to heel. He couldn't just trot up any little heiress and expect to succeed."

"A rather good point," the captain said, puffing on the pipe, new clouds billowing to the rafters. "How exactly did you approach the earl with your plan?"

"I work for Quentin. Finances and such—" She waved her hand negligently, not getting to the details. "And the earl, he came all the way from England to persuade Quentin it was high time he marry. I overheard a terrible argument, not intentionally, you understand."

Both men appeared on the edges of their seats. Surprisingly, the first officer, who had spent most of the day scowling at them, had become their stern advocate after only the third bottle.

"I was rather fond of Quentin by then," Leydi said, picking up the deck of cards and beginning to shuffle. "When I approached the earl, he was . . . very amenable. Something about desperate times requiring desperate measures."

The lieutenant nodded his head and popped a candy into his mouth. "There wasn't a mama on the island that didn't scheme to get his lordship ankling up the aisle with their daughter, sir. I'm telling you, the man was notorious for his determination to avoid the noose of wedlock."

"And you're Rutherford's . . . woman of finance?" the captain inquired, still not sounding quite convinced.

Leydi shuffled again. "I expect it is an unusual occupation for a woman. Still, it's what came naturally to me. Perhaps I can impress upon you my talents. Surely a captain with a commission in the Royal Navy could use some advice. If you were to, let's say . . . invest your moneys wisely."

The captain laughed. "You think to give me financial advice, dear?"

"Captain." Leydi met his eyes squarely. "Most likely you've been investing the little money the government deems to pay you on something solid like government papers and such. If I may make a suggestion, there is a promising prospect in a new shipping line, the Bombay Company. It's about to merge its interest with a more established concern with contracts in the Far

East. You could triple your money in . . . let's say conserva-
tively . . . five months."

She knew she'd caught his attention. A new gleam of respect
sparked from his eyes. Leydi smiled. Dear Mr. Stevenson had
always taught her to use her talents wisely. So far, her aptitude
at cards and finances and a strong stomach for liquor had served
her and Gabby well.

Gabriela leaned forward and added, "Did Lieutenant Bishop
ever mention how he came to discover Kincaid's supposed hideout?"

The captain took another drag of his pipe, turning to Gabby
thoughtfully. "No, that he did not."

"But that Frenchman was always jabbering about it," the lieutenant said. "And by Jove, you know, Captain, I do believe he
spouted some nonsense about being kidnapped."

"Captain," Gabby implored, her emerald eyes flashing, her
full mouth plumped in the most charming of pouts. "Isn't it
unlikely these men were held captive by one of the most notorious pirates of our times—and yet they were never harmed, just
released to reveal Kincaid's whereabouts?"

"That does seem rather tolerant of a pirate," the captain con-
ceded.

Gabriela glanced at Leydi and bit her lip, looking quite convincing in her reluctance to speak. Leydi nodded sympatheti-
cally, as if urging her to tell all.

Gabby sighed, the sound coming long and sweet. "Perhaps if
I explain that—after Lieutenant Bishop agreed to bring you
here—he received a message informing him that I was expecting
his child." She looked down at her folded hands demurely, then
flickered her gaze up at the captain and lieutenant. "You might
better understand his change of heart in bringing you here?"

Now the captain leaned forward on the table, his thoughtful
look becoming one of understanding. "That would certainly account for his strange behavior."

"And, Captain," Leydi said, seeing that indeed the man was
beginning to believe their story, "Quentin Rutherford's fleets
have been raided quite frequently by Kincaid. Can you really

believe he and Mr. Bishop are acting rationally protecting a pirate?"

The captain kept his steely gaze on Leydi. "Quite irrationally."

"What we did—we realized it was wrong," Gabby said. "After all, you can't bully a man into marrying you. That's why we let them go, hoping if they loved us enough, they would come back."

"And they did come back," the lieutenant added as if it were a charming end to a fairy tale. He gave a poignant sniff. "Oh, that's a lovely story."

"We never intended to involve the Royal Navy," Leydi pressed. "Captain, you can search and search—but I assure you, Kincaid is not on this island. There's simply no pirate to hand up to you come morning. But if the men should find out about what we've done . . . well, not only will they not marry us, I'm afraid they shall never forgive us."

"Won't you let us send a message to the earl to meet with you?" Gabby added persuasively. "We have proof . . . undeniable proof . . . that the island doesn't belong to Kincaid."

Leydi held her breath and waited.

"Well," he said, letting out a long stream of smoke. "I suppose I could at least listen to this proof." He picked up his glass, lifting it for yet another drink. He frowned, glancing at Leydi. "However did you come up with this outrageous plan of yours, Miss Carstair?"

"Have you read the book *Constant Constance?*" Leydi asked. When both men shook their heads, Leydi gave a mental *good.* She slanted a look at each. "Quite ingenious, that Lady Constance. Got herself a title just the same way."

Chapter Thirty

"Well, Captain," the earl asked, "will we be clapped in irons?"

The captain stood over Kincaid's desk, examining the documents laid across the seaweed marquetry, papers Quentin had doctored to show one Earl of Carrick owned the small island just east of Dominica by grant of King George himself. Also laid out for him were the meticulous plans Leydi had devised for a sugar plantation, the years of toil that had gone into those papers clearly not the work of overnight scheming.

The captain shook his head. "It's all very convincing, I must say. These plans, the experimental fields you showed me."

Right then Lieutenant Thompson entered the room, followed by a bank of red-coated soldiers. "It's just as she said, Captain. Not a trace of pirate treasure or any signs of Kincaid. Just a simple village with blacksmith and dairy. All very straightforward."

"It appears I owe you an apology," the captain said to the earl. Then he turned to Leydi and Gabriela. He paced across the room to stand before the two, giving them a studied examination. "Or that I have just been charmed by two of the best," he said under his breath so only the women could hear.

"Will you tell Lieutenant Bishop?" Gabriela asked, her anxious plea just the right touch to wipe away the captain's doubts.

"No," he said with a smile. "I think not. Though you're damning him to believing he has betrayed his office as a member of the Royal Navy." He frowned. "Which he has, though only in mind and not in deed." He rocked back on his heels. "And what will you two do when Kincaid never shows up?"

"Oh, we plan to confess," Leydi whispered conspiratorially.

Gabriela patted her stomach significantly and said, "In about nine months time, you understand."

The captain winked, then turned back to the earl. "And you went along with this scheme?"

"What could I do, sir? My son threatened to leave everything to escheat to the Crown."

The captain shook his head. "Such an impetuous young man."

"Indeed. And with my failing health—" The earl gave a discreet cough and shrugged. "I became quite desperate when Miss Carstair approached me."

The captain leaned forward, speaking in a whisper only Leydi and the earl could hear. "I must applaud your decision, sir. I suspect after the nuptials you'll have the place crawling with heirs."

The earl's gaze met Leydi's eyes. "My plans exactly."

Bishop and Rutherford were ushered into the room. Bertie and Cy followed a discreet distance behind. With a wink to the earl, the captain turned to face the men who'd been carefully kept waiting outside. The captain had held to his promise not to reveal the ladies' wiles. The men had been told only that the captain would look over the papers that proved their innocence.

"I find the evidence presented quite credible," the captain said affably. "You're all free to go. But, Lieutenant"—he turned to Felix, his eyes searching for artifice or guile—"I must ask one final question. On your honor as a British citizen and a naval officer, did you ever lay eyes on this Kincaid?"

Felix looked straight at Gabriela. Standing beside her was Daniel Kincaid, the most notorious pirate of the seven seas.

"No," Felix answered. "No, I never saw him."

Without another word Felix moved to stand at Gabriela's side. He took her hand and gave it a squeeze.

"Well, there you have it," the captain said. With the aplomb of a gallant, he swept up Leydi's hand and kissed it. "You are an incredible tactician, madam," he whispered. "Perhaps if you have some time, we might plan a few naval strategies?"

The earl wrapped an arm around the captain's shoulders and steered him toward the door. "Now, about that splendid brandy," he said, guiding the captain from the study he'd adopted as his own, playing his role of gracious host.

Through the open floor-to-ceiling windows the sound of Hugh's voice bleating out the name of his newest love flitted into the room, bringing a begrudging smile to everyone's face. Bertie laughed and took up Cy's two hands in hers. She leaned up to give his bearded cheek a smacking kiss.

"It looks like we are going to have to work *very* hard, *meu amor,*" she whispered up to Cy, "if I am going to make that fool jealous."

"Aye," he answered with a spark in his eye. "And I'm a hard-working man," he finished, enveloping her in a searing kiss.

Gabriela smiled at the sight of her mother in the arms of a man she knew would always care for her—perhaps always had. She stared up at Kincaid, then turned to Felix, holding her breath.

"It's all right, Gabriela," Felix told her. He embraced her in his arms, repeating, "It's all right now."

Gabriela saw the healing in his eyes and the love. With a sigh she determined it was time for some healing of her own. She stepped away from Felix and turned to Kincaid. She kissed her father's cheek, whispering, "Thank you."

Outside in the corridor Quentin tugged Leydi down the hall. She stumbled along behind him, both of them laughing as they found the old room where he'd been kept prisoner. He swept her inside and shut the door behind them. He pressed her up against the paneled wood, bracing his body against hers. In a long, poignant moment, his dark blue eyes centered on her face. His hands cradled her head as if she were infinitely precious. The longing so clear in his expression made her feel cherished.

He kissed her hard, letting her know just how dear she was to him.

He shook his head, muttering between kisses, "Your story. It sounds so insane, I almost believe it."

Leydi smiled, stroking his cheek. She sighed.

"What is it?" he asked, stopping his kisses.

"It was so much like one of my dreams—a rich heir to an earl marries the daughter of an indentured servant on his plantation. That's why it was so easy to make up." She glanced up at Quentin, shaking her head. "But I don't want dreams anymore. I want real life. A life with a man I can love. And who loves me."

"And you're worried that I don't?"

"I want to believe . . ." she said helplessly.

He wrapped his arms around her, letting her know by the strength of his embrace and his tender touch just how much he loved her. "If you don't let me love you, if I can't spend the rest of my life beside you, giving you the children of my heart . . . I will die a lonely man, without soul or hope to save him."

He tipped her face up to his, looking deeply into her eyes. "Leydianna, I love you. There, I said it." His hands caressed her hair, twining in the short curls. "I was afraid to come here. Afraid you could never forgive me . . . But I won't let the past defeat me—defeat us. I thought I didn't deserve love. Show me I'm wrong. Give me that happy ending you promised."

She hugged him fiercely, seeing the ghosts of his past finally laid to rest. "Just close your eyes and hold me tight and you'll feel it right there between us, Quentin. I love you," she whispered in his ear. "And I'll always love you. You have all my happily-ever-afters."

Epilogue

Quentin stepped into the receiving chamber, casting a furtive glance over his shoulder. He shut the door behind him with the heel of his boot and concentrated on the swaddled bundle in his arms. His son gurgled up at him, a slobbering smile dominating his cherubic features.

"Alone at last," he whispered.

Making silly faces that seemed to enchant Jared, Quentin paced across the carpet. The baby reached up with his hands for his father, cooing deliciously. Swept clear of its past deluge of papers, the receiving room had at last become a place of welcome. No business was conducted there. It served strictly to please family and friends.

Quentin stepped around Nigel. Aloysius lurked in the corner, his ginger tail flicking in the air as he waited to pounce on the ribbon trailing from the iguana's neck—a favorite pastime of the cat's that Nigel admirably allowed. Quentin settled into the armchair, happy for these quiet moments with his son. His finger flicked lovingly through the wisps of brown curls. He stroked Jared's soft cheek, thinking his son had his mother's charming eyes and giving smile.

These days Rutherford Hall was filled with the hustle and bustle of servants and visitors. If his father wasn't living with them, Kincaid would come nosing about, complaining about the retirement Leydi had forced on him. Gabriela often brought over Elise, her daughter, though not often enough for Leydi's taste. Felix and she lived on Devil's Gate with Kincaid, Felix having renounced the navy to become a successful planter.

Cy and Bertie, too, were a common sight, living as they did in Basse Terre. Even Hugh would make frequent visits, though it was always a different "love of his life" draped on his arm.

There was only one set of visitors Quentin could do without: Argus and Elaine Carstair. Of late, there had been talk of leaving the island and returning to good old Mother England, a plan Quentin did his best to encourage.

He nuzzled against the warm baby skin, inhaling the milk-and-honey fragrance of his son. He cooed gently, then glanced up at the angels painted on the ceiling. "Thank you," he said out loud.

The door creaked open. Leydi walked into the chamber dressed in a brilliant emerald wrapper trimmed with tiny pink roses. She wore matching slippers and a ribbon swirled through her shoulder-length curls. She rubbed her eyes and yawned.

"I thought you might be here," she said with a smile to her husband. Sitting on his lap, she twined her arms around his neck as they held the baby between them. "Mrs. Bailey complained you'd disappeared with Jared when she wanted to give him a bath."

"Mrs. Bailey always has some plan for Jared while you sleep. Today I thought I should get a turn at him."

Leydi watched their baby boy grab at her finger. "He is quite wonderful."

"Yes. Wonderful enough that I'm always fighting someone off for him. Mrs. Bailey, Stevenson, my father—Kincaid." He gave Leydi a kiss on the cheek, so content with his life, it almost hurt. "I don't deserve you."

She laughed softly, leaning her cheek against his.

"What?" he asked.

She tapped his nose with a kiss. "I was just thinking that the sign of a good business arrangement is when all parties think they received the better bargain."

He hugged her tighter. "You always had a good head for business, Viscountess."

They stayed quiet, watching their son. Jared smiled and gurgled, playing with the buttons of Quentin's waistcoat. Then suddenly, he reached higher, as if something else had caught his eye.

Quentin looked up. On the cove ceiling above, his painted angels smiled down at them. Though they had never spoken to him, he couldn't help but give those angels some of the credit for his happiness.

He stroked his son's cheek as he held his wife, then mouthed another, "Thank you."

In the corner, the angel mouthed back, "You're welcome."

It happened in a split second, so fast, he could have imagined it. He glanced down at Jared, now giving baby chortles of glee as he continued to reach toward the ceiling. Quentin looked up at the angel again. Nothing but paint and stucco.

"Leydi, have you ever noticed . . ."

"Yes, darling," she said in a sleepy voice.

But the question was too preposterous to even voice. "Never mind."

He watched the angels suspiciously as his son continued to giggle up at the ceiling. Why not believe in his painted angels? he thought with a smile. In his lap sat the daughter of a pirate, in his arms the heir he'd sworn never to have. And his heart was brimming with the happiness of it all.

This time he stared up at the angels, unafraid of the miracles he might find there.

And he could have sworn the angel in the corner winked.